P9-DCC-435

"Lora Leigh delivers on all counts."
—*Romance Reviews Today*

Praise for Lora Leigh's Novels of the Breeds

Mercury's War

"Erotic and suspenseful . . . Readers will laugh, readers will blush and readers will cry."   —*Romance Junkies*

"With two great twists, fans of the Breeds saga will relish [*Mercury's War*]."   —*Midwest Book Review*

"Intriguingly powerful with plenty of action to keep the pages turning. I am completely addicted! A great read!"
—*Fresh Fiction*

Dawn's Awakening

"Leigh consistently does an excellent job building characters and weaving intricate plot threads through her stories. Her latest offering in the Breeds series is no exception."
—*Romantic Times* (4½ stars, top pick)

"Held me captivated."   —*Romance Junkies*

"Heart-wrenching."   —*Fallen Angel Reviews*

"Erotic, fast-paced, funny and hard-hitting, this series delivers maximum entertainment to the reader."   —*Fresh Fiction*

Tanner's Scheme

"The incredible Leigh pushes the traditional envelope with her scorching sex scenes by including voyeurism. Intrigue and passion ignite . . . Scorcher!" —*Romantic Times* (4½ stars)

"Sinfully sensual . . . [This series] is well worth checking out."
—*Fresh Fiction*

continued . . .

HARMONY'S WAY

"Leigh's engrossing alternate reality combines spicy sensuality, romantic passion and deadly danger. Hot stuff indeed."
—Romantic Times

"I stand in awe of Ms. Leigh's ability to bring to life these wonderful characters as they slowly weave their way into my mind and heart. When it comes to this genre, Lora Leigh is the queen."
—Romance Junkies

MEGAN'S MARK

"A riveting tale full of love, intrigue and every woman's fantasy, *Megan's Mark* is a wonderful contribution to Lora Leigh's Breeds series . . . As always, Lora Leigh delivers on all counts; *Megan's Mark* will certainly not disappoint her many fans!"
—Romance Reviews Today

"Hot, hot, hot—the sex and the setting . . . You can practically see the steam rising off the pages."
—Fresh Fiction

"This entertaining romantic science fiction suspense will remind the audience of *Kitty and the Midnight Hour* by Carrie Vaughn and MaryJanice Davidson's *Derik's Bane* as this futuristic world filled with 'Breeds' seems 'normal' . . . [A] delightful thriller."
—The Best Reviews

"The dialogue is quick, the action is fast and the sex is oh so hot . . . Don't miss out on this one."
—A Romance Review

"Leigh's action-packed Breeds series makes a refreshing change . . . Rapid-fire plot development and sex steamy enough to peel wallpaper."
—Monsters and Critics

"An exceedingly sexy and sizzling new series to enjoy. Hot sex, snappy dialogue and kick-butt action add up to outstanding entertainment."
—Romantic Times

BENGAL'S HEART

LORA LEIGH

BERKLEY SENSATION, NEW YORK

THE BERKLEY PUBLISHING GROUP
Published by the Penguin Group
Penguin Group (USA) Inc.
375 Hudson Street, New York, New York 10014, USA
Penguin Group (Canada), 90 Eglinton Avenue East, Suite 700, Toronto, Ontario M4P 2Y3, Canada
(a division of Pearson Penguin Canada Inc.)
Penguin Books Ltd., 80 Strand, London WC2R 0RL, England
Penguin Group Ireland, 25 St. Stephen's Green, Dublin 2, Ireland (a division of Penguin Books Ltd.)
Penguin Group (Australia), 250 Camberwell Road, Camberwell, Victoria 3124, Australia
(a division of Pearson Australia Group Pty. Ltd.)
Penguin Books India Pvt. Ltd., 11 Community Centre, Panchsheel Park, New Delhi—110 017, India
Penguin Group (NZ), 67 Apollo Drive, Rosedale, North Shore 0632, New Zealand
(a division of Pearson New Zealand Ltd.)
Penguin Books (South Africa) (Pty.) Ltd., 24 Sturdee Avenue, Rosebank, Johannesburg 2196,
South Africa

Penguin Books Ltd., Registered Offices: 80 Strand, London WC2R 0RL, England

This is a work of fiction. Names, characters, places, and incidents either are the product of the author's imagination or are used fictitiously, and any resemblance to actual persons, living or dead, business establishments, events, or locales is entirely coincidental. The publisher does not have any control over and does not assume any responsibility for author or third-party websites or their content.

BENGAL'S HEART

A Berkley Sensation Book / published by arrangement with the author

PRINTING HISTORY
Berkley Sensation mass-market edition / August 2009

ISBN: 978-0-425-22902-6

BERKLEY® SENSATION
Berkley Sensation Books are published by The Berkley Publishing Group,
a division of Penguin Group (USA) Inc.,
375 Hudson Street, New York, New York 10014.
BERKLEY® SENSATION and the "B" design are trademarks of Penguin Group (USA) Inc.

PRINTED IN THE UNITED STATES OF AMERICA

10 9 8 7 6 5 4 3 2 1

ACKNOWLEDGMENTS

Thanks to my wonderful editor, Cindy, for her patience and understanding. This was a hard one, and your understanding made all the difference.

To Sharon, just because you're you and you know what that means to me.

And to Lee Stepp. Your Munchkin never forgot.

BENGAL'S
HEART

· PROLOGUE ·

BREED PROGRESSIVE TRAINING FACILITY, GERMANY

It was a scene out of a nightmare. Something so horrific, so bloody, as to defy the imagination and leave Cassa gasping in shock.

"We have to find the release," she screamed in horror as her husband stood beside her, the camera on his shoulder trained on the viewing area of the rumored death pit.

It was more than a pit of death. It was a place of such torturous agony and evil that Cassa struggled with the ramifications.

A dozen Breeds, nude, tiger stripes gleaming against their flesh, moved frantically to escape the long, lethally sharp blades that played a horrendous game of hide-and-seek with them.

Blood sprayed against the steel walls, pooled on the floor beneath the bodies of those who'd had the misfortune of not moving quickly enough. And still the others fought to survive and to protect.

A savage roar of rage tore from the tallest, the most powerful of the Bengal Breeds doomed to die, and echoed through the intercom. He fought to shove the others aside, to save them, to find some way to stop the mechanical thrust and parry that sliced into vulnerable flesh.

"Douglas, help me," Cassa sobbed as her husband stood silent and still, the camera recording the brutality of the Genetics Council and their so-called progressive training.

How had this happened? She flipped a switch and slammed her hands onto the release plungers, but the blades continued to slice and dice their way through even more Breeds in their path.

The roars of fury crescendoed, the raw animal rage sending shards of terror racing down her spine as she grabbed her husband's arm and jerked him toward her.

She saw it then. Frozen, immobile with shock, she saw the morbid pleasure in his gaze and the satisfaction on his face.

Like a key finally releasing the lock on months of suspicion, Cassa blinked at the truths that finally slammed inside her head. The group of men and women who had come to this small country to find this particular lab and rescue the Breeds here had suffered through too many unfortunate accidents and false trails. For days now, the commander, Jonas Wyatt, had treated the group as a whole with icy suspicion. Because of one man.

"You." She felt herself shaking apart. Felt something breaking inside her at the realization that she too had played a part in the deception that was now killing the very men and women they had been sent to save. "What have you done?" She screamed the accusation at him, watching the smirk that curved at his lips as his pale blue eyes glittered with fanatical anticipation.

"What have I done? No, Cassa, what did you do? I couldn't have gotten on this team without your help." He laughed in her face. She felt the amusement, the hated, mocking arrogance in his tone, as more cries echoed through the control room.

He was her husband. He had used her connections, her friends, to ensure that he was chosen as her cameraman to document the rescue of the rarest of the Breeds ever created. The Bengal Breed.

"Help me release them," she shrieked, her palms slamming into his shoulders, knocking the camera loose and jerking it free of its mooring on his shoulder.

The crash of the equipment to the ground was only a distant sound of destruction as Douglas used his fist to send explosions of brutal pain tearing through her head, and she fell to the cement floor.

Agony lanced through her, and Cassa couldn't stop the whimper of pain that fell from her lips. Okay, she could forget getting any help from him.

She pulled herself up to the control panel, tears spilling from her eyes now as she began to press, punch and slap any lever or button she could find.

Sirens began to blare, strobe lights flashed in red and blue. A mechanical voice began spitting warnings and directions in a coded gibberish that made the pain in her head intensify.

"You damned, stupid bitch!"

Cruel hands latched onto her hair and jerked her to her feet.

Cassa didn't bother to scream. There was no one to hear her cries, there would be no one to care. Her hands jerked to the hand gripping her hair as she began to claw at his fingers with her nails.

Struggling, she was only dimly aware of the enraged, horrific roar that sounded too close, too furious.

"You ignorant little whore!" Douglas yelled again, his expression twisted into lines of rage as he shook her by the hand in her hair. "Do you know what you're doing? They're abominations. Fucking animals pretending to be human." His free hand slapped her across the face, causing her head to ring with explosions of light as another warning blared through the control room, followed by a roar of animalistic rage unlike anything she had ever heard.

Cassa cringed at the sound as Douglas suddenly stilled.

"You knew," he snapped as he flung her away from him.

Her legs wouldn't hold her up. Her head was filled with clashing cymbals reverberating with agony. She collapsed to the floor, shaking her head. "I didn't know," she cried out, forcing herself to stare up at him. "You're a monster, Douglas."

The smile that curved his lips was one of triumph. "You told me the plans to get in here, Cassa. You told me the animals they were going to free, and you told me, dear wife, of the repercussions to the Council if they were freed." He kicked out at her, laughing as the toe of his boot connected with her side and sent her scrambling in an attempt to crawl from his reach.

"Ten million dollars, Cassa, in an overseas account. Who the fuck needs you or your connections now? You gave me the means to betray these crackpot idiots that want to suck up to animals. Now you can live with it."

A piercing animal scream exploded through the room. Through the veil of her hair and the tears filling her eyes, Cassa watched as Douglas paled, glanced to the sealed doors to the pit, then turned to run.

It happened so fast and yet Cassa swore she watched each detail of movement as though in slow motion. She saw the only Bengal still standing, his enraged, demonic eyes spitting amber fire. Blood dripped along his body. His face, his shoulders, the stripes that extended from his buttocks around his thighs— blood flowed over the heavy muscle and lean lines of his golden body. He lifted a broken steel stake and hurled it past the slowly opening cage door, swashing through the control room windows with deadly force.

The wickedly sharp blade buried itself at the base of Douglas's spine. He screamed as he went down and his head arched back on his shoulders as he screamed again.

The stake protruded from the base of his spine as blood spurted around the wound. He convulsed, agonizing sounds of horror and twisted pain escaping his lips, as Cassa watched the only Bengal to escape the pit.

He was the one the others had fought to save. She had seen that much. She had watched as they had sacrificed themselves to save this one.

A mechanical warning sounded through the room. "Alert! Alert! Enemy forces are now entering level zero corridor. You have fifteen seconds to evacuate. Fourteen. Thirteen."

Cassa stared at the creature that turned on her now. Long, once golden hair was streaked black with blood. It hung limply to his shoulders as the golden flecks of rage gleamed in a backdrop of forest green eyes.

His lips drew back on a snarl, exposing the wicked canines at the sides of his teeth.

She shook her head. He would kill her now. He'd heard everything Douglas had said, every charge he had made. She had betrayed the very creatures she had fought so hard to save. It didn't matter that she had done so unwittingly. It didn't matter that she would have died to protect them.

"I'm sorry," she cried hoarsely as he paced closer. "Oh God, I'm so sorry."

"Sorry is a weak man's excuse," the creature growled, his voice filled with dark purpose.

Her shoulders shook with the sobs she fought to hold back,

the terror that cascaded through her. Blood dripped to the floor in front of her, each small droplet a brilliant, enraged red, as he paced closer.

It dripped to the toe of her boot, the hem of her jeans. The next splattered on the jersey material of the T-shirt that covered her breasts.

She swore that small droplet seared her flesh as she stared up at him, grief and pain racing through every nerve in her body.

"Twenty-four Breeds dead," he growled, the sound of his voice so rough, dark and rasping it scraped over her senses. "Bengals. Each one fought every second of their miserable existence for freedom." His lips lifted into a snarl as he glanced to the pit, then back to her. "All dead."

A sob tore from her throat a second before his fingers were latched around her neck, pulling her to her feet as she struggled against the knowledge of death.

He didn't hurt her, when he should have. She had been responsible. She had trusted. She had betrayed.

"I should toss your body in there with them," he roared in her face as she screamed in fear.

His lips curled back from his teeth, and she could almost feel the sensation of those wicked incisors tearing at her neck.

She wanted to excuse the betrayal. She wanted to explain, but there was nothing she could say, nothing she could do to excuse it. She had told her husband. She had discussed it with him. She had overlooked the fact that he wasn't the man she once believed he was; she had tried to believe in that last vestige of humanity she thought he possessed.

Her hand lifted. She touched the blood that ran in a slow, crooked stream down his hard cheek. She touched it, fingers trembling, and bringing it to her lips, closed her eyes.

She tasted the blood she had spilled. Her father had said before his death that men should be made to taste the blood they spill, to experience death, to know the horror they perpetuate.

She knew. She accepted her fate. She tasted his blood as another sob tightened in her throat yet never fell past her lips. She hung in his less than gentle hold, expecting the pain at any moment. Expecting death. She had trusted the man she had given her heart to, and she had learned the cost of that trust.

"I own you."

Her eyes jerked open to see his, too close, glaring back at her. Nearly nose to nose, the heat of his breath caressing her cheek, the sharp canines too close to her flesh.

"What?" the question was instinctive.

"I own you," he growled again. It was the animal, not the man, that she faced. This Breed was nothing like the civilized Breeds she had been following for so many months for the newspaper she worked for.

"No." She tried to shake her head, but the fingers wrapped so cruelly around her throat refused to allow her to move.

"I know your secrets," he snarled. "And I'll know more. This." He looked around the control room, rage flashing in his face as his gaze landed on the entrance to the pit once more. His eyes flashed back to her. "You owe me for their lives. You owe me for his sins." His gaze returned to Douglas's fallen form.

She tried to shake her head again, but his hands only tightened mercilessly, as his expression became harder, colder.

"Brothers and sisters," he snapped at her. "My family, not my pride, and they lie dead because of his perfidy."

More tears slipped free. Guilt was a ball of flame in her chest. Grief was the knot of agony in her throat that his fingers clenched into.

She was going to die here. She could feel it, and perhaps a part of her would even prefer it. If she lived, she would have to face this, she would have to deal with it. She had seen the blood, the lives wasted in that pit, and she didn't know if she could bear the weight of knowing they had ended because of her ignorance.

Dear God. She might as well have killed them with her own hands.

◆   ◆   ◆

Cabal St. Laurents. They were named in these labs. They were given an identity when it would have been far kinder if they hadn't been. It was a reminder of what they were not. Never free. A reminder of what they were, always tied to their creators.

He was a Bengal, and the animal inside him refused to relent. It rejoiced in the blood of the enemy. It plotted with his humanity, planned and sought the death of every creature that would stand in the way of escape.

Now the man was ready to kill. The human wanted to taste the blood, and the animal held back.

His captive was female. It was the most corrupt of any species. It was the reason those that shared his blood now lay in that same blood that had gushed from their bodies. He held her now, his fingers gripped around her throat, his teeth aching, his tongue nearly tasting her flesh. And he couldn't harm her. The animal drew back, the feral intensity that had driven him to escape the pit receding.

He released her slowly, watching as she crumpled at his feet. She wasn't sobbing for mercy. Her head bent, her long, burnished, dark blond hair flowed around her. It touched the floor, and his blood stained the ends of it.

An agony of rage shuddered through him. The roar that raced through his throat and exploded from his lips brought an unwilling sob past the female's lips. But still, he didn't strike. The animal stood back, watched, waited. For what it was waiting, he wasn't certain, but he admitted he had no desire to take this woman's blood.

She had been foolish. He could smell the scent of her husband on her body, knew the pain that tormented her. She had betrayed them unknowingly, but how could he ever forgive the death of those he had held dear?

"I own you," he repeated, stepping back from her as he felt the weakness of blood loss creeping through his system. "When I call you, you'll come. Whatever I ask of you, you will give." He reached down, and gently, so gently, when rage and the need for violence poured through his system, he gripped her chin and lifted her head until he could see into the dove gray of her eyes, inhale the scent of her and know her forever. Know her and always remember this day. The day a woman had destroyed everything he had held dear.

"And one day," he swore, "you'll pay."

He stumbled. Weakness rushed through him.

He'd lost too much blood. His strength was depleted. There was nothing left but the aching rage, the agony of loss and the taste of defeat. He had sworn to save them, and because of this woman's thoughtlessness, because of her trust in the wrong man, he had lost everything.

He stumbled again, going nearly to his knees before he caught himself. Swaying, he forced himself upright as the sliding metal doors into the control room were pushed open, and the scent of Breeds filled the room.

There was no threat, no feeling of danger. The animal inside of him recognized the animals rushing in. The rescue forces the scientists had been so worried about. Headed by a Breed that even the Genetics Council was rumored to fear, Jonas Wyatt.

Cabal lifted his head and stared back at them, noting their expressions of disbelief at the sight of the male dying on the floor and the female staring up at him with equal parts fear and anger.

She recognized him for the animal he was and she knew he had stamped her with his ownership. She would walk his line and by all that was holy, he would ensure that she paid the price if she ever allowed another to touch her.

He almost stopped in shock at that thought. He would have, except one of the men stepped up for the woman. His hand reached out to grip her arm, to pull her to her feet. And Cabal was there.

He locked his fingers around the man's wrist and snarled out a warning. A primal, feral sound that had the female flinching.

What was this imperative need inside him? What had the animal driving forward once again in rage where this woman was concerned? He should want her out of his sight, out of his mind. Never did he want to have to think of the horrors he had faced here or the mutilations that had occurred within that devil's pit of death.

He could still smell the blood of his family. They shared his blood. Each of them, created of the same DNA from the same Bengal, created of the sperm from the same donor. They were true family. Blood family. And he had lost them all.

"Mine," he snarled back at the other Breed male, ignoring the arrogance, the dominance in the swirling gray eyes that stared back at him. "Her debt belongs to me."

The male looked from his wrist, where Cabal held him firmly, back to Cabal's eyes. There was an edge of danger in the stranger's silver eyes. An edge of pure, primal command. The scent of it was in the air and Cabal was aware that even at full strength he would be hard-pressed to defeat the strength and power of the animal.

"You're wrong." The dark, even tone had the hairs at the back of Cabal's neck lifting in warning. "You're hurt, and weak, Bengal," he said softly. "I'll let this one go. But she's not one you can use, and she's not one you can harm."

"Her debt is mine," Cabal hissed again, baring his canines as he pushed his face closer to the other Breed's. Nearly nose to nose now, the battle of wills was one Cabal feared he might well lose if pushed. But he would fight. He would fight to his last drop of blood.

"She owes no debt," the other warned him, his voice lowering further. "Don't make this mistake."

Cabal's gaze moved to her husband and back to the Breed male determined to stand in his way now.

"She trusted him." His tongue felt thick, awkward. "She touched him, followed him. He betrayed you all." There was a sneer in his voice now. The bastard would have never betrayed him. Cabal would have smelled the scent of his deceit from the first meeting. He would have never allowed such a creature to live.

"Her debt is not his," the other repeated.

"She is mine!" Cabal snapped in reply. "Interfere with this Breed and you'll die."

He could smell the weapons trained on him, sense the other Breeds as they watched the confrontation.

"Please." Her voice stroked over his senses. Weak, rough with tears, shaky with fear. "He's right, Jonas," she whispered then. "Let it go. Please."

Jonas. *The* Jonas Wyatt. The Bengals had rated him the most commanding of the Breed generals, one of their strongest strategists. Well, wasn't he just feeling satisfied? Wyatt had strategized an entire race of Breeds into extinction.

"Yeah, Wyatt, let it the fuck go," he growled viciously, even as he swayed on his feet.

He damned the weakness of his own body. He damned Wyatt to hell for not planning better and as he stared at where the woman gazed back at him, tears and regret mingling in her eyes, he damned himself for not killing her, just as he had killed that bastard of a husband she possessed.

He inhaled roughly. She stank of that human. The smell of him was an affront to Cabal's senses, an affront to his sense of justice.

"Remember me." His whisper was more of a hiss. "Never forget, woman, because I won't. And the day will come . . ." Darkness swirled through his vision then. His knees buckled. He'd lost one ounce too much of precious blood.

He was unaware of his body crumpling to the floor or of the

cry the woman gave as she tried to catch him. He didn't feel her hands touch him, he didn't feel the racing of her heart or the tears that touched his neck.

"Cassa, we have him."

Cassa was only barely aware of Jonas lifting her away from the fallen form and handing her to another Breed. She felt numb inside, even as the fear exploded and ricocheted through her. She felt cold, yet she was flushed with heat. She felt dead, yet she knew she was still living.

Tremors worked through her body as the Breed that held her helped her out of the room. He lifted her into his arms as he stepped over her husband's body. Cassa wanted to feel remorse. She should have felt grief. But instead, she felt only hatred and a sense of freedom.

Douglas was dead. He had been the instrument of his own death, just as he had been the instrument of her fears for so many months.

God, she should have known. When he was chosen for this team, she should have warned the Breeds that she no longer trusted him as a husband. The problem was, she had trusted him as a supporter of the Breeds. He had been there with her when news of the incredible creatures first hit. He had been during the first of the riots against Breed Law, and had expressed his outrage, his concern on their behalf. And all the while, he had been selling them out.

She should have suspected. It wasn't the first assignment they'd had that had gone horribly wrong. Each time, the blame had fallen to others. Just as the blame would fall to her now.

She had trusted him, as the Bengal had stated. She had led him here, she had allowed him the opportunity to deceive and to plot against the Breeds. He'd tried to profit from their deaths, and he had paid for it.

As they exited the room and headed along the corridors, she was aware of the majority of the Breeds staying behind. They were like that. They cleared out those who weren't Breeds, and they grieved for those lost before wrapping their bodies and carrying them to a safety that would be eternal. The Breed cemetery in Virginia, not far from Arlington, was a testament to the dedication that the Breeds felt for one another. They had fought for it, won it, and they carried out their own ceremonies without the benefit of any humans in attendance. As at Sanctuary, the Feline Breed compound, they grieved the loss of their own and buried them with all the gentleness and humanity that they hadn't known in their lives.

"He won't let me live," she whispered, more to herself than to the one who sat her slowly back to her feet and began leading her through the corridors she had raced through earlier.

Her life was forfeit. Once that Breed healed and regained his strength, she would die. She had seen it in his eyes. Hell, she had tasted it in his blood. She could still taste it. Dark and feral against her tongue. She was marked, and she knew it.

"Breeds have an amazing sense of justice," the one that led her through the facility stated softly. "You'll live. But only because he knows you'll suffer more for it."

She looked up at him. There was an edge of wisdom in his amber gaze, a sense of regret. Mercury Warrant. His lionlike features were stoic and solemn, his gaze understanding despite the fact that she feared she didn't deserve such a thing.

"I have no doubt he's right," she said tonelessly, forcing herself to walk, to place one foot in front of the other, to leave the facility and to face the blood and death that awaited outside as well.

Breeds and humans alike had died here, because the labs had been warned of the rescue force's arrival. The Coyote and human soldiers that had awaited them had shown no mercy. Not that the rescue force hadn't expected it once they realized what they were up against.

Many had known they would die. It had been par for the course in the past months, as betrayal after betrayal had marked each facility they had breached. It seemed there were as many willing to kill the Breeds among the humans as there were those willing to save them. And telling the difference between the two would never be easy.

"He was my husband," she whispered.

"They're usually the ones you can trust the least," he responded.

She almost laughed. And how would he know? How could he ever understand that even though Douglas hadn't been a good husband, still, he hadn't been one she had seen as evil.

Abusive? Yes. A killer? No. She would have never imagined that he could see death in terms of profit.

"I'm so screwed," she whispered painfully.

"I have no doubt," he agreed, his voice cooler now. "It's the price you pay, Cassa. And it's not always a kind one."

No, the price she would pay wouldn't be a kind one.

· CHAPTER 1 ·

WOLF MOUNTAIN, COLORADO
WOLF BREED BASE, HAVEN
ELEVEN YEARS LATER

Cassa Hawkins slipped silently through the shadows of the Wolf
Breed compound of Haven as she tried to ignore the misty rain
falling and her own sense of anticipation. She felt like a ghost,
like a shadow, unseen, unheard. It was a heady sensation to slip
past Breed after Breed, undetected.

The chill night air wrapped around her and penetrated the
black clothing she wore. Even the snug black cap that covered
her hair did little to keep out the cold or the dampness. It added
to the thrill, to the sense of disbelief and impending danger. She
was insane, creeping around like this and she knew it. She
couldn't get far. It wasn't possible that a drug had actually been
created that could fool the Breed senses and allow her to get
much farther past the sentries posted throughout Haven.

Someone was playing with her, allowing her to get only so
far. That was the only explanation for the distance she had gained
between the cabin she was assigned and the main offices of the
compound, because there were too many Breed sentries posted.
Breeds who had an incredible sense of smell. They were chosen
for their positions simply because they were impossible to get
past.

It wasn't possible that such a drug could have been created, a drug that would fool the Breed's superior ability to scent others. Was it?

According to the emails she had received and the small bottle of round white pills that had arrived at her apartment the week before, it was definitely possible. And she had been crazy enough tonight to actually take one. To slip it onto her tongue, to allow it to dissolve and enter her system before she left her cabin.

The reckless decision had concerned her, but only for brief moments. As many of her fellow reporters knew, Cassa had often been known to dare death. It was one of her faults, many said. She considered it one of her strengths. After all, her days were numbered and she knew it. She might as well get away with as much as possible until the day of reckoning arrived. Cabal may have allowed her to live this long, but she doubted that decision would last much longer.

In this case, intuition had spurred her on. The pictures of bloody bodies, the emails that had warned her that a rogue Breed was taking vengeance for some unknown crimes, and then the drug that arrived with the unsigned note that said the past always returned no matter how hard one fought it. The past was indeed always there. It hovered at her shoulder, ran through her nightmares and glittered in the golden flecks of Cabal St. Laurents's eyes every time he looked at her. The past was alive and well. She didn't need a killer to remind her of that. Just as she didn't need anyone to remind her of the truth of her own actions.

The truth.

The truth was, Cassa had spilled blood herself. The truth was, once her secrets were revealed, she would die. The Breeds would never allow her to live once they knew the truth. She was lucky that the small team of Breeds who knew the truth had kept their mouths shut all these years.

She slipped past yet another Breed guard. Mordecai. One of their best trackers, rumored to be one of their most merciless Coyote Breeds. On silent feet, she moved slowly through the shadows, along the wet ground, heart racing, mouth dry, until she was a safe distance from him.

The chilly winter air gave no hint that spring was just around the corner. The cold penetrated flesh and bone, but nothing could still the excitement racing through her now. It was working. They hadn't scented her, they hadn't sensed her.

God, this couldn't be possible.

Pressing her back tight to the thick trunk of a pine, she stared up at the moonless sky and whispered a silent prayer that neither one of the Breeds patrolling the area would scent her.

A drug like this could be deadly, just as her source had warned her.

Pushing away from the tree, Cassa skirted around several maples bare of leaves and dripping a chilly rain. She slid through the night.

There was a whisper of voices ahead, the sound of soft footfalls coming nearer. Ducking behind the evergreen shrubs that grew around an enclosed picnic area, she waited for them to pass.

"Are you certain of your information?" Jonas Wyatt's voice came through the night clearly as the pair grew closer.

"Five dead, Jonas, that's hard to mistake. Each one was rumored to be a part of a twelve-man hunting party that came together several times a year to hunt down escaped Breeds. Each one was killed in the same manner, using the same pattern. There's no mistake."

The voice that answered had Cassa's heart tripping, then speeding up in awareness. She fought back the response, bit her lip and prayed that little miracle pill would cover the scent of arousal as well.

Cabal St. Laurents had a voice that made women want to melt to the floor in a puddle of orgasmic bliss. It rasped over the senses with a velvet cadence Cassa had never been able to ignore. It was a seducer's voice, and she had been seduced long ago, even when he'd stared at her with death in his eyes.

"Hell." Jonas paused, no more than four feet from where she crouched.

As badly as she wanted to peek over the border of shrubs, she didn't dare. The scent of her body might be masked, but there would be no way in hell she would escape their exceptional eyesight.

"That's a good description of what we're facing," Cabal answered. "It's not over. The hunters are becoming the prey, and if the first five are any indication, we could be looking at some pretty high-profile individuals. The former mayor that disappeared last week was a well-known individual throughout the nation. We're looking at a PR nightmare here."

Cassa felt her mouth dry. The former mayor who had disappeared recently was David Banks, a proponent of Breed rights. He had argued for Breed Law, and had been known to host several charity parties a year in honor of the Breeds. Now he was also rumored to have been a member of a group of men that once hunted Breeds?

She could believe it. She had never liked Banks, but she knew his popularity. His smooth, charming smile and soft-spoken voice had fooled more than one journalist.

"PR is your brother's area," Jonas growled. "I'll let Tanner worry about the sugar coating. I want the killer caught, Cabal. That's your job."

Jonas's voice was commanding, harsh in its reminder. Yes, that was Cabal's job, to do the things that the more public enforcers couldn't do.

"It's hard to do a job when there's no evidence to go on, Jonas," Cabal snapped, irritation clear in his voice. "There's no DNA left on the scene, and no scent. We were notified within hours of the mayor's disappearance. When we arrived, you could smell the scent of his terror, but the scent of his kidnapper was nowhere to be found."

"Find something, Cabal," he was ordered. "We're working on borrowed time here. If you don't find the killer before news of these murders, possibly committed by a Breed, leaks to the press, then we're fucked."

"It looks to me as though we're fucked either way," Cabal informed him, his voice cold. "Horace Engalls and Phillip Brandenmore are making certain of that."

Brandenmore and Engalls, the owners of a pharmaceutical and drug research company, were under indictment for the drugging of the Breed doctor, Elyiana Morrey, and conspiracy to murder in several Breed deaths. They had been caught attempting to buy from her two assistants research conducted by Dr. Morrey, and were rumored to be researching a de-aging phenomenon the Breeds and their wives were supposedly experiencing.

There was no supposition to it. Cassa knew the truth of it. The Breeds were experiencing an aging decrease once they went into mating heat. The phenomenon was making Breed doctors crazy trying to figure it out, and sending the Breed Ruling Cabinet into a frenzy each time the gossip tabloids came up with another angle to tell the story from.

So far, it wasn't being taken seriously. But that couldn't continue much longer. It had been eleven years since the Feline Breed alpha had announced the existence of the Breeds. Ten years since he or his wife had aged in any noticeable way.

Cassa was one of the few people who knew the truth, and she knew the consequences of ever writing that story or revealing her knowledge of it. The nondisclosure agreement she had signed, in return for special consideration in interviews and breaking Breed stories, had been frightening. She was certain she might have signed away her soul, her firstborn child and her cat's blood. Or something close.

"Engalls and Brandenmore are being dealt with," Jonas drawled, his tone one of pure ice. "I'm more concerned with a rogue Breed's indiscriminate killings. Find him, Cabal, or we could all be up shit creek without a paddle."

Cabal grunted at that. "I thought we already were."

"No, at the moment, we have a paddle," Jonas informed him sarcastically. "Now find that bastard before he kills again. I'll be damned if I want to try to clean up another mess like the last one. I'm certain there are still pieces of him missing."

Cassa forced herself to silence. She had the pictures of that killing, she was certain she did. That one, and three others. Pictures that had been sent via secured, untraceable emails that accused the Breeds of hiding a killer.

She hadn't doubted they were capable of it. She just hadn't imagined that even a Breed could do the damage that had been done in those pictures.

Trepidation built inside her as she felt the sweat that began to trickle down her temple at the thought of being caught now. She knew Breed Law, and she knew the price of eavesdropping on this conversation. Like David Banks, she could disappear and her fate never be known.

There was once a rumor that Jonas had a fondness for throwing his enemies into volcanoes. She really didn't doubt it. It sounded like a very "Jonas" thing to do.

"You're pissing in the wind, Jonas," Cabal informed him. "We have nothing to go on here. No suspects, no clues. Until I have one or the other, then there's not a lot I can do."

"Get it." Jonas's voice became dangerous, clipped. "Quickly, Cabal."

"Yeah, I'll get right on that, Director, just as soon as you tell me who the hell I'm looking for." Cabal's voice lowered until it vibrated with suppressed menace. "Until then, there's not a hell of a lot more I can do."

"Banks was from Glen Ferris. Get back there, see what you can find out. We're supposed to be searching for him. Investigate it from that angle."

"Just what I need, you telling me how to do my fucking job," Cabal grunted.

"I could be telling you how to find your mate," Jonas drawled with a hint of amusement. "I'm certain she's around here somewhere. What do you think?"

A dangerous growl filled the air as Cassa felt her heart sink in her chest. Cabal was mated? No, that couldn't be true. Breeds did not ignore their mates, and they sure as hell didn't fuck around with anything in a skirt as Cabal was known to do. The man had a virtual harem kneeling at his feet, begging for the privilege of pleasing him. It was enough to make her teeth clench in irritation.

Jonas had to be talking about a mate in general, not one in particular. Such as in a seek and ye shall find, why aren't you looking for your mate type of thing. That had to be it.

"Don't fuck with me, Jonas," Cabal warned him. "I'm not in the mood."

Jonas chuckled. It wasn't a comfortable or amused sound. It was, frankly, frightening.

"I'm not the one you have to worry about fucking with you, my friend," he drawled. "I do believe though that our intrepid little reporter, Ms. Hawkins, could give you lessons in it."

Cassa felt her lips part in shock. There was a hint of amusement in Jonas's voice now, but none in Cabal's rumbled snarl. The sound was sexy as hell even as it sent chills racing up Cassa's spine—and a flood of warmth between her thighs.

Jonas knew exactly how Cabal felt about her; he had been there the morning Cabal had killed her husband and nearly killed her. She could still feel Cabal's hands around her throat, see the fury and the need for blood in his eyes.

"Drop it, Jonas," Cabal warned him.

Yes, Jonas, please drop it, Cassa moaned silently. She was becoming aroused by his voice, despite her best efforts not to do so. She was worried that whatever that pill did, it would be little defense against the scent of her need. And she was definitely needy. In the eleven years since her husband's death, she had never been so turned on as she was when she was around Cabal St. Laurents.

"Fine, consider it dropped." She heard the shrug in Jonas's voice. "The heli-jet will be ready to fly you to Glen Ferris in the morning. Investigate Banks's disappearance further. We might get lucky and you'll find a suspect while you're there."

"Keep hoping," Cabal grunted. "Trust me, if they're hiding a feral Breed in their midst, they're not going to turn him over simply because I ask nicely."

The residents of Glen Ferris would be more likely to shelter and protect a feral Breed, no matter the risk to themselves. Hell, they'd been doing it for years; there was no reason to believe they wouldn't do it now.

"You know how to ask nicely?" There was a wealth of sarcasm in Jonas's voice.

"Go to hell." There was a wealth of arrogance in Cabal's.

Cassa wanted to laugh at the confrontation, even as she filed away the surprising information that had come her way. Everyone suspected that Banks was dead at this point. It had been a week since his disappearance, and there were no leads on what had happened to him. The river had been dragged, search efforts were still ongoing, but there wasn't a clue to his whereabouts.

David Banks had gone for his evening walk one night in the little town of Glen Ferris, West Virginia. He hadn't been seen again. His body hadn't been found. There was no trace, no clue where he might have gone or what might have happened to him. Until now.

"I'll return to hell, you check on our nosy reporter." Jonas's voice echoed with command once again as Cassa gave a small start of fear. "She was too jumpy at the reception tonight. Make sure she's where she's supposed to be rather than someplace where she shouldn't be."

Cassa sensed the air of hesitation that filled the area on the other side of the shrubs.

"Is she becoming a problem?"

She definitely didn't like the flat, cold tone Cabal used now. He'd claimed he owned her the morning of his escape from that pit, and he took every opportunity to remind her that he could enforce that claim anytime he chose.

"She's always a problem whether she's here or at Sanctuary," Jonas answered.

Cassa's eyes narrowed. She was never a problem at Sanctuary. The Feline Breed stronghold was homier and a damned sight more welcoming to her than the Wolf Breed compound she was in now.

"You don't know how to handle her," Cabal injected.

Handle her? No one handled her, period.

"Only with a whip and a chair," Jonas growled. "Callan and Merinus give her much too much freedom in Sanctuary. She thinks she deserves it elsewhere."

"And this is my problem how?" Cabal argued. "She's a reporter. You should have known better than to allow the invitation she was given to stand."

Bodies shifted. Cassa was dying to look over the top of the shrubs, but she leaned to the side instead, to try to get a view through the open foliage of thick branches.

The glimmer of light from a nearby building revealed the two men. Jonas was still dressed in his tuxedo. Cabal though had changed into jeans, T-shirt and a rain-resistant jacket and boots. His black-striped golden blond hair dripped with the misty rain and fell long to his shoulders.

His shoulders were broad, his waist lean, his thighs muscular and his legs long. Standing there in the rain, he looked like the animal he was. In his prime, ready for action. Sexy as hell, mouth-wateringly male.

She breathed in slow and easy, and felt the familiar slick warmth between her thighs.

"Just make certain she's in her cabin, and well guarded, if you don't mind," Jonas ordered in a drawl heavy with mockery.

"And if I mind?" Cabal asked carefully.

Jonas's teeth flashed in a hard, cold smile as the chilly rain dripped along his face and saturated his short, clipped hair.

"Then I might make you part of her protection detail rather than sending you to Glen Ferris. Come to think of it, that might be a good idea after all."

Cabal's brilliant green eyes narrowed, and Cassa could have sworn she saw the glitter of the amber flecks within the green as he stared back at the other Breed.

"I'll check on her." The hard fury that echoed in his normally cold voice surprised Cassa and sent a chill racing down her spine. Fine, so he didn't want to be anywhere near her. She didn't want him anywhere near her either. She would consider herself lucky if she didn't have to run into him again, period, and she didn't appreciate Jonas sending a babysitter to make certain she was in place.

She had to get back to her cabin before Cabal arrived there. If he found her missing from her cabin or, God forbid, sneaking around in the rain, she could just imagine the consequences. She'd lose every privilege she had gained in the past years where Sanctuary was concerned. Not to mention the fact that she would have to deal with yet more of his arrogant *I own you* bullshit. She almost snorted at the thought of that.

She slid back from her position silently. Heart racing, she fought to move slowly, carefully.

She was running out of time anyway, with the single pill she had taken. Two hours, the information had warned. She had spent most of that time testing it against the Breeds patrolling the compound.

Once the time limit was reached, her natural scent would return quickly, which meant she had less than half an hour to get back to the cabin.

She couldn't let Cabal know she hadn't been there all along, and she damned sure couldn't face him while that drug was still in her system.

They continued to discuss her, much to her dismay, as she slowly retreated. She could hear their voices, but not what they were saying. Once she reached a safe distance, she straightened again and moved hastily through the shadows back to her cabin.

She used the heavy trees that grew throughout the compound to hide her return. Skirting the areas she knew the Breeds were prone to guard more heavily, she made it back to her cabin within twenty minutes. The delays were nerve-wracking as she waited for sentries to move slowly past her, or when she was forced to backtrack to avoid them.

Rushing back through the unlocked window of her cabin, she raced to the bathroom as she heard a vehicle pulling up in the small driveway outside.

Hell. For once, Cabal hadn't wasted any time in following Jonas's orders.

Twisting the knobs to the shower, she quickly adjusted the water and stripped the wet clothes from her body. Tossing the saturated fabric into a nearby closet, she grabbed her scented shampoo, squeezed a large amount into her palm and worked it quickly into her long hair before snatching the bottle of bath gel from a shelf and soaping up a sponge.

She needed scent, lots of it. Pear-scented shampoo in her hair, apple-scented bath gel. Lather built over her body from head to toe as she fought to make damned certain Cabal had plenty to smell when she faced him.

Rinsing quickly, she beat back the racing of her heart, forced herself to remain calm and assured herself the drug had time to get out of her system by the time she conditioned her hair with the pear-scented conditioner, rinsed it and shut the water off.

Minutes later she left the bathroom, her hair bound in a towel, a heavy robe wrapped around her and plenty of apple-scented body lotion smoothed over her. She smelled like a damned orchard.

Normally, she would have used the products sparingly. She preferred unscented shampoos and conditioners, even soaps. The heavy scents bothered her, as well as the Breeds she interviewed or worked with. Tonight was an exception, and she was thankful her assistant had once again slipped the scented stuff into her overnight pack.

Kelly thought everyone should smell like a fruit stand just because she did.

Calm, poised, Cassa stepped out of her bedroom into the wide living room and came to a stop at the sight of a damp-haired, much too handsome Breed, sitting in the large easy chair across the room.

It was no more than she had expected, and it wasn't the first time she had walked into a room that should have been hers alone to find a Breed waiting for her. Though, she admitted, it was rarely this particular Breed. Thankfully, Cabal had kept as much space as possible between the two of them in the past eleven years.

"A little late for a visit, isn't it?" She tugged at the towel around her hair as the mocking question passed her lips.

She didn't miss the flicker of his gaze to her hair as it fell around her shoulders, curled down her back and landed just above her waist. Damp, riotous curls snaked over her shoulders and fell down the front of the robe to lie over her breasts. His gaze touched there, and Cassa was suddenly thankful for the thick material. It hid the hardening of her nipples, but she knew nothing could hide the scent of her arousal now.

Cabal's nostrils flared, his eyes narrowed and his muscles

bunched as he rose slowly from the chair to a very impressive height of six feet, four inches tall. Too tall for her, she thought.

She felt dwarfed by him, despite her own five feet eight inches. She felt too feminine, and too physically weak. She felt like those silly little twits that cooed and ahhed at the sight of him. The ones she hated because they lusted after him with such determination. The slinky little redheads that hung to his arm. The vapid little brunettes she had seen him squire around. She detested each and every one.

"You're normally up rather late," he stated, his voice low as his gaze flickered to her laptop. The one she hadn't turned on all day. "I expected you to be working on whatever story you were coming up with." There was an edge of suspicion in his voice.

Could he smell her nerves along with her arousal? Probably. But who wasn't nervous around him?

"I don't consider the story or my hours any of your business." She shrugged, moved across the room and headed to the open kitchen. "I'm going to fix a pot of coffee. Interested?" In the coffee, she should have said. It was rarely a good thing to leave a question or a sentence open around a Breed.

She felt him follow her. Like a heated breath of air at her back, she could feel him behind her as she moved into the kitchen and headed for the counter.

"Nothing for me."

No coffee, tea or me, she thought sarcastically.

She lifted her shoulder negligently. "Suit yourself."

Silence filled the room as she programmed the coffeemaker and flipped it on. Within seconds, the scent of hot, rich coffee began to fill the room.

Cassa turned then and faced the one man, the Breed, she couldn't seem to help but be fascinated by, despite her own best efforts.

He looked far different now than he had eleven years before, during his rescue from the labs in Germany where he was being held.

There, he had been bloodied, slashed, bruised, near death, but still fighting to survive, in a pit filled with stakes and slashing blades. His pride had fallen around him. Women, children, young men. His screams of rage still haunted her nightmares, as did the knowledge that she had played a part in the horror he had experienced. And he knew it.

Guilt seared her with a slash of pain that raced across her chest, and a sense of fear that never failed to weaken her knees. And he sensed it, just as he always did. She watched his eyes darken, his body tense as the scent of it reached him.

"I haven't killed you yet," he growled. "I'd imagine you could drop the fear now, Cassa."

"Perhaps it's just a case of feminine wariness?" She asked a question rather than making a statement. Breeds could smell a lie, and she wouldn't give him the satisfaction of smelling hers.

"And arousal?" His head tilted to the side as though the knowledge of it were a curiosity to him.

"I bet a lot of women are aroused by you." She was careful to keep her tone even, calm. No nervousness, no hint of guilt. She'd learned over the years how to cover most responses when around Breeds. They sensed too much, knew too much. And Cassa had far too many secrets.

"That doesn't answer my question," he stated, as he continued to watch her much too closely. "Why fear me now?"

Cassa could only shake her head. And stare. She stared at those golden flecks in his eyes, unable to break the hold they had on her. She wanted, no, she ached to touch him, and that was by far the most dangerous impulse she had ever known. And the thought of that need infuriated her. He was the last man in the world she should ache for. The last one that she should need, and she knew it.

"What do you want, Cabal?" She bit the words out as she tried to hold back her anger and her need.

His gaze narrowed. The look was a warning, and it was one that common sense suggested she heed. Unfortunately, common sense had never been her strong point.

"I hear you've been spending quite a bit of time with the Feline Breed doctor, Ely Morrey," he stated. "Why?"

Why? Why, because she was afflicted, that was why. Because her body insisted on retaining some damned hormone within it that she had picked up when she had lost her sanity eleven years ago.

She remembered the moment clearly. The second she had touched her fingers to her lips and tasted Cabal's blood on them. Such a small thing. It shouldn't have been enough, and actually, it hadn't been enough to begin mating heat. But it had been enough to affect her in curious ways. Ways that Dr. Morrey was still attempting to decipher.

Mating heat was the Breed curse. Some Breeds claimed it was their strength; others saw it as a weakness. Of course, it did depend on whether or not the Breed was mated.

"I'm working on a story." That was definitely a lie, and there was no way to hide the scent of it.

A dark blond brow lifted with mocking curiosity.

"I hate it when you lie to me," he warned her softly. "You've been making visits to Ely for the past several years on a regular basis. You would have written the story by now."

Cassa's chin lifted at the deliberate arrogance in his tone.

"Ely's a friend of mine, Cabal, just as the other wives at Sanctuary are friends. I don't need an excuse to visit with them any more than you need an excuse to visit with your pride leader, Callan."

It was a deliberate attempt to get him off the subject of Ely. Everyone knew that Cabal recognized no Breed as his pride leader. He had lost his pride, his family, during a rescue that had gone to hell, and he claimed no other.

"Stop trying to distract me," he growled as he moved closer.

Cassa could feel that nearness. She swore her body heated by several degrees when he moved closer.

"I wouldn't dare attempt to distract you." She shoved her hands into the pockets of her robe as she glared at him. "Don't you have better things to do than to harass me? Shouldn't you be out shooting at Breed enemies or lurking in the shadows for some reason?"

His jaw tightened. To say he was displeased would be putting it mildly. But she had never pleased this particular Breed in any manner. She doubted she would begin tonight.

"Are you in mating heat?"

The question had her staring at him in shock. Excitement raced through her now, just as it always did anytime they came anywhere close to a confrontation. She could feel her body flushing with heat, her heart racing furiously.

"If I were, would I be here arguing with you?" she snapped back. "I'd be with my mate, wouldn't I?"

Unfortunately not. Her mate was standing in front of her, and he was known as the Breed poster boy for sexual excess. The

son of a bitch had had more women under his belt in the past
eleven years than most men could achieve in two lifetimes. He
was a tomcat, plain and simple.

She watched as his jaw tightened further, as his nostrils
flared in his attempt to catch the scent of mating heat.

Cassa wondered how the mates of Breeds could stand knowing that any Breed in the vicinity could tell when they were in
heat and aroused. It had to be horribly discomforting. She knew
for a fact that the physical discomfort could become excessively
painful, and in some cases, dangerous.

She would have preferred to have stayed as far away from
mating heat as possible.

"You're up to something." His lip lifted in irritation. It was
incredibly sexy the way he flashed a single canine while glaring
at her.

She scoffed at him in reminder. "I'm a television investigative reporter. We're always up to something, Cabal. It's part of
our job description."

For some reason, he liked to forget that little fact. Then she
forgot it as well, as he moved closer. Just that quickly, his harder,
stronger body was flush against hers, as she backed herself right
into the wall.

She stared up at him in shock. A distant part of her brain
quickly analyzed the strange sensations that shot through her.
Flames seemed to scorch her flesh; she swore she broke out in a
sweat, and her nerve endings became so sensitive that even the
whisper of his breath against her cheek was a stroke of pleasure.

Sweet Lord have mercy, she thought. She was throbbing from
head to toe, and so ready to throw him to the floor and fuck him
that it was pathetic. She wanted to ride him. She wanted to feel
all that male power and sleek, hard muscle brushing against her
naked flesh, driving inside her.

Her vagina clenched, her womb spasmed and the liquid heat
that trickled between her thighs should have been embarrassing.
She was so ready for him her knees were weak.

But if she was ready for him, it was nothing compared to how
ready he was. His cock pressed into her lower stomach through
their layers of clothes, his expression gone enigmatic, but his
eyes, the gold flecks in his eyes, were richer, deeper than ever
before.

"This is your warning," he growled, as his hands clenched

against the wall by her head. "Keep pushing me, Cassa, and I won't stop next time."

"You'll stop." She could barely speak. Excitement churned through her system, making her voice as weak as her knees. "You won't rape me."

"I won't," he agreed as his gaze flickered over her face. "But we both know mating heat will. Don't we, mate?"

Her lips parted in surprise. She had known, but she hadn't realized he had. How long had he known? For how many years had he been screwing everything in skirts when he had known all along what was building between them?

Before she could blast him, deny him or spurt out a protest, he pushed away from her, turned his back and strode from the kitchen. The only sound in the house after he opened the front door was the sound of that plate shattering on the door where his head should have been.

"You bastard!" she yelled furiously, anger churning inside her now. "You tomcatting, whore-mongering snake." Another plate flew for emphasis and shattered against the wall. "Your mate my ass!" She kicked an end table. "Not in this lifetime." Would she ever admit it? she finished to herself silently.

Because to admit that, she would have to admit so much more. To needs that haunted her through the night, and truths that dogged her through the day. She would have to admit she loved him. And that was something Cassa refused to do.

· C H A P T E R   2 ·

It began here. In this unassuming little town. In the savagely hewn, subtly cruel mountains of West Virginia. Hell began here. A nightmare began here.

It began with one man, one woman and a vision of monsters, of creatures that could be controlled.

So long ago. A lifetime ago. A heartbeat in time, a drop of red in an ocean of blood.

The mountains rose around the peaceful little town of Glen Ferris, nestled in the mountains like a babe in a mother's arms. It hadn't changed much, despite the passage of time and the technology that had birthed a new species. Glen Ferris remained more or less the same. Sleepy, quiet. Quaint.

There was no sign of the vast network that had once worked to shelter and protect the Breeds that had known this area as one of safety. There was no hint on the quiet streets, or in the mountain homes, that these people had once risked their own lives, and the lives of their families, for creatures that weren't man and yet weren't animal. Just as there was no hint of the evil that had once visited and stayed much too long.

It had begun here. Despite the attempts of the citizens of these mountains to save those Breeds that had been brought to them, still, hell had begun here. A hell that so few had known of. A hell that had birthed a darkness that wouldn't disappear, that growled in the night, that screamed in silence.

Here. Within these mountains. Within the home of a man and woman, and with the knowledge and cooperation of those who looked on.

There was no forgiveness. There would be no mercy.

Glen Ferris had been a haven for many, and yet for a few, it had been an agony worse than anything that could have been suffered in those labs. Those Breeds who escaped, they couldn't have known the hell that had existed on the perimeters of freedom.

And now it was time to pay for that hell. It was time for one man and one woman to know that vengeance awaited them.

They had created hell. They had created the means to their own destruction.

Horace Engalls and Phillip Brandenmore had experimented on Breeds. Breeds had been tested, dissected, experimented upon for years untold by a brother and sister, by a wife and husband.

It would be over soon. Soon, the world would know more than they could have ever imagined. Just as they would know those who had helped.

"The past never dies." It was a whisper caught by the night breeze. "It lives on in my memory. Ashes to ashes, dust to dust."

Those who had died in the past months were no more than peons to the powerful family. Two-bit ass kissers who had carried out orders and begged for favors. A doctor, a police officer, a lawyer, a former sheriff and a former mayor. They had participated. They had helped, but none had done so much to collaborate in that hell as the one that would die this night.

H. R. Alonzo. So few knew who he was, what he was. The great-grandson of the man who had donated his sperm to create the first Breed. A man who should have aided, who should have protected those his great-grandfather had fought to protect.

Vanderale had seen to his son's rescue, his freedom and his safety. So long ago. More than a century had passed since the escape of the first Leo, aided by his father, a high-ranking member of the Genetics Council. Alonzo should have continued that aid. He should have donated his fortune to protecting rather than destroying. He should have never reached out to destroy the Breeds. He should have never searched for what was never meant to be his.

Drawing Alonzo back here had been so very easy. Laying the groundwork for what was to come had been a stroke of genius. Engalls and Brandenmore had begun their own downfall with their experiments into the phenomenon the Breeds were experiencing known as mating heat. They alone had believed they could duplicate the antiaging that those mated Breeds were experiencing. They hadn't found the fountain of youth they searched for, but they had found something else. A drug that would deceive those Breed senses, that for a time hid the scent of man from the senses of the animal.

But the secrets they sought still eluded them.

They had failed. The information they had nearly killed to obtain had been denied them. But it was the opening needed. It was the first crack in an impenetrable shield that Brandenmore and Engalls had kept around themselves. It was a shield that would be further damaged by the death of one man.

H. R. Alonzo.

The Reverend Alonzo.

He waddled along the forested path now, a flashlight in his fat little hand, his face sweating, glistening beneath the moonlight. He waddled like a duck, tromped through the forest like a fat little lamb to the slaughter.

How very apt.

"Insane is what this is," he muttered, the sound of his voice carrying clearly through the night. "Son of a bitch, ordering me to a meeting like this," he continued to mumble aloud. "As though it would matter if we met at the house."

The house. It wasn't a house. It was hell. It was a place of pain, of blood and of death. It was where it had begun. And now the ending was within sight.

The night was a whisper of cool spring air. The trees swayed with the breeze, a ripple of water could be heard as it played along the stones and boulders of a centuries-old stream. The scent of fresh, clean water filled the air, almost washing away the smell of sweating human flesh and an evil, rotting mind.

Alonzo. His vast fortune supported the efforts of the Genetics Council. His rhetoric argued against the humanity of the Breeds, argued for their imprisonment, their death.

"Come alone," Alonzo continued to snarl as he made his way

to the small clearing he had been directed to. "As though it matters now."

Had it mattered then, so many years ago? Had it really mattered where Alonzo had met his cohorts? They had thought it had. As though it had been some secret little game. Meeting here, in this clearing, where the blood of Breeds had soaked the ground more than once. Where bodies were still buried. Where the screams of Breed children could still be heard. Where one agonized scream still echoed through the mountains.

Alonzo huffed and puffed, his light wavering as he reached the clearing and slowed to a stop.

Right there. How many times had he stood right there, beneath the breadth of a huge oak, and stared into the clearing with a smirk? Chuckled gleefully at the screams that echoed around him. Participated in the torture and in the pain of creatures that hungered only for freedom.

"So where the hell are you?" Alonzo called out. "I don't have time for games tonight, Phillip."

"Phillip doesn't play games here anymore."

Alonzo's obese, foul body swung around. His florid features reflected first surprise, then shock.

"Who the fuck are you and what do you want?"

There was a hint of fear now. That provided the needed edge of satisfaction.

"I'm the past, Reverend," he was informed softly as the satisfaction and pleasure grew. It always did, when the prey finally knew fear itself. They had once played here, and now they could play again.

Playtime. A smile came and went. What was play? What Breed could answer that question or understand that ideal?

Alonzo's beady little eyes narrowed. "How do you know about this place? Phillip would never have told you."

"Phillip has actually told me many things." She shrugged negligently. "Tell me, Reverend, do you still enjoy playing with death?"

Oh yes, death was returning to these mountains. Blood would stain the ground here once again, and it would begin with HR.

The fat little bastard's face paled. "Phillip wouldn't dare have me killed. You better check your orders, because he knows what will happen if anything happens to me."

Ah yes, the ever present threat.

"Yes, Phillip knows well what will happen." A breath of a promise, of death, filled the air.

There was no secret there, not because Phillip or his insane little wife had told it, simply because the Deadly Dozen, as they had once called themselves, always protected their own asses against one another. That fact had been learned the first time the blood of a member had been shed. The others should be worried by now. HR should have been concerned enough to use caution in coming here.

Tonight, death would lose another member of its evil little group.

Alonzo could sense it, it was there in the waves of fear beginning to fill the air. His heartbeat echoed in the night, the stench of his cowardice wrapped around the senses.

"You're not going to kill me." The bastard tried to bluff. He should know better.

Canines flashed in the night. Alonzo's gaze locked on the sight as his heavy jowls trembled.

"You were here. You smiled." Agony twisted and bloomed in colors of red. *"You laughed as they died. I'll laugh now as you die."*

Forcing back the pain didn't always work. It was always there, always spearing the soul like a poison-tipped sword as the voice weakened and became hoarse.

Alonzo swallowed; a whimper nearly left his throat.

"You'll never get away with it." Terror was thick in the mountains once more, but this time, it wasn't a Breed's terror. It was just a human's. A human of no worth.

"Perhaps getting away with it isn't my aim."

"You'll destroy the Breeds," Alonzo charged furiously as he began to back away. *"My death won't go unnoticed."*

"They don't even know who I am, why should I care about them?" It was a hiss of fury, of hatred. *"Let them deal with it however they will. You are no longer an equation in their battle."*

He stumbled, then righted himself. His eyes widened. His face went white.

"You don't want to do this."

"I did the others. The doctor, the lawyer, the sheriff and the mayor, the police officer." The words were a sigh of pleasure, almost of ecstasy. *"It was good, Alonzo. I tasted their fear, I feasted on their blood. And it was good."*

He froze. Like a deer caught in the brilliant rays of a head-light.

"You," he breathed. "You're the one that killed them."

A chuckle filled the night. The last Breed they could have suspected. It was perfect. It was just perfect revenge. Just a study in exacting revenge.

"It was I." It was a soul stained with blood, with death, with the need for more. "And now it's your turn."

His head shook. His body shook. What was the saying? Like a bowlful of Jell-O? It wiggled and trembled and swayed with terror.

"You can't do this," Alonzo wheezed.

Canines flashed again. Sharp, extended. Prepared.

"Good-bye, you little motherfucker. May you burn in hell."

He turned to run, but there was really no place to run. His screams tore through the night, but there was no one there to care. The gurgle of death, the spurt of blood, the sound of flesh ripping open was a symphony that filled the soul, as the taste of tainted blood touched the tongue.

It had begun here. In these mountains. The dream of freedom had turned to horror. Pain and death and the knowledge that there was no true life, no true freedom. There was this though. The taste of blood. The feel of a diseased soul leaving the body, and the sound of a scream of triumph as life slowly gave its last gasping attempt to survive before succumbing to death.

Alonzo had once sought a Breed known for her killing abilities. She had been called Death. But she hadn't been Death. She had been living, breathing. She had a soul, a mate and a life. That wasn't true death. Death had no soul. It had no mate. It had no life. True death had no dreams and no heart.

Crouched over Alonzo's lifeless body, tasting his blood, feeling it like warm silk flowing through fingers that knew only cold, knew only pain. This was Death.

And Death screamed in triumph rather than pain. Death howled in pleasure rather than horror.

Or was it all the same?

NEW YⴲRK CITY

The email arrived after midnight. Cassa Hawkins stared at the pictures in the file and tried once again, without hope, to use the tracking program she'd installed to track the origin of the email.

User location unknown. The answer was always the same, but this file, just like the others that had come in the past few weeks, held blood and horror. They were emails she knew the Bureau of Breed Affairs was tracking as well, straight from her damned computer. Her tech person still couldn't figure out exactly how they were doing it, but she knew they were. Jonas Wyatt, the Bureau's director, had been quite clear when he had called the day before and warned her to stay out of Breed business.

Cassa stared at the photos. The violence in them sickened her, causing her to swallow tightly to hold back the bile that would have risen in her throat.

She should call Cabal, or at the very least Jonas, she thought. She should do something more than the attempts she had been making to track the emails and the locations of the deaths.

Unlike the others, this email contained at least the location of the murder. The killer had even been nice enough—she snorted at the idea—to send a detailed map of where the body could be found, as well as a letter.

> *Good evening to you, Ms. Hawkins. You will find enclosed the proof of H. R. Alonzo's execution, completed on this day, just after midnight.*
>
> *Glen Ferris, West Virginia. It began here, Ms. Hawkins, and with God's help, it will end here. You should know, the past never dies. As long as there is a memory, there is life. I hold the memories. I hold life. And I'll take yet more.*
>
> *I've tasted their blood and now I hunger. I've warmed myself with their fear, and I've laughed in joy at their deaths. And there will be more.*
>
> *Six down.*
>
> *Six to go.*
>
> *Tell the world. There is no honor, there is no hope. I am what was created.*

Tell the world. Grief ripped through her chest at the thought. If she actually went on the air with a story showing a Breed kill, the consequences would be horrendous. The world, unstable as it was in its opinion of Breeds, would turn against the creations instantly.

Their safety depended on the world believing in the justice and the honor that Breed Law demanded. It depended on the goodwill of citizens who were as fickle in their loyalties as they were in their trust.

She pushed her fingers through her hair and swallowed back a curse before saving the file and encrypting it on her laptop. She couldn't risk its discovery, not yet, not until she figured out exactly what was going on in Glen Ferris.

The story involved more than just the deaths Jonas and Cabal had spoken of the night before. It involved much more than the Reverend H. R. Alonzo's execution at the hands of the very creatures he preached as abominations and the scourge of God. This involved the preservation of an entire race of individuals fighting for survival.

HR was executed just after midnight. She looked at the time on the laptop. It was just after one in the morning. One hour.

She covered her face with her hands and blew out a hard breath. She couldn't report this, not yet. But she couldn't let it go either. She needed to know more.

Jumping to her feet, Cassa jerked the silken robe from her shoulders and tossed it to the bed. She threw open the doors to her closet and pulled out jeans and a sweatshirt, before striding to her dresser for socks and underclothes.

Glen Ferris, West Virginia, was perhaps a nine- to ten-hour drive. She could make it. She'd be dog tired by the time she got there, but she could do it.

Twelve hours, she guessed, before she could even get started finding the location. And if the body were still there? The ramifications of what she was preparing to do began to flash through her mind.

She dressed quickly, threw several outfits into a bag and grabbed an additional, already packed overnight bag from her closet. She shoved hiking boots into her bag as well as a pair of flat dressier shoes. She laced sneakers onto her feet, then grabbed her purse and cell phone.

She was hitting speed dial as she packed her laptop.

"Marv, it's Cassa, wake the hell up," she snapped into her news director's answering machine. "I don't have all night here."

She tapped her foot, waited until the machine beeped, then hung up and called back.

"What the bloody fuck do you want, Hawkins?" Marv Rhinard snarled with sleepy ill humor as he answered the phone.

"I'm out on a story," she told him as she zipped up the laptop bag, pulled the strap over her shoulder and headed for the door. "Have Shelley cover me. I'll call you and let you know what's going on as soon as I know."

"What's the story?" Marv was definitely awake now.

Cassa didn't fly off on wild-goose chases, and he knew it. If she was dumping her airtime on her stand-in, then there was a reason, and usually a damned good reason.

"I'm not sure enough of the details yet, Marv," she informed him as she locked the door and moved down the hall to the elevator. "I'm heading to Glen Ferris, West Virginia, now. I'll call you once I'm there."

"It's those damned Breeds." Frustration filled Marv's voice now. "Do you know those bastards are causing hell's own mess from one end of the planet to another? There was a report last week that Wyatt threw some scientist into a volcano. I needed you in Hawaii to check that out."

"I'd love the vacation, Boss, but no go. The volcano thing is old news and lies at that." Or so she hoped, though she doubted it. Jonas Wyatt would definitely go for the volcano if it was feasible. "This is bigger, if it pans out. I'll let you know more as soon as I can."

Marv cursed again. "Fuck. I hate it when you do this. The viewers don't like Shelley nearly as well."

"Well, they'll have to suck it up or watch the competition. Tell Shelley to flash cleavage and maybe a little thigh while she's reporting. Ratings will skyrocket."

Marv was likely foaming at the mouth, if the virulent string of curses she heard was any indication.

"Look, I have to go," she stated imperatively as the elevator doors opened in the lobby. "Shelley will do great. The stories are waiting on her, or you can rerun some of the older stories. Try the one about that Breed Mathias and the kid he and his wife adopted. That was an interesting piece."

The former Breed assassin and his wife had rescued an abandoned baby several months before and were now trying to adopt it.

"God, you're pissing me off," Marv snapped. "Fine, I'll go through the old footage and see what we can set Shelley up with. But this better be damned good, Cass. I better see blood at the very least."

Her stomach was still roiling at the thought of the blood she had seen. She didn't think Marv really wanted to be a part of the massacre of the Breeds that would occur if that were shown.

"I'll see what kind of gore I can get you, Marv," she promised as she entered the garage and headed for her car. "I'll call soon. I promise."

"Better be damned soon or—" Cassa cut off the *or else* that usually followed. Marv was damned good with the threats and even better at yelling for hours on end if anyone was willing to listen to him.

She tossed her bags into the trunk of her car before sliding into the driver's seat and hitting the ignition. A ten-hour drive was going to suck. Too bad the news station didn't have their own plane; she could have used the lift.

Tossing the phone to the seat beside her, she roared from the parking garage and headed out of the city. Her hands gripped the steering wheel tightly as she fought to keep from speeding. She needed to be there now. She needed to find out what the hell was going on and why a Breed was now attempting to turn world opinion against them.

It didn't make sense. The Breeds could be merciless, she knew it, she had seen it firsthand. But never without reason. And though H. R. Alonzo no doubt deserved a bloody death, if even half of the charges the Breeds laid against him were true, still, there were courts and trials for a reason.

Breed Law protected the Breeds against men like Alonzo. It was the reason the law had been written and was now the framework for justice at any time that Breeds were involved.

The Bureau of Breed Affairs had been established to ensure that Breeds, as well as non-Breeds, followed those mandates, and that the creations man had made were preserved in both safety and freedom.

For the most part, the world supported them, but if those pictures were flashed across the news screen without a damned good story in Breed favor to back them, then world sentiment would turn against them fast.

She glanced at the cell phone as she pulled to a stop at a traffic light and debated calling Sanctuary. She could talk to Merinus and Callan; the pride leaders of the Felines would send a team to investigate, and they would assuredly give her the story. If Jonas Wyatt and Cabal didn't poke their busy little noses into it, just as she knew they would.

The deaths documented in the files she had received were the very ones Jonas and Cabal had been discussing the night before at Haven. Except, H. R. Alonzo hadn't been on the list.

Alonzo had been a thorn in the Breeds' sides since they first revealed themselves. According to Cassa's research, he was also most likely a part of the shadowy organization known as the Genetics Council, though she doubted he was part of the inner twelve.

It was a story she was working on. Alonzo and several others who spoke out often against the Breeds were rumored to have ties to what was left of the Council. Most of the organization had been disbanded once the members themselves were revealed and convicted of having conspired to create, torture and murder the creations known as the Breeds.

Now Alonzo was dead. Who else would die?

Cassa breathed out roughly as she left the city, hit the interstate and sat back for the drive ahead. If she got there fast enough and managed to locate the area where Alonzo's body was now lying, then she might have a chance to find a few of the answers she needed.

Eleven years as a television investigative reporter had given her the experience; a knowledge of the Breeds was an additional bonus. Now she could only hope that she was the only one who had received that file. If she was lucky—and she was praying she would get lucky—then she might have something to bargain with when she was forced to call Wyatt.

Her own pictures. She would need those. The file was good, but it wasn't good enough. Pictures could be faked. Technology was amazing and still growing at a rapid pace. There was no way to prove those photos were, in fact, pictures of men who had died at the hands of a Breed.

Only Banks's body hadn't yet been found. Alonzo's was a new addition, but she had no doubt that Jonas would ensure that his murder was covered up. Jonas was damned good like that. So good, a shiver of fear snaked up her back.

But Jonas wasn't the only one with a knack for doing whatever was needed to protect his people. Cabal was also slowly gaining that reputation. The playboy of the Breed society. The whore-mongering tomcat. He was also whispered to be one of the Bureau's best silent assassins.

He wasn't an enforcer. He wasn't even listed with the Breed registry. For a reason, she guessed. Breeds listed with the registry had to turn in blood and DNA samples. They couldn't turn in fingerprints because those had been burned away in the labs.

She knew what those labs were, the hell the Breeds had endured. If one was now taking vengeance, then God help her, she couldn't blame him. But she knew that the rest of the world would do more than blame the Breed, they would turn on all of them.

There was only one way to ensure that didn't happen. She needed to know why. A face had to be put to the killer, a history. That was her job.

Now she just prayed that Jonas, and most especially Cabal, wouldn't catch her before she managed to do it. If they did, then she didn't have a chance in hell.

· CHAPTER 3 ·

EIGHTEEN HOURS LATER

Cassa was beginning to learn to hate the dark, and as she crashed down the mountain she was cursing her own lack of foresight in not having taken one of those nifty little scent blocker pills. Of course, she was on foot. The tangle of brambles and trees in this part of the forest was too thick for her Jeep to make it through.

Slapping at the vines as she crashed through them, she cursed herself, the Breeds and whoever the bastards were chasing her down the mountain.

She had a feeling that if they were Breeds, then they weren't the friendly sort. She'd gotten an inkling when her attacker had jumped from a broken cliff above her position and snarled in a less than friendly manner.

The curved canines were her first clue that she was in trouble. The Coyote Breeds had curved canines, and for the most part, if they were chasing her now, then they definitely were not the friendly sort.

She heard a low, vicious growl behind her. The sound of it sent her heart rate spiking and her legs attempting to pump faster. She stumbled and rolled down a steep incline before gaining her feet once again.

This was insane. Coming here at night rather than waiting

until morning. She'd been too impatient. The trip to West Virginia had been a nightmare to begin with. A flat tire, then a traffic jam along the interstate that had lasted long enough for her to take a long nap, due to the tanker that had collided with a guardrail before slamming into the face of a mountain.

She'd arrived in Glen Ferris just after dark and had taken the time to do nothing more than check into a hotel before setting her personal GPS with the coordinates that had been sent in the email. After dark.

Her father had warned her before his death that she was going to end up racing into more trouble than she could get out of one of these days. She was certain she had finally met up with that day.

"Nosy little bitch!" The snarl drew her up short as the body of a tall, muscular male Coyote Breed jumped in front of her, blocking her exit.

Cassa let out a girly scream. A high-pitched, surprised scream that pierced her own eardrums before she skidded to the side, went down on one leg and slid past him.

Oh God. Angels watch over her. Jesus, Mary or Joseph, whoever was listening to prayers tonight, just get her out of this one. Get her out of this and she promised she wouldn't harass Marv for a week. No, make that a month. She'd fix coffee for him. She'd call her old biddie of an aunt, send her flowers or something. She would find some kind of good deed worthy of saving her skin.

A low, dark laugh echoed behind her. "Run, little girl," the wicked voice called out, the pitch low, the amusement in the tone sending fear snaking down her spine.

She could feel her own breath laboring in her chest and wondered if this would be the last time she would feel it.

"Did someone forget to post the 'No Reporters' sign?" A hard laugh sounded behind her again.

God, they were playing with her. Coyotes were like cats playing with mice when it came to their victims. And like the mouse, she was running, running, running, and still they were thrashing behind her, shaking the brambles, crunching through the dead leaves and laughing with evil amusement.

She should have thought, should have put more planning into this.

She should have brought a flashlight. The third sharp branch of the night jumped in her path, and this one slapped her broadside, left her cheek stinging and brought tears to her eyes a second before a sharp tug at her jacket jerked her back and tossed her to the ground.

She kicked and struck something hard, a second before a furious yelp was heard, then she rolled and scrambled to her feet again.

She was almost back up and running. She had her foot planted on the ground, ready to sprint, when a hard hand gripped her jacket again and threw her back.

This time, the breath whooshed from her lungs as she hit the ground. The impact sent pain racing through her, and just as she felt the hard fingers touch her next, she heard a hard, furious animalistic roar echo through the night.

The brilliant rays of a full moon broke through the clouds, illuminating the sight of the darkened figures no more than several feet from her.

Six Breeds—she knew they were Breeds—surrounded three others, quite possibly the Coyotes that had chased her through the forest. But in the center of the small clearing, there were two others facing off. A feral Feline roar sounded through the night once again. It was followed by a low, amused chuckle.

"Cabal, you're following in your brother's footsteps a little too closely here. Losing your mate in the forest? Quite possibly a very dangerous thing to do."

Dog.

Cassa recognized him then. The mocking smirk on his face, the glitter of hard, cold eyes as he faced off with an enraged Bengal Breed.

Both men were tall, bold, powerful. Cassa felt the tension that filled the air now, and stared at the Coyote in amazement as he chuckled once again.

"What the fuck are you doing here, Dog?" Cabal snarled. "Last I heard you were leashed."

Dog moved with smooth, lithe grace. A second later a match flared and the tip of a cigar glowed almost merrily, lighting his expression with a red, dangerous glow.

"Last I heard, you had a hold on one nosy little reporter," Dog growled back. "She's none the worse for wear from my gentle handling. A few bruises perhaps."

Cabal snarled again, the sound sending a flare of trepidation surging through Cassa.

"Shall we call this one a draw then?" Dog questioned mockingly as he glanced around at the Breeds surrounding the men with him. "Three against six seems rather unfair odds to me."

"You didn't answer my question," Cabal snapped. "What the hell are you doing here?"

"Perhaps the same thing you are, but with quite possibly different reasons," he answered. "We're searching for the same Breed, I do believe, Bengal. Shall we lay odds on who finds him first?"

They were both searching for a killer. Well, my, my, my, didn't that just make three of them?

Cassa rose slowly to her feet and brushed off the seat of her jeans with what she hoped was a carefully casual move. She bit back a wince at the bruises she knew would be showing soon.

Placing one foot behind the other, she stepped back once, then again.

"Go home to your handler, Coyote," Cabal ordered him coldly. "Or I'll have you carted home."

Cassa took another step backward. Just a little farther, she thought, then she might have a chance of actually getting out of Cabal's sight before he decided to focus on her. If angels were watching out for her, then she could actually make it back to the Jeep and to her hotel without having to face him.

"You have such an amazing capacity for self-confidence, Bengal," Dog drawled. "Sorry, but I'm here to stay for the time being. There seems to be quite a bit of a mess that needs to be cleaned up in these mountains."

A mess? That was an understatement if she had ever heard one.

One more step back.

"Cassa, make another move and you won't be sitting on that perky little ass of yours for a week."

The utter sincerity in the threat had her freezing.

"Dog has taken care of that for you," she snapped out, glaring at both men. "I won't be sitting for a week anyway."

When Cabal moved, it was with such swiftness that even Dog's rumored lightning fast reflexes couldn't help him avoid that fist that planted itself in his face.

He hit the ground with a thud that Cassa swore she could feel even from where she was standing.

To give Dog credit, he didn't come back swinging. He rescued his cigar from the ground, brushed the tip off and replaced it between his obviously swollen lips before breathing out heavily.

"Bengal, that one's free," he stated as he propped himself up on his elbows and stared up at Cabal. Cassa swore she saw a gleam of red in his eyes. "Don't try it again."

"Touch her again and I'll kill you." The promise was harsh, Cabal's voice vibrating with rage.

"Felines are so dramatic," Dog sighed, rising lithely to his feet as he glanced at Cassa.

"Drama" wasn't exactly the word she would have used for it.

"They're something, that's for sure," she muttered. It wasn't a compliment.

Dog gave a brief, hard laugh. "He's Bengal. You should have him explain exactly what that means."

It could be worse than just being a Breed? She eyed Cabal suspiciously. She'd hate to imagine he could be more arrogant or stubborn than most Felines. It would be her luck though.

"Shut up and get the hell off this mountain," Cabal snarled. As he spoke, Cassa cocked her head and listened. Swinging around, she turned and lifted her head. The silhouette was dim. The black against the clouded night sky was hard to detect, but the gleam of metal and the soft, almost undetectable hum was unmistakable. A Breed heli-jet.

She had been so close, almost within sight of the little valley she had been searching for. And now it would all be gone: Alonzo's body as well as any proof that it had ever been there.

She turned back to Cabal slowly, feeling that familiar sense of betrayal rising inside her.

She should be used to it by now. Any story that might actually give her an insight into the Breeds, or might shed some light on the hell they still lived through, and she was blocked. Anytime she came close to the truth, it was covered up.

"Bastard!" She glared at him furiously before turning on her heel, despite his warning, and moving back along the path she had followed in.

Damn him.

"Cassa. Stay where you are!" Hard, cold demand filled his voice.

"Go to hell!" She tossed the words back at him, intent on getting just as far away from him and as fast as possible.

"Give him hell, Ms. Hawkins," Dog laughed. "This is almost as good as actually catching Jonas covering up a crime. Perhaps we'll be luckier next time and really find something. Don't you think the Breeds should be revealed for who we are? You are a reporter after all. Doesn't the story matter?" She could hear the smirk in his voice.

As if she wanted to find anything while he was in the vicinity. The next time she would make certain she blocked her scent first. That way, nosy Coyotes couldn't stop her, harass her or otherwise endanger her self-preservation, where Cabal was concerned.

"I said hold up, dammit." Hard fingers wrapped around her arm and dragged her to a stop, despite her struggles. "You're not going anywhere."

She wasn't going anywhere? Cassa lowered her gaze to stare at the sight of his darker, broader fingers as they encircled her wrist, holding her in place. There was just enough light to make out his features, to detect the glitter of gold in the forest green eyes, and the hint of red as moonlight glinted within them.

Animal eyes. He was a Breed, and she often let herself forget that one little point. He wasn't a normal male, and the reaction she had to him sure as hell wasn't normal.

"You can file a complaint for harassment," Dog's voice echoed in the night again. The Coyote was damned brave considering he and his two men were surrounded by well-armed Felines.

"Shut up, Dog." Cabal's tone was just hard enough to hint at the tension that suddenly flared between them.

Cassa felt it. She watched his nostrils flare, knew he was drawing in her scent, that he could smell her arousal as well as her reaction to the clasp of his fingers.

Such a simple touch, yet the powerful dominance and clear arrogance that was so much a part of him wrapped around her tightly.

It was just his fingers, but she felt so much more. She swore she felt his touch traveling through her body, through her veins, soaking into her pores.

"Let me go, Cabal." Mating heat had started with much less than such a simple touch.

Dog's chuckle echoed through the night again. "Boys, this could get interesting. These Felines get a little intense over their women. And she smells like a hot one."

Heat flamed through her face. Cassa could feel the wave of angry embarrassment that washed through her as she glared back at the Coyote. Her angry look was met with a flash of strong white teeth in the darkness.

"You shouldn't have come here," Cabal warned her, the softness of his voice sending chills racing down her spine.

"Of course I shouldn't have," she agreed sarcastically. "I should have just let you have your little party alone. Let you hide the truth and bury my head in the sand just as everyone else does, shouldn't I?"

She watched his face. Even in the darkness she could detect the tightening of his features and the sudden lust that flared in his eyes.

"That's exactly what you should have done," he snapped back at her as he turned and began to move, practically dragging her behind him.

"Like hell!" She jerked at the hold he had on her. "Dammit, Cabal, stop pulling at me."

He stopped suddenly, turning on her, his eyes shining in the darkness. "Are you going to come with me peaceably?"

"I doubt it." She would have kicked at him if she thought it would do her any good.

"That's what I thought," he snarled. "Lawe, finish up here, and escort those damned Coyotes off this mountain," he suddenly ordered. "I'll meet you back at base."

Where the hell base was, she had no idea, but before she could protest or question anything, he was pulling her down the path once again. Where the hell he actually thought he was taking her, she wasn't sure. The one thing she was certain of: She most likely didn't want to be there with Cabal.

"This isn't going to work," she hissed furiously.

"It's working fine for me."

Of course it was working fine for him. She had no doubt in her mind.

If there was one thing she knew about Cabal, it was that his superior arrogance worked perfectly. For him. What it did for others was another story.

The path veered to the left, the opposite direction of the valley she had been heading for. This was just her luck, of course. And there wasn't a chance in hell that Cabal was going to let her in on whatever was going on here.

"This won't stop me." She didn't fight his hold now. She'd learned over the years of watching mated couples what came of pushing a male Breed too hard. Especially when he was agitated. Cabal was definitely agitated.

Poor fucking kitty.

She hated this. She hated being dragged behind him and forced away from the direction she wanted to go in. She hated being forced into anything anyway. He was taking her choice away from her, with no explanation, with no reason.

"Ignoring me won't work either," she informed him, hearing the shakiness in her own voice.

He was affecting her, she couldn't help it. There was something about being this close to him that made her too warm and made her too damned nervous.

"I'm not ignoring you," he informed her shortly. "Just shut the hell up, Cassa, until I can get over the fact that a fucking Coyote was chasing you through the forest. Do you have any idea what it did to me to see him on your ass like that?"

Anger filled his tone now.

"So why didn't you just shoot him?" she asked with mocking sweetness. "Or dump him in a volcano? Isn't that the preferred method of disposing with irritating Breed enemies this year?"

"That was last year. This year it's a pit of alligators. Didn't you get the memo?"

"Do I ever get the memo?" she muttered. The Breeds didn't inform anyone of anything. They made a point of being close-mouthed and stubborn.

"I'll make sure you get the next one."

She just bet he would. There wasn't a chance in hell he was going to tell her anything, unless he was forced to. If he kept dragging her around like a child, then he was going to find out just where he could shove his memos.

Tightening her lips to hold back the angry words eager to fall from her tongue, Cassa tromped behind him until they came to an area where their wicked black mountain Raiders were parked. The powerful, high four-wheel-drive vehicles held four easily, and if she wasn't mistaken, one of them was outfitted with a lethal automatic rifle on the roll bar that encased the top of it.

"Get in." He jerked open the passenger door to the nearest vehicle.

Cassa eyed the darkened interior suspiciously before eyeing him more so. "Why?"

"Because I said to." Before she could do more than draw a shocked breath, he had lifted her into the seat and slammed the door closed.

She should jump right back out of the vehicle, she thought furiously, but that little click she'd heard a second after the door slammed was probably a lock. And more than likely it would take her longer to figure out how to unlock it than it would for him to get into the vehicle and stop her.

Instead, she crossed her arms over her breasts and glared out the windshield as he moved into the driver's seat and started the ignition.

The soft hum of the motor was barely detectable as he slid the Raider into drive, turned the steering wheel and began maneuvering down the mountain.

He made a path where there were no paths. The mountain-adept vehicle traversed the rolling dips and maneuvered around ages-old trees until they hit the graveled road.

Cassa stayed silent, watched the night beyond the headlights and attempted to get her head on straight where this man, this Breed, was concerned.

They had a past, too much of a past to ever be able to get to the point where other mates were. Those she knew who had mated, loved. They loved each other with a depth and dedication that brought tears to her eyes if she thought too long on it. They adored each other, they trusted each other. And that trust was something she knew she would never have from Cabal.

"Why the hell are you here?" he asked as he turned on the blacktop road that led back to Glen Ferris. "You're supposed to be back in New York."

"Obviously I'm not," she stated quietly. "I'm here."

"Why?"

"I received a tip." She shrugged. "Reporters get those, you know, they follow them to get stories. That's what we do."

"There's no story here, so go home." His voice rumbled dangerously.

Cassa almost smiled at the sound. It would have been intimidating if she didn't hear it damned near every day of her life from one Breed or another. They were always rumbling, growling or roaring. It was their nature.

"Where you can be found, a story can be found," she grunted. "Give me a break, Cabal."

"Give *me* one. Where did you get your tip?" The question was more a demand.

Cassa gave a brief, hard laugh. "Why don't I just give you that information?" There wasn't a chance that was happening.

She turned and glanced at him in time to see his jaw tighten angrily.

"Don't make me dig for the answers, Cassa," he snapped. "Where or who did you get the tip from?"

"Anonymous source," she answered truthfully, knowing it would make him crazy.

She was right. A little growl vibrated in his chest as he glanced at her.

"What did your source say?"

"That you could go to hell," she bit out angrily. "Leave it alone, Cabal. I'm not in the mood for your questions, and I'm sure as hell not in the mood to give you any more information than you're giving me. Now, if you want to try a nice little exchange here . . ." She left the question open.

"Exchange of what?" he asked suspiciously.

Cassa smiled. "Information of course. I don't bargain with anything else. Especially with you."

"Especially with me?" If his tone of voice was anything to go by, he was becoming angrier by the second.

That should concern her, she thought, it really should. Only a fool deliberately teased the tiger.

"Of course." She shrugged again. "I like to think I'm smart enough not to want to mate with a Breed, Cabal. This reaction building between us isn't on my list of things to deal with this year."

And, of course, that comment didn't please him in the least. His expression became darker, tighter.

"And if I decide I do want to deal with it?"

Cassa laughed at that. Trust a Breed to only want to do something if challenged.

"I'd tell you to check your little black book for the name of one of your little playthings then." She heard the contrary tone of her own voice and assured herself that she wasn't jealous.

She had been assuring herself of that for years. She didn't believe it now any more than she had believed it then.

Hell yes, she was jealous. Every time she turned around there was another woman on his arm. Even after she had learned about the mating heat, and learned that the reaction had begun all those years ago in that facility, still, he'd ignored her. She'd begun taking the hormonal treatments to contain the arousal that bloomed inside her at the most awkward times, while Cabal had satiated his lust with other women.

There were days she was thankful that he avoided the heat with the same dedication she did. There were other days that she thought she just might hate him for it.

"So we're going to just keep pretending we're not dying for each other?" he asked, as he pulled into the parking lot of the inn.

Cassa could hear the throb of lust in his voice. It was hard to miss. The dark, husky pitch was a vibration of hunger and need.

"That was my plan." She ignored the regret that ached inside her just as she ignored the loneliness that wracked her at night.

She'd found over the years that there was more to this reaction than just the physical. There were the nights when she'd lie alone and wonder which woman he was with, and hate them both. And there were nights when she wished she was the one he was lying beside.

"Think that plan is going to work?"

She turned to him as he asked that question. "It's worked so far."

He nodded slowly, then reached out to touch the hair that had fallen over her shoulder.

"It won't work if you stay here."

Cassa felt her breath lodge in her throat as the backs of his fingers brushed over the material of the thick shirt covering her breasts.

"Meaning?" She was breathless now, waiting, telling herself she wasn't going to let him torture her even as she almost welcomed the surge of sensation that tore through her body.

"Meaning, you're too close," he explained, his voice dark, filled with hunger. "Meaning, Cassa, get the hell out of Glen Ferris, or you're going to find yourself mated. And I promise you"—he leaned closer as she fought to breathe through the stifling atmosphere of lust that suddenly filled the vehicle—"you won't be writing this story then. You'll be too exhausted to consider a story. I'll make damned certain of it."

Her teeth snapped together in offended fury as she curled her fingers into fists and leaned just close enough, just far enough that she knew he could feel her breath on his lips.

"And I promise you," she stated tightly. "Nothing you do, no matter how you do it, is going to keep me from this story. Remember that, Cabal, before you make the worst mistake of both our lives."

Before he could reply, she hit the latch at the side of the door. When she jerked the handle back to open the panel, it flew open and she jumped from the seat without bothering to look back. Back straight, pride bruised, she strode for the door to the inn.

She could feel him watching her. She could feel him wanting her. And she could feel every hair at the nape of her neck lifting in warning at the thought of exactly what he could do to her.

He could possess her. He could make her beg, and he could break her heart. And Cassa knew, breaking her heart was the one thing that could very well destroy her.

She wanted his love, not just his body. She had a very bad feeling though that love was the last thing Cabal wanted to give her.

CHAPTER 4

Cabal watched her, and he wanted her. Four hours after she left the inn two days later, he was still watching her broodingly.

What was it about her that had made nature decide that she belonged to him?

He tilted his head and watched as she walked down the bank of the Gauley River, following the path David Banks, the former mayor of the city, often took for his evening walks.

She had a nice, long-legged stride, though at the moment her slow, careful walk disguised it. He watched as her jeans conformed to the twin globes of her nicely toned ass. The low band of her jeans enticed him as well. It would take very little, so very little to touch the sweet mound of her pussy at the front of those jeans. The tip of his finger inserted beneath the snap.

He tightened his jaw, his teeth clenching together furiously as the riotous hunger raced through his system. His tongue was swollen; the glands beneath it were spilling the spicy taste of the mating hormone.

The Breed curse. That was his definition of it; others saw it differently. Those couples that had mated called it a gift. Cabal saw very little in the demented reactions of mating that could be a gift.

At the moment, every sense he possessed was focused on the woman rather than the mission he was on. The mission was close to taking a backseat to the mate he had denied himself for so many years.

And why had he denied himself what nature had decreed was his and his alone? What had made him insane enough to believe that he could ever be in the same vicinity without taking her?

Anger. A sense of betrayal. He could still see that flash of knowledge in her eyes when her husband had accused her of knowing what he was doing. Something inside her had already warned her of his deceit. Unless she had truly loved him. Love was blind, Cabal understood that; he saw it on a daily basis with the mated Breed couples. It was blind faith, blind trust, and it took the ultimate evil to tear away those rose-colored glasses.

Her husband had done that. In one moment, whatever she had sensed inside her husband had become clear, and she had seen him for the evil he was.

She should have seen it sooner, the jealous part of him argued. She should have sensed the evil of the man she slept with.

And there they were. The second reason why Cabal had restrained himself. Because she was his mate, because mating brought out the animal within the man and because it kept the man from hiding the true core of his nature.

He was a Bengal Breed—in some ways more, in some ways less, than most Breeds. More animal, more cunning, more savage and vicious and much more deceptive than the normal Breed. And less human.

It was documented, proven. It was what the scientist who developed the Bengal genetics had worked toward. Unfortunately, Bengals didn't fare well in captivity. Those that had survived were impossible to train, as proven by Cabal's team. His pride. Those that he considered his family.

A dozen male and female Bengals. Cunning, fierce, they had been working within the facility for years against the Council. They had smuggled out information, destroyed targets that were Council friendly as well as the targets the Council had sent them after.

They had shed innocent blood, that was true. But they had shed more enemy blood than innocent. And they had saved those that they could.

Cabal had played the reluctant Bengal. Attention was focused on him, while those considered weaker worked around the scientists, trainers and psychologists to destroy them.

So many had died. It was believed that all but Cabal had died; that was a belief that Cabal perpetuated. Those who lived should live free for a change.

Cunning was their strongest weapon, and his people were cunning. They were surviving outside the Breed communities. Cabal was surviving, barely, within it. The restrictions often chafed at him, smothered him. The hunger for freedom after the years of captivity was still a gnawing ache inside him.

The hunger for his mate was growing even stronger than that for freedom. The possessiveness, the need, the demand that he claim her was becoming overwhelming. And with it came the anger.

Cassa was the hardest battle he had ever faced, and he admitted it. He had admitted it more than once in the years since he had nearly killed her along with her husband.

Douglas Watts had been an abusive bastard. Cabal's initial investigation into the man's background had turned up surprising information. Information such as the fact that he had abused several ex-girlfriends. Yet there had been no proof that he had abused his wife, but Cabal knew in his gut.

Cabal hadn't needed proof; he knew instinctively that Watts had to have abused his wife. He wouldn't have changed his pattern, even for love. If he had known *how* to love, and Cabal had no doubt in his mind that Watts had not loved his wife. The investigation he had conducted had shown several instances where the man had cheated on his new wife.

Did Cassa know that her husband of barely a year had had a new lover every other month? Mostly one-night stands. Women he had barely known. He'd had the perfect, faithful wife, and he had betrayed not just her emotions and their vows, but the principles she had lived by and the battle that she had accepted as her own.

Breed freedom. He had sold Breed freedom for a paltry couple of hundred thousand dollars. He had sold information on the majority of the rescues he had covered with his wife. Not all of them, he'd been smarter than that, smart enough that he'd managed to slip past Jonas Wyatt, and that wasn't an easy feat.

And here Cabal was, more than eleven years later, still in conflict with himself over Watts' wife. Over his own mate.

He watched as she continued her slow stroll along the bank of the river, obviously scouring the area for some clue as to the missing former mayor's fate.

There was nothing to find. Cabal and his team had searched that bank more times than they should have. There were no clues, it was that simple. Just as there had been none at the scene of Alonzo's murder. It was as though David Banks had simply walked off the face of the earth. Or had been jerked from it. Which, Cabal couldn't say for certain. The only thing he was certain of was that Banks had been a part of the Deadly Dozen, the group of men responsible for the abductions and deaths of Breeds who had escaped the labs before Breed Law.

Banks, as well as Watts, had been a close associate of Brandenmore and Engalls, the pharmaceutical giants currently under indictment for the attempted murder of Breeds as well as suspected illegal Breed genetic research. Both men had been known to hunt with the pharmaceutical family, for the four-legged variety of prey as well.

Watts had been as evil and as vicious as his scent had indicated seconds before Cabal had killed him. But did his wife know what he had been?

Cabal clenched his teeth at the thought of Watts touching her. For eleven years it had tortured him, knowing that she had been married to Watts. Tortured him? It enraged the man as well as the animal that lived within. It was like an acid burning in his gut, knowing she had lain with him, that she had loved him.

He watched her now, the glands beneath his tongue throbbing as he tasted the hormone seeping from them. The spicy taste was stronger now, the need to claim her growing more desperate.

He had to get away from her. If he didn't, he was going to destroy them both. He could feel the need to snarl in rage at the thought of Watts touching her. The fact that he had been married to her didn't matter. Cabal didn't give a fuck. She'd had no business wearing Watts's ring, allowing his touch.

And Cabal also knew he had no business blaming her for it.

He shook his head. He was falling into the same pit he fell into each time she was too close for too long. The same conflicts. And the same angers.

He saw her, ached for her, and each time he saw the men and women who had died in that pit, because of her husband. Not because of her. It wasn't her fault, he knew that. Douglas Watts had betrayed those rescues on his own. He hadn't even needed his marriage to Cassa to do it. He had already been chosen to cover those rescues. So what the fuck was Cabal's problem? Other than a green-eyed monster that refused to fucking let him go. And a hunger that threatened to destroy him.

His brother Tanner had warned him this was coming. The brother he hadn't known he'd had until his rescue. His biological twin brother. Tanner had known on sight what they were to each other; it had taken Cabal a few months to accept it.

But only his blood could be as damned conniving as he was himself. Yeah, Tanner was his brother, and Cabal had accepted it. Just as he'd finally accepted that Cassa was his mate.

◆　　◆　　◆

Cassa paused at the edge of the water and stared into the rock-strewn edge as minute waves lapped at the darkened soil.

This was the path David Banks normally took for his evening walk. He had been seen here the evening he had disappeared. Right here, in this very spot, below the falls and the old water management plant.

She stared across the water at the brick building with its hollow spillways and boarded windows. In the overcast light it appeared brooding, sinister.

Kanawha Falls. The water that crashed into the small lake ran its course back into the river and continued along its way. And here David Banks had been standing, staring up at the old plant, the last time he had been seen.

That had been two weeks before.

There had been an extensive search of the river. Divers had been called in, satellites had been aimed into the murky depths and remote search bots had canvassed the water for days. Nothing had been found.

The sheriff, Danna Lacey, had led search teams through the area. Not so much as a clue to what had happened to the former mayor had been found. It was as though he had disappeared off the face of the earth.

Shaking her head, Cassa turned and stared up the sloped bank that led back to the parking area and a small picnic location. Winter-dried bamboo saplings waved in the breeze, while the hulking skeletons of bare trees cast dark shadows out over the bank and reminded her that nothing in this beautiful little town was as it seemed.

Breathing out roughly, she made her way back up to the parking area before turning and heading into the edge of the trees that led back to the main river on the other side.

There had been nothing to indicate that David Banks had walked into the forested area. It wasn't part of Banks's known walking trail, and it had been searched many times. She didn't expect to find anything to indicate that he had been there; rather, she was making note of whom she saw and what she saw.

One thing she had made note of was the fact that she was being followed by none other than Cabal himself. She had seen two other Breed Enforcers in town earlier, at the small café where she had breakfast. Rule Breaker and Lawe Justice had been quietly amused as they watched her. They had then traded off duties with Cabal after she left the café.

He'd been following her ever since.

Didn't he have his own investigation to see to? She was certain he had more resources in the area than she had managed to dig up, despite the fact that she was acquainted with several of the journalists in town, as well as the sheriff.

There was a dead end here on Banks as well as H. R. Alonzo's murder. And what made it even worse, one of the first news stories of the morning was the report that H. R. Alonzo had died in a blaze that had swept through his Missouri home. The cause of that blaze was yet to be determined, but the unofficial report was that HR's fireplace and the fire that had burned within it had somehow been the cause.

It would be ruled an accidental death, just as the others had been. Jonas Wyatt and the Bureau of Breed Affairs were amazingly efficient, at all times.

It would make the story she was working on more difficult. It was hard to report someone had been murdered by a Breed when a human coroner ruled the death accidental. The pictures she held were next to worthless, but not a total loss.

What the hell was going on? She couldn't believe the Bureau would turn a killer loose, but she knew Wyatt and his enforcers. If there was a rogue Breed out there threatening the stability of the Breed community, then they would have neutralized that threat as quickly as possible. Which meant they didn't know any more than she did.

More than likely, they were being led on the same wild-goose chase she was being led on, and refused to admit to it.

"Ms. Hawkins, you do like to live dangerously."

Cassa came to a hard stop as Dog stepped just far enough from the other side of a tree to allow her to recognize him.

The overcast day lent a brooding, harsh quality to his expression. It cast shadows that did nothing to soften his features or to help him appear less threatening. Though Cassa doubted anything could make the Coyote Breed appear less threatening. And considering the fact that Cabal was likely not far behind her, the situation had turned into one with the potential to become rather dangerous. At least for Dog.

"And you say I like to live dangerously." She gave a short, sarcastic little laugh. "You must be suicidal."

"That's the general opinion." His lips quirked into a rueful, if not mocking, smile, and his strong white teeth gripped an ever present cigar. "But you're definitely showing signs of following in my footsteps."

She gave a false shiver of dread. "Bite your tongue, Coyote. I can't think of anyone who would want to do anything so fool-hardy."

For a second, something dark and bitter flashed in his gaze, but then it cleared and the familiar icy disdain replaced it.

"Neither can I actually," he drawled. "Which leads me to wonder exactly why you're still in Glen Ferris. You should be in Missouri covering H. R. Alonzo's accidental death." His lips tilted in a cruel, cold smile. "Poor bastard burned himself to a crisp."

"So I heard." She shoved her hands into the pockets of her leather jacket as she watched him warily.

"Coroner ruled an accidental death. Did you know his will states a wish to be cremated? Ashes to ashes, dust to dust." His canines flashed warningly.

Alonzo didn't die in a damned house fire and he knew it. Dog had been in those mountains the night before, most likely for the same reason she had been there. To find proof that the Bureau was hiding a rogue Breed. Unlike Dog though, it wasn't the killings she wanted to reveal, it was the reason behind them. She wanted a story that wouldn't destroy the Breeds, while she was certain Dog was more inclined to see the worst possible scenario revealed. He was rumored to be part of whatever was left of the Genetics Council. He was the muscle—no one had quite figured out for certain who held his chain.

"Why are you bothering me today, Dog?" She crossed her arms over her breasts and faced him suspiciously. "I think we're both aware Cabal isn't too far away."

"Yeah, those Felines have a rather good habit of keeping track of their mates," he commented with a slow nod of his black-streaked gray head.

The breeze whispered through the dark and light strands of hair as he turned his head against it and stared out at the river once again for long seconds.

The coarse strands rippled over his shoulders and down his neck. Long hair for a Breed, she thought. She much preferred Cabal's golden blond and black hair. It was soft to the touch; she remembered that suddenly. Feeling his hair against her face as he leaned into her so long ago.

I own you.

"I hope the memory is a pleasant one."

She was jerked out of her reverie by Dog's mocking voice. She stared back at him suspiciously, watching the slow, cold grin that shaped his lips.

"You're picking into things here that you need to stay out of, girl," he finally drawled warningly, those cloudy gray eyes flashing dangerously. "You need to get the hell out of Dodge, as they say."

"And you need to get the hell out of my business," she stated tightly.

His lips tightened around the cigar he still held between his teeth, before he reached up and lifted it free with two fingers.

"Girl, you need to heed a warning now and then," he snapped back at her. "Let me help you out here. You and your mate. Drag his ass to the nearest bed, get yourself nice and warm and sit this one out. Let it the fuck go."

"And why would I do that?" She narrowed her eyes back at him.

"Because you don't want the answers you're going to find here. And trust me, Jonas doesn't want you to find them. That could make for a very sticky situation for both you and Cabal."

"And you care for what reason?"

He stared back at her speculatively before answering. "I'm not really certain. Maybe I've found a conscience."

"In a Cracker Jack box?" she snorted. "Give me a break, Dog, we both know better."

He laughed at that. She had researched Dog, perhaps almost as much as she had researched Jonas Wyatt. The two men were like the opposite sides of the same coin. Not exactly a good-and-evil type thing—shades in between, but poles apart.

Dog wasn't a man that would listen to a conscience, even if he had one. She had her suspicions about who and what he actually was, but she kept them to herself. There were levels of being wrong. If she was wrong about him, then it could be such a major wrong as to be fatal.

"Cracker Jack box," he repeated musingly. "Interesting. But, as I was saying, it's time for you to leave Glen Ferris. I figure I'm the Breed to ensure you do just that."

"And you're going to accomplish this how?" She laughed.

Cassa was almost amused. She had to admit, Dog taking an interest in this made her distinctly uncomfortable—an interest in her that she didn't particularly like right now.

He inhaled slowly. His smile was positively even more evil than before.

"I have my ways," he drawled, then stepped forward.

Her hands dropped from her breasts as she tensed, stepping back.

"You know he's watching," she whispered, feeling her heart race as panic began to override the normal calm she always fought to achieve.

"Of course he's watching." His smile was predatory, his demeanor threatening. "He's always watching you, Ms. Hawkins. If not him, then someone he directs. You are always being watched, at all times."

She swallowed tightly. Cabal wouldn't do that. He wouldn't have her watched like that. She shook her head, trying to understand why he would do such a thing, if he was.

"You've got a screw loose," he said softly. "Dangerously loose. Do you think he wouldn't see the threat you could be?"

"So you're going to do what? Kill me while he watches?" she snapped back, her head swinging around as she fought to catch sight of Cabal. He wouldn't do that. He wouldn't allow anyone to harm her, ever. If he was going to kill her, then he would do the job himself, it was that simple.

"Kill you?" He chuckled at the suggestion, as his eyes glinted with brief amusement. "I have no desire to kill you, Ms. Hawkins. But I have to admit, I was wondering how sweet your kiss would taste. Tell me, has he kissed you yet? Touched you?" There was an edge of anticipation that surrounded him now, that filled his expression. An edge of hunger.

"He'll kill you."

He laughed again. "You think you know him so well, don't you, Ms. Hawkins? Well enough to believe he would lose his mind if I touched his woman."

"He came after you last night," she reminded him.

"He did." He tilted his head in acknowledgment. "I knew he would. He's a Bengal. I was chasing you, he was chasing my team. You were an incidental."

An incidental. Yeah, that sounded like the story of her life. Incidentally left out in the cold and in the dark.

"For whatever reason," she replied. "He'll kill you if you touch me."

"He's a Bengal." Hard, sharp canines flashed in the dreary light. "He'll wait. He'll watch. At this moment he's calculating the chances that I'll actually touch you. He's deduced there's a ninety percent chance I will, and he's deliberating his move. He's a Bengal, my dear Lady Hawkins. Cold. Manipulating. Calculating. Deceiving."

"Bored." Cabal's voice seemed to echo inside her head as he stepped around the trunk of a nearby tree, his broad shoulders rippling beneath the dark long-sleeved T-shirt he wore, his arms resting casually at his side. Black jeans conformed to long, powerful legs, while black biker boots gleamed with a dull, dusty edge on his feet.

Cassa's heartbeat kicked in; it slammed against her chest as her womb gave a surge of complete feminine surrender and a slick, wet heat dampened the flesh between her thighs.

Out of hand. He might as well have kissed her already, mated her, because her body was more than interested in giving up any fight her mind might want to wage. Traitorous hormones surged and rioted through her body, even as she fought back every reaction that weakened her knees.

His amber-flecked green eyes glittered in his bronze face; a stubble of a beard darkened his lower jaw and gave him a rough, dangerous appearance. Even more so than Dog.

And he did look bored.

Dog turned a knowing look on her, a sandy brow arching in mocking acknowledgment of his own assessment.

Looks were deceiving, Cassa knew, and as Dog had said, Cabal could be manipulative, calculating, deceiving. She wasn't a Breed; she couldn't smell the danger in the air, but she could feel it. Cabal was anything but bored. He was controlled, a quiet, ready control that filled Cassa with tension.

"She thinks she knows you, Bengal," Dog drawled as he flicked a glance back at Cabal. "She thinks you're possessive of her."

Cassa took another step back. There was something about Dog's tone, about the mocking amusement suddenly filling it, that warned her the situation could deteriorate. Quickly.

Unfortunately, Dog wasn't using what should have been his normally superior Breed senses, because he followed her step for step. A move Cabal watched with predatory awareness.

"Does she then?" Cabal asked, the smooth, dark resonance of his tone sending a shiver racing down her spine as he followed each move Dog made.

Cassa stepped farther away, but to the side, edging closer to Cabal as he turned his hand, palm up, toward her. That smallest indication had her heart tripping with something other than dread or fear.

It was that slow outreach of his fingers. At first, a casual movement, nothing to really suggest anything emotional, anything to attach hope to. But those fingers, long and broad, powerful, his palm held out to her. It became a lifeline to something she wasn't certain of, something she knew she couldn't refuse.

Keeping her eye carefully on Cabal, she moved for the safety of that touch. Something urged her, warned her, that if she didn't get to him, if she didn't hold on tight, then she would never be safe.

"Not quite yet."

· CHAPTER 5 ·

Startled, a weak cry fell from Cassa's lips as she felt Dog's fingers wrap around her wrist, holding her in place. There was no pain. She knew with full mating heat that the female mate couldn't tolerate the touch of a male other than her mate.

She stared from Dog to Cabal. Her gaze met cloudy gray eyes then amber-flecked green as a low growl emanated from Cabal's chest. She could feel the tension rising in the air around them as Dog's fingers wrapped around her wrist.

"What are you trying to prove?" She stared up at Dog suspiciously as Cabal paced closer, his gaze narrowed on them.

"I warned you, didn't I?" he said softly. "He's a Bengal, Ms. Hawkins, I warned you of that. He won't risk his mission for you."

"Dog, you're pushing your luck," Cabal warned him, his voice rumbled and deep. "Let her go."

Dog's lips quirked as he lifted his brow inquisitively toward Cassa. "His brother is much more volatile with his mate."

It was a well-known fact that Tanner Reynolds would attack any man that dared to touch his mate, Scheme.

"We're not mates," she said, fighting to tamp down the anger and the disappointment that Cabal wasn't doing exactly what she knew any other Breed mate would be doing.

Dog merely chuckled again, but seemed to pay no attention as Cabal stepped closer. Cassa could see the fury sparkling in Cabal's eyes; the amber flecks were almost neon now. Dog on the other hand looked as calm and cool as a man contemplating a cold beer rather than one going head-to-head with a Bengal.

"Oh, you're mates," he drawled, his eyes flicking back to Cabal. "Tell me, Cabal, why are you letting your woman roam alone? It could get dangerous around here."

"Not for her," Cabal stated, his tone rough and deep, the fury in it sending chills racing over her body now.

Dog's fingers caressed her wrist. The feel of it was uncomfortable, wrong. Like nails over a chalkboard, it almost had her wincing in distaste.

"Dog, don't make me kill you," Cabal warned him. "Release her."

Cabal could feel the fury building inside him as he watched the Coyote Breed, fingers wrapped around Cassa's wrist, holding her in place.

What the bastard was up to, Cabal hadn't figured out yet. There was no air of intent where the Coyote was concerned, no sense of threat. Rather, Dog was playing, pushing, for what reason Cabal couldn't decide.

He should kill him, Cabal thought. Hell, he should have killed him a long time before this, but for some reason Jonas had a "no kill" attached to this particular Coyote. He was no doubt one of the fucking pawns the director of the Bureau of Breed Affairs so enjoyed using. Cabal called them Jonas's pets. Enemies, or at least perceived enemies, that Jonas was somehow using in one or more of his little games.

Though Cabal had a feeling Dog was much more than that. This was a Coyote that no one, not man, woman or Breed, would use without Jonas's express permission.

If Dog didn't take his hand off Cassa though, Cabal was going to ignore that "no kill" order. The Coyote was going to die—now.

Cabal could feel the need for blood rising inside him, trying to overpower, overwhelm the cold, hard calculation that was so much a part of him.

She was his mate, and not just another man was touching her, but another Breed. This woman—her body, her hormones, her very essence—was the perfect match for Breed mating, for Breed conception, and another Breed was daring to touch her.

He felt the low growl that built in his gut, rumbled in his throat. He had to force himself not to clench his fists, not to jump for the bastard. Not to tear his woman away from the Coyote and place his mark on her immediately.

The urge was desperate. It pounded through his veins, throbbed in his head. The need to mate her, to slam inside her was a pulse of electric hunger rioting inside him.

Arousal was reaching critical mass. The urge to mate her, to mark her, was threatening his control.

"Let her go." Cabal stepped closer, every sense he possessed focused on the hard fingers around his mate's wrist, holding her back from him.

Dog tilted his head to the side and gave a slow, hard grin.

"I'd like a taste of her first."

Cabal saw red. As Dog jerked Cassa against his chest, a little cry fell from her lips and she reacted to the unwanted hold. Cabal saw her knee slam upward even as he moved.

He wouldn't allow Dog's lips to touch his mate's. He wouldn't allow the other Breed to claim what was his. Spicy heat filled his mouth and infused his senses. The mating hormone, its taste brighter, hotter, enflamed an arousal already building past the boiling point.

As Cassa's knee connected with Dog's hard thigh, Cabal was pulling her from the other Breed's grip as his fist slammed into the hard, rough contours of Dog's face. A snarl tore from Cabal's lips even as he tried to hold it back.

Pure bloody rage consumed him. A rage unlike anything he had ever known, unlike even his fury when his pride had been thrown in that damned pit.

Mating heat and possessive fury swirled through him as he felt the soft heat of his mate's body come against his own. Heard the crack of his fist against Dog's jaw and felt the animalistic instincts he kept tamped down roaring to the surface.

"I'd rather face terrorists than Breeds." A hard hand slammed into his chest, almost knocking him back in surprise as Cassa struggled in his arms, almost pulling away from him.

"Stay still." He clamped his arm around her, holding her in place against his side as Dog quickly righted himself.

"Where's that cold calculation everyone thinks you have, dumb-ass?" she yelled furiously, slapping at his shoulder once again.

Cold calculation? It had gone the way of common sense the moment he first laid eyes on her. When it came to Cassa, there was nothing cold about him, no matter how hard he tried to pretend.

"My, my, the Bengal has snapped," Dog drawled derisively. "Was there an error in your genetic sequencing perhaps?"

"Fuck off, Dog!" Cabal bit out crudely.

Dog's answer was a low chuckle as Cabal struggled to hold on to Cassa in all her fury. That fury, the feel of it, the scent of it, wrapped around his senses and challenged the animal rising inside him.

He could smell Dog's scent on her. It enraged him. The genetic coding that made him the most fierce, the coldest of killers, was receding beneath the demand that he protect and mark his mate. Nothing else mattered.

"Come on, Bengal, be a good little kitty and share a little bite." Dog laughed.

The Coyote had a death wish.

Cabal forced back the rage, clamped his arm around his struggling mate's waist and leveled a hard glare on the Coyote. Cold. Calculating. That was what he was. He had his mate. She was safe, secure, by his side, if reluctantly. The calm he needed slowly infused his being, though the animal still growled, if silently, in impatience.

"You're both dead," Cassa raged at him. "Infantile. Morons. You're like two bullies playing schoolyard games."

She continued to struggle, and Cabal continued to hold her. Right by his side, where the warmth and softness of her seemed to sink into his flesh through the layers of their clothing.

"The game is over," Cabal informed her as he stared back at Dog. "Find another playground, Dog. Now."

Rather than replying, Dog pulled another cigar from his shirt pocket, lit it and smirked. Cabal kept his eyes on the Coyote, his senses trained on Cassa. He could smell her anger, her arousal. And her fear.

"Bengal, I think you're the one that needs to find another playground," Dog stated then. "I'd watch out for that pretty mate if I were you. She's a luscious little piece, Bengal. Tempting, if you know what I mean."

Tempting. The scent of her called to him, even with that hint of fear. The fear of the unknown or fear of him?

"Touch her again, and I'll kill you."

He watched Dog's gaze flicker then. It was a promise Cabal made, it wasn't a threat, and the Coyote recognized it for what it was. But the damage had been done, and Cabal knew it. He could feel it pounding through his veins, rushing through his heart and tormenting the glands beneath his tongue.

Mating heat was a fury burning through his body now. His cock was thick, hard. Blood pounded in his tightened balls, sending a wave of lust rushing through his body.

His woman. His mate. That was all that mattered, all he cared about. Claiming what belonged to him. Eliminating any threat that could be made to his position as her mate.

Logically he knew that it wasn't possible for such a threat to succeed. This woman was designed for him; no other could mate her. Or so the Breed doctors and scientists claimed. But the animal inside him refused to listen. It wouldn't listen any longer.

Finally, Dog inclined his head and backed away. It was only then that Cabal realized that his voice when he uttered that final threat had been more a savage snarl than a recognizable human voice. Not that he was human, but never had he heard that tone in his voice before.

It had silenced Cassa as well. She was standing still now, tense, waiting.

"Take care of her, Bengal," Dog stated quietly as he moved farther back. "You may be the only one who can. She seems to have a bit of a reckless streak."

A reckless streak didn't describe it. She was independent, stubborn. She was the woman nature had declared would belong solely to him. If he claimed her.

"I hate Breeds," she muttered at his side as he stepped back, moving toward the parking lot of the Kanawha Falls Park.

His truck was parked there. It was a short distance, and from there the ride back to the hotel would be brief. If he made it back to the hotel before he mated her.

He was dying to kiss her. He was all but carrying her as he kept his gaze firmly on Dog's receding form. His nostrils flared as he tested the wind, searching for any hint, any scent of an enemy, Coyote or human.

"This is insane, Cabal. I have a job to do here." But she wasn't struggling. He could feel the anticipation moving through her, building in the air around them just as it was building inside him.

The anticipation of the mating, the arousal. Pleasure. There was said to be no greater pleasure than that of a mating. Cabal was about to find out.

"I told you to get the hell out of here," he bit out harshly as he turned and moved for the truck.

Hitting the remote, he strode quickly to the truck, threw the door open and lifted her into the passenger seat. He didn't give her a chance to slide around into the seat. Gripping her hips, he pushed himself between her thighs, notched the hard length of his cock there as he gripped her hair, tilted her head and took the kiss he had been dying for, for eleven long, lonely years.

· CHAPTER 6 ·

It was fire and ice. It was a kiss unlike anything Cassa had ever
known. It was infused with passion, with hunger, with the spicy
taste of the mating hormone and the dark seductive taste of the
man himself.

The taste of the man himself was more potent in ways than
even that of the mating hormone she could feel rushing through
her system. Like the strongest narcotic shot straight into her
system, it produced a sense of euphoria, of need, of a clamoring,
fiery hunger invading her body.

It wasn't much different from the needs that had filled her
before his kiss. The only difference was the physical burn, the
taste, the sudden, overwhelming need for more. Now.

Her hands dove into the thick gold and black strands of hair
that lay to his shoulders. Her fingers clenched in the coarse mass,
pulling him closer as she took his tongue again and again, accepted the taste of the mating hormone and gave herself to him.

She had fought it. She really had. For over ten years she had
tried to ignore it, just as he had. They had stayed as far apart from
each other as they could. Now there was no ignoring it. There was
no way to hide from it. They would never be able to hide from it
again.

Lips and tongues melded, stroked and sucked. His hands pushed beneath her T-shirt and Cassa felt the shudder that tore through her body as his calloused hands touched her bare back.

She remembered the sensation of his skin touching hers, even before the hormonal influx that spilled from his tongue. So long ago, his hand around her neck as he swore he owned her. The touch of his hand then had nearly overwhelmed even her fear. Now his touch sent a rush of sensation, hard and brutal, to strike to the very core of her.

It was too much, too soon. The hormonal fluid from the glands in his tongue shouldn't react on her this quickly, not this hard. Not considering that for the past five years, she had been taking the hormone treatments given to mates. She shouldn't be reacting this strong, this fast. She shouldn't be, unless the hunger of the mating heat was reacting to her own desperate need for his touch.

And it was desperate. It had been desperate for years. He had been the focal point of her deepest fantasies, her every desire, and she needed him.

She needed him and she was going to take him. They could run from the need, but they couldn't hide from it. For eleven years both of them had run, and now the running was over.

"Damn you!" His growl was one of frustration and driving need as he tore his lips from hers long enough to watch, the amber in his gaze flaming, as he jerked her shirt over her breasts.

The cold air met her heated flesh, adding another sensation. It was surrounding her, rushing through her until she could barely breathe for the need.

"Damn you," she panted brokenly. "You've screwed everything in sight for eleven years. You've ignored this. Ignored me." And she hated him for it. Hated him for the years she hungered for him, the years he had kept that distance between them.

"I spared you this!" His hand tightened in her hair as the fingers of the other flattened at her waist, stroked upward, then cupped one hard, aching mound of a breast.

Cassa sucked in a hard, deep breath at the feel of his hand through the lace of her bra. The heat of his touch was brutal. The feel of his fingers was like a fever raging in her blood.

"You didn't spare me anything," she gasped, glaring back at him even as her body rioted for more of his touch.

"I spared myself then," he snarled, a second before his head lowered, the sharp tips of his canines raking her neck as a growl rumbled in his throat.

Sweet heaven that was good. Her head fell back for more, the feel of his lips, his teeth against her throat was both ecstasy and frustration. It was edged with a sharp pleasure that raked across nerve endings too sensitive to bear.

She felt his hands, one cupping her breast, the other supporting her back. She felt his teeth raking her flesh, and shivered at the electric sensations racing over her.

"I've needed you." She hated the whimper, the weakness she revealed with those three little words, with the way her hands tightened in his hair, with the huskiness of her voice.

She had needed him since that fateful day that the husband who had sworn his loyalty to her had betrayed everything she believed in. She had needed him, needed the power and the promise in the very threat she knew he was to her self-control, to her very survival.

"God, Cassa." He nipped at her neck, his fingers tightened on her nipple.

Between her thighs Cassa could feel the growing wetness, the slick, heated essence of arousal coating the lips of her pussy, sensitizing them as her clit began to throb with erotic pain.

She had waited so long, fought so hard to run from it, only to end up right here, in his arms. Finally.

The same place so many other women had been.

"I hate you." The sob in her voice belied the words.

"You'll hate me worse before the day is over." He pushed the cup of her bra over the throbbing flesh of her breast, and she lost her breath.

Capturing a hard, too sensitive nipple between his fingers, he rolled the calloused pads against it and sent her senses spinning with the pleasure.

They were in public. The park might be deserted now, but they could be discovered at any moment. God only knew where that hateful Coyote was, probably spying on them. She didn't care if a whole damned pack of Coyotes were spying. She didn't want to let him go. She didn't want to lose this touch, his kiss.

Gripping his hair, she fought to draw his lips back to hers. She wanted more than the spicy, addictive taste of the hormone that spilled from the glands beneath his tongue. She wanted more than just his touch. In his kiss, there was an intimacy she couldn't define. As though only there, he allowed her to have all of himself.

And he gave it to her. His tongue licked at her lips, his teeth nipped, lips rubbed then devoured her breathless moan as she arched closer to him.

The naked peak of her breast rubbed against the rough material of his shirt. She wanted flesh against flesh. She wanted to feel the tiny, silken hairs that she knew covered his body. She wanted to see the stripes that were rumored to be so damned sexy.

She wanted her Bengal. Her mate. She wanted what she knew no other woman would ever have with him, had never had with him.

This. Mating heat.

In the next instant, his lips lifted from hers as the words tore from them: "I'll end up fucking you here."

Cassa stared up at him. The amber in his eyes was almost neon against the velvety dark green. Intense eyes, filled with hunger. His expression was drawn with the lust surging through him, his lips swollen from their kisses.

Cassa stared at the strong, savagely hewn features and felt her heart trip from more than just the lust surging between them. There was such strength, so much hunger, and yet a thousand betrayals reflected in his eyes, in his expression. He could lust for her, hunger for her, but as she stared into his oddly colored eyes, there wasn't a hint of the emotions, or the wellspring of need that she felt rising inside herself.

Mates loved. Every mated couple that she knew loved, and they loved deeply.

"Cassa." His head lowered as he whispered her name once again, a grimace contorting his face as he took a quick kiss. Then another. The third became deeper, longer.

Cassa felt herself falling beneath the pleasure of his touch once again. She lost time and place. She lost herself. There was nothing but this pleasure, this kiss, this man.

"We have to get the hell out of here." In the next second he was pushing away from her, taking the heat and the promise as he straightened her T-shirt before pulling back and pushing her into the seat.

Cassa watched him as he closed the door, sealing her into the truck rather than the Raider he had used before. Pushing away from the door, he loped around the front of the vehicle to the driver's side, got into the truck and started the engine.

He didn't pull out of the parking lot. He caught the back of her head in his hand, pulled her head back and filled her senses with another of those long, deep probing kisses.

Her nails dug into his arm as a whimper of need escaped her lips. She wanted him now. Waiting until they reached the hotel room was quickly becoming a hazy notion. She was beginning to wonder if it wouldn't be possible to slip in a quickie in public after all.

"Damn you. I knew you'd be fucking dangerous." Cabal's voice was tortured, as tortured as her feverish mind.

And she wasn't the one that was dangerous. It was him. His kiss, his touch.

Breathing harshly, she forced herself to sit still, to keep her hands to herself. She wasn't going to start stripping his clothes off in the pickup, but it was close, really close.

He had a body to die for. Or one a woman would kill for. And if rumor was to be believed, then once those clothes came off, the hungry, powerful male animal beneath was unleashed.

The thought of that was both anticipatory as well as irritating. Rumor came from all the damned bigmouthed women who thought they had to brag about sharing his bed. From the women who had touched him when he belonged to her. The women he had warmed through the nights when she had lain alone, wishing, dreaming, regretting.

Thankfully, Glen Ferris wasn't a large town; the inn she was staying in was only a few miles from the falls. Cabal pulled into the parking lot, shut off the engine and threw open the door. He didn't bother striding around and helping her out on her side. Impatient Bengal that he was, he pulled her across the seat, ignoring her breathless little cry, before gripping her hips and setting her on the ground.

Within seconds the vehicle's locks were clicking in place and he was gripping her hand, pulling her toward the front entrance.

Cassa could feel her head spinning. She wanted to protest, something. She wanted to demand more, but she wasn't certain what she needed to demand. All she knew was the sudden need for the spicy taste of his kiss, for the heat of his touch. Just Cabal. The years of dreams and fantasies were finally coming together, and she found herself suddenly unable to wait. Unable to function without his touch.

The journey to her room seemed to last forever, yet when Cabal took the key card from her hand and opened the door, she suddenly wished it had taken longer. Just a few more minutes to anticipate, to think, not that she was thinking much past the touching him, kissing him. But while her body knew what it wanted right at this moment, her emotions were screaming for more time to adjust, more time to center themselves.

"Come here." His voice was a deep rumble as the door slammed closed behind them and he pulled her into his arms.

Cassa found her palms flattened against his chest as his gaze caught and held hers.

"It happens so fast," she whispered, feeling the effects of the mating hormone as they rose inside her. The arousal she had felt for him in the past eleven years was nothing compared to what she was feeling now.

She felt naked, though she was clothed. Vulnerable when she needed to be strong, needed to sort through the emotions tearing through her.

"Sweet Cassa." His voice was low as his hand rose to cup her cheek, his thumb playing over her swollen lips as his brows lowered over brooding, intent eyes. "I tried to spare us both."

"With every woman in the continental United States," she bit out querulously. "Maybe I should have taken your example and chosen a few lovers myself."

Except, it wouldn't have helped. The hollow emptiness of shallow sex was something she never wanted to experience again. She'd had that in her brief, bitter marriage.

"Only if you'd wanted to see blood spilled." His hand cupped her jaw as his gaze glittered dangerously. "I would have killed any man that I suspected shared your bed."

Cassa shook her head. She wanted to argue that point, she wanted to rage over the years she had watched him screw his way through the groupies that followed the Breeds around. But her thoughts were too fractured, her desires rising too heatedly.

She watched as his nostrils flared then, as he caught the scent of the moisture gathering between her thighs. As she watched, her gaze locked with his, his other hand lowered, flattened on her stomach and created a path of heated pleasure as his fingers pushed between her thighs.

He cupped the swollen, aching flesh of her pussy, causing her to rise, to lift against him, to arch into the arm that suddenly curved around her back to support her.

"Damn you,' she whimpered. "Oh God, Cabal."

It was too much pleasure. Even through the material of her jeans and the damp fabric of her panties, she could feel the heat of his flesh, the power in his touch. His fingers cupped, his palm ground against the swollen knot of her clit and nearly sent her senses exploding.

"I can smell how sweet you're going to taste." He nipped at her jaw, his canines raking her flesh erotically. "You always have the sweetest scent, Cassa."

She shivered at the sound of his voice. It was dark, rough, as potent as the strongest liquor.

"Come here, baby." He moved, backing toward the bed as his palm continued to rub against the sensitive mound of her pussy. "Let me taste you. All over."

Cassa felt mesmerized. The cadence of his voice stroked her senses as his hands stroked her body. A whimpering protest fell from her lips as his hand slid from between her thighs to grip the hem of her shirt. He drew the material over her head, lifting her arms until he could pull it free and toss it aside, leaving her clad in jeans and her bra.

"So beautiful." His hands cupped the hard mounds of her breasts, his fingers finding her nipples through the lace of her bra. "I've dreamed of sucking those hard little nipples, Cassa."

The front closure to the bra flicked free, and a second later he was pushing it from her shoulders and staring down at the rapid rise and fall of her breasts.

Cassa couldn't make her mind work, she couldn't make her body do anything but lean into him, as his head lowered and his lips wrapped around one agonizingly sensitive point.

The sensation of his lips drawing on her sent a shaft of pure pleasure striking from her nipple to her clit, as though the two were connected by nerve endings she had never known existed. Her hands dug into his hair. Her back arched and a strangled cry tore from her throat.

She was only barely aware of his fingers at the band of her jeans, loosening them, spreading them apart. His fingers stroked her lower stomach and sent juices spilling from the aching flesh beyond.

"Shoes," he growled, his voice growing rougher. "Push them off, Cass." He kissed the mound of her breast, licked it, then nipped it.

She toed off her sneakers in record time, and he rewarded her by pushing her jeans and panties over her hips. Bending as he pushed them over her legs, he spread a series of kisses from her breasts over her stomach, her abdomen, both hip bones.

By the time he pulled the material over her feet, she was a shaking mess of arousal. She could feel her juices dampening her thighs, hot and slick as her body prepared itself for him.

"God, your scent." He buried his head against her lower stomach, his hair caressing the flesh there as his hands gripped her thighs. "Sweet Cassa. I want to bury my tongue in your hot little pussy and feel you come for me. Taste you coming for me."

She nearly came in that second. The eroticism of his words struck an explosion that shuddered through her womb.

Her fingers tightened in his hair as she fought to steady herself against the explosions of pleasure tearing through her body. She was only barely aware of him straightening, rising above her as he tilted her head back and took her lips in another kiss, this one hotter, hungrier than ever before, as she felt the world spinning around her.

When his head lifted, she lay on the bed staring up at him, fighting to breathe as he jerked his shirt off. Sitting on the edge of the bed he pulled off his boots, then rose to his feet and undid his jeans.

It was the most erotic thing she had ever seen, watching him undress. Watching the denim material clear his thighs, revealing those darker gold stripes, edged with black as they curved around his hips and thighs and led to the thick, heavy weight of his cock.

The mushroomed head pulsed erratically, the darkened flesh glistened with pre-cum, as the wide shaft rose from between his thighs.

He looked like a sex god. Like the most erotic pleasure a woman could ever dream of.

Before she could reach out to touch him, he was moving to her. His lips came over hers again, his tongue pumping into her mouth as he spread her thighs, his fingers testing the dampness that covered her pussy before circling her aching clit.

Cassa arched into the pleasure, a cry tearing from her lips as her thighs tried to clamp on to his hand, only to be held apart by his powerful thighs.

The fiery taste of the mating hormone filled her senses, spread through her body and left her gasping for breath as his head lifted.

He had no intention of giving her a chance to catch her breath though. In the next second his lips were on one nipple, then the next. He sucked them into his mouth, tormented them with his tongue, drew on them, nipped at them and left her forcing herself not to beg for more.

"Cabal." Desperation filled her voice as he pushed her breasts together, bringing her nipples close to each other and licking them.

The slightest roughness of his tongue could be felt there, rasping over the tender peaks and sending pleasure surging through her system.

Arching against him, Cassa writhed in tormented ecstasy, reaching for that one touch, that one caress that would send her over the edge.

"Not yet, baby." He gave another lick across her nipples before his hands caressed down her sides to her hips, holding her in place as his lips trailed down her torso.

She arched to him, her fingers gripping his shoulders, nails biting into his flesh as his lips, teeth and tongue created a path of incredible sensation to the curl-covered mound between her thighs.

He paused there, his breathing rough, ragged as Cassa stared down at him. His gaze was broody and hungry, his lips parted in intent.

"What are you waiting on?" She'd waited for what seemed a lifetime for this, and he seemed too determined to make her wait that much longer.

"How bad do you want it?" His husky question was breathed against the swollen bud of her clit.

How bad did she want it? She was ready to die for need of it. Her pussy pulsed in demand, her clit was throbbing in an agony of need. She wanted to grip his hair and jerk him in place.

"Would it matter how bad I wanted it?" Her heart was racing in anticipation. She wanted this touch so bad she was ready to scream for it.

Her fingers dug into the blankets, her nails curling into the material as she fought to keep from begging.

"Does it matter to you?" he responded. "Tell me what you want, Cassa. Tell me how bad you want it."

The hell she would. Her hips arched though as he blew a subtle breath over the curls between her thighs once again. One hand lifted from the blankets, her fingers latching in his hair as the heated air stroked across her sensitized clit. Her head tossed against the pillow and she had to fight back a moaning plea.

"Damn you," she cried out furiously as a rumbled growl vibrated in his chest. "Do it."

"That doesn't answer the question, mate." The backs of his fingers ruffled over the curls. "How bad do you want it?"

Bad enough. Bad enough that her fingers tightened in his hair, her hips arched and a strangled cry tore from her throat.

"Do it," she demanded. "Damn you, eat me."

As though it were a trigger, a fuse to a detonation, a half snarl, half growl left his lips an instant before they covered the saturated folds of her pussy and sucked her clit into his mouth.

His tongue flickered over the tortured little bud as he drew on it. One hand pressed her thighs apart, the fingers of the other caressed through the narrow slit and found the tender entrance to the needy tissue beyond.

Cassa felt herself shaking, shuddering as pleasure gripped her, tore through her nerve endings and left her trembling with the need for climax.

"Oh God!" She nearly screamed out the prayer as she felt two fingers press inside her, stretching apart the tight flesh.

Calloused fingers worked inside her pussy, caressed and stroked the inner muscles until she writhed beneath him and nearly screamed out his name.

She was going to come. She couldn't hold back, she didn't want to hold back. She felt the vibrations of the inner explosions building inside her, tightening her muscles, wetting her vagina. Her juices flowed around his fingers, easing his way and sensitizing her further as he began to fuck inside her, slow and easy, then fast and hard, then slow and easy again, until she felt as though every sense she possessed was careening out of control.

"Not enough," she gasped, the raging need building inside her until she wondered if she could breathe through it. "More, Cabal. Please. Please. More."

She felt him growl, the sound vibrating around her clit as his fingers thrust hard and deep inside the trembling grip of inner tissue. Waves of sensation built inside her, exploded through her system and sent ecstasy breaking over her, until she was arched hard and tight into his grip, her fingers latching onto his hair as she fought to scream through the most incredible pleasure she thought she could experience.

Until seconds later. Until she learned there was more. There was Cabal coming over her, fitting the wide crest of his cock into the spasming entrance and working inside with quick, deliberate thrusts. There were his teeth raking her shoulder. There were the pinpoints of pleasure-pain as his thighs pushed hers farther apart, his hips rocked powerfully against her and the heated length of his cock filled her, overfilled her, until the sensations had her seeing stars with the pleasure detonating in her body.

She was at a loss to understand it, at a loss to process her body's reaction to Cabal's touch. Each stroke of his fingers, each caress of his lips, oh God, the rasp of his teeth and tongue against her neck, the strokes of his cock inside her overly sensitive pussy were too much. She felt as though she were burning, as though each touch was too painful to bear and yet too much pleasure to ever escape.

"Help me," she cried out, as she arched closer, begged for something she didn't understand.

It wasn't enough, and yet it was too much. Tears filled her eyes as her hips arched closer, the muscles of her vagina clamping down on his cock.

Powerful shuttling thrusts filled her, stroked her until she felt the stars, the moon explode inside her. Sensation became rapture, it became ecstasy as her orgasm rushed through her.

Cassa's nails bit into his shoulders, her lips opened on a soundless cry. Bucking against him, she fought for a control that didn't exist, and one she didn't want. She felt his thrusts increase as the first wave of pleasure tore through her. She felt his teeth rake her neck, heard his growl, felt the bite that pierced her shoulder. Inside, held within the tight grip of her vaginal muscles, his cock began to pulse, thicken, a second before she felt the hardened thrust of the Feline Breed barb become erect beneath the mushroomed head of his cock. It thickened, locked into place inside her, stroked hidden nerves and sent her careening into another harder, more heated orgasm. Crying out his name, Cassa felt herself melting, burning inside with each pulse

of his semen as it filled her. She felt her muscles tightening to
the point of pain, and yet pleasure rushed through her in waves.

Her head lowered to his bare shoulder. As his teeth pierced
her flesh, she raked her teeth against his skin and bit down.
Hard. She didn't tear the skin, didn't pierce it, but the very act
was enough to send them both racing higher, farther, crashing
into a sea of exquisite ecstasy before sinking into a pleasure as
deep and as dark as the night itself.

She was possessed.

She was taken.

She was mated.

Now, she wondered, would she survive the fallout?

· CHAPTER 7 ·

The fallout was always sure to suck. Cassa had learned that years ago, the morning after the rescue and the deaths at the German facility where Cabal and his pride had been held.

The fallout was slipping from the hotel room while he showered and trying to run, to hide, not just from Cabal, but from herself.

What the hell had she done? She had all but dared him, all but begged him to mate her, even knowing what she would be facing. What she was facing now. The sensitivity of her flesh, the emotions that roiled within her, the need that attacked her clitoris, that kept her nipples tight and hard.

She wandered through town until she found herself once again on the bank of the river where the missing former mayor had last been seen, staring across the distance at the old water management plant once again.

The place looked dark, sinister. Like some specter of death that overlooked the small lagoon and falls before the water spilled back into the main river.

Its appearance suited her morbid turn of mood.

She may as well be contemplating a prison sentence, she told herself. Or remarriage. Hell, this was going to be worse than remarriage, because you didn't divorce your mate. There was no cure for mating heat. Too bad, so sad, she thought sarcastically.

Crouching at the water's edge, she stared into the cold ripples of water swishing back and forth against the sand and frowned at her own thoughts.

She was doing what she had sworn she would never do again; she was tying herself to another man. And this time, she was doing it in a way she couldn't escape.

She had allowed Cabal to mate her. He had taken her, not just once through the night, but almost continually. Tirelessly.

She closed her eyes and forced herself to breathe through the ripples of remembered pleasure. She could almost see him as he had been the night before, his body sheened with sweat, his muscles rippling in his chest and arms as he rode her with a strength that still amazed her.

God, she was insane. She had lost her ever lovin' mind somewhere, and evidently she wasn't about to find it anytime soon.

The hormones she had been taking for the past five years evidently did little to help assert common sense when a woman was around the Breed that her hormones went crazy for. Because the treatments sure as hell hadn't helped. This morning she had taken two pills to compensate, but she had a feeling the compensation wasn't going to last past her own hope that she could exist away from him for more than an hour or two.

She was demented.

She almost smiled at the thought as she shook her head and picked up a small, mineral-stained pebble, wishing the chill in her hand would extend to other parts of her body. Like the flesh aching between her thighs, dammit. And even worse, and this truly was the worst part, the incredible need just to be held. Something he hadn't given her.

She threw the pebble and watched the ever widening ripples as it hit the water.

Damn him.

She tried to fight back the emotions tearing at her. She hated it when she allowed herself to be hurt. When she let her expectations build despite her efforts not to.

And that was exactly what she had done. Over the past years she had watched the Breeds and their mates. She had seen their devotion to each other, the silent though passionate and emotional air that surrounded each couple.

She had allowed herself to dream. She hadn't thought she had; she had thought she was controlling it. She had been wrong. This morning she had learned exactly how wrong she had been. When she had turned to him, half-asleep, wanting his arms around her, he had turned away instead.

She rose quickly to her feet, blinking back her tears as she turned and stared around the forested little park once again.

Why the hell had she come back here anyway? Why hadn't she just packed her shit and returned home once she realized the problems she was going to have with the story she was investigating?

It wasn't as though she was actually going to report the damned murder anyway, unless someone else did. Her loyalty to the Breeds was so well known that it had begun affecting her professional standing.

It sucked to be an unwanted mate. But it just might suck worse to be an unloved mate.

Her teeth snapped together at the thought of love. She had never allowed herself to think of Cabal in terms of love. She had deliberately forced herself to never think in those terms. Unconsciously though, perhaps she had thought in those terms anyway. After all, she knew how mated couples loved, she had seen it, envied it over the years.

What had made her think that simply mating her would make Cabal love her?

Because she loved him?

She shook her head and turned around to stalk back to the parking lot. As she neared the pavement, her gaze was caught by the car pulling into the entrance to the park and the curly red hair of the man driving.

She almost smiled.

She had left a message on the reporter's cell phone as she left the hotel earlier, though she hadn't expected him to show up rather than calling her back.

"Look what the cat dragged in." A quiet smile crossed Myron's freckled face as he opened the car door and stepped out of the car. "I heard you were in town before you called. Heard you were being shadowed by some Bengal with an attitude too."

"News travels fast." Cassa shoved her hands into the pockets of her leather jacket as a capricious wind tugged at her hair and whipped it across her face. "Is the Bengal why you haven't checked out the rumor?"

She had expected to hear from Myron earlier. She hadn't called before now because she knew his wife, Patricia, could be a jealous little shrew. She liked Patricia, but she didn't want to be the cause of yet another fight that Myron had to deal with because she had called.

"The Bengal might have had something to do with it." A rueful grin tugged at his lips as he pulled his denim jacket closer and gazed around the park rather than meeting her eyes. "This place has been getting a lot of attention lately. Ever since Banks's disappearance, you can count on seeing at least a couple of Breeds a week here. Not to mention the government types that have made an appearance."

"Government types?" Cassa tilted her head to the side as she stared back at him, noting the somber sadness in his pale blue eyes.

Myron shrugged at the question. "There was a government agent roaming around a few days before your Bengal showed up. Just after he arrived, a team of Coyotes showed up. I didn't know Banks was that damned popular. Personally, I think the world is a better place without him."

Cassa watched him in surprise. "What did you know about Banks that no one's telling me?"

Myron snorted at that. "Plenty. You don't live here, Cass. I've tried to tell you about small towns and you never want to listen."

Myron had always said they were a law unto themselves, and that it was that simple. That they band together to protect themselves or fight the enemy. They were independent and headstrong.

"So what are the good citizens of Glen Ferris banding together to hide?"

He shook his head before plowing his large hands through the shaggy, fiery curls that covered his head.

"Banks was a bastard." He breathed out roughly. "He and his buddies got together around here about once a year. Brandenmore and Engalls and a bunch of others. They liked to hunt." A shadow passed across his expression for a brief second.

"I've heard they liked to hunt two-legged prey more often

than four-legged," she guessed. "Banks was rumored to be a part of a group of men that hunted Breeds."

Myron's nostrils flared as a cold breeze whipped around the lot.

"A lot of Breeds were hunted in a lot of places," he snapped out. "Not just here."

He knew more than he was telling, Cassa could feel it. She knew Myron. They'd worked together before her marriage, and after Douglas's death, it had been Myron who helped her through the first bitter months of realization. She knew him as well as she could know anyone.

"What's going on, Myron?" She pushed her hair back from her face, her gaze turning to the entrance of the park, where several cars pulled out and another pulled in.

"You should go home, Cassa."

She was getting really tired of being told to go home.

"Rather than what?" she asked quietly. "I'm here to find out what happened to Banks, not to turn tail and run because no one wants to talk."

"There's no fucking story," Myron bit out angrily. "Banks was a crazy bastard that liked to drink. He's probably drifting in the current of that damned river somewhere and just has yet to surface. Give the fucker time, he'll show up."

The wealth of hatred in Myron's tone had Cassa staring back at him, more than surprised now. She was shocked at the fury that brightened his gaze and flushed his face.

"He was mayor here for eight years," she said quietly. "Voted in and supposedly loved by all the citizens of the county. Then he just disappears and the sheriff can't get so much as a dozen citizens together to search for him."

"'Good riddance' is pretty much what we thought about it," Myron grimaced. "Cassa, dammit. No one cares if he's dead or not. No one cares and you shouldn't either."

"Why shouldn't I? He's not the first casualty here, Myron, and you know it. People are dying in the mountains here and no one seems to care."

Myron stared at her silently for long moments. His expression flashed with such bitter pain that Cassa actually felt the hurt herself for a moment.

"People have always died in these mountains," he finally said softly. "No one cared then either."

Breeds had died here. The information she had stated, more than one had died here, and many had suffered at the hands of the Deadly Dozen, once they were captured.

"Why did Banks stay here?" she asked. "If what you say is true, then he couldn't have had much peace."

"He had what he wanted." Myron shrugged. "His nice house on the hill, his guns and his hunting buddies. Banks didn't give a damn about much else."

"Did his hunting buddies give a damn about him?" Cassa moved closer to the warm car. The engine was still running; the warmth flowing from it eased the chill that raced over her on the outside.

Myron leaned against the car door as he turned to look at her.

"You're not going to let it go, are you?" he asked.

Cassa grinned back at him. "You know better than that, Myron. Might as well help me."

"You lost your senses somewhere," he accused her. "Even I'm not following up on this story, Cassa. As much as I hated Banks, I'd still like the answers to what happened to him. But things happen here in these mountains, and a smart man knows when to back off."

That internal reporter radar went off like a siren. The blood was suddenly pumping through her veins and curiosity was slamming in her head. Of course, that surge of adrenaline was causing other, less comforting sensations as well, but she could handle those for the time being.

"I don't know of anyone who knows you that's accused you of being smart when it came to backing off on a story, Myron," she reminded him.

"Naw, Cassa, that was you," he sighed.

Her lips parted to ask more questions when a black-and-white sheriff's cruiser pulled into the parking lot on the other side of Myron's car.

Cassa lifted her brows as Myron's head lowered and another rough breath passed his lips.

What the hell was going on here and just how many people were involved in it?

She watched as the sheriff, an older female, stepped out of the cruiser and settled her official hat on her head.

Danna Lacey. At forty-five years old, her short black and

gray hair framed her slender face and emphasized her dark green eyes.

"Myron, how are you doing?" The sheriff's eyes were curious as her gaze went between Myron and Cassa.

"I'm doing fine, Danna," he stated with a tinge of mockery as the sheriff moved around the car. "You?"

She nodded slowly, her gaze staying on Cassa now.

"Doin' good. I noticed your car over here and thought I'd stop by and let you know that Patty was looking for you earlier."

Myron frowned at that, as he pulled his cell free of his jacket pocket and flipped it open. "She didn't call."

Danna's smile was a bit rueful. "She lost her cell phone again, Myron. She's at the diner. I told her I'd let you know if I saw you."

Myron rolled his eyes. His expression was a cross between impatience and impotence.

"Time for me to go." He opened the car door as Cassa straightened from the car and glanced back at him. "Tell your Bengal hello from me, Cassa. Make sure I get an invite to the joining, wedding or whatever the hell they're calling it this month."

The reference to the different titles given to mating ceremonies had a frown flashing across Cassa's face. There was a hint of knowledge in Myron's tone that shouldn't be there. As though he knew more about the ceremonies, and the joining, than he should.

"Yeah, I'll make sure to make a note of that," she promised mockingly, as he got into the car and slid it smoothly into gear.

He drove off as Cassa turned and lifted a brow in the sheriff's direction.

Sheriff Lacey grinned at the look. "Patty's my cousin," she stated. "She's been having a hard time lately. I didn't want rumor circulating that Myron was seen having a nice little visit with a strange woman."

At least the sheriff was honest.

"Cassa Hawkins." Cassa extended her hand to the other woman. "I'm a fellow reporter. Myron and I went to college together."

"He's mentioned you actually." The sheriff nodded with a smile. "You were there with him during the first interview with Callan Lyons, when he revealed the existence of the Breeds."

That historic occasion was one that Cassa had nearly missed.

The notice had gone across the nation that a breaking story in Ashland, Kentucky, was going to blow the top off a top secret private and military experiment that had been over a century in the making.

Cassa and Myron had met up in West Virginia and driven in at near breakneck speed. They had questioned Lyons, gone over the medical evidence and seen the truth for themselves, along with dozens of other reporters.

"I was there," Cassa admitted.

That had been more than a decade ago. Hell, it was probably closer to twelve years before. So much time had passed. So many lives had been lost as well as created in that time.

So many years, and still the Genetics Council that had created the Breeds, then tried to destroy their creations, was hampering their freedom.

The Council funded pure blood societies, incited those groups against the Breeds and, in some cases, recaptured their creations and finished the destruction.

"There were a lot of us that threw a party the day Lyons revealed what was going on." Danna nodded. "I was part of the Breed Freedom Society," she revealed. "The battle isn't over, but reporters such as yourself and Myron have definitely made the world safer for them."

The Breed Freedom Society had disbanded a few years after Sanctuary, the Feline Breed compound, had been created.

They had created themselves as a group dedicated to the lives of the Breeds who managed to escape and to finding them. They hid them in the mountains and in their own homes, or smuggled them to other states. Whatever it had taken to protect them.

"Lyons coming forward made it much easier to protect them," Cassa agreed. "The battle isn't over yet though."

"No, not quite," the sheriff agreed as Cassa fought back a cold shiver.

The temperature felt as though it had dropped on the outside, while on the inside she was beginning to burn with disastrous results.

"The Breed Freedom Society is almost as legendary as Lyons himself," Cassa told her. "Your group was together for more than two decades trying to protect the Breeds that came here. You did a wonderful job."

"Did we?" The somber curve to the sheriff's lips couldn't be called a smile. "We did our best, but it was rarely enough." She turned and stared at Myron's vehicle as it turned back to the main road. "He was married to a Breed, you know."

She hadn't known.

Cassa turned her head quickly to the rapidly disappearing car before turning back to the sheriff.

"I had no idea."

Had Myron mated his Breed?

"She was killed a few years before Lyons came forward," the sheriff said. "An entire group of Breeds was killed that night. It was Valentine's night. She was pregnant at the time with their first child. David Banks was part of the group that hunted them down, though we couldn't prove it."

Good God. David Banks had been part of the Deadly Dozen, she had known that, or at least her informant had claimed he was, and Cassa hadn't doubted it. But to hear this, to know he had killed so indiscriminately, for the fun of it, still had the power to shock her to the core of her soul.

"I've known Myron a lot of years," Cassa said. "I had no idea."

Danna shrugged. "It's fairly common knowledge here in Glen Ferris. For a while, we didn't think Myron would survive her death. He was in bad shape." The sheriff shook her head in concern. "When he finally pulled himself out of it, he just wasn't the same anymore. A few years later he married Patricia, but she knows Myron never forgot his first wife, Illandra."

Which explained why Myron's wife was so possessive and jealous. She had a man who she knew belonged to another woman. It wouldn't matter if that woman had died, or if she was living, in her heart Patricia knew that his heart belonged to another.

"You talk to enough folks and you'll hear about Illandra," Danna sighed. "We all loved her, especially those of us who were part of the Freedom Society. If we'd known who the men were in that hunting party, we would have done a little hunting of our own."

Cassa saw the rage that flashed in the sheriff's eyes, the pain that filled her face for the briefest second. She knew Myron was close to all his family. He thrived on family, and evidently Danna did as well.

"Anyway, just be careful where you meet him and who sees

it," Danna advised. "Patricia's been sick lately, and she doesn't need any more grief than she's already dealt with here."

Cassa nodded slowly. She could relate to that, she could understand it. Cassa had her own ghosts, her own regrets that she knew would follow her probably even into death.

She understood Patricia a little better now though, where she hadn't before. She'd always liked Myron's wife, but she'd always known that Patricia had hated it when Cassa met with Myron over the Breed revelations more than a decade ago.

If Myron had mated his Breed wife though, would he have eventually been able to wed and to have children with another woman? And there was no doubt those children were Myron's. They looked just like him.

She wished now that she had questioned her friend more extensively when she first learned that he had been part of a group that had smuggled Breeds through the States after their escape. She wished she had delved into more than the fact that Breeds had been escaping those labs for decades.

There was so much information to process at times with this new species of humanity though. Sometimes Cassa could well relate to the average citizen's fears and phobias where the Breeds were concerned.

Breeds had been created with one purpose in mind: to kill, and to do so savagely and without mercy. To look at them, to see the near perfection of their bodies and their features, it was hard at first to imagine that killers lurked behind their charming smiles or saddened eyes.

But that was exactly what lurked there. A creature that had been bred with the intent to bring out the most animalistic instincts that could be imagined.

"I better be going then," the sheriff finally announced as she turned away. "If you need anything, Miss Hawkins . . ."

"Actually, I do," Cassa informed her.

The sheriff turned back to her slowly with a frown. "How so?"

"I need to know more about David Banks and his disappearance. There's been no body, no clue to his whereabouts or who may have wanted him dead. This is my story, Sheriff Lacey. I'm going to need information from somewhere."

A smile flashed across the other woman's face. It was tinged with a hint of knowing mockery as well as friendliness.

"So, since you can't meet with Myron, you'll just ask me?"

Cassa lifted her hands with amused helplessness. "We do what we must."

The sheriff laughed at that. "That we do." She shrugged her shoulders beneath the heavy jacket she wore. "But, where Banks is concerned, there's not a lot I can tell you. I know his ex-wife, his kids, in-laws and grandkids. I know his birthday, I know where he ate when he ate out and who his golfing buddies in town were, but that's about it."

Cassa pulled the notebook and pen from her back pocket and flipped it open. "Who were the golfing buddies?"

Danna's eyes glittered with amusement as she shook her head. "You're a quick one. No one knows anything, but I'll give you names."

The sheriff gave her names—names of the golfing buddies, Banks's favorite waitress and his banker. By the time they'd finished talking and Danna was driving away, Cassa was left with a head full of information that she had no idea how to categorize at the moment.

She was also left to face the mating heat and its building effects. The burn between her thighs, the light sheen of sweat between her breasts and the knowledge that, on more than one front, running from Cabal wasn't going to work.

Even more, running from herself wasn't going to work. The old saying *you can run but you can't hide* more than applied at the moment. She was running from the emotions she had hid for far too many years, and now she was going to have to figure out exactly how to deal with them.

Tucking her hands back into the pockets of her jacket, she turned and headed out of the park for the walk back to the inn. It wasn't a short hike, and it would be hell with the mating heat rising inside her body. It would give her time to think though. And right now, she needed plenty of time to think.

· **C H A P T E R   8** ·

Cabal followed his mate as she made her way back to the inn and to her room. He'd shamelessly eavesdropped on her conversation with both the male she had met with as well as the sheriff that had arrived later.

Following her smacked of deceit, especially considering the night that had just transpired between them. But he'd be damned if he knew what else to do at this point.

For the first time in his life, Cabal was conflicted.

Emotions. He knew what they were; it wasn't as though he didn't have feelings. He just made certain he didn't have them often. He was immune to having a conscience—with the blood that stained his hands, he'd be crazy not to be immune to it. He liked sleeping at night, and worrying over lost lives outside his control wasn't conducive to sleeping.

Or were feelings out of his control?

He shook his head at the thought, as his hands clenched at his sides. He was lingering outside Cassa's room like a damned stalker uncertain if it was time to strike.

She was his mate. He had every right to be in that room with her. To touch her. Except there were other responsibilities that came with touching, responsibilities he just didn't know how to carry.

As he stood there staring at the door to her room, he was reminded of another young woman, who had often given him cause to think of Cassa.

Jolian. The little Jaguar Breed had been young, clumsy, uncertain with herself and her place in Sanctuary. She had also, for a brief time, been suspected of spying within the Feline Breed compound.

She'd died when the spy they had overlooked had attempted to kidnap Cabal's sister-in-law, Scheme. She had died as she attempted to fix a misunderstanding that she feared had angered Cabal. Because she had been infatuated with him. Because she hadn't wanted him upset with her. She had given her life to explain that to Scheme. She'd stood between Scheme and the kidnapper.

He remembered sitting next to her still, lifeless body and staring into her pale face. He'd cared for her, even though he hadn't wanted to admit to himself that he had. Not as a mate, not really even as a lover. But he had cared for her because what came so hard to him was easy for her.

Emotions. She had cared about him, and she had gone out of her way so many times to show it. Her smiles, her attempts at laughter, even the nervous little twitter that had often been in her voice and the scent of anticipation and hopelessness that often filled the air around her.

She'd had very little respect from other Breeds, simply because of her lack of confidence. As he sat beside her that day, he'd realized she hadn't had enough respect from him.

She had died feeling unloved, unwanted and, even worse, untrusted by the man she had thought she loved. She had let her heart, her emotions, get in the way of her training, and she had died because of it.

Now Cabal was facing the fact that something he didn't want to admit to was getting in the way of his mission: his emotions, his hunger for Cassa, his need just to be close to her.

Yet when she had tried to curl up against him this morning, what had he done? When she had sought a bit of solace amid the tempestuousness of the mating heat, he had moved away from her, uncertain how to deal with it.

He could deal with the sex. The physical part of mating heat wasn't a hardship. It was damned exciting and more pleasure than he'd ever had in his life. It was also causing some of the damnedest feelings to rise up inside him. Feelings he didn't want to face and didn't want to admit to. Heading the list was the need to hold her.

He'd run from her this morning like a fucking coward. Now he was hanging around outside her door like a worse fucking coward.

Son of a bitch.

Because the mating heat was doing something odd to him. He didn't have the need to just fuck. Hell no, it couldn't be that simple. Just getting his rocks off wasn't going to be enough with this woman, as it had been with others.

He wanted to feel her. He wanted to feel her rubbing against him, her skin stroking his, her hands caressing him as he stroked and caressed her. He wanted her laughter, God help him, even her tears.

It was the strangest thing. He'd never had the desire to be close to any woman, but this woman, he wanted to sink into her flesh and be consumed by her.

She was dangerous. The animal inside him had realized that the night he escaped from that pit, lured by the scent of her fear, her rage and his own fury. He had realized it in that one instant when he saw her pale face, her agonized gray eyes, and knew that she belonged to the man who had betrayed the lives of his family.

She was dangerous because she slipped past his training as well as his determination not to care, for anyone. He cared for his brother, Tanner; he had no choice there. Tanner hadn't allowed him a choice. He cared for Tanner's mate, Scheme. That perhaps was instinct. She belonged to Tanner, therefore she was Cabal's responsibility to care for.

But this woman?

He strode down the hall before turning and contemplating the closed door once again. This woman he had no ties to, he had no reason to care if she was warm, if she needed affection or needed to be held.

Yet he did care.

Clenching his teeth, his muscles bunched to move. Before he could make the trip back to her door, the cell phone at his belt vibrated imperiously.

Throttling a growl, he jerked the phone from its clip, checked the number, then flipped it open and brought it to his ear.

"What the hell do you want?" he answered.

"A few manners would go over very well tonight," Jonas replied sarcastically. "A little discretion wouldn't be amiss either."

"I haven't had witnesses in years," Cabal snapped. "And we were taught not to spill blood in public, remember? So what the hell are you talking about?"

The silence on the line was telling. Jonas's patience was being tested, and wasn't that just too damned bad.

"I have pictures," Jonas finally said, ice dripping from his voice. "A pretty little park, a pretty little mate and a Bengal Breed all over her in the front seat of his truck."

"Pictures?" Cabal asked carefully. No one should have had pictures. He hadn't sensed anyone watching, nor had he sensed any danger.

"Isn't that what I said?" Jonas stated calmly. "The memo attached states that one Cabal St. Laurents seems to have 'mated' the Breeds' favorite reporter." There was a short, tense silence. "We have a problem here, Cabal."

Mated. The very fact that the word had been used was cause for alarm. So far, they had managed to ensure that exactly what mating heat was remained hidden, and the term "mate" wasn't something used lightly. Someone knew. Which meant Cassa could be in danger. The Council would love nothing better than to get their hands on a Breed mate. Especially the mate of a Bengal Breed.

"We have a Breed watching us," Cabal stated. "Have you checked out Dog's interest in the area?"

"This isn't Dog," Jonas replied, his tone certain.

"Is Dog here at your request?" Cabal asked then, knowing the machinations that the Bureau director was often involved in.

"He's not there at my request, but neither is he considered a danger at this point."

That told him more than he wanted to know, Cabal thought. Dog wasn't under Jonas's control, but the reasons he was here benefited Jonas or the Breeds in some way. With Jonas, it was all about the Breed society, something most people rarely understood when it came to his games and calculations.

"So what the hell do you want me to do?" Cabal finally growled. "You have pictures and a message that she's my mate.

Our killer is a Breed; there's every chance he well knows what a mate is."

"And every chance that he's deliberately pulled in the one person that could distract you," Jonas pointed out. "Which means he has some connections into the community."

"We've gone over this ground," Cabal sighed. "I know she's being watched. We already suspected she had been deliberately brought in, now we know why."

"Now we know why," Jonas agreed. "Have you mated her?"

Jonas was always inordinately curious when one of his enforcers or, in Cabal's case, one of his covert enforcers mated. Strangely enough, he kept up with them, even after the mating, even after the initial danger. Cabal bet Jonas could name every mate, every potential and suspected future mating, and list any variances in the mating heat that showed up on the scientists' tests.

"She's my mate," Cabal affirmed. "That's all you need to know, Jonas."

"Her file shows Ely's had her on the mating hormone for the past five years. Were you aware the effects had progressed to the point that she required the treatments?"

He hadn't. Cabal turned and paced back to the end of the hall, where he moved to the wide window that looked out over the Gauley River.

"I didn't know," he finally admitted.

"She told Ely there had been no physical contact other than the night of your escape from the facility. She stated she tasted your blood."

Cabal closed his eyes as a wave of agony swept through him. Emotion. Regret. He remembered the scene clearly. Tears had poured down her face, saturating her features as her body shuddered with her sobs. Trembling lips had opened as her fingers shook, touched the blood on his face, then touched the tips of those fingers to her tongue.

She had tasted his blood.

"Hell," he muttered. "There were no signs of heat then."

Jonas grunted at that. "Snarling that you owned her didn't count, huh?"

"Reflex," he growled.

"Or instinct," Jonas suggested. "Tell me, Cabal, have you told her yet that the man she believed was her husband is still alive?"

Cabal froze. A sense of predatory rage built inside him until the growl that came from his throat was more enraged animal than furious male.

"I'll take that as a no." Jonas's tone was coldly disapproving.

"As far as she's concerned, he's dead," Cabal snarled. "He can rot in whatever prison he's sitting in."

A heavy silence filled the line. Cabal understood it. His boss was giving him the chance to reconsider the decision. There was nothing to reconsider. The moment he had learned that the marriage Douglas Watts had perpetuated between himself and Cassa hadn't even been legal, he'd made the decision for her.

He'd be damned if that bastard would ever shadow her life again. He wouldn't have it.

"Cabal, you could be making a mistake," Jonas warned him quietly.

"It's no mistake," Cabal snarled. "He's been in a Breed organized prison since his recuperation. That was his choice. That or death. He chose the prison. He wasn't given the option of informing the woman he'd continually lied to."

He heard Jonas breathe out heavily. "Very well. For now, we can play this your way. The day may come though that the game shifts. What will you do then?"

"She is my mate." His voice was clipped, cold. "He has no hold on her that I can't top. Period. If that day ever comes, then I'll deal with the choice I made. Until then, fuck the bastard. I only wish he were in more pain."

He was paralyzed from the hips down. There was no sensation in his legs, or in other areas that had been important to Watts. Confined as he was in a high-security overseas prison created and manned by Breeds, there wasn't much chance of Cassa ever learning the truth.

"I just hope you know what the hell you're doing, my friend," Jonas stated, his tone concerned now. "She's a good woman."

"She allowed the man she loved to use her," he growled. "He used her to kill, to maim, and he received pay for it. She should have chosen more wisely."

A part of him protested the statement he'd made. The human part, he decided. The weaker part. That internal voice was forever harassing him where she was concerned. His conscience? Hell, he thought he'd killed the fucker years ago.

"Perhaps she should have." It didn't really sound like an

agreement; it sounded more like a chastisement, and not of Cassa.

Cabal tightened his lips, refusing to argue the matter further. It was a done deal. Douglas Watts was no more than a shadow of himself that existed in a hellhole of a prison. There were no televisions, video games or computers. There were few comforts. The food wasn't too bad, unless you were used to better.

Sucked to be Watts.

"I have things to do, Jonas," Cabal finally stated harshly. "If this was all you wanted, then you're wasting my time."

"I have no doubt." The heavy mockery pricked at Cabal's temper. "Take care of your mate then, Bengal. Give me a report whenever you have one."

"Until then you can get your report from Rule or Lawe," Cabal snapped. "Since they're obviously not here just to see the sights."

"They're not mated," Jonas said quietly. "Their heads are still clear, Cabal. And that's what I need. Enforcers with clear heads. Remember that."

Jonas disconnected before Cabal could tell him to get fucked. But one thing the director had done was to remind him of the fact that mating Cassa, tying her completely to him, was of the utmost importance.

If she ever learned about Watts, she might be a little upset. He didn't want to have to do without one of the few benefits that came from mating heat. Especially the one that put her screaming in pleasure beneath him.

He'd deal later with Rule and Lawe sticking their noses into his business. For the moment, there was the scent of his mate in the shower, the smell of feminine cleanliness and sweet, hot woman.

She was aroused. The mating heat was building inside her. She could take the hormone treatments until hell froze over, but it wasn't going to cure the effects of his kiss, his touch. She should know that by now. Nothing could combat that, though the scientists were still trying.

Unfortunately, they couldn't hide mating heat forever. There would be a day—and it was coming soon, Cabal knew—that the world would learn about mating heat, just as it had learned about the Breeds to begin with.

It had been more than ten years, closer to twelve, since Callan Lyons, the alpha leader of the Feline Breeds, had mated his wife, Merinus. Neither Callan nor Merinus had aged appreciably since then. Doctors had determined that their bodies had aged merely one year in all that time. Their bodies' aging process had slowed down dramatically, and from all the scientists had learned, especially since the first Leo's appearance with his own mate, it seemed that the aging process would remain incredibly slow for years to come.

The first Leo was over a hundred years old, as was his mate. They both appeared no older than their late thirties, and their bodies were in peak condition.

Mating heat could become the Breeds' worst enemy if the public at large learned of it. For now though, it was the greatest pleasure Cabal had ever known in his life. His emotions were in chaos, hell if he knew what to do with them, but he knew that nothing in this world or any other could be as good as touching his mate.

He strode to the door, slid the key card through the security lock, waited for the light to turn green, then twisted the door latch.

The door swung open, and he was confronted with a sight that made the blood in his veins boil with lust.

His mate. His woman. And she was beautifully, splendidly naked as she froze in place, just outside the bathroom door.

Cabal now felt the heat rising inside his body like an inferno. How the hell was he supposed to stay sane, to keep his head straight, when the sight of her bare body made him dizzy with fucking lust?

Maybe having Rule and Lawe here wouldn't be a bad idea after all, he thought, as he tore off his jacket.

The denim material dropped to the floor as he watched her eyes widen.

"Don't you dare move," he growled as she started to step back into the bathroom. "For both our sakes, Cassa. Stay still."

He swore he could feel a ringing in his ears as he tore off his T-shirt before turning his attention to loosening the material of his jeans.

His cock was so damned hard it felt like steel, so hot he wondered why he wasn't blistered.

She stood there like an angel, wide-eyed, almost innocent. Her long hair lay around her shoulders and down her back, thick and heavy, darker with dampness. High, full breasts were topped with hard, reddened nipples. Her slender waist and softly rounded hips led to smooth, creamy thighs and a patch of soft, dark blond curls to entice him.

He inhaled her scent again, growing nearly drunk on the smell of her arousal. It hit his head like a potent drug, almost making him dizzy as he tore his boots, then jeans from his body.

She just stood there, watching him. A damp sheen covered her shoulders; there was a single drop of water lying against her breast. Her nipples were peaked so hard they looked like ripe berries, sweet and ready for him to taste.

Another man had once touched her body, he thought with rabid fury. Had kissed her, stroked her. His scent no longer lingered on her, but Cabal clearly remembered a time when it had.

He needed that memory wiped away. He needed his scent to become so much a part of hers that when he smelled her sweetness, there were no lingering memories of any others tainting her.

She was his. She carried his mark on her shoulder. Her scent was infused with the mating heat now, but soon, so soon, it would change. Her scent would meld with his, creating something different, something unique. She would be marked by him, into her very DNA. She would never escape him.

"I told you." His voice was rough when he wished he could make it softer, gentler for her. "I own you."

What did the tone of voice matter though, when stating such a harsh claim? he asked himself.

Her eyes narrowed as he faced her, naked and aroused.

"You wish you owned me," she stated clearly, enraging the animal inside him. "No man owns me, Cabal."

He reached her in a few long strides, his fingers sliding into her hair to grip her head and hold her still.

"You're mine."

"In your dreams." Confidence and steely amusement glittered in her gray eyes. Damn her. She would never admit what he knew they were both well aware of. She belonged to him, there was no way her body could deny him.

His head lowered, his lips covering hers without preliminaries, sinking against the soft silk of them, his tongue pushing into her mouth to release the hormone that gathered in the glands beneath his tongue.

She took it, she took him. A little moan whispered into the kiss as her soft hands lifted to grip his biceps, as though she needed to hold on through the storm raging between them.

"Deny it now," he bit out harshly as his lips lifted just enough to allow her to speak.

"My body can't deny you, Cabal," she stated, her voice husky with arousal now. "That's all you own. And its probably all you'll ever own."

There was an edge of bitterness in her voice that bothered him, a faint sadness. It reminded him of her attempt to curl into his arms that morning, and his rush to escape the swirl of emotions that had swept through him.

His fingers tightened in her hair. Soft, dark blond lashes drifted over her eyes in pleasure as he did so. She was so easy to pleasure, he thought. Each touch he had given her the night before had had her turning to him with eager need. With hunger.

His cock throbbed at the thought. That unruly organ was insistent that he take her again, now. Preliminaries be damned. To spread her thighs, grip her ass and push hard and deep inside her.

"Cabal." She whispered his name as he realized his hand was cupping her ass, his fingers only scant inches from the dew-soaked folds of her pussy. And he was lifting her to him.

"I need." His eyes closed as he tried to block out the need he heard in his words and saw in her eyes. The need for more than just this.

This being him, lifting her, bracing her against the wall as he shifted them to the side, spreading her thighs, tucking the head of his cock into the slick, hot folds of her sex.

"I wanted to give you more." The words tore from him as he pressed inside her. Slowly.

Ah hell. It was so fucking good. A heated silken glove enclosed his tortured flesh, stroking it with pleasure, rippling over it with hungry demand.

He braced his feet apart, his hands tightened on the globes of her ass as he pressed deeper and growled with the sensations of not just his own pleasure, but hers as well. He could feel the silken muscles tightening, gripping around him as her sharp little nails bit into his shoulders.

He felt her legs wrap around his hips, gripping him as he surged those final inches inside the heated, ecstatic grip of her hot little pussy.

"You make me crazy." He nipped at her jaw as he forced himself to still inside her, to luxuriate in the pleasure.

"It's just the hormone." There was a sob in her voice that he hated to hear. Part pleasure, part pain. "It's just the hormone."

No, it wasn't just the hormone, he knew that. It was so much more; he sensed it, felt it. She was his match, his mate; nature had only ensured that the stubborn human part of his genetics didn't fuck up and walk away from her.

And he would have. He would have continued to run for as long as possible. He would have denied the animal's insistence, because she fucked with his head, not just his arousal. And even worse, she fucked with his cold, icy heart.

"Fuck that damned hormone," he snarled, wishing he could recall the words.

Clenching his teeth, he forced back words he refused to release. To say them was to mean them. To mean them was to accept that he needed more.

He couldn't allow himself to need. To need invited weakness. It invited danger.

He would not allow himself to endanger her.

He wanted to fuck her, that was all. The hormone be damned, that didn't make him fuck. It just made him want to fuck more, harder.

Holding tight to her, he moved his hips, rotated them, thrust and plunged inside the velvet grip of rapture. So much pleasure. It washed through him like a tidal wave, tearing past his consciousness, sinking into the animal that lurked inside him.

It roared in triumph. The sound slipped past his throat, mingled with her cry as he felt her tighten in orgasm. He felt her juices, sweet and hot, flow around the erection thrusting harder, faster inside her.

God save him, he was dying inside her.

He couldn't hold back the pleasure or the need. He couldn't hold back the victorious snarl, or the ecstatic groan as she bit his shoulder. It wasn't a timid bite. Her sharp little teeth latched onto him and refused to let go.

He could feel the brutal ecstasy rushing over him now. His cock thickened, tightened. His balls drew up tight to the base of the steely shaft, and when he came, it was death. And it was re-birth.

The thumb-sized extension became erect beneath the head of his cock, thickened and distended, revealing the Feline Breed male barb and locking his cock inside her. His hips rotated, shifting until it was lodged comfortably, pleasurably. Then a throttled roar left his chest as his semen began to pump hard and deep inside her.

Each fierce spurt sent a surge of blistering electric sensation tearing up his spine, wrapping around his body. His muscles drew tight, his head lowered; his teeth locked into the mating mark at her shoulder as his tongue licked and stroked, spreading the hormone into the tiny bite. Marking her more, marking her deeper.

Sweet Cassa. His mate. His woman. She was the one thing in this world that he knew was his alone. The woman created for him. The one woman that could destroy him.

· CHAPTER 9 ·

Cassa was silent as Cabal carried her to the bed, tucked her in, then went to shower. She stared up at the ceiling for long moments, a frown on her face as she fought to work through her own feelings, her own emotions.

The sex was good. It was damned good. It was like flying, free-falling. But when it was over, it left a hollow little ache inside her chest that she couldn't escape from.

Sighing heavily, she moved from the bed. What the hell did he expect her to do? Spend all her time in bed? She had work to do, and it was obvious she had her job cut out for her.

If the killer had contacted her, there was always the chance that he had, or could, contact another reporter. She needed to get her facts together and find the answers she was looking for if she was going to have her story ready.

After pulling on her robe, she moved to the laptop and the flash chip of information she'd hidden in her laptop bag. She inserted the small chip and pulled up the information, went over it once again.

Six men were dead, all with ties to Phillip Brandenmore and Horace Engalls, owners of the pharmaceutical and research company currently under indictment for illegal Breed research, conspiracy to murder and conspiracy to buy stolen medical and personnel files of unnamed Breeds. The two men shared a hunting cabin in the mountains of the Hawk's Nest–Gauley Bridge area.

Cassa had confirmed Brandenmore and Engalls's ties to the victims over the past weeks, after the anonymous emails had begun coming through with their bloody pictures attached.

Dr. Ryan Damron. Phillip Brandenmore's father had paid Damron's way through college and medical school. The forensic pathologist had at one time been under scrutiny for having worked with the Genetics Council that created the Breeds. He had been charged with performing autopsies on live Breeds. He had escaped Breed justice though, just as so many had during those first trials.

Officer Aaron Washington had been a New York City police officer of little rank or notoriety. His connection to Brandenmore and Engalls stemmed from off-duty work he had once done as a security guard for the pharmaceutical labs just outside New York City.

Attorney Elam March. He had been one of Brandenmore's best friends in college.

The former Glen Ferris mayor David Banks had grown up in the area with Brandenmore and was known to have frequented Brandenmore's mountain cabin often.

And finally, H. R. Alonzo, the great-grandson of one of the founders of the Genetics Council. He spoke out often against the Breeds and contributed heavily to organizations rumored to often strike out violently against them. There was little connection between him and the pharmaceutical and research giants though.

Staring at the screen of her laptop, Cassa frowned and hit another button, pulling up an outdated, grainy photograph that had been included in one of the files her anonymous source had sent her.

There was no identifying all the men in the picture, though Cassa had been able to recognize Brandenmore and Engalls, and pinpoint the six men that had been killed in the past months.

Six down and six to go, she thought as she squinted at the picture and tried to make out facial features of the men she couldn't identify. She'd run the picture through several identity programs, and had a list of names as long as her arm from them.

The picture quality was just too damned poor to do anything with. But there was one face that kept niggling at her with its near familiarity. She could never pin down what bothered her though.

Sighing, she closed the files, backed them up and stored the small chip of information in a protective case before hiding it in her purse as she heard the shower shut off.

She wasn't a fresh reporter with no experience backing her, she thought mockingly. She knew better than to allow Cabal to catch her with that chip. Every piece of information she had stayed backed up and as secure as she could make it. She had learned that lesson early in her career, and she made certain it was a habit she adhered to.

The ties the six men had to Phillip Brandenmore and his brother-in-law Horace Engalls placed the two men right in the forefront of early Breed killings, during the years before the Breeds were public knowledge, when they were shadows sliding on the outskirts of human knowledge.

There were accusations against the two pharmaceutical and research giants, that they had experimented on captured Breeds in the past years and used their physiology to come up with several revolutionary drugs. The primary drug in question was one now being used with a high success rate in the fight against cancer.

If it was proven that the two men had been involved in those early activities, it could mean a trial involving Breed Law— namely, the law that called for the punishment of death against those who experimented on, or contributed to the deaths of, Breeds after the establishment of the laws.

Breed Law was a complex set of rules and regulations adopted by the U.S. and several other countries to allow the Breeds a measure of autonomy, to police themselves and their communities, as well as protection against the factions and societies intent on destroying them.

So far, Breed Law hadn't been used to kill, at least not that anyone knew. There were rumors that the Bureau of Breed Affairs, or namely its director, Jonas Wyatt, exercised Breed Law outside the dictates of a public trial.

Cassa didn't doubt it, but neither could she blame him, in most cases. When compared to the world population of humans, Breeds were few. Little more than a thousand at the last count, with less than a half dozen children. Without Breed Law they would have been decimated by now.

Brandenmore and Engalls were already close to facing Breed Law. If evidence showed they had indeed conspired to steal information, were behind the drugging of Dr. Elyiana Morrey, and conspired to kill several Breeds within Sanctuary, then the panel convening to weigh the evidence could rule that they go to trial under that complex set of laws. And that they could be put to death without appeal or a waiting period.

So far, that extreme measure hadn't been practiced on any of the Breeds' enemies that had been put on trial, but Cassa knew for a fact that it was being considered now.

Cassa could imagine the protests against the Breeds, should that happen. Already Brandenmore and Engalls were being defended by many of the press, as well as many political figures. Enacting an execution based on Breed Law could do more harm than good. But not doing so could send just as destructive a message to others.

Either way this went, the damage that the Breed society faced would be harsh. Cassa ached with that knowledge. The Breeds had endured hell in ways most men and women couldn't comprehend. She would hate to see their independence and freedom being limited any more than they already were, because of the evil of two men.

Pacing her room, she moved to the wide windows that looked out over the Gauley River. Frowning down at the winter gray choppy water stretching out below her, Cassa let herself remember, just for a second, the night she had realized the horrors the Breeds had actually faced.

In a little-known valley in Germany, in the middle of a storm, watching blood mix with mud and pour over the landscape, she remembered the battle to free the Breeds in that hidden lab.

The plans put in place to rescue that lab had been precise. There should have been no lives lost. But the Council soldiers and Coyotes had been waiting for the rescue forces. They had been warned that they were coming, from which direction, how many and the strength of their weapons.

She closed her eyes, trying to block out the memories, but they refused to dim. They refused to give her any peace. She had been the reason her husband had been allowed on that team. The trust the Breeds had placed in her had been extended to Douglas.

And her husband had betrayed her.

She remembered the blood and the death. The image flashed through her mind of the flight through the facility to the underground pit where the Bengals were being killed.

Douglas hadn't let go of that camera even once. He had tracked every move, recorded it. Through the mic he'd worn at his cheek, he'd recorded his observations, and in his voice she'd heard his excitement and his pleasure.

"There's no saving this batch of the bloody bastards," he'd commented as they raced through steel-lined halls. "We can hear their screams even from here. The blood has to be ankle-deep in that pit if the reports are anything to go by. Hopefully there'll be a way to get a shot."

He'd wanted to see the blood, the death. The camera had been his proof that he'd ensured their deaths, as well as his own private adventure in the making.

She'd been desperate to save lives. He'd been desperate to watch and record the deaths.

She rubbed at her arms to chase away the chill that invaded her. Her husband had died that night, by Cabal's hand. But so many Breeds, as well as the humans fighting to rescue them, had died as well. Within the heavily fortressed compound, the Breeds the scientists suspected would turn against them once the rescue began had been placed within a pit of churning blades.

Two dozen. Men and women that Cabal had led. His pride. His people. His family.

They had died. All except him, and his rage had been like a living flame within his eyes as he pushed past the slowly opening panel Cassa had managed to release.

Cassa had known the second she stared into Douglas's eyes in that secured room that he had betrayed her and the Breeds. It had been there in his eyes, in the smirk at his lips and the knowledge he could no longer hide, that he intended to benefit from the blood shed that day.

How had she not known? How had she managed to fool her all those months that they were working with the Breeds?

A chill raced down her spine again, the cold invading her as she realized that this was why Cabal held himself from her. He'd always blamed her for those deaths. He'd never forgiven her, and she couldn't blame him.

Why hadn't she thought of that before she had allowed him

to touch her? What had made her think that mating heat could ever dim his hatred over those deaths?

She'd been warned she couldn't escape the past much longer. The anonymous killer in the first email he had sent of the first murder had said as much: *I know who you are. I know who you were. The past is never dead, my friend, it now haunts not just the prey, but the hunter as well. Beware you don't become the hunted as well.*

The words were impossible to forget, just as it was impossible to forget the pictures that had come in that first email. Dr. Ryan Damron, his expression contorted into lines of horror, his neck torn out, the ragged, bloody wounds attesting to his pain-filled death. Along with the pictures of the victim were the pictures of the dark figures removing him.

Two days later it was reported that Dr. Damron had died in a fiery crash as his vehicle plunged down the cliffs outside his California home.

More pictures, more messages, more assurances of death had come in over the months. Someone was working steadily, quickly to take out what he called the Deadly Dozen.

They were hunters who had tracked escaped Breeds and turned them over to Phillip Brandenmore for research, or returned them to the labs. At least, those that had lived through the hunts.

"Such morose thoughts reflected on such a pretty face."

Cassa swung around, her heart tripping, pausing before racing in sudden fear and arousal as she found Cabal standing just inside the room, closing the bathroom door behind him.

How had he managed to slip up on her so easily? How had she not heard him?

Breed stealth, she thought. It was becoming legendary.

"I don't recall my thoughts being very important to you at any other time," she snapped, as she drew the belt of her robe tighter.

Suddenly, she felt underdressed, exposed to him. They'd had sex repeatedly, but being naked in front of him, or even half-clothed now, suddenly made her uncomfortable.

"You didn't check the fine print in Breed Law." His lips quirked, a sexy male smirk in his sun-darkened face as mockery reflected in his eyes. "You should be more careful in the future. I'm certain that particular stipulation is there."

"I'll be certain to do that and lodge my complaint at the same time," she bit out, as her arms tightened across her swelling breasts. "I believe precedence for separations has already been established by the Coyote Breed alpha and his mate. I could sue for my own."

He shook his head, the silken strands of his gold and black hair brushing against his shoulders. Her fingers itched to tunnel into the mass of oddly striped hair. To clench and pull, and drag his lips down to her own.

She swore she could taste him in her mouth. A taste of heated spice, a need, a hunger she fought to hide from.

"I wouldn't try that if I were you," he warned her, his voice dangerously soft now. "You'd not get out of bed for months, Cassa. I'd make certain of it. And I'd make certain there was no thought of separation once you did manage to actually rejoin the human race."

She had no doubt she wouldn't protest it either, she thought furiously. She'd probably help him keep her in that damned bed, if the sudden flurry of aroused sensations rushing through her body was any indication. He wasn't helping matters by strutting around naked, and aroused.

Her gaze flickered to his erection before jerking back to his shoulders and the bite mark there. The mark she had left, similar to the one he had left on her shoulder.

Damn, he was making her as wild as he was.

"Come here," he suddenly growled. "If you want to stare at me with those hungry eyes, then come to me, Cassa. Let me sate you."

Did she look like a fool? On second thought, she didn't want to answer that question.

"I think I prefer to keep a very careful distance between us at the moment," she informed him. "I have things to do this evening, and being distracted by you isn't one of those things."

His eyes narrowed on her as he moved to his discarded clothing and pulled his jeans from the pile.

"What did you have planned?" he asked, as he pulled the denim over those spectacular legs. "I thought we'd have dinner together."

She suddenly wished her evening was free after all.

She was too easy, she told herself. A wimp. A wuss. A horny fool.

"Regretfully, I have to decline."

Actually, she was ready to dress and run home right now rather than face the pain she knew was coming. If it weren't for her own past and the knowledge the killer evidently had, then she would do just that. Maybe.

Her gaze flickered over him again, from his muscular legs encased in denim to the dark bronzed flesh that stretched across his chest. He was one of the most handsome men she knew, and one of the most alluring Breeds she had ever met.

It was truly not fair that man had created such animalistic beauty in so many different forms. Breeds were known not just for their genetics, but for their intense good looks and superb physical condition.

"You're aroused." His sudden statement sent heat coursing through her face. "You're always aroused around me, Cassa, yet you've never flirted, never given any other hint of interest. Why is that?" Suspicion darkened his eyes.

"Because I didn't like the games you played?" She arched her brows. "You and your brother are known for more than your good looks, Cabal. Playing with your toys together is one of the nicer descriptions that I've heard of your little playdates."

They had, at least at one time, been known for sharing their women.

A smile creased his lips then. "Tanner's mated now, you know that. We no longer share our toys, as you call it."

That smile was too knowing and too damned sexy. Cassa stared back at him with an impending sense of finality. The past was indeed catching up with her, in the worst possible way.

She breathed out roughly. "I don't have the patience for Breed games this evening, Cabal. I have a job to do here. Maybe I'll see you tonight."

She moved for the change of clothes she had laid out on the dresser earlier.

His arms dropped from his chest as he advanced into the room, his head turning, his gaze roving over the small living area and the laptop.

When he stopped, he was only a few feet from her, his gaze pinning her as his expression turned dark and foreboding. "Stay out of the park area," he told her, his voice chilly with warning. "It's not safe right now."

"It doesn't work that way," she answered firmly, when everything inside her was warning her to back down. "You don't tell me what to do simply because you've mated me."

His lips thinned. "Make it work that way, Cassa."

"Then give me the information I need," she told him. "Tell me what the hell is going on and why Breeds are cleaning up after a killer."

He knew what she knew. He had been in that valley, he and Dog, possibly working together, had ensured that she made it nowhere near the area.

Cabal's brows lowered heavily over the glitter of gold in his green eyes. Irritation marked his expression as well as his gaze.

"You don't want to be a part of this," he finally told her, his voice low. "The killer has targeted you, Cassa. I know you were contacted. Jonas has already talked to your editor concerning it. Go home, let me take care of this. That's my job."

At least he wasn't lying to her anymore.

"You had no right to talk to my editor, and I'm already a part of it," she argued. "Your killer made certain of it."

"And haven't you questioned why?" he snapped furiously. "You're a target most likely because of that bastard Watts. He was involved with the Deadly Dozen up to his fucking eyeballs and you know it."

Yes, she had suspected that much. One of the men in that grainy picture, the one more hidden than the others, the one she couldn't quite place, resembled Douglas too closely.

"I've always been a voice for the Breeds, Cabal," she informed him. "If Tanner is the face of the Breeds, then I'm the voice, you know that. I've made certain of it. The killer is obviously targeting the Breeds and their standing in society. If Douglas was part of the Dozen, then that would make it even sweeter for the killer. It discredits me if the world finds out. It would make it appear as if I were playing favorites to make up for his sins."

He shook his head. "And the killer is targeting much more than Breed standing in society, we both know it. Now I'll ask you again. Why are you involved in this?"

"Because I'm involved with you." That was the truth. Not enough of the truth, but enough that he couldn't smell a lie.

Cabal frowned at the answer. "We're not involved. You've made certain of that."

She shook her head. "I was there when your facility was rescued. I reported it. That story and the pictures taken of it rocked the world with the brutality of the Council, you know that, not to mention the airtime Douglas's death received. You're investigating these murders; you have been since the first. Naturally the killer would tie us together."

It was logical, and the only reason she could come up with that didn't truly terrify her.

He shook his head. "You're reaching."

His gaze flickered over her again. The caressing look had heat chasing away the chill of fear. This was the danger in being around Cabal. She forgot to beware of him. She forgot that he was as much a danger to her as an attraction. She forgot this wasn't a love match, it was a hormonal phenomenon. That was the greatest danger, because forgetting that could destroy her.

She shrugged nonchalantly at the accusation. "It makes perfect sense to me."

"Only to you," he grunted as he looked around the room once again, before turning his gaze back to her. "I want you to drop this, Cassa. Let me do my job here, then I'll give you the story. Stay out of it for now. Don't endanger both of us."

Cabal caught the scent of her anger, her refusal, seconds before her eyes narrowed on him and her face flushed a becoming shade of pink.

She was pissed. That anger infused her arousal as well, to create a scent that struck straight to his balls. They drew up, tightened and clenched with a surge of lust that almost took his breath. He could take her again, he realized. Right now. It would be no hardship to lay her back on that bed and fuck her until they were both screaming with the pleasure.

"Not going to work." She jerked her clothes from the dresser before stooping to pick up a pair of hiking boots. "Sorry, babe, but I have a date I can't miss. Have fun without me."

Have fun without her? He almost snarled at the thought of her having fun without him. He didn't think so. There wouldn't be a date she'd be attending without him overseeing.

"You're being foolish, Cassa. You know the danger that exists here."

"My job description doesn't mention safety," she informed him coolly as she headed for the bathroom. "Don't worry, I'm fairly certain you don't have to be concerned about me whoring around on you." There was an edge of pain in her voice now, a bitterness that had nothing to do with him.

"I'm not Watts." He made the statement simply, coldly. "Don't apply his treatment of you to me."

That too had been in the investigation that had been done on her after Watts's so-called death. The man had treated his wife like a possession. He had made painful false accusations to control her. He'd made certain she stayed on a very short leash. Not because he loved her, but so he could control her.

She paused at his command. Her lips thinned angrily as she watched him, evidently sizing up exactly how far she could push him. At the moment, the boundary was a near one.

"Then don't try to control me," she suggested, the scent of her anger nearly overwhelming the arousal now. "You can share this little venture with me, or we can just keep muddling along on our own. Either way, this is my story and I'll finish it."

Cabal could feel the hunger moving inside him now. Her deliberate defiance had his animal instincts rising, the need to dominate her nearly overwhelming his control. She was his mate. He was the more powerful, he was the leader and she was deliberately endangering herself, placing herself in the line of fire.

Humanity insisted he step aside and let her do what she needed to do. The animal was roaring in rage though. This was his woman. His mate. Without her, what would he be? How would he function?

He had to get her out of the area. He had to get her far enough away from him that she was no longer in danger. He would have called Jonas and requested his help except he was pretty certain he would be denied. The bastard would only be amused by the request.

He watched as she stared back at him. His gaze locked with hers, willing her to do as he ordered, to save them both, because he couldn't leave. Even if he wanted to.

"I can't leave, Cabal, even if I wanted to."

He almost flinched as her words reflected his own thoughts. He wanted to clench his fists with the need to touch her now, to claim her again, to force her to think of her safety first.

"You never did understand the meaning of personal preservation, did you, Cassa?" Cabal heard the rumble of his voice in his chest and almost winced.

"And you never did understand the meaning of personal choice," she retorted. "I don't need your permission, Cabal. Don't pretend that I do."

Animal genetics sucked on a good day, and today was definitely not one of the good ones. The dominance that was so much a part of the Breeds could rise within seconds, as it was now. She was defying him in a situation where he needed control, needed to control the players involved. But even more than that, she was his mate and she was placing her life in jeopardy.

The human part of him accepted the logic that she had a free will of her own, but the animal part of him, the part that knew the preservation of the Breeds depended on mating, felt otherwise. She should be safe, behind strong walls, enclosed in a secure environment. She shouldn't be placing her life in danger, no matter the situation or the reason.

It was typical Breed arrogance and even though he fought it, he feared he would eventually lose the battle.

"Personal preservation was never high on my list of priorities anyway." She shrugged and he knew she meant it. "You only live once, Cabal. If you hide and bury your head from the world around you, then you aren't living. You're existing."

"You're an adventure junkie," he accused her.

She laughed at that. He watched her lips tilt in sudden amusement, saw the laughter that crossed her gaze.

"Is that what you call it? My father used to call it insanity."

She had lost her family just before meeting Douglas Watts and marrying him. Perhaps that was why the bastard had managed to fool her so easily. He had been no friend of the Breeds, and his coverage of the rescues had always been subtly biased.

"Insanity is a good word for it." He moved closer. Damn if he could help himself. He wanted to feel the warmth of her, wanted to touch her satiny flesh, taste it. She was naked beneath that robe, for now. If he didn't move quickly, she would be dressed and gone.

"Cabal." Her voice was breathless.

It was breathless in passion as well, he remembered. Sweet and husky, drawn from deep within her chest as pleasure stole through her. He wanted to hear it again, her soft little cries, her mews of need and ecstasy.

"I dream of you." The words were dragged from him. He

hadn't meant to whisper those words, hadn't meant to reveal that information to her. "I dream of touching you, of licking every inch of your flesh."

She shivered. Cabal watched the betraying little ripple as it rushed across her body. Wide gray eyes stared up at him, a little bemused, a lot wary. He could see the hungry need in her eyes, in the ripening of her lips, in the flush of her cheeks.

He couldn't force himself to move from her path, to allow her to walk from the room and into danger. His sweet, sweet mate. Why would he do something so insane when he could have her beneath him, arching into his touch, begging for the completion that only he could bring her?

"Cabal, don't do this."

He paused, his lips a breath from hers as he watched the conflicting emotions chase across her face, smelled them in her subtle scent. Anger. A shade of pain and bitterness. And determination. She was determined to do what she had come here to do, and he was deliberately standing in her way.

Mating heat was one thing, but at this moment he was deliberately igniting those fires to keep her here. To keep her safe.

"Letting you go tonight isn't going to change anything," he warned her softly. "You can run forever, Cassa, and I'll be right behind you."

Her lips trembled, and it was all he could do to keep from catching them beneath his own and loving them with all the hunger he could feel building between her and him.

She was his. God had created her for him, matched her to him. Heart and soul, she had been meant for him.

"I'm a possession," she whispered painfully. He could feel the pain, smell it on the air around them. "A mate. That's all, Cabal."

"My only mate," he reminded her, his voice harsh. "You should be thankful I haven't loaded you up in a heli-jet and had you whisked back to Sanctuary."

"You should be thankful that I didn't shoot you first." She was nose to nose with him now, anger overwhelming arousal, pride adding its bittersweet scent.

She wanted to deny him, but her fingers were holding on to his arms, the tips massaging his flesh. She was denying him, even as she held on to him.

"I should show you how good staying here could be," he whispered.

He wanted to act on it. His tongue wanted to act; the glands beneath it were swollen, hot, the mating hormone begging to be released into the warm depths of her mouth. He could just lick her. Just lick over the lush curves of her lips. It would take no more than that. The mating hormone in the glands of his tongue was eager, ready for release once again.

Cabal clenched his teeth, fought for control. Just a little control. Now was not the time for this. He had his own meeting to attend and arrangements to make to ensure her safety.

But how fucking sweet she was. He knew her now, knew the taste of her and the intoxicating effects it would have on him.

So intoxicating.

A growl rumbled in his chest. One hand lowered, fingers cupping the curve of her rear as he jerked her close, lifted her, ground her against the erection throbbing hard and hot beneath his jeans.

He could have her now, he could take her. All it would take was a single kiss. One hot, desperate caress of his tongue against hers and she would belong to him. She wouldn't be able to deny him.

"Cabal." If it was a protest, then it was a weak one.

Her head fell back as his lips moved to her jaw, her neck. He didn't lick, though he wanted to. He was dying to.

Instead, his lips only parted, his teeth raked over the sensitive flesh as his cock jerked at the sound of her sudden, needy little moan.

Sweet heaven. That was what he needed from her. The sound of her pleasure. Not her protests, not the look of wariness or fear in her eyes. But just this, Cassa's pleasure.

· C H A P T E R   1 0 ·

She was dying in his arms.

Cassa could feel the waves of heated, intoxicating need rushing through her system; she embraced it even as she fought it. Her nails dug into his forearms as her head fell back helplessly, her senses trained on the intensity of sensation rushing over her neck. The sharp tips of the wickedly long canines raked against her skin and sent spirals of exquisite pleasure racing in their wake once again.

Her toes were actually curling against the carpet as she tried not to lift closer to him, and failed. As his thigh slipped between hers, pressing against the desperate need throbbing between her legs, a moan left her throat. Her hips undulated as she rode the hard muscle; her nails dug into the material of his shirt, and she felt the rush of wild wetness spilling from her sex.

She ached for him. Never had she ached for anything or anyone as she ached for Cabal. Just this fast, just this soon after he had taken her last time, and she hungered for him with the same desperate intensity as before.

Mating heat. That chemical reaction that was racing through the Breed community, tying couples together, refusing to allow them to separate. It was a feral, hungry heat, one that refused to be ignored, one Cassa knew was taking her over, stealing her soul. Cabal had already stolen her heart. Now he was taking anything that might have been left.

"Damn you." He growled the curse at her ear. "Do you know what you do to me, Cassa? Do you know what this will do to us?"

"One question at a time." She panted breathlessly as his thigh pressed harder against the robe-covered flesh of her sex. "My multitasking abilities aren't working today."

She could have sworn she heard a chuckle at her shoulder as he buried his face against her neck.

"You damned smart-ass," he accused her.

"You damned Breed." Her lashes refused to lift, to open as his hands gripped her back, massaged, stroked over the material of her robe.

It shouldn't feel so good. The feel of his hands stroking up her back, his fingers finding her spine, shouldn't fill her with this insane, crazy need to bite him again.

His neck was there beneath her lips. He would bite her again if he took her again.

And she could bite him as well. She could bite to her heart's content, taste his flesh and revel in it now without worrying about the consequences, because the consequences were already here.

Her lashes lifted, pleasure rushing through her like a narcotic as her head lowered and her lips touched the tough, hard flesh of his neck.

The sound that rumbled from his chest sent a chill of fierce sensation rushing down her spine. Part fear, part pleasure and a whole lot of feminine satisfaction.

No matter the reason—chemical, biological or just plain fate—she would please this Breed as no other woman could. The womanizing, charming and fierce Cabal St. Laurents would never know pleasure like he knew with her, simply because she was his mate.

For a moment, the fear overpowered every other sensation. Because the same held true for her. There would never be any pleasure as fierce as this with anyone else.

"Cabal, we have to stop this." She spoke the words, but her thighs tightened on his, her hips worked against the hard muscle pressed between them and her juices flowed thick and hot from her vagina.

She had never needed anything as desperately as she needed Cabal. Again. Right now.

"You ache," he whispered at her ear. "I sense it, Cassa. You need me."

She needed him now. She had needed him before she had ever known what mating heat was, before she had ever been close enough for the phenomenon to flare between them. She had needed him a second before she had parted her lips and tasted his blood.

Yes, she needed him, but she knew the depth of her need went far beyond the physical. Even as she felt one hand slide from her back to her stomach, she knew she couldn't have his heart as well.

But that didn't stop her from whispering his name as she felt the belt of her robe release. And it didn't keep her from sucking in her stomach as she felt the ends part.

"Just a touch." He nipped at her ear and sent an explosive flare of ecstasy shooting through her body.

Bare flesh, his fingers calloused and sure as they slid against her lower stomach.

"Cabal, this is crazy. We both have things to do." Her protest was a thin, pleasure-filled cry as his fingers slid between her thighs, the tips feathering the damp curls that hid the sensitive folds of her sex.

Her hips arched closer, trying to recapture the pressure of his thigh as he drew back. A second later they stilled at the feel of his fingertips pressing into the curls at the top of her mound.

How hot his flesh was. Pleasure intensified and exploded through her system as she felt her clit swelling, felt the folds of her sex becoming drenched in her juices. Her body was so primed for him, so desperate for his touch that it left her helpless in its wake.

"I can smell how sweet and hot you are." His lips smoothed over her neck, to her shoulder, as he pushed the neckline of her robe aside with his chin. "I can feel it, Cassa."

His fingers slid lower, sliding past the desperate throb of her clit, stroking around it with the lightest touch before delving into the drenched, slick essence spilling from her pussy.

"We can't do this right now." She wanted to cry at the knowledge of what was coming, the ties that would bind them even closer together, and would eventually destroy them both. Each time he touched her, each time he possessed her, she lost more of herself to him.

"We can't? But, baby, we're already doing it. Have already done it."

She went up on her tiptoes as his finger slid lower, curled and thrust wickedly into the tight, desperate entrance that throbbed for his possession. A wailing, desperate sigh fell from her lips. Her head pressed into his shoulder, her hands tightened on his forearms.

Cassa could feel herself shaking, coming apart from the inside out as his finger thrust inside her. Her muscles clamped around the intruder, tightened. The heated wetness increased, making his way slick and hot as his finger pumped slow and easy past the tightening tissue.

"I need to be inside you," he growled, his jaw pressing against hers now, the feel of his muscles clenching in the side of his face reminding Cassa of the control he was imposing upon himself. "I need to lay you down, Cassa. To touch you. I could spend hours, days, just touching you. Tasting you."

Oh God. She lost her breath as white-hot need slammed into the muscles surrounding his stroking finger. Her womb clenched and tightened, and if she wasn't mistaken, she was bare seconds from the most intense orgasm of her life.

"Do you want me, Cassa?" The question was an insidious promise of both pleasure and pain as he whispered the words. "Do you need me?"

She needed him like she needed air to breathe.

A whimper left her throat as his finger pulled back, and when it returned, another made the fit tighter, stretched her, burned her with a pleasure she couldn't fight.

She had never had a problem fighting against desire, or attraction. Not since she was too young and too stupid to know any better. Not since she had learned the true depths of betrayal that loving a man could bring.

But now, the pleasure was too intense, too deep to ignore or to deny. His fingers fucked inside her with slow, deliberate movements while his thumb circled the swollen bud of her clit and had it throbbing with the need for orgasm.

She was close. So fucking close. If the pressure was just a little firmer, just a little harder.

"Cabal, please." Her hips jerked against each slow, deliberate thrust. "Don't tease me."

"I would never tease you, Cassa."

She wanted to scream at the next thrust. The feel of his fingers pushing hard and deep inside her, sending a surge of violent pleasure rushing through her system, shocking it, and nearly stilling her heartbeat with the extremity of it.

She should be used to this by now. She should know his touch, be immune to the excitement that was just as fierce, just as hot as the first time he had touched her.

When her breath returned, it was in a rush, a cry as the next thrust sent her to her tiptoes and had her fingernails tightening at his biceps now. Close. So close. She was going to explode. She was going to destroy them both with the response beginning to build inside her.

"Come for me, Cassa." His voice rumbled at her ear. "Let me feel it, baby. Let me feel you coming for me."

She cried his name, tightened. She could feel the fragile threads of ecstasy closing in around her clit. Felt the need coalescing within her.

As his fingers plunged inside her once more, filled her, stretched her, the need began to expand, began to beat in a hard, rapid demand through her bloodstream. It was inside her, around her, amassing through her.

"Ms. Hawkins, it's Sheriff Lacey." The voice was an intrusion, a hated, horrible sound as she felt Cabal still. "Ms. Hawkins, are you there?"

She wasn't here. She couldn't answer. The breath was trapped in her throat as surely as Cabal's fingers were trapped inside her sex.

A growl, harsh and dangerous, rumbled in his throat.

"Ms. Hawkins, open the door or I'm going to have it opened." Sheriff Lacey's voice firmed, became cold and warning. "Are you all right, Ms. Hawkins?"

The sheriff would have checked to be certain she had come back to her room. The receptionist at the front desk knew she was there.

Cassa shook her head.

"Answer her," Cabal demanded.

A whimper left her throat.

"Now, Cassa." His fingers slid free of her, and she wanted to scream in rage at the sheriff.

"Just a minute." Her voice was hoarse, filled with the agony of a release slipping slowly out of her grasp.

"Is everything okay, Ms. Hawkins?" Sheriff Lacey's voice became more demanding.

"Fine. Fine," she snapped. "Just a minute."

She was weak, too off balance even to realize that Cabal was fixing her robe until he had already completed the job.

His expression was tight with lust, his eyes greener, the amber flecks in them more brilliant as he stared down at her.

"We're insane to have let this start," he stated harshly.

She could have cried. She wanted to cry. There was nothing like the regret when a man she was tied to forever stated his own regret that they were tied. Oh yeah, this little relationship was going to be tons of fun.

"Your hand was in my robe," she reminded him, her voice tart. "Not the other way around. I remember telling you I had things to do this evening." She would have preferred Cabal not know about this meeting though.

Her body was still singing, the need for release still tearing through her, as Sheriff Lacey knocked on the door once again.

Wiping her hands down her thighs, Cassa drew in a hard breath before pulling her control around her and moving to the door.

She looked back at Cabal, wishing she could still her response to him as easily as he seemed to be stilling his to her. She would have taken more time to get herself under control, to stop her hands from shaking, if the sheriff hadn't pounded on the door again.

Clenching her teeth, she gripped the doorknob and pulled the door open, stepping back and facing the sheriff as the other woman's gaze sliced into the room and settled on Cabal.

For a moment, Cassa felt the tension and the certainty that the sheriff and Cabal knew each other more than either of them would want her to realize. It was in the tension that tightened in the other woman's shoulders, and the suspicion that filled her hazel eyes.

"I hope I didn't interrupt anything." The sheriff's tone was wry, her smile friendly, though the knowledge that she had indeed interrupted something was clear in her gaze.

"Not at all," Cassa assured her. "Please come in, and thank you for taking time to see me again."

"When I received the message that there was possible Breed violence in the county, I admit, I rushed right over. You didn't mention that earlier today."

Great. Cassa glanced at Cabal and watched his eyes narrow.

"Is Mr. St. Laurents involved?" Slender, tall, the sheriff hooked her thumbs in the pockets of her jeans as her gaze raked over Cabal. "I always did think he was a rather suspicious character."

There was an edge of laughter in the sheriff's voice, and one of familiarity. She wasn't trying to hide the fact that she knew Cabal, but there was no sense that she knew him too well. Cassa tried to still the jealousy rising within her, both surprised and horrified as she recognized the emotion.

She didn't do jealousy. She did not, she would not, become jealous of a man. There was no quicker way to self-destruct than to give in to that emotion. And Cassa refused to ever self-destruct again.

"Mr. St. Laurents, I'm certain, is most likely involved some-how." Cassa felt the tightness of her smile as well as the cer-tainty that Cabal had come here tonight for no other reason than to influence her against the investigation she had come to Glen Ferris for.

Danna Lacey stepped into the room, her gaze going between Cassa and Cabal as a dark brow lifted curiously.

Dressed in jeans, an official shirt and boots, Sherrif Lacey looked the quintessential country girl. Her shoulder-length hair was pulled back into a sleek braid that fit well beneath her offi-cial sheriff's hat and showed off her high cheekbones perfectly.

Green eyes twinkled merrily, but they held a hint of cyni-cism. She was amused though well acquainted with dealing with Breeds and very well aware of their deceptions.

She should be. Danna Lacey's department had been one of the first to sign on to cooperate with Breed Law in its efforts to incorporate Breeds into the law enforcement communities and to enforce the new laws governing violence against Breeds.

"So, what's the problem?" Sheriff Lacey looked between the two of them. "Usually the Bureau of Breed Affairs contacts me if any violence has occurred involving Breeds. Not reporters. And you didn't mention any of this earlier, Ms. Hawkins."

"Ms. Hawkins is merely concerned, I believe," Cabal drawled.

"We've been conducting training exercises in the national forest and she came upon one of them the other night."

Oh, that was a good one.

"Not quite," Cassa objected. "The last I heard, Coyotes in the employ of John Bollen don't exactly cooperate with the Bureau or Sanctuary."

John Bollen, formerly second-in-command under General Tallant, a once high official with the Genetics Council, had taken over after Tallant's death. The Tallant organization, now called Bollen Enterprises, supplied security guards, personal protection and other services where muscle and weapons were required. It had, under General Tallant's ownership, also supplied subversive teams to strike against Breeds.

What it did now, where Breeds were concerned, was anyone's guess. Bollen kept his business quiet, but the general consensus was that the Breeds were now in more danger from Bollen than they ever had been when the organization was under Tallant's leadership.

"Bollen's Coyotes are in the national forest?" Sheriff Lacey directed her question to Cabal. "During Breed training exercises?"

Cabal directed a chiding look to Cassa before turning back to Lacey.

"Come on, Danna, you know how it works. We spy on them, they spy on us. No one was armed, no one was hurt."

Sheriff Lacey grimaced at the comment before directing her attention back to Cassa. "Then where does the violence come in?"

Cassa knew immediately that the sheriff, though sympathetic and likely prone to disagree with or outright disbelieve Cabal, wasn't about to involve herself in investigating something Cabal was so clearly warning her away from.

"I was ambushed in the forest," Cassa stated, hiding her anger now. "I thought you should be aware that Coyote soldiers are roaming the area and I did feel threatened. Had Mr. St. Laurents not been in the area, then the three soldiers I faced could have become dangerous."

Lacey's eyes narrowed. "Do you know who they are?"

"Only one." Cassa shrugged.

"It was Dog and his two lieutenants, Butch and Mongrel." Cabal spoke up with a cold smile.

Sheriff Lacey shook her head at the information, her expression becoming sober as she gave a sharp nod. "I'll alert the forest rangers to be on watch for them," she promised. "As well as the local police and my deputies. We can't throw their asses out of the area, but we can keep an eye on them." She looked back at Cassa. "How much longer will you be here?"

Cassa crossed her arms over her breasts, aware that the sheriff was probably hoping her stay would be brief.

"I'm not certain," she stated. "Should it matter?"

The sheriff grimaced. "You're like gas poured on a Breed fire," she said. "You could be the reason the Coyote soldiers are here, Ms. Hawkins, as you're well aware. The few times Dog has shown up in your reports, you've not exactly been tactful in regards to your opinion of him."

"I'm not paid to be tactful." She felt like a ten-year-old being taken to task for causing trouble.

"And I'm not paid to babysit reporters who go looking for trouble," the sheriff shot back. "Stay out of the forest until the Coyote soldiers are gone, that's the best advice I can give you."

In other words, it would be really nice if she just packed up and left town. Cassa mentally scratched the sheriff off her list of persons to contact should she actually need any help in her own investigation.

"Thank you so much for your time, Sheriff." A patently false smile spread her lips as she strode to the door and opened it for the other woman. "I'll be sure to let you know should I need any additional help."

Sheriff Lacey breathed out wearily as she shook her head and moved to the door. "Ms. Hawkins, Breed Law states that I can't run these guys out of town, nor can I officially protest their presence. As much as I hate it, I have to put up with the likes of men like Dog and his lieutenants until they actually mess up and give me a reason to contact the Bureau or throw their asses in jail."

"Until then, I'll just hide in my room and pretend I'm having fun," Cassa stated sarcastically. "I'll be sure to mention that in the pleasant little story I had planned about the area."

"And while you're mentioning that, please mention that you created this situation for yourself by plastering Dog's picture all over the damned air at that station you worked for last year," the sheriff reminded her. "'The once anonymous Coyote Breed, suspected of drug and weapons smuggling, violence against Breeds and stealing candy from little children,'" the sheriff quoted her mockingly as she shook her head in amusement. "Really, Ms. Hawkins, did you think he was going to be pleasant when you met up with him in the forest? You were lucky Cabal and his team were there."

At the moment, lucky wasn't exactly how Cassa felt. But she kept her mouth shut, kept her opinion to herself.

"Good day, Sheriff." She smiled tightly at the sheriff, then she turned to Cabal. "You can leave now too."

Her body was still humming. Sexual need was still a hunger that ached to be assuaged, even as anger poured through her. He had to have known she had contacted the sheriff. That was why he was here, the nosy bastard. She should have filed a damned report about the attack the night before and she should demand an investigation now. But to do that, she would actually have to come up with a reason why she had been in the forest herself.

Normally, that wouldn't be a problem. But she wasn't normally so aroused that her brain refused to work.

"Come on, Breed," Sheriff Lacey ordered, her voice firm. "Let's see if you'll be any more forthcoming about the reason you're here as well, while you file the report you obviously forgot you're supposed to file when conducting exercises in my county. I have a feeling you two are going to be more trouble than Dog and his men."

The look he shot Cassa promised retaliation of a kind that would no doubt leave her screaming in pleasure and begging for more.

"Getting rid of me for a while isn't going to make this situation any better," he warned her softly as he moved closer, his gaze locked on hers now. "Don't fool yourself, Cassa."

"Bet me," she muttered.

"I'll bet you." He stopped in front of her, his head bending until his lips rested at her ear. "I bet you, sweetheart, one hard, hot kiss. I bet you ignoring it is something you won't be able to do."

Jerking back, Cassa glared up at him. The blood was thundering through her veins again, and she could have sworn the fresh, winter-night smell of him was a taste against her tongue.

"I'll catch you later, Cabal." She had to force the words past her lips even as she had to force herself to step back from him before she took that kiss now. "Have fun with the sheriff."

His lips quirked in mocking amusement before he straightened and did as she asked. Turning, he strode to the door, gripped the doorknob and pulled the panel closed behind him.

The sound of the door quietly latching had Cassa closing her eyes in relief as well as regret. The regret was something she wasn't going to allow herself to face. She had turned on her heel and started for the shower when a muted beep from her laptop alerted her that mail had just been received in her inbox.

She turned back to the room and strode to the desk. Having typed in the passcode to access the screen, she stared at the subject line of the email.

You're going to fail.

Failure wasn't an option.

Cassa opened the email.

More blood is being spilled. The Deadly Dozen are deadly no more. I've given you enough time. My prey comes here each year. He dines in splendor. He charms without prejudice. How handsome he was, how handsome he is. How evil is his soul, how corrupt is his heart. The land that would have hid and cherished the children of the wild will now taste the blood of their enemies once again, Ms. Hawkins. Beware that one day you don't become the prey as well.

The ever present warning, that one day she would become the prey. Cassa had no doubt that that day was growing ever nearer.

◆   ◆   ◆

Cabal followed Danna Lacey from the inn, his stride even, matched to hers until she drew abreast of the official SUV she had driven there.

"Stay out of this, Danna," he warned her as she unlocked the driver's door and glanced back at him.

Her expression filled with mocking amusement. She knew the investigation he was working on, she knew the danger involved, and yet there wasn't so much as a hint of fear in her eyes.

"Who do you think you're talking to, Cabal?" Her voice was gentle, despite the hint of arrogance in it. "I'm not a Breed sol-

dier under your command, nor do I heel so well. You'd do well
to remember that."

"Just as you'd do well to remember exactly what we're facing
here. Not just the Breeds, but this community as well. Stop feeling sorry for Cassa and start worrying about yourself."

He could smell the sympathy, the compassion that rolled off
her in waves. That was just Danna. He would have never thought
she had the emotional strength for the job she held. As a sheriff
of a small town, she saw the cruelty inherent in people she must
have surely once seen as friends, as neighbors.

"I always worry about myself first, Breed." She chuckled as
she reached in, pushed the key into the ignition and started the
vehicle.

"Stay out of my way, Danna," he warned her again. "Don't
let Cassa put a fire under your ass where this is concerned. I
don't have time to battle you."

She gave a graceful little snort. "As though there would be a
battle to it," she drawled. "Really, Cabal, you should know better.
I'm fairly lazy; I don't put myself out any more than I have to."

Cabal knew that statement for the lie it was. Danna was anything but lazy.

She laughed at his dark look, refusing to show so much as a
hint of trepidation or fear. And he doubted she felt either emotion.

"Yes, Cabal," she continued, "I'll just put my little head
down and run around barefoot and pregnant to suit the Breeds.
Satisfied now?"

Cabal grunted at that. No, he wasn't really satisfied and he
didn't appreciate her humor either.

"You just be certain you do that," he muttered. "While you're
at it, see if you can get some information on Banks that I don't
already know. That would please me immensely."

Danna shook her head with a laugh. "You have what I have,
Bengal. I can't do you any better than I've already done for you."

And she had done a hell of a lot of legwork for them. At forty-
five, single and independent, the sheriff had given uncounted
hours through the first few days of Cabal's investigation.

"Stay the hell out of trouble, Danna," he warned her, even as
he wished he could warn Cassa.

"I could say the same to you, Bengal, but I suspect you'd pay as much attention to me as I'm going to pay to you." She rolled her eyes at him, but he saw the hint of worry in her gaze.

Glen Ferris was her territory, and from past experience he knew she didn't take well to Breed interference in what she considered her domain.

He shrugged the thought off. No one took that well, but it was now a fact of life. To survive, Breeds needed a measure of autonomy. Breed Law had given them that autonomy for a period of five decades. They had fifty years. Cabal had a feeling it wouldn't be nearly enough time.

A restless night filled with broken, erotic dreams haunted Cassa until the first fragile rays of light began to spill over the Gauley River that flowed beyond the window of her room.

Rising from bed, she stared into the churning, murky winter water, not for the first time, frowning at the sense of excitement and trepidation that filled her.

She should have been furious. She hadn't seen Cabal the night before. Whatever business he'd had to do had taken him much longer than hers had. Of course, hers had amounted to no more than tracking down Banks's golfing buddies. None of whom had any information that could have led to the cause of the former mayor's disappearance.

She had returned to her room at midnight, disgusted and aroused. Mating heat sucked, but at least Ely's hormones were keeping her from searching out Cabal and demanding sex.

She didn't want to face what she knew was happening to her own body. She wanted to question someone, anyone. She just wanted a few ideas on how to handle a very stubborn Bengal Breed. Surely that wouldn't be too much to ask.

Merinus, the Feline pack leader's wife, or Scheme, the wife of the Felines' head of public relations—anyone but Cabal, because

God only knew he'd never tell her the truth. But she knew better. If she talked to anyone, then she was sealing her own fate.

Somehow—no, not somehow, she knew how—mating heat was beginning to affect every facet of her life. It would only get worse, she already knew that. As the days slipped by, her need for him would only grow, until the initial phase of the heat eased. After that, she could expect a few days to a week each month that the symptoms were worse. Ovulation always triggered it, made the need for sex more insistent. Ely had already pretty much told her what to expect.

Wrapping her arms across her chest, she breathed in slow and easy, feeling the hard tips of her nipples, the swollen contours of her breasts. It was more of an irritant, at the moment, rather than being painful.

She gave her head a hard shake before turning and striding quickly to the shower. Despite the cool temperature that she'd set the thermostat at the night before, her body was still overheated.

A cool shower eased it, but only marginally. Two hours later, dressed in jeans, a white blouse, leather jacket and hiking boots, she slung the small backpack she carried for personal use over her shoulder and left her room.

She'd wasted enough time the day before. There were answers in this small town, she could feel it, as well as a story that went much deeper than the murders of men who had once hunted down and aided in the torture of Breeds.

She had felt that knowledge each time the anonymous emails came through. She had seen something beyond the pictures of death that were attached to the later emails, and the threats that her own secrets could be revealed. She had no secrets that she knew of. There wasn't a day in her life that the Breeds hadn't thoroughly investigated.

Those deaths had a purpose though, a reason that went far beyond Breed rage. Cassa wanted to know what that purpose was. For the first time since the Breeds had revealed themselves, one of them was stepping past the careful control she had always glimpsed within them. One of them was taking personal vengeance, and he had come here, to Glen Ferris, a place where Breeds had once taken refuge, to do so.

Leaving the inn, she opted to walk rather than drive the few blocks to a nearby diner and the breakfast meeting she had set up with Myron, hoping to get more information than she had the day before. He knew something. She had sensed it, felt it.

She wanted to know what he wasn't telling her, and why he had never told her about the Breed wife he'd had before he met and married Patricia.

Pushing through the door to the diner, Cassa gazed around the large, crowded room until she caught sight of Myron. His bright red hair stood out in relief. Cut much closer to his head than it had been years before, it lay around his freckled features and threw his pale blue eyes into stark relief.

At the side of his eyes deep lines were carved into his face that she hadn't noticed the day before. She would have called them laugh lines, but Cassa had never seen Myron laugh. The same grooves bracketed his mouth, and across his forehead deep frown lines were displayed with the shorter cut of his hair.

But his face was lean, and he looked years younger than his forty-two years of age. He had been one of the guiding forces in the movement to find a safe place for the Breeds to hide before their presence was revealed eleven years ago. He and his father had worked tirelessly for years to hide the Breeds, who had often arrived near death, in the one area rumored to offer a measure of safety.

Moving across the dining room, Cassa caught sight of two Breeds drinking coffee in a corner behind and to the side of Myron. They were dressed in jeans, flannel shirts and ball caps. She would have never picked them out for Breeds if she hadn't familiarized herself before she arrived with the Breeds known to be in the area. They looked like farmers. Hell, they might well be farmers. Many of the Breeds that had been hiding in these mountains had been smart enough to carve a living out for themselves in the area.

"Myron, I hope you have coffee coming." Cassa slid into the booth as she smiled back at the reporter, taking in the ever present suspicion in his pale eyes and the deepening of the frown lines at his forehead.

Lifting his head, he nodded toward the counter.

"The waitress was waiting on you," he told her as he laid aside the newspaper he had been glancing over. "What do you need now? I told you, Cass, I don't know anything about Banks's disappearance."

He had been in a better mood the day before, which wasn't saying much.

"I wasn't going to ask about Banks." She waved the subject away. "It's been a while, Myron, maybe I just wanted to catch up."

He shook his head at that. "You don't have time to catch up, Cass. I follow your stories, you know. Last I heard you were chasing down the location of Breed scientists known to have been involved in the Coyote Breed genetics. What happened to that?"

"I'm still working on it." She shrugged. "There were rumors that two Coyote Breed scientists had survived an assassination attempt by the Coyote Ghost and were now actually residing in the Coyote stronghold. All I've heard are rumors though."

Myron lifted his red brows in surprise. "Surprising that the Council allowed them to live, even if the Ghost did. The Coyotes were their most secret creations."

"And Breeds as well as human scientists are still trying to figure out why," Cassa agreed. "Perhaps this marriage between the Coyote alpha, Del-Rey Delgado, and Anya Kobrin will shed some light on those scientists."

Myron snorted at the thought, though she saw a flicker of worry in his gaze.

"I wouldn't bet on it," he muttered.

"I don't bet on anything where getting information out of Breeds is concerned." She almost laughed at the thought. The definition of "Breed" was "closemouthed and unpredictable."

Myron smiled at that, then gave her a probing look as he sipped his coffee, before saying, "I hear you have a particular Breed on your ass at the moment. What's up with that?"

Cassa affected an innocent look. "Just a particular Breed? If there's a Breed around, then he seems to be nosy about my business."

"Comes with the territory?" He chuckled. "You've turned yourself into the bane of their existence with your reports. You're not just a nosy reporter, but best friends with two of the Breed alpha mates. Be careful, you might become a liability next."

Cassa rolled her eyes at that. "Maybe I've already become one." She had no doubt that was how Jonas and Cabal both saw her now. It was a dangerous position to occupy.

"That could explain that Bengal Breed shadowing you." My-ron folded his arms on the table and glared at her warningly. "Stay out of trouble, Cassa. I'd hate to see you get hurt here."

Now there was a shift.

"There was a time when you would have helped me get into trouble," she reminded him with a small smile.

Myron only shook his head as he sighed roughly.

"So have you found out anything about Banks?" He lifted his coffee to his lips as the waitress set another cup in front of Cassa along with a menu. "It's obvious you don't intend to stay out of whatever stink you're trying to stir up."

"I could only wish." She tried for a smile as she poured cream in her coffee and watched Myron through the veil of her lashes. "Did you know Brandenmore and Engalls very well? I know they have a hunting cabin in the area."

Myron's eyes narrowed on her. "It's a small town, Cassa. Of course I knew them. We didn't socialize together though."

"Did you suspect then that they were involved with Breed deaths?"

Myron's expression hardened further as his jaw tightened.

"If I had suspected then, they wouldn't be alive to continue to torture Breeds now."

Myron was being extremely closemouthed on the subject. That wasn't like him. He was a reporter. He should have already gotten most of the information that she needed to continue her own investigation.

"Did they have a connection to the Breeds that you knew of?" She frowned at the feeling that she was having to drag an-swers out of him.

"They hated the Breeds and you know it." Myron grimaced. "Look, Cassa, if anyone around here knew anything that would help you or St. Laurents, trust me, you'd have the information. We want to see those two taken down as much as anyone else does. We'd be doing ourselves, as well as the Breeds, a favor."

"There's a rumor that someone is doing the Breeds other fa-vors as well. That someone has identified the Deadly Dozen and they're taking them out." Cassa reached into her bag and pulled out the picture of the valley she had been searching for in the mountains. Watching him closely, she laid it on the table. "One of the Dozen could have died here."

Myron's gaze flickered over it before his expression tightened with what she was certain was recognition. He knew the area, and he knew that location.

"Do you recognize that valley?" she asked him.

When his gaze lifted, the look in his eyes was flinty and hard.

"That could be anywhere," he said tonelessly.

Cassa frowned down at the picture before looking back at him suspiciously. She had seen his reaction; she knew he recognized that valley.

"Its about four miles past the north fork, along the eastern portion of the largest ravine that runs down the mountain."

"That could be anywhere," he repeated, his tone stiff.

Cassa sat back in the booth and stared at Myron in confusion. What had happened over the years to change his attitude toward her? They used to be friends.

"What's the problem, Myron?" she asked quietly. "You and I have exchanged information for years, what makes this time different? What makes today different from last year?"

His lips thinned as he looked away, his gaze focused outside the large windows of the café. When he turned back to her, the animosity wasn't there, but neither was the friendliness she was used to seeing in him.

"You should stay out of the forest at night, especially if there's something going on up there concerning Breeds and the Deadly Dozen," he finally said, his voice pitched low as he leaned forward. "Listen to me, Cassa, these mountains are brutal, and I'm not just talking about the nature of them. Whatever you're looking for here, let it go."

Cassa sipped at her coffee as she gazed back at him. There was a darkness in his gaze, a warning that she couldn't ignore. When she set her coffee back on the table, she made certain her expression reflected the determination she could feel inside to figure out what the hell was going on in Glen Ferris.

"You know me better than that, Myron," she warned him firmly. "Just as I know you. You know what's going on up there, don't you? Is this something you're working on yourself? We've worked together before; we could do it again."

He had to know. She could see it in his face, in his eyes. And he wasn't mentioning his first wife, or her death. He never had. Suddenly, she had a feeling that Myron was covering up much more than he had ever revealed to her about the Breeds. She knew he was.

"I stay out of those mountains now," he snapped, his voice still low. "And that's the advice I'd give anyone else. Stay the hell out."

"And ignore the fact that people are dying. Again. Just as your first wife died."

Myron flinched before he breathed in slowly as she spoke. She watched his nostrils flare, watched the dilation of his eyes and the flicker of his gaze toward the Breeds in the room.

No doubt they could hear exactly what was being said. A Breed's hearing was excellent, much more sensitive than a human's and she had a feeling they were there just to listen in on this particular meeting.

"People or monsters?" he snapped back. "I'm not worried about the death of something evil, so don't look at me as though I should be. The Deadly Dozen should have been exterminated before they ever came together. You know that as well as I do. And I don't discuss my first wife. Ever."

"And if a Breed is doing the killing?" she hissed back at him. "What happens when he's caught, or when that Breed sends the proof to a reporter who doesn't care about anything but flashing it across every paper in the nation? Does that make up for your wife's death, Myron? Or will it just see more Breeds murdered?"

His lips thinned. "Justice, Cassa. It would be no more than justice. You know that."

"And if that justice is going to be used against the Breeds?" She lowered her voice further as his eyes narrowed on her once again. "What if I told you that the killer intends to frame the Breeds with certain murders? That there are pictures of the victims, their throats ripped out, their bodies clawed? What if, Myron, there were pictures of a Breed cleanup crew?" She nearly mouthed the last question. "What do you think that would do to everything we've both fought to save?"

She watched his expression closely. All emotion seemed to have been wiped from it, as a bleak anger flickered in his gaze.

"You know what's going on here, don't you, Myron?"

His lips parted.

"Myron." A deep male voice voice piped up from behind Cassa. "There you are. Your wife's looking for you, buddy."

It seemed his wife was always looking for him.

Cassa watched, eyes narrowed, as the older gentleman slid into the booth beside Myron. "She was getting a little irate that you weren't answering your cell phone."

"Cell phone's turned off," Myron muttered as he slid out of the other side of the booth and stood up. The look he cast Cassa was that of warning, and concern. "If you need a ride to the airport tonight, let me know."

With that, he grabbed his jacket and stalked from the booth. That was the warning. To leave now. It did nothing but make her more determined to stay.

"More coffee, Debra, if you don't mind and a slice of that banana cream pie if you have any left."

Cassa watched the stranger silently. In his fifties, with a wide, friendly smile and dark brown eyes. Thick, coarse gray hair was brushed back from his face, revealing strong, prominent bones.

Farmer Brown. A country boy in his maturity. He was the epitome of the strength and endurance of the mountains.

"A few slices, Walt, and it's fresh." The youthful Debra flashed the stranger a smile before turning to Cassa. "Anything else for you?"

"I'll take the pie as well," Cassa said. "And more coffee."

Debra moved off as Cassa turned and glanced over at the Breeds still sitting several booths away from them.

"You have excellent timing," she told Walt with a mocking smile. "Though I doubt Myron was going to tell me anything more than he already had."

Walt arched a brow. "Really? Most people say my timing sucks. But that's okay, whatever you think." He leaned forward slowly. "Don't change nothin' though. Myron's wife is lookin' for him. And I think he said something about you needing a ride to the airport."

Cassa almost grinned.

Cassa refused the offer. "Not quite yet. I haven't seen Myron for a while, I would have liked to have caught up with him."

Walt breathed out heavily at that. "He and Patricia have been having a hard time lately. When I saw him in here, I thought I'd let him know she was looking for him."

Cassa frowned at that. Myron and Patricia were always at odds with each other. There had been times over the years that Cassa had wondered why they stayed together. And now she was beginning to wonder why everyone thought they needed to rescue Myron from Cassa.

"I know Myron knows you pretty well," Walt stated as Debra set the coffee and pie on the table before leaving. "He's spoken of you often."

"Has he really?" Cassa ignored her own pie and braced her arms on the table as she watched him curiously. "Good things I hope."

Walt laughed at that. "Pretty much what Cabal says about you. Stubborn. Tenacious. A bulldog when you're after a story. I consider those compliments."

Cassa continued to stare back at him with a hint of a question. Namely, why the hell Cabal would discuss her with anyone, let alone this old man.

"Cabal's discussed me with you?" There was a tinge of anger in her voice that Cassa fought back. She had to ignore Cabal and any emotion that arose in her concerning him. She couldn't allow herself to be taken by a man that would see her as no more than a possession. He would try to wrap her up, lock her up. And he'd proven he'd go to any lengths to do it.

Walt gazed around the diner, his eyes lingering on the two Breeds with narrow-eyed intent. Seconds later the two men glared back at him irately, but rose from their seats and headed to the counter to pay for their coffee.

"I'm impressed," Cassa told her. "They don't seem the sort to give up so easily." Most Breeds didn't.

Walt laughed at that, his hazel eyes twinkling. "I know them. They're nosy as hell, but not really much trouble."

Not exactly an honest description of any Breed. They were all trouble with a capital T, and those two Breeds were more than just nosy.

"So tell me, Ms. Hawkins, what are you looking for in Glen Ferris that has Myron looking as hunted as a Breed in Council territory?" Walt stared back at her curiously, his rough-hewn face creased into lines of sincerity.

Small towns, you had to love them, Cassa thought.

"David Banks. Anomalies. Anything to add to my story about his disappearance," she answered blithely as she pulled her notebook free, snapped her pen open and then stared back at him expectantly. "Do you have any information?"

Walt laughed. "Banks was liked by some, hated by others.

There was no in-between." He shrugged. "I suspect he managed to slip and fall into the river. I figure they'll find his body sometime around spring or so. Hell of a way to go if you ask me."

She tilted her head and watched him silently for long moments.

"You seem pretty certain that was how he went," she commented.

"Certain as I can be," he drawled as he finished his pie. "Banks liked to play with Phillip Brandenmore and Horace Engalls quite a bit as well. Maybe they offed him."

Or maybe someone was trying to throw up a hell of a smoke screen.

"Maybe." She smiled tightly, pulled some money from her jeans and laid it on the table for the pie and coffee that she had barely touched. "Thank you anyway, Walt."

She rose from her chair to leave, aware that the old man rose as well and followed her out of the restaurant.

"Ms. Hawkins." Cassa paused as Walt's voice hardened.

"Yes?" She turned back to him with a frown.

"Whatever you're looking for here in Glen Ferris, you can trust me, if you'd be honest enough to let me know exactly what you need," he said, his expression sober, sincere. "Let me help."

"I'm sure Cabal wouldn't approve," Cassa warned him mockingly. "Jonas definitely wouldn't."

If the old man knew Cabal, then no doubt he knew Jonas. Cassa couldn't bring herself to trust him though, whether Cabal or Jonas approved or not. There was something about "Walt" that warned her he was hiding much more than he was revealing.

Walt snorted at that. "Those two don't scare me. They never have, and they won't start now. You just have to know how to handle them." He winked back in amusement. "A long chair and a sharp whip. It works every time."

Cassa laughed, shaking her head. No truer words were ever spoken.

"Until they take the whip and break the chair?" she asked as they moved down the sidewalk.

"Well, there's always that." Walt laughed. "The idea though is to keep them from getting that close."

As Cassa started to laugh at the comment, a shadow moving at her side had both her and the old gentleman twisting around.

Cabal lounged against the brick face of the café, his dark gold brow arched, a knowing smile on his lips.

"Breeds aren't that easy to control or to contain," he informed them both, as he straightened and regarded them with mocking amusement. "But you can keep dreaming if you like." He turned to Walt with a slow grin. "Good to see you, old man. How's the fishing?"

"The fishing is damned good," Walt assured him with an easy grin. "You should go out with me one day."

"When time allows, Walt," Cabal promised. "I'm a little busy right now."

Cassa felt her heart spike, her flesh grow sensitive. Her breasts became swollen, her nipples pressing hard and tight against the bra she wore beneath her shirt as he turned his gaze back to her.

"So, you going to take Walt's advice on how to handle Breeds?" he asked, his smile wicked.

"Fairy tales aren't my thing," Cassa informed him. "Unlike Walt, I know you and Jonas much too well to fall into that trap."

But that didn't keep her from flushing with heated hunger as his fingers wrapped around her upper arm. She swore she could feel his hand through the material of her jacket and the T-shirt she wore beneath. The heat of his fingers, the raspy feel of them, calloused and sensual—she swore she could almost feel his touch straight to the aching center of her clit.

She was wet, sensitive. The brush of her silk panties against her folds had her restraining a shiver of pleasure. And he knew it. Damn him.

"Oh, I know them well enough." Walt smiled. "I just prefer to see the good in them rather than the bad. If there's any bad to see." He winked back suggestively. "Hell of a position for an old man to take, huh?"

It was a hell of a position for anyone to take in any situation. The rose-colored glasses were always put on at the most painful of times, and recovering from them wasn't always possible.

"It's a hell of a position for anyone to take," Cassa muttered as she tugged at the hold Cabal had on her arm, before glaring at him. "Let me go."

"Say please." His smile was predatory and sent a tingle of arousal rushing through her body.

He knew what he was doing to her, and he was doing it deliberately. She could see it in his face, in the glitter of his green and amber gaze.

"Please." She pushed the word through clenched teeth.

She didn't like the feeling of warmth that overcame her, or the hunger she could feel rushing through her system. She didn't like the emotions or the sensations that swept through her each time he was near. She especially didn't like them amped up as they were now.

"I'll be more than happy to after we talk," he assured her, before turning to the old man with a brief "Later, Walt."

His grip firmed on her arm as he began moving down the sidewalk, ignoring her silent protest as she tugged at his grip once again.

He was too forceful, too dominant. She wanted to kick him, but she had a feeling it would do very little good. Damned Breeds, stubborn bastards.

"Stop fighting me, Cassa," he growled as she tried to jerk her arm out of his grip once more. "It's time we talk."

"Time we talk or time that I listen to you order me out of town again?" Her voice was sugary sweet. "Sorry, Cabal, but I'm rather busy today. Perhaps tomorrow."

Turning the corner, he yanked her into the diner's parking lot and strode along the parked cars. His fingers were still locked around her arm, pulling her behind him. Fighting his hold only made her angrier, simply because he acted as though he didn't even notice the attempts.

"Here we go." He stopped at the black SUV parked at the back of the lot and pressed the remote. The doors unlocked, and he gripped the handle and opened the driver's side door. "Will you get in and stay put?"

"Not on your life." She smiled back cheerily. "Want to tie me in the seat?" She looked around, and wasn't it just her luck, there wasn't a damned soul anywhere near. "Looks to me like the coast is clear if that's your intention."

"I'm going to get tired of these accusations, Cassa," he said softly. "There is no way I'd hurt you, and you know it."

His gaze flickered over her, heated and intense. There was sex in his eyes. Lust tightened his features and gave him a savage, honed appearance.

"I need you, Cassa. Now," he growled.

Cassa lost the sarcasm. She felt her expression go blank with the hunger that rumbled in his voice and reflected in his gaze now.

"And that's all that matters? Where were you last night? This morning?"

Where had he been when she awoke needing his touch? Needing him to hold her. She could feel the hunger for him deepening now though, the need, a steady ache blooming in her womb. She had always known it would take little more than one of those sizzling looks to have her melting at his feet. And she was right. That was all it was taking.

"Like you, I had things to do." He reached up and touched her jaw with the backs of his fingers. "You're taking the hormones, and evidently they're working. You would have called my cell otherwise."

"Begged for your attention, you mean?" She huffed bitterly. "Yeah, let me get right to my knees and start on that."

"You wouldn't have to beg, Cassa." His tone became seductive, deep with sensual promise.

She wanted to shake her head, but could only stare up at him in surprise now.

"You're playing a game." She knew he was. "You think you can seduce me out of this story."

His head jerked back as anger lit his gaze. "Seduction?" He growled. "I barely think so, mate. I doubt I could seduce you into agreeing the sky was blue if you wanted to believe it was green. I have no pretenses that you could ever be persuaded so easily to give up a story."

"But you'll try," she accused him, anger and knowledge churning inside her as the need wrapped around her senses, tormenting her.

Touch. He was touching her, and touch was something she had denied herself for far too many years. She needed him. Ached for him.

His head lowered again, his gaze locked with hers as his lips whispered a kiss along her lips. "So resist me, Cassa. That's all you have to do is walk away. If you can. Walk away, or accept the fact that the fight is over. You're my mate. And that's something that may well destroy both of us."

· CHAPTER 12 ·

He couldn't touch her skin-to-skin, but now that he had, he didn't want to stop. He couldn't kiss her lips-to-lips, but once that line had been crossed, he hungered for her kiss. He'd told himself for so long that he couldn't have her. It was his place to protect her, his place to hold back the mating heat and ensure her safety, her security.

The past years had been hell, forcing himself to stand back, to stay away. Refusing himself the slightest touch of her soft flesh.

"You could try telling me what the hell is going on."

Cabal wanted to howl in fury as she pulled back, crossed her arms over her breasts and glared back at him. She was good at that. The woman could glare with those stormy gray eyes like no man's business.

"I could try." He eased back, his gaze going over the parking lot as he tried to sort out the emotions that assailed him each time he was near her.

"But you won't?" Her gaze narrowed on him and he wanted to smile. Damn her, she made him forget all the reasons why he shouldn't have allowed the mating heat to begin here.

"I didn't say that." He gripped her arm again, pulled her back from the SUV and opened the door.

"Manhandling me only pisses me off." She managed to jerk her arm out of his grip as he stared back at her in surprise.

"Manhandling you?" he questioned her abruptly. Was that why she fought his hold each time he tried to keep her in place? She thought he was manhandling her? "Cassa, you're like a damned windup toy. You never stand still for too long. How the hell am I supposed to keep you covered if I can't keep you within a safe area?"

She knew the Breeds were still targets, and their women even more so. He could feel the gun sights on him, even now. He was always watched, always threatened—and yet she seemed oblivious to it.

"I don't need you to keep me safe," she snapped back. "I'm not the one that's a target, Cabal. Worry about your own safety and I'll worry about mine."

His teeth clenched almost violently as a wave of lust shot through his senses. Damned independent woman. It was like dealing with a Breed. He wondered if she had any concept of how well she resembled one. It was obvious she had been around the alpha mates too long; their independent, argumentative ways were rubbing off on her.

"How about I do what I do best, and watch both our backs?" he growled as he waved her into the passenger seat. "Now, would you like to talk, or do you want to stand here arguing for the rest of the day?"

He saw the brief battle in her eyes and swore she was debating whether or not to stand there arguing with him.

"Talk?" she finally asked.

"What the hell do you want me to do, promise I'm not going to touch you? We're in the middle of mating heat. I want to fuck you so bad that my dick's throbbing like an open wound." He could feel every muscle in his body tightening in protest. "Get in the vehicle, Cassa, before I go about my own business and leave you standing here."

In the cold and the wind? That wasn't likely; his protective instincts toward her were becoming much too honed, too sharp to ever allow him to do that. She was aroused, nearly to the point that she was in pain herself. He wouldn't allow that to last much longer.

"A promise would have been nice," she muttered, but she moved past him, ignored his outstretched hand and hopped into the seat.

Cabal closed the door before allowing a rumble of displeasure to vibrate in his throat. He *would* have a mate with a mouth that would sear a man's flesh at fifty paces.

His brother sometimes said that at least he was never bored since mating his wife, Scheme. Tanner often remarked that life was interesting now. Cabal definitely wasn't bored with Cassa, could never imagine himself being bored, but damn if he wasn't ready to pull his own hair out.

Jumping into the driver's seat, he slammed his door, started the ignition, then backed out of his parking slot. Remaining quiet, he turned onto Main Street before heading out of town to the small cabin he'd rented in the state park.

Cassa remained silent as well, which only had the tension tightening through his body. He could smell her emotions, her arousal and the hint of fear she always carried whenever he was around.

It tore at something inside him to know that she feared him, even a little bit. And it *was* fear of him. He knew the scent of it, he smelled it often enough from others. Where it rarely bothered him at any other time, it bothered him now. To know that something so elemental as her trust in him was denied him sent a shard of disappointment raging through him.

Maneuvering the SUV along the mountainous roads, he glanced over at her from time to time, taking in her calm profile. The thick waves of her dark blond hair flowed around her face and shoulders, fell over her breasts and down her back.

His fingers itched to bury themselves in that silken mass, and he found that denying himself was only making the hunger grow. He felt lost in the need rising inside him. That need was threatening his control and the assignment he was on. *She* threatened the assignment he was on.

By the time he pulled the vehicle into the small driveway of the cabin he'd rented, Cabal felt as though his control had been stretched to its limits. It was the scent of her. Subtly sweet, heated with a hint of wild desire.

That was what tempted him past bearing, he decided, as he stopped the vehicle in front of the wide front porch and turned off the ignition. That hint of wild spice in her arousal.

"Here we are," he announced as he turned to her.

"Convenient." Her smile was tight as she turned to him before opening her door. "What are we, a few miles from that little valley I was looking for?"

Two maybe. He was surprised that she realized that.

"You have a damned good sense of direction," he said, complimenting her as he opened the door and stepped out of the vehicle, before loping to her side to help her out. Not that she needed any help. She was jumping out of the SUV as he moved to open the door. He should have known she would be too damned independent to wait for a man to do anything for her.

"My sense of direction has always been excellent," she informed him as he placed his hand at the small of her back and led her to the front door.

The cabin was large and roomy. The lower floor, with its wide living room, spacious kitchen and spare bedroom, was neat and open. Upstairs, the master bedroom overlooked the door, and held a large master bath.

The rental cabin was built for year-round stay, and afforded plenty of room for the additional Breeds working the assignment with Cabal, when they were needed.

"Nice place," she said as he closed the door behind them, then silently locked it.

"It works." He shrugged, moving ahead of her. "Coffee?"

The last thing either of them needed was coffee. The caffeine played hell with mating heat and they both knew it.

"Sure." Her smile was knowing, mocking, as she followed him into the open kitchen. She knew what caffeine did to the system, and she was daring him just as fiercely as he was daring her now. "Then we can talk."

Talk wasn't exactly what he had on his mind. Laying her down and licking her from head to toe—now that idea held some merit. He was curious though. How much longer would the mating hormone treatment she was taking allow her to hold out? She was doing damned good. A hell of a lot better than he was actually.

"Sure, we'll talk." He wasn't promising what they would talk about though.

Awareness of her tingled over his flesh like an invisible caress and sent a shard of aching loneliness tearing through him. He knew what he was missing by holding back; he knew the completion he could find by claiming his mate.

   But he also knew what he was risking if he allowed his emotions to become involved any more than they already were. He
was risking his very soul, as well as hers. Unlike other Breed
enforcers Cabal was a covert enforcer. He was unregistered and
known for his complete lack of regulation. He was a suicide
operative. He took the jobs the other enforcers couldn't because
of Breed Law or protocol. He took the jobs with a fatality rate
much higher than most.
   He was a mate now though. If anything happened to him,
then the hell Cassa would live through was something he didn't
want to contemplate.
   Once this mission was over, his enforcer status would have to
be reconsidered. There were plenty of other Breeds who could
take his place, and honestly, he thought he might be more than
happy to step aside for them.
   "What do you intend to talk about then? The fact that you
don't want me for a mate, or the one where it's already too damned
late to do anything about it?" There was a snap to her tone that
had him turning and staring back at her silently.
   Hell, he wouldn't have imagined that mating could have
started with something so simple as his blood against her tongue.
She couldn't have done more than taken a drop of his blood, but
somehow, it had been enough.
   Bullshit. He'd become more enraged than ever when he'd
seen Cassa and her husband in the control room of the facility
he thought he would die within. He'd watched her fight to release him, watched Douglas's glee at the blood and death.
   He'd claimed her then, he thought. Before he'd ever escaped
that pit, he'd known he would claim her.
   He could smell the scent of her desire now, almost taste it on
the air around them. The night of his rescue he had smelled her
fear, her anger. He'd smelled her rage and her pain. And when
she had touched her finger to his face, then brought that finger to
her lips, he had sworn he had tasted her tears and her regret in
the air around them.
   "Or we could talk about H. R. Alonzo's dead body and the
reason why the Breeds are protecting a killer."
   He could tell by the sound of her voice exactly which subject
she was forging the most interest in. Her body was heating by
the moment, but that sharp little mind of hers wanted answers
first.

"The Breeds are not protecting a killer," he informed her as he finished preparing the coffee and turned back to her. "We're investigating David Banks's disappearance, Cassa."

She gave a delicate, ladylike snort. "Bull. You know the information I was sent, Cabal, don't try to lie to me. I know you've managed to access my files as well as the emails from my server. You have my laptop tapped. I'm not stupid. You know exactly what I have, just as I know what you're covering up."

She was enough to make a hardened, coldhearted Breed want to laugh, or to at least smile.

She was right. He knew the information she had. He was doing nothing more than delaying the inevitable by pretending that he didn't.

The soft metallic ring of the coffeepot completing its cycle sounded behind him. Grabbing two cups from the hooks beneath the counter, he poured the aromatic, decaffeinated brew into them and carried the cups to the long counter that separated the kitchen from the dining area.

He might want to silently dare her where the mating heat was concerned, but he wasn't going to deliberately see her in more discomfort than need be. The caffeine in coffee aggravated the systems of mating heat, not the coffee itself.

"Lying to you isn't something I had in mind," he told her as she slid onto one of the bar stools across the counter from him. "I am investigating Banks's disappearance."

"As well as Alonzo's death," she pointed out knowingly.

"As well as several deaths." He wasn't going to admit to Alonzo. Admitting to anything where this woman was concerned was the same as giving her express permission for an interrogation. She should have been a prosecutor rather than a TV reporter.

"And you think I don't know exactly how many deaths there are? The killer contacted me, Cabal. You know that. You're more than aware of it, and you think you can continue to play this damned game with me?" Her voice rose as amazed anger began to fill her, to scent the air around her.

She was coming to the end of her patience. Cabal knew it, recognized it. Just as he knew that he was going to have to make a choice soon. Make her hate him forever by pulling them both out of the game, or allowing her in. Neither choice was one he wanted to face.

For a second, the barest second, his self-control slipped.

Anger surged through him at the thought that she honestly believed she could so carelessly endanger her life and he would do nothing to protect her.

"I have the right to protect my mate." He pushed his face close to hers, felt her surprise, saw it in her rounded eyes and the flush that suddenly mounted her skin as his voice rumbled dangerously. "However need be, Cassa, I claim that right. You're in danger here. The very fact that that bastard contacted you tells me that he's already targeted you. You know that as well as I do."

"Well, you can unclaim that right." Suddenly, she was nose to nose with him, her stormy eyes darkening further as they narrowed back at him angrily, daring him, challenging him. Hell, he was going to come in his jeans now. "Don't think I'll tolerate force, Cabal. Not from you or any other man. Never again. And don't for one minute think that you can force me out of this. Mating heat be damned, I won't allow it."

Cassa could feel the anger she had been trying to stem over the past days rising inside her now, trying to break free of the careful self-control she used to maintain it. She'd focused on the story she'd come here to uncover; she'd even allowed herself to focus on her own guilt rather than his actions. That tunnel vision was beginning to expand though and her ability to continue to ignore his actions was eroding.

He had dared to manhandle her, to all but lie to her. He had frightened her, deliberately in the forest her first night here, and in the back of her mind she admitted to herself that she had always believed that no matter the circumstance, her Bengal would never treat her in such a way. He would never allow another Breed to chase her, nor would he try to push her out of something that was so important to her.

"Never again?" The golden glitter of the amber flecks in his dark green eyes intensified. "I know I've never forced anything from you, Cassa, so who the hell are you talking about?"

His voice lowered. There was a throb of latent violence in it now that sent a chill up her spine and made her wonder if the man she had been married to wasn't lucky to be dead. He'd died easy. The look on Cabal's face made her suspect he could make a man die hard.

"You deliberately allowed me to be chased through that forest," she accused him furiously. "You let Dog terrify me. You let him run me from that valley so you wouldn't have to deal with it. What you did was terrifying and painful and something I would have sworn you could never do to a woman, let alone your mate."

She watched his jaw clench, the muscle ticking furiously beneath the flesh as he glared back at her. Let him glare. She felt like raging—hell, she felt like hitting.

"How dare you!" she yelled as she moved from the stool and slapped her hands furiously on the top of the counter. "How dare you do that to me."

"How dare you risk your life in such a manner!" he yelled back at her. "How dare you to think I'd allow any Breed, no matter the reason, a chance to so much as breathe your air. Damn you to hell, Cassa. I nearly broke my own fucking neck getting to you that night."

"Then you should have done more than attempt to run me off later!" she yelled. "You have zero respect for me, Cabal. And even less understanding of who I am, or you wouldn't think you can lie and connive to get me off this story."

"What the hell did you expect?" he growled out. "You're like a fucking bulldog with a bone. I doubt death would stop you."

She rolled her eyes at his male outrage. "Oh, forgive me for doing my job," she bit out sarcastically. "Excuse me for giving a damn if the Breeds are framed or in danger of losing all this great public sentiment they've acquired over the years."

"Public sentiment my ass," he growled, and she couldn't blame him. The majority of goodwill and expressive sympathy toward the Breeds was no more than an attempt at political correctness for many of the high-profile individuals that spouted it.

"I've worked hard, Cabal, as have other journalists that I work with, to make certain the Breeds are portrayed in the best possible light, while still staying within the bounds of truth. You aren't helping me at all here."

"Truth?" He came around the counter, his body tense, wired for action as his expression tightened in outrage. "What truth, Cassa? If you found a Breed bending over a bloody body, what would you do then?"

"The same thing I'm doing now!" she yelled, her hands going to her hips as she faced him defiantly and loved every second of it. "Investigating, Cabal. I have the pictures of an obvious Breed attack and death. Do you see any damned thing in print, or do you see me trying to figure out who the hell is trying to frame the Breeds and why?"

"I see you trying to get your ass killed. That's what I see."

She almost laughed at his expression. It was completely male, infuriated and filled with frustration. And she wasn't frightened. She was facing him defiantly without fear.

He wouldn't hurt her. He hadn't allowed her to be hurt that night in the forest, and he wouldn't do it now. He had frightened her, brought back memories of a past she wanted to forget and pissed her the hell off, but he hadn't hurt her.

"Well, I guess you'll just have to let me continue on my merry little way and hope I get lucky," she snapped. "Because there's not a chance in hell, Cabal, that you're going to stop me."

Cabal could feel the heat and hunger rising to a boiling point inside his mind. She knew better than this. He knew she knew better than this. She had been around Breeds long enough, especially mated couples, to know what such vocal and physical defiance did to a mate.

"We are not normal combatants, Cassa," he warned her, his voice dropping as the growl in his throat echoed inside it. "You know what you're doing."

Her brow arched mockingly. "Do I really?" She turned away from him and paced a few feet before turning back. "What am I doing, Cabal? Refusing to give you your way? Poor little Bengal Breed. He's been so spoiled by his little toys that he thinks all women are going to kneel down and worship those pretty little stripes he has on his ass. Sorry, babe, not me. Your arrogance is pandered to enough the way it is."

The thought of those women, a damned parade of them who had visited his and his brother's bed, was enough to set her teeth on edge. There were times she was certain that pissed her off more than the way he'd manhandled her and fought to keep her from getting to the truth in Glen Ferris. If there was a Breed groupie he and Tanner had missed over the years, then it wasn't because he hadn't tried to screw them all.

"Leave the stripes out of this." He paced closer, his growl warning.

She should have known better than to mention the stripes; Cabal was also rumored to dare his lovers to mention them. It was said he hated the Bengal stripes, the oddly colored fine hairs that ran from a point along each buttock around his leg to end in a point on the inside of each thigh.

The unusual markings were highly erotic. She wanted to kiss every damned one of those hairs but hadn't yet found the courage to try.

She widened her eyes in false innocence. "You mean all those snickering little debutantes you've fucked over the years didn't dare mention them to you all? Why, Cabal, they were quite remiss. They're sexy. They make me wet." She was nose to nose with him. "They make me just want to pet you all over."

His eyes narrowed on her. "You're daring me," he stated, his voice so dark and warning that it sent chills racing down her spine. "Why, Cassa? Why push me like this when you know where it will lead? Do you think I want to take you without thought? Without consideration? Why push me like this?"

If the glitter in his eyes was anything to go by, then he was more than ready to find out if he could make time.

"I never was one to enjoy playing second best." She crossed her arms over her swollen, sensitive breasts and tightened her jaw as anger surged through her. "How many women have you had since you first suspected I was your mate, Cabal? One dozen? Two?"

"At least make the number believable," he snarled back at her.

Cassa's lips tightened in anger. She had watched him fuck his way through countless women over the years. He and his brother had once shared those women, had played sex games that would make most grown men blush.

"The number is very believable to me," she stated coolly. "Really, Cabal, your lack of fidelity amazes me. I thought Breed males were supposed to be faithful from the moment they first realize who their mates are. What? Are you an exception to the rule? Need a harem rather than a mate, do you?"

She needed her head examined. She was pushing him, daring him to take her, and she knew it. Somewhere between last night and this morning she had misplaced her sanity.

"And here I thought you were here for a story." The rumble of his voice made her clit throb. "I didn't know you had come to claim your mate, Cassa. You should have said something beforehand. I would have made certain to take time to accommodate you."

Angry heat flooded her face at his tone.

"You insulting bastard," she snapped. "Go to hell. And while you're at it, tell Jonas Wyatt to kiss my ass. I'll just report on what I have so far. I bet it gets me a Pulitzer for revealing the real face of the Breeds."

Not that she would ever do it. She couldn't do that to the people she knew as friends, even for a story. But damn him, he deserved to sweat over it, and so did Jonas.

She turned to stomp out of the kitchen, to get as far away from him as fast as she could. She'd walk that lonely mountain road in the dead of night to get away from him. Snarky, snarling prick. She needed to be tied to a Breed like she needed a hole in her head. Especially this Breed.

She'd had no idea how much it had infuriated her that he had been denying the natural impulse to take her, to claim her. She knew she had denied it. She knew why she denied it. He didn't have an excuse, nor did he have a reason for it that he could justify to her.

He was a tomcat. Plain and simple. He wasn't taking her because *he* didn't want to be tied down. He couldn't play all his cutesy little sex games with her or make nice with every woman willing to lift her skirt for him.

"Like hell you're leaving."

His voice was animalistic; it throbbed with lust and with demand as she felt his fingers curl around her arm, drawing her to a halt as he pulled her around to face him once more.

Bracing her hands against his wide chest, Cassa stared back at him, refusing to be intimidated by the sudden hunger reflected in his eyes.

"Like hell. You better believe I'm leaving. I'll be damned if I need anything from you, Cabal. Need or want. I'll just tromp my merry ass back to Sanctuary, have Ely increase the hormonal treatments, and you can go to hell." She pushed against his chest, even as she knew he wasn't about to let her go.

She could feel the power of the intent in his gaze now, the hunger and the lust that suddenly churned the air around them.

"You believe I didn't claim you because of something so trifling as a desire for other women?" His fingers flexed on her arms. Not painfully, but as though his need to touch her, to caress her, was overriding whatever demands he was making on himself otherwise.

"I really don't care why you didn't *claim* me, as you put it," she sneered back in his face. "I will never be claimed by you, Cabal. Not in this lifetime or any other. I was willing to work with you, to be a partner—there's a difference."

Work with him, and maybe learn what this hunger for him was all about, how the mating heat could give her something she had never had. Something of her own. A man to love her, a man to care for her. She hadn't wanted him in her bed because he was forced there by the mating heat. She'd wanted him to want her. And she'd been too damned naive to realize it couldn't work that way for her.

She'd been warned that mating heat was something that couldn't be denied, even in its mildest form. She hadn't believed it until the day she met Cabal St. Laurents face-to-face. Until she saw the torment that lined his face, saw the loneliness in his eyes and ached for everything he had lost in his life. Even more, she had ached for her part in what he had lost.

The need to go to him after his rescue all those years ago had nearly overwhelmed her common sense. She'd wanted to touch him, to ease him. She'd ached to do something, anything, to ease the pain she knew he had to feel at the loss of the pride he'd loved so dearly. She'd wanted to make up for what Douglas had done. She'd wanted to make certain he was safe. She'd just wanted to be a small part of his life. Something more than a bad memory.

"You're a torment." He pulled her closer, her breasts against his chest, his heavy thigh pressing against her legs as he pushed her back to the wall. "You torment my thoughts. You torture my body with need. Why the hell you'd walk into this mating as blithely as you have confuses the hell out of me, Cassa. You knew what you were facing by pushing me here. Admit it. You've always known."

Yeah, no one had ever nominated her for the common sense prize, and they sure as hell weren't going to do it now. It had been evident with her deceased husband that she had lousy taste in men, and Cabal was only proving that theory. Problem with this one was, it wasn't just her fault. For some reason nature had decided to get in on the fun and help her screw her life up even more.

"Please be so kind as to excuse me for pushing you in any direction," she ground out between clenched teeth. "Honestly,

Cabal, all I want from you is the damned story. That's it. Tell me what I need to know and I'll just go on my merry little way and let you continue to screw yourself through the rest of the female population. Isn't that what you want?" Was it even possible? She knew female mates couldn't bear another's touch, but could males?

She tried to push away from him again. She tried to ignore the feel of his erection pressing into her stomach, hard and insistent between the layers of their clothes. And she tried to ignore the need beginning to whip through her, the sudden desire for the taste of his kiss, the feel of his hands stroking over her flesh.

She wanted to deny it all.

"Damn you," he growled. "I knew you would do this to me."

"What? Refuse to let you think you're lord of all you survey?" she bit out furiously.

One hand moved from her arm, cupped her cheek and held her head firmly in place as his head lowered.

"I knew you'd shred my fucking control," he whispered, his voice tormented now, deep and dark and echoing with the same needs she couldn't control any longer. "Damn you, Cassa. I knew you'd end up destroying me."

Her lips parted to argue that statement. She even had an excellent comeback poised to shatter his ego. Before she could speak, before she could flay him for making such a ridiculous statement, his lips covered hers. His tongue pushed into her mouth. The taste of cinnamon and spice filled her senses as heat exploded through the rest of her body.

Cabal's taste. She loved the taste of him. His kiss. She ached for the feel of it again. Her fingers clenched on his forearms and she lifted to him. Her tongue touched his, tasted the spicy heat of the mating hormone, and she knew she was lost. Or was she found?

Lips, teeth, tongues. The taste of lust, of need and heat, seared Cassa's senses as Cabal jerked her to his chest and took the hungry caress with a force that fired her desires.

It was better than the last time. It was hotter. It was brighter. Sweet God have mercy on her, it was like being thrown into a vortex so blistering, so bright, that nothing mattered but the sensations ravaging her now.

Arrogance was so much a part of him. It echoed in his hungry growl as she tried to jerk back from him, and it added dominance to the hold he had on the back of her head to keep her in place for his kiss.

Cassa moaned as his tongue swiped over hers and spilled more of the spicy taste she was rapidly becoming addicted to.

She had definitely lost her sanity, because she had known what she was facing in accepting this, in daring him to take her as she had. She had known there could be no easy ending to it, but the need, oh God, the need was tearing her apart, driving inside her like steel stakes burning with hunger.

"Damn you." The light nip at her lips had her lifting to her toes, desperate for more now. His kiss, even without that damned hormone speeding through her system, was still more than any other kiss she had ever known.

Hungrier, greedier, filled with more desire, with more lust than anything she had ever known.

Tugging at his shirt, she fought to touch skin, to stroke his body as his lips came over hers again, his hard body pressing her closer to the wall at her back.

Her breath hitched as his hands clenched on her ass, lifted her and jerked her closer. Her thighs parted over his. His cock, covered by a layer of denim, was still hard and hungry as it pressed into the cradle of her thighs and stroked over her clit.

Cassa wrapped her arms around his neck and held on for dear life as her hips moved of their own accord against him. Thrusting, stroking against the rigid mound pressing against her, she drove herself mad with the arousal burning through her now.

Her fingers threaded through the silken strands of his hair, the caress of it against her fingertips, erotic, sensual. Everything about Cabal was too erotic, too sensual. She had been losing this battle for months, and she had known it.

"No. Please." She gasped out the plea as he jerked her head back, one hand gripping her hair to hold her in place as he glared down at her.

"You know what you're doing," he stated, his voice like a caress of a hot summer night. "Tell me, Cassa. You know what you're doing."

"I know what I'm doing." Her fingers clenched in his hair to drag his head back. "You're damned right I know what I'm doing."

He was hers. A part of her refused to accept anything less than the fact that he did belong to her. She would pay for it later. She might well die for it later. But for now, he would belong to her. Hers to hold. She had never had anyone, or anything, belong solely to her, until Cabal. And she had never belonged, not really, not where it mattered.

"It doesn't change anything." He lifted her closer against his body and began to move through the cabin to the stairs that led to the loft bedroom. "Nothing, Cassa. This story is still off limits to you."

That was what he thought. Let him think it. Let him believe whatever he had to believe for now; she'd show him different later. She wouldn't be dictated to in this mating any more than she had been dictated to before it.

Her lips parted, and she allowed her teeth to nip at the line of his lower lip as he moved slowly up the stairs. Her tongue licked over the little wound and she wished she knew how to purr, because she would have purred with the pleasure coursing through her now.

"Stop ordering me around," she panted as his hands clenched on her ass. "Kiss me again, Cabal. Just kiss me."

His lips covered hers again as a soundless cry vibrated in her throat. It was a kiss made of gossamer desire and fiery need. It stroked over her senses as his tongue stroked over her lips, then her own tongue. The spill of the hormone spread through her, slowly at first, heating nerve endings, throwing her body into chaos as she felt herself being lowered to a bed.

Cabal's bed.

Her arms lifted as he caught the hem of her T-shirt and pulled it slowly from her body.

The chill of the room washed over her lace-covered breasts for only a second. Only as long as it took for him to toss the shirt away, and for his palms to cover the heavy, swollen mounds.

"So pretty," he sighed, his voice thick and husky. "I dreamed of caressing your breasts, Cassa. Of holding them in my hands and seeing that pretty flush on them."

She looked down. Sure enough, her breasts were as flushed as the rest of her body felt. Her nipples pressed hard and demandingly into his palms, and she knew they'd look ripe, cherry red with the need for his touch, his kiss.

She was almost panting as his hands moved, his fingers flipped over the closure of her bra and peeled the fabric away while she fought to hold back a cry of complete surrender.

It was a cry that fell from her lips anyway, as his head bent and one of the hard, tight peaks disappeared into the heated depths of his mouth. His lips closed over her, his cheeks drew on the sensitive point and sent shards of pleasure racing to the throbbing knot of nerves in her clit.

The feel of her juices flowing between her thighs had her hips flexing, arching against him. She wanted him naked, she wanted to be naked with him. She wanted to feel every inch of him caressing her, touching her.

When his head drew back, his lips releasing her damp nipple, she nearly orgasmed from the sight of it. The look of building lust on his face, the hunger that suffused it.

Reaching down, he gripped the hem of his T-shirt and jerked it off, displaying the impressive muscles of his chest and abs. The tattoo of a blood-dipped fang lay against his shoulder. The opposite bicep held what was becoming known as a Breed tribal tattoo: barbwire, canines and daggers in a circle around his muscle. It was impressive, sexy as hell, and looked as dangerous as she knew the Breeds could be. Funny that until now, she hadn't paid as much attention to the tattoo. She'd seen it, known it for what it was, but it had been on the periphery of her attention before.

Her hands moved, her fingers gripping the hem of his jeans as she pulled and popped the first metal button free. The head of his cock peaked above the opening now. Wide, flushed, throbbing for attention.

"Not yet." He pushed her hands back to the bed. "Later."

"Like hell later." She panted, fighting to get her fingers back in place to touch him. "I didn't say you get to make the rules here, Cabal."

He chose that moment to release her jeans and jerk the tab of the zipper down. The low-rise jeans parted, revealing the flesh of her lower abdomen as she froze beneath the hunger in his look.

She couldn't move beneath his gaze. His expression was absorbed as he moved lower, pulled her boots and socks from her feet, then gripped the bottom of her jeans and shifted them down along her legs.

Cassa was mesmerized by his eyes, by his expression. The glitter of gold in a field of vibrant dark green as he revealed her.

Silken panties came down with the jeans, removed with a long, slow caress of his calloused hands and dropped to the side of the bed along with the denim.

She was naked beneath him now. Chill bumps of sensation raced over her flesh as his palm pressed against her belly, stroked over it until his fingers encountered the soft curls between her thighs.

"The mating hormone treatment," he growled. "I can smell it on you. It's what's allowed you to stay away from me."

"It's allowed me to survive," she informed him tartly. "I'm not a mating puppet, Cabal. I refuse to be one."

She watched as his eyes narrowed on her, his lips curling in amusement as his fingertips moved slowly through the saturated center of her body.

Cassa gasped and arched against the caress. She swore she could feel flares of explosive heat in each pore that his fingers touched.

"Trust you to keep trying to stay a step ahead of me," he murmured before moving back, his fingers going to the metal buttons of his jeans as he toed his boots from his feet.

"Who's trying?" She could barely breathe, let alone talk. "I succeeded."

He grunted at that, but arguing wasn't her first impulse as the impressive length of his cock was revealed, along with the subtle Bengal stripes on his thighs.

Cassa shivered at the proof of the animal inside him and how close to the skin it truly was. The orange stripes, three in all to each side, curled around the teak flesh from the outside of his thigh to the inner flesh.

The stripes flexed over the muscle as Cassa's fingers curled with the need to touch them, to run her nails along them.

"I love these stripes." A wave of sensuality raced through her belly as he placed his knee on the bed and moved closer to her.

"The stripes aren't up for discussion," he warned her, his look completely carnal.

"Yet," she agreed, entranced by the gold glitter of need in his gaze as he came over her.

"Never."

His lips cut off any protest she may have had in mind to make. They covered hers as she felt his hard, naked body come over her. Heavily muscled thighs parted her slimmer ones, and the tip of his cock kissed the heated wetness of her inner lips.

Cassa reached into the kiss with a desperation she had never known for another's touch. Her arms curled around his neck, her fingers dug into his hair. She could feel her thighs clenching on his as her hips arched in a wild attempt to force the hardened flesh of his erection deeper into the embrace of the wet folds between her thighs.

"Not yet." He pulled back, his lips moving down her neck, sending hot pulses of pleasure racing along the nerve endings there. "Not yet, baby. I get to taste first. You've tempted me with the scent of your arousal; now you'll give me a taste."

She shuddered at the dominance in his tone, at the need.

Cassa lifted her head to watch as his tongue licked over her nipple, then he began moving down her body. A kiss here, a nip there. His tongue played over her flesh and left her shaking for more as he moved down her abdomen to the blazing heat of her sex.

"So sweet," he whispered, his voice rough. "You smell as sweet as sunshine."

His tongue swiped through the narrow slit as something part growl, part purr left his throat and sent a punch of lust flexing through her womb. Her hips arched closer, her hands dug into his hair and wicked flares of sensual heat began to ignite through her senses.

Her head tipped back as the pleasure wracked her. Cabal's tongue was wicked. It stole her senses as it caressed around the sensitive bud of her clit, then swiped over it before his mouth drew it in.

"Cabal." Her cry was a thick wail of hunger as pulsing shards of need echoed through her flesh.

Arousal was a never-ending hunger. It throbbed and ached from her clit to her nipples and beyond. Each inch of flesh was sensitized, each portion of her mind consumed by it.

She could feel the drugging response of the hormone whipping through her bloodstream, burning through her veins. She couldn't get enough. She needed his touch, needed all of it.

"Oh God!" She nearly screamed the prayer as she felt his fingers burrow into the clenching depths of her vagina. They stretched her, burned her, thrust inside her until she was certain she couldn't hold on to the last shreds of her sanity.

Cassa couldn't stop her hips from moving, from driving onto his fingers. She felt as though she were being torn apart by the need now, the desire to be filled, to be taken. She was lost in the pleasure burning through her, and she had no desire to be rescued from it.

Cabal's tongue raced over and around her clit. He suckled at it delicately, then firmly. All the while his fingers fucked her slow and easy, pushing her past the point that she could keep so much as a measure of control.

A control she didn't want in his arms.

"More," she panted out breathlessly, her fingers digging into his shoulders as she arched closer.

Her legs opened wider, desperate for more kisses, more touch, more of anything he wanted to give her, because she had no idea what the hell she needed other than to be possessed by him.

She had sworn she would never allow a man to possess her. She had made that promise to herself when she realized her husband was more monster than lover. Now, eleven years later, she wasn't lying to herself. Her lover was more animal than man, and she promised herself that this time she would handle her emotions, she would handle what she didn't have, for this. For what she could have.

She could immerse herself in this. Here and now. She twisted beneath him, pressed her hips higher, drove her clit deeper into his mouth as she felt the winding pleasure tighten through her warningly.

"Cabal." She cried out his name when she fought and couldn't hold back the sensations.

His answer was a low growl, a flick of his tongue over her clit and a sudden, powerful thrust of his fingers inside the core of her.

Pleasure exploded through her, shocking her with the strength of it, the force of it. Her body tightened with the suddenly harrowing pulse of release and the fire streaking through each cell of her body.

She could have sworn she heard herself scream his name. She was certain she had, despite her attempts not to. Her fingers were locked in his hair, holding his lips between her thighs as she jerked and shuddered beneath him.

Perspiration soaked her body even as sexual need climbed through her again. Writhing beneath his caresses, Cassa fought to find the relief she needed from the heat flooding her senses.

"Hell yeah, baby." The animalistic growl echoed around her as Cabal suddenly came to his knees between her thighs. "Come for me again."

She stared down her body, watched his fingers curl around the heavy length of his erection as he bent to her. She watched, entranced as the broad head parted the swollen lips of her sex, her juices glistening as he parted her farther.

"You're mine, Cassa," he stated, his voice uneven, rough, as he began to press inside her.

She wanted to laugh at the claim but couldn't find the breath. Instead, she stared back at him fiercely.

"Other way around," she gasped. "Mine."

She wouldn't let him possess her. She would possess him. She wanted to wrap him so deep inside her soul that when the truth came out, he could never walk away from her. So deep that he would try to see, try to understand what she knew could never be understood.

A hard, heated chuckle met her statement before her eyes widened and jerked back down the line of her body. He was entering her, pushing inside her. She watched, sobs of need leaving her throat as her flesh parted for him, burned around him.

He filled her. Inch by inch as she felt another contraction of release tear through her. She hadn't thought it was possible to orgasm with no more than the act of penetration. Just the feel of him pushing inside her, the heavy length of his cock caressing her sensitive inner muscles. She threw her head back as pleasure suffused her in a violent cascade of light and color. It whipped through her senses, tore through them and left her shaking as Cabal began to thrust inside her with deep, measured strokes.

His body covered hers; his hands held her hips to him as his lips moved to her neck, her shoulder. She could feel each harsh growl that rumbled in his chest, as it echoed through her chest. She felt each pulse of blood that throbbed in his cock as it shuttled inside the tender tissue of her sex.

Her moans echoed around her; his harsh, rasping breaths filled her senses. Wrapping her legs around his hips, Cassa fought to hold on to something, anything, that would anchor her to earth as the spiraling ecstasy began to tighten inside her.

She couldn't bear it. She could feel it burning, racing, creating a whirlwind inside her that she didn't have a hope of resisting.

Pleasure had never been like this. Lust had never been like this. She had never known anything as deep, as filled with pure ecstatic sensation as the feel of Cabal taking her.

It shouldn't be like this, she thought distantly. Just lust wasn't this consuming, this dangerous. She could feel things she didn't want to feel, a connection, a bond through the pleasure that terrified her.

It was just a chemical reaction, she warned herself. That was all. She had to make herself remember that. She couldn't let love interfere. Cabal didn't love her. He wasn't going to love her. She couldn't allow her own love for him to get in the way of this.

His hand smoothed along her hip as he held his weight on one elbow. It caressed up her side, cupped her breast. His fingers flicked over her tight nipple as his tongue laved at her shoulder and his hips moved faster. Harder.

His cock thrust inside her with powerful, even strokes. Sensitive nerve endings fired further to life. Cassa felt her flesh becoming swollen, felt her womb tightening, her clit throbbing.

So close. She could feel her orgasm moving through her, feel it building, edging closer. It was tightening, drawing her body closer to him, making her arch and writhe against him as the wildness of it began to burn through her.

Her legs tightened around him, her nails dug into his back. She could feel it, it was there, so close, so filled with sensation that when it poured over her, she swore she was dying.

Cassa heard herself scream his name as his canines sank into her shoulder. Then she felt her breath lodge in her throat, her body contract, her sex swelling with rapture, as the barb, the small, thumb-sized erection, swelled from the flared head of his cock, locking him inside her and spilling its hot hormonal essence into her, binding her further to him. There were no words for the ecstasy shooting through her now. There was no way to explain or to describe the strength, the depth of her release.

She felt as though she melded into him, became a part of him. She felt her body taking him, accepting him, and knew that in her lifetime she would never know this pleasure with another man. She had never imagined such pleasure could exist.

The feel of the barb locked inside her was animalistic, ecstatic. It was hers. This happened with only one woman, she knew. That additional erection happened only with a mate, no other. She was the only woman Cabal would ever know this with. And she was the one that had betrayed him.

She buried her face against his chest as he shuddered above her, his own release jerking through his body as Cassa fought back the tears that would have dampened her eyes.

For now, she held him. He would belong to her as much as she would belong to him. He couldn't deny her now. He couldn't make her leave; he couldn't turn her away. The mating heat would ensure that. For now, he would have to share himself with her, and not just physically.

She felt his bite at her shoulder like a brand into her flesh, marking her forever. The little wound would never fully heal. It was a physical mark that would never go away entirely, just as she knew that her own bite on his palm still hadn't fully healed.

The Breed's and the mate's bodies changed during mating. They shadowed each other, the essence of each blending. Cassa knew that, just as she knew that there hadn't been a mating that hadn't ended up in love. In a devotion between the two mates that had always made Cassa envious.

There was no longer a need for envy.

"My mate," he growled at her shoulder.

Cassa held on to him tighter. She was his mate, for now. She would revel in him while she had him. She would pit her will against his, enjoy the hell out of the time they'd have together, but she promised herself she wouldn't let herself depend on it. She would never fully become her Bengal's heart, because she'd betrayed him. She would lose him. She was resigning herself to it. But she had never expected the pain that was coming from it. It had done her no good to steel her heart against this man, because she had a feeling it was going to be ripped from her chest anyway.

Losing him might well kill her.

◆   ◆   ◆

Cabal held on to Cassa, his arms wrapped tight around her as he slowly loosened the bite against her shoulder. He could taste the primal mating hormone in his mouth as he licked against the wound, spreading it over the tiny bite marks he had left in her flesh once again.

Mating wasn't easy, it wasn't gentle. He was still shuddering at the force of the pleasure that had torn through him. The violence of his release left him shaking and suddenly much too aware of what would happen to him if he ever lost this woman.

Brushing her hair back from her perspiration-damp face, he let his fingers caress her cheekbone, her jaw, as he stared into her dove-soft gray eyes.

His woman.

He fought to hold back the possessiveness rising inside him, the feeling of something belonging to him. Just to him. He knew fate, and she laughed at him for sport. She snatched happiness from his fingertips with a sneer and a laugh.

He stared into Cassa's eyes, and once again saw a flash of that ever hated fear in her eyes. Even now, seconds after the most incredible pleasure he had ever known, he still sensed her fear of him.

Perhaps it was something time would take care of for him, if he had time with her, he told himself. She would learn she had nothing to fear.

He would give his life for hers without thought. He knew without a shadow of a doubt that living without her now wasn't something he could face doing. This hunger, this need, this total fulfillment of sexual pleasure was unlike anything he had ever known in his life.

And her touch. Her touch was a stroke of pleasure and of comfort. Living without that comfort wasn't something he wanted to ever risk.

She was the other half of him, the one thing he had longed for ever since he had learned of the mating phenomenon. She was the part of his soul that had been missing and was now complete.

"I don't like seeing that fear in your eyes," he told her softly as the barb slowly receded and her inner flesh released its grip on it.

Her eyes flickered and he saw the lie coming. Placing his fingers over her lips, he held back the words.

"No lies, Cassa," he told her softly. "If you can't tell me why, then don't bother to tell me I'm not seeing what I know I see."

Her lips were pressed tightly together as a frown worried at her brow.

"When you're ready to discuss it, then I'll be here," he told her rather than demanding the answers.

A man didn't get far when demanding anything from Cassa. She was as willful as a woman could get, and twice as independent.

"Will you?" she finally asked, her lips whispering over his fingertips. "Will you, Cabal? Or will you walk away like you always do?"

His lips quirked mockingly at the thought of walking away now.

"I think we're both very well aware of the fact that there's no walking away now. Even if it was something either of us wanted to do."

He moved against her, his hardening erection filling her flesh as her breath caught.

"See, Cassa? There's no walking away, honey. We're bound. Just as you knew we would be."

He could see it in her eyes, in her expression. The knowledge, and the fear.

CHAPTER 14

Death smiled at the sight of the lights flipping off in the cabin. Death would have laughed, but something deep inside a frozen heart refused to allow the amusement to go quite that far.

It was a mating. There was no doubt of that. Cabal St. Laurents and Cassa Hawkins were mates. It was one more sin to add to Death's conscience.

Death touched the shoulder that was still sensitive, even after twenty years, and still bore the bite of a mate. A mate long dead.

Snow drifted in the air; the cold formed like freezing vapor and eased along the forest floor. The mist from the gorge not far away sent frozen fog to cover the land, even now, so close to spring. So close to the anniversary of Death.

There was a job to be done, and it didn't matter the regret now, or the fact that a mate would soon be lost once again. The past refused to die; Death had to help it along. That meant they all had to die. Everyone who had been a part of that massacre so long ago had to be taken from this world.

It didn't matter that Cassa Hawkins hadn't been a part of that massacre at the time. Truth was, she had been a part of her husband's life later, and her husband had been part of that massacre.

The husband would come now. He would find a way, he'd slip from his hole and come here once he learned his precious wife had mated a Breed.

Douglas Watts had been so young the night Death had been created, barely eighteen and following in his father's evil footsteps. But still, it was an evil that refused to die. And Cassa, his precious wife, had helped him later to betray the Breeds—that put the mark of evil on her soul as well.

As far as Death was concerned, Cassa was as much a part of the Deadly Dozen as her husband had been, and she would have to die.

Luring her here had been easy. The pictures, the emails, the threat of framing the Breeds. The world would one day know that Breeds were no more than humans and humans were no more than Breeds. They all had the ability to kill, and they could all die. Proof of that had already begun.

Death hadn't expected the mating though. That thought flitted through a mind that was torn with the decisions made that now must be followed through. Losing a mate was a horror no creature should have to endure. It was a pain unlike any other. Each breath taken without that mate was a nightmare that never eased.

Death slid slowly back from the cabin, easing along the path that the snow hadn't yet covered but would soon. It wouldn't do to leave proof that eyes watched and an enemy waited. The Breeds that chased Death through the silence of the night could never understand the mission that lay ahead. They couldn't understand why their lives didn't matter any more than those of the humans.

Cassa's day would come. It was right around the corner, her blood marked to be spilled if her husband didn't arrive. But first, another's blood would soak the valley of Death. Another's blood would still the demons rising inside Death, tearing at the mind, searing the soul.

The seventh of the Deadly Dozen. It was time for him to die.

◆　　◆　　◆

Cabal curled around Cassa like a living blanket, keeping her close to his chest, holding her warmth inside each pore that he could press against her.

He was a man that had never relished sleeping with others.

He had bedded enough women over the years, but as his brother could attest, the intimacy of sharing a bed with them was something Cabal hadn't found much pleasure in.

Until Cassa. He had fought it at first. He'd tried not to need it, to need her. Now he would have dared Cassa to find another place to sleep, at any time, after tonight. She would spend her nights here in his arms, no matter what he had to do to achieve it.

He brushed back the long, tangled strands of her hair to stare at her sleeping profile. She slept deep, hard, her slight breathing brushing against his arm where she lay. She had slept the night away with the same deep intensity. But he couldn't say her sleep had been dreamless. She had shifted about throughout the night, muttering to herself a time or two, a frown working between her brows.

Did she relive the horrors she had seen during her years as an investigative reporter? he wondered. She had been there the night his lab was attacked, and during his rescue. She had seen the slaughter that had taken place in the pit of death; she had seen his wounds and his rage during his rescue.

He stared across the room, fighting those memories himself now. That was a place within his soul that he tried not to revisit too often. Too many of his family had died in that pit. A dozen men and women who had given their lives to ensure that he lived, despite his protests. They had thrown themselves in front of him, blocked him, kept the blades that sliced through the metal walls from impaling him.

So much blood had filled that pit before he had managed to escape. So many lives had been lost. Because a betrayer had been harbored in the midst of the rescuers. Because Cassa's false husband had betrayed them all.

Damn, Douglas Watts had sowed a hell of a mess. He was still living, albeit a bit miserably, but those whose lives he had touched carried the bitter wounds of his actions.

What would she do if she learned the bastard lived?

He stared down at her, questioning within himself the decision he had made so long ago to allow Watts to continue living.

It had been that cruel streak he harbored within him. To kill Watts would have been too easy. Too merciful. He'd wanted the man to suffer and to suffer hard.

Had Cabal instigated the demise of his own future with that decision though? Would he be the first Breed to lose a mate to a former lover, to a man who had lied even to the point that the judge who had wed them had been false?

Once this assignment was completed and the identity of the Breed killing humans was revealed, then, Cabal promised himself, he would take the time to learn more about his new mate. More than just her stubbornness and her loyalty. He would learn what made her laugh, what made her find joy. He had a feeling that Cassa hadn't known great joy in her life.

And then perhaps he would know if he had her loyalty over that which she had once given the man she believed was her husband.

Glancing toward the window, he drew in the scent of the snow outside. The late winter air gave the forest a fresh, clean scent as well as a blanket of white to wrap the world outside within.

The fire he had laid just after Cassa went to sleep was still burning, the glowing embers and low flames lighting the bedroom through the open ceiling of the living room.

Moving from the bed, he tucked the blankets carefully around his sleeping mate before pulling on his jeans and easing from the bedroom. He could hear the Breed Raiders easing up the road to the cabin. Jonas would be in one of the vehicles, he knew. The director rarely left anything to chance, especially in a mission as delicate as this one.

A rogue Breed killing humans wasn't something to ignore. As Cassa had stated the night before, it could show the world the true face of the Breeds, and that was something they weren't quite ready for.

Moving to the front door, he watched as the two Raiders, the powerful ATVs the Breeds used in mountainous and desert settings, pulled into the drive.

Leaning against the door frame, he watched as Jonas moved from the first vehicle, followed by his bodyguard and driver, a human simply called Jackal. The second vehicle held the two enforcers, Lawe Justice and Rule Breaker. The names rarely failed to cause Cabal's lips to twitch in amusement.

It wouldn't do to let either Breed see that amusement though. They were rather proud of the names they had chosen for themselves.

As Jonas neared the house, he paused, his eyes narrowing on Cabal as his nostrils flared. Cabal knew the director was taking in the scent of the mating, as well as Cassa's scent as it surrounded Cabal's body. Now there would be no doubt in Jonas's mind that the mating was completed.

"Hell, I thought you'd at least wait until this assignment was over," Jonas growled.

Cabal narrowed his gaze back at him. "I'd waited long enough."

And that was the damned truth. He'd held back because he'd sensed Cassa's need to do so. That need was no longer there, for either of them. He should have held back for the sake of the mission, but the animal inside him didn't give a damn about the mission. It cared about the mate, and the animal was closer to the skin than he had ever imagined.

He watched as Jonas grimaced before staring back at Lawe and Rule.

"Hey, Boss, don't look at me," Lawe ordered him. "I told you, I'm steering clear of that mating shit."

"It gives us the heebie-jeebies," Rule drawled.

Jonas grunted at that. "At least someone is still sane." The look he gave Jackal was mocking.

The other man stared back at him stoically, as always. Jackal didn't talk a lot. He did his job and spoke when he had to.

"Coffee's inside," Cabal informed them. "I have caffeinated for the four of you."

He'd stick to the decaf for now. He didn't need any additional problems where the mating heat and Cassa were concerned. Caffeine tended to make the symptoms worse. If his current state of arousal was any indication, he didn't need anything to hype them.

Jonas looked around the clearing, his jaw tense before he shook his head and moved for the porch. "Pack up. You can head back to Sanctuary with your mate," he stated as he reached the steps.

Cabal chuckled at the thought. "Forget it, Jonas. This will finish out here, and we both know it."

"Not with that mate of yours tracking every move you make," Jonas said coolly. "This investigation is too serious, Cabal. We can't risk her."

Cabal shook his head at that. "She already knows just as much as we do. The killer sends it to her whether we want him to or not, Jonas. We can't afford to ignore that."

He hated it. There was nothing he hated more than the fact that a killer was drawing his mate into these murders, but he couldn't stop it. In the early hours of the night he'd admitted that he couldn't keep her out of this. As long as there was a Breed going rogue, as long as he was drawing Cassa into this, then there was no way to keep her out of it.

"Hell, just what we need, a damned journalist involved in my business," Jonas cursed.

"Come on in, Jonas," Cabal sighed. "We don't have a lot of time before she wakes up."

Not much time at all. The mating heat was a fever that couldn't be ignored for long, and Cabal knew it. Already the need to touch his mate, to taste her, to possess her was rising again within him.

The hormonal treatments she had been taking over the past years had helped those first few days. Adjustments were always required as time went on though, and Cassa hadn't had an adjustment to counter the rise in hormones that mating heat was causing.

It wasn't as hard on the male as it was on the female mate. At least Cassa had had the foresight to start the hormonal treatments ahead of time. That would ease it for her, delay conception, sometimes, and lighten the stress on the body from the need for sex.

It didn't take away the need. There was no way to eliminate it, or to allow for the separation of mates for long periods of time. Jonas was stuck with Cassa in Cabal's life for the moment.

"We don't need this, Cabal," Jonas growled as they entered the cabin and headed for the kitchen. "This situation is too damned delicate. We have to find this Breed, and when we do, we can't risk a journalist being aware of the fact that I have no damned intentions of turning him over to Breed Law."

Yeah, that was pretty much what Cabal had suspected. The rogue Breed had managed what no one else had. He killed without leaving a scent or a trace of his identity. There was no way to track him, no way to identify him.

"I'm sure you'll find a way to hide the fact that the bad guy doesn't die in the end," Cabal muttered. He knew Jonas. The man had the ability to make things work out in his favor.

"You're going to completely fuck this assignment up, Cabal,"

Jonas bit out as Cabal moved to the coffeepot. "He's going to kill again, and soon. We both know he will. Do you really want your mate in the middle of that?"

Hell no he didn't, but he knew there was no way to get her out of it now. Not without making her hate him, making her run. He wasn't about to force her again, he'd already tried that once. It hadn't worked then, it wasn't going to work now.

Cabal prepared the coffee before saying anything more. He didn't have an argument for Jonas and he knew it. There was no damned way to explain to the other man that Cassa would hate them all if she was pulled out of this.

He'd wrestled with it most of the night. He'd come up with a thousand different ways to pull her out, and he knew that not a damned one of them was going to work.

"Cabal has a point, Boss." Lawe spoke up as Cabal poured the coffee. "The killer contacts her when he doesn't contact us. We could use that."

"You don't use my mate." Cabal turned back to him with a snarl.

Jonas's bark of laughter echoed through the room as Cabal jerked around to meet the other man's mocking gaze.

"Hell, Cabal, it was no more than you were suggesting yourself," Jonas informed him angrily. "Get off your mating high horse and settle the fuck down. If we're going to figure out how to handle this situation from here on out, then I need your head clear, not filled with the need to fight or fuck."

That was Jonas, blunt to the bitter end.

Pushing his fingers roughly through his hair, Cabal paced to the other side of the room as Jonas moved to the coffeepot. Cocking his head, he listened for any signs of movement from the bedroom and prayed Cassa would sleep just a while longer.

"Have you found anything out?" Jonas finally asked.

Cabal shook his head at the question. "Not enough. David Banks had a meeting in Charleston the day before he disappeared. He met with Brandenmore and Engalls, but we already knew that. The afternoon he disappeared he was supposed to meet with a reporter here in town, Myron James. He never showed up for that meeting."

Jonas rubbed at his jaw thoughtfully. "We weren't aware of that before."

"Sheriff Lacey mentioned that Banks asked her for Myron's phone number. When I questioned Myron about it, he admitted Banks called and requested a meeting. Said he had some information Myron might be interested in."

"Any idea what the information was?"

Cabal shook his head. "He didn't tell Myron, or Myron wasn't telling me. I couldn't sense any deceit though. There are secrets in this town, Jonas, plenty of them, but Banks didn't seem to be privy to many of them."

"He was a former mayor," Lawe pointed out. "Mayors get all the gossip."

"Not all of it," Cabal said. "The movement that began here about thirty years ago to hide escaped Breeds wasn't well known. There was only a small group of men and women involved in that. Banks wasn't one of them."

"We know all that," Jonas pointed out.

"What we didn't know was that Banks was originally part of that group," Cabal told him. "Myron remembered his father mentioning that Banks was part of the group until they began to suspect that he had betrayed one of the Breeds early on."

"There weren't a lot that came through here," Rule stated. "A few dozen."

"But compared to those created, that's a high number," Cabal pointed out. "A few dozen escaped Breeds during that time would have been a problem for the Council."

"And the Council would have made it a problem for the Deadly Dozen," Lawe stated. "They were the trackers when everyone else failed."

"Because they had connections where they were needed to track escaped Breeds," Cabal agreed. "Banks was one of the Dozen, there's no doubt of that. But why wait this long to strike back at the group? And how many of them were located in this area?"

"Most of the escaped Breeds were hiding in this area," Jonas stated.

That was true. For some reason, the West Virginia, Tennessee and Kentucky mountains had been the preferred haven for Breeds escaping across the world.

One here, a few there—somehow most of them had made it to the States, and into the few groups within a three-state radius willing to hide them. Few of the groups knew about one another. Many of the Breeds were unaware of other individual groups. It was a matter of safety. If others didn't know where they were located, or the Breeds in each group, then they couldn't be betrayed under torture.

"What I'd like to know is how Brandenmore and Engalls managed to capture Breeds in this area and experiment on them without the Council or the groups aiding the Breeds knowing about it," Lawe growled. "You'd think someone would have put a stop to it long ago."

"The Deadly Dozen worked not just for the Council, but also for Brandenmore and Engalls," Jonas pointed out. "They bought captured Breeds off the Dozen. When they returned to the Council with a dead Breed, they were paid again. It didn't matter how they died, all they needed was their heads. Brandenmore and Engalls didn't mind in the least removing a head."

It was sickening. The horrors the Breeds had faced in their attempts to be free had sometimes been as harsh as the horrors they had faced within the labs.

"What I'd like to know is how the hell the killer is creating this carnage without leaving so much as a scent of himself on the victim. He rips their throats out with his teeth. There should be DNA, something."

There should be, but there wasn't, not so much as a trace.

"We were trained not to leave anything to identify ourselves," Jonas stated. "That means scent, saliva, whatever. There are ways to hide it."

"But there was only a very small group of Breeds with that advanced training," Rule pointed out. "It wasn't general knowledge."

"Coyotes weren't trained in the more advanced covert areas," Jonas mused. "Jaguars were, Lions were."

"Wolves were also left out of that training for the most part," Cabal stated as he remembered the lists of training areas and the Breeds considered the strongest in each of them. "Jaguars and Lions were considered their best killers."

"Yeah, we rock." Lawe snorted at that statement.

"At least we were considered good at something," Rule stated mockingly. "It kept us alive."

"Six deaths and not a single clue, none of us were that good," Jonas said coldly. "Even I'm not that good. Scent is something you can't hide. You can mask it, but there's not even a sign of masking. It's as though a ghost is attacking and killing these men. And, gentlemen, I don't believe in ghosts."

Did any of them? Hell, ghosts, fairies, happily ever afters— they were all lumped into the same category. Fairy tales.

"So where does that leave us?" Lawe asked. "Six dead men and no clue to the killer. You know he's going to strike again, and soon. Banks and H. R. Alonzo were just the beginning. He's not sticking to the no-names anymore. He's going after the big guns."

They hadn't even been aware that Alonzo was part of the Deadly Dozen. Only after his death had they found proof that he had been a part of the hunting group.

"High-profile names," Jonas growled. "Just what the hell we need."

"And a reporter on our ass," Lawe grunted as he glanced at Cabal with a mocking grin. "We're going to have fun hiding this one."

"You won't hide much from that woman," Jonas informed them all.

Cabal felt a burst of pride at the disgust in Jonas's voice. Cassa was known for her ability to ferret out information despite Jonas's wishes otherwise. She wrote the stories he hated and published them whether he liked it or not. Not that she ever published anything damning, but she didn't mind a bit to tell the truth about what she did publish.

For a long time they had been able to keep her from learning anything that could hurt them. Those days were over. She already had information that could destroy the Breed community, but she had held back.

"So what are we going to do?" Lawe asked. "Let her in, or what?"

"Or what," Jonas snapped. "Yeah, let's let her in. Let's just tell her how we've been protecting a rogue Breed and allowing him to kill our enemies for us rather than sending out teams to protect those we suspect of dying next."

Cabal almost grinned at the thought of that.

"Do we even know who might be next?" he asked the director. He had no doubt that Jonas had a clue somewhere. The man usually did.

"Not yet," Jonas snapped. "That's not the point. Hell, if I did know, I'd still stand aside and let him finish it. He's better at it than I am."

"Sooner or later someone is going to accuse the Breeds of these murders," Cabal warned him. "The Dozen know they're being hunted now. One of them will start squealing in fear sooner or later."

Jonas's smile was tight and hard. "That's what I'm waiting on. We get one of them, then we get them all."

Cabal had already figured that plan out. Jonas ran from murder scene to murder scene cleaning up the mess. He searched for clues; he was looking for the killer, but even more, he was waiting on one of the members of the hunted group to raise his ugly little head.

"How much longer do you think it will take?" Cabal questioned the other man.

Jonas shrugged. "Alonzo is the most high-profile of the six dead. We'll let him remain missing. Tanner has a handle on public relations, and we've managed to get a few rumors started that the Council itself was fed up with him, but his buddies will know differently. I'm hoping his death will force one of them out."

"Six left to go." Lawe shook his head. "Do you think they're all still alive?"

"That kind of evil rarely dies young," Jonas stated as he poured himself another cup of coffee and paced to the window of the kitchen.

Cabal watched as the director frowned out the window, staring into the snow-laden dawn.

"Evil rarely dies young, period," he finally said as he turned back to them. "And what we're dealing with here is a Breed that's trying to change that. I want him caught, but I'll be damned if I'll force a human's justice on him."

"Murder is murder, Jonas," Cabal reminded him. It was something Jonas had preached at them often enough when it came to a Breed's death.

"There's a difference between murder and survival," Jonas snapped back at him. "We've managed to cover up these deaths to this point, and I'd like to keep it that way." His eerie silver eyes flickered in anger. "And need I remind you the hell these men visited on Breeds in the past? They didn't just capture a few and return them to the labs. They sold them for research. Research that if our information is correct was more horrendous than anything the Council did. They deserved their deaths."

Cabal couldn't argue that point. The information they were slowly amassing against Brandenmore and Engalls was enough to give even a Breed more nightmares. If they could manage to acquire proof, or a single witness to those horrors whom they could force to talk, then the two men that headed one of America's largest pharmaceutical and research facilities would be subject to Breed Law. And Cabal had no doubt in his mind that Jonas would push for the limits of punishment where the two men were involved.

"Now figure out how to catch our Breed," Jonas ordered him. "And while you're at it, see if you can't figure out why the hell the bastard doesn't have a scent."

"Possibly because he's hiding it."

They all turned to the door. Weapons cleared their holsters and aimed at the nosy little reporter poised at the entrance to the room, as Cabal jumped in front of her, his heart racing in horror at the threat those weapons posed.

She didn't flinch; she didn't back away. Her long hair lay in tangled waves against the material of one of his shirts as her bare toes peeked out of the hem of her jeans.

She looked like a little girl playing grown-up games. Games that could get her killed.

As he shielded her body, several things registered at once. She had managed to slip up on them, something that should have been impossible. Unless she had no scent. His nostrils flared as he tried to draw in the essence of her, just as he knew the others were doing.

There was nothing there. No mating scent, no arousal, no smell of his lust on her body. It was as though Cassa were a ghost, with no substance, with no scent.

He turned, gripped her arms and stared down at her in shock as he fought to smell the woman he had just spent the night spilling his seed into. There should be some trace of a scent. Any scent.

"What the fuck," Lawe muttered to his side. "Jonas?"

Behind him, he felt Jonas shift, move. He knew the other Breed was doing exactly what Cabal was doing, trying to find a scent so elusive it didn't exist.

Cabal narrowed his eyes on her, searched her face and realized the implications in a single heartbeat.

"Gentlemen, here's your killer's secret." She lifted her hand and in the middle of her silken palm was a small white pill. "A scent blocker. Sent to me by the killer, reportedly created by Brandenmore Research. This is how your rogue Breed is getting by you."

· **C H A P T E R   1 5** ·

Cassa watched Cabal's profile several hours later as they made
the trek back down the mountain in the all-terrain Raider he
was driving.

He was still angry. His profile was hard, his expression cool,
and she'd noticed that the amber glitter in his eyes seemed
duller. That was rage, because the dark green was more brilliant
and seemed alive with the anger surging through him.

Panic had threatened to overwhelm her ever since morning,
when she had given Jonas one of the small pills that had been
sent to her, and explained just how well they worked. Jonas
hadn't been happy that she had eavesdropped on his conversation with Cabal the night of the Coyote alpha's wedding reception. Cabal seemed even less pleased with her.

She remembered her first, ill-fated marriage. Whenever
Douglas had become angry, she had carried the bruises, sometimes for weeks at a time.

Now, more than a decade later, she was sitting in a vehicle
with a lover whose anger swirled in the air around her. There
was an edge of fear, uncertainty. She hadn't allowed herself to
ever be placed in a position again where she had to worry about
a lover striking her. She was beginning to wonder if perhaps she

had bit off more than she could chew with Cabal. If she thought Douglas was dangerous, then her Breed lover was a hundred times more so.

He was angry with her, and what made the situation even more precarious for her was that she wasn't certain why he was so furious.

Her interruption of his meeting that morning could be the cause, she thought. It had been a rather dramatic entrance. She had taken the pill when she had heard the Raiders advancing up the driveway, not long after Cabal had left the bed.

She'd had every intention of telling Cabal about the drug. It was too dangerous to hold secret for very long. If the Breeds' enemies got their hands on it, then Sanctuary or Haven, either one, could be breached easily by the Council's Coyotes and soldiers. No Breed mate would ever know a moment's security, and every Breed child born would be at risk.

"Your attitude is starting to irk me." Cassa forced herself to go on the offensive. "If you're pissed off, then you could do me the courtesy of telling me why."

He shot her an irate glance. An irate Breed was really rather commonplace, she assured herself.

"You could have warned me about that pill before Jonas arrived," he pushed between gritted teeth. "And what the hell are you doing risking yourself by just taking some damned drug that an anonymous killer sent to you? Have you lost your mind?" There was the anger. His voice rose with it.

"Don't yell at me, Cabal," she ordered him with more bravado than she felt. What she felt was sheer panic. He was angrier than she had first thought. "I took a risk admittedly, but it was one that paid off."

"It could have paid off with your life." His hands clenched around the steering wheel as he navigated the mountainous path. "Son of a bitch, Cassa. Did you even think before you did it? Did you even consider the risks?"

She gave a little shrug. "I always consider the risks, Cabal. Whoever sent that drug and the proof of those killings doesn't want me dead yet. He has something to prove. To the Breeds as well as to me. Killing me wouldn't serve his purpose quite yet."

Because the past hadn't come full circle yet. Cassa knew that. The killer had other plans in store for her, the only question was whether or not she would survive them.

Was it foolhardy? Risky? No doubt. She had admitted that going in. But after more than a decade of doubts, recriminations and guilt, she knew she couldn't do anything less than see this through now.

She had dropped the ball during the rescue of the German facility where Cabal had been imprisoned. Because of her husband, so many had died. Because she had trusted Douglas to care about the story even though her marriage was failing. And she had been wrong.

Now she had a chance to make certain that this rogue Breed didn't destroy the Breed community as a whole. She refused to drop the ball on this one. She refused to back down.

"And all you thought of was yourself?" he asked, his voice lowering, darkening.

Cassa gave a bitter little laugh. "Who else should I consider?"

"Friends?" He snarled. "I know you have many of them, don't deny it."

She didn't try to.

"Look, this is my job. It's my life." Cassa turned to him, her own anger mixing with her fear. "I weighed the consequences and took the risk. It was my choice to make."

His lips thinned as he narrowed his gaze at the road. His hands didn't relax on the steering wheel.

"You knew we were mates when you took it," he accused. "Did you consider me?"

"Oh yeah, let me think about that one," she bit out sarcastically. "No, I didn't consider your opinion of it quite simply because I assumed you really didn't give a damn. It's not as though you gave the impression that you were ready for a mate, Cabal. A harem maybe."

She hated that. The playboy of the Breeds. Or at least he'd been considered one half of a play team before his brother Tanner mated.

She watched as his jaw bunched, and she wondered if his molars were strong enough to stand the force of his teeth gritting together.

"I've never had a harem," he stated angrily.

"Whatever." Cassa blew out an irritated breath and flicked her fingers in his direction. "You were just fucking your way through the world. I understand."

And she hated it. The thought of those women touching him, having him, touching those sexy-as-hell stripes while she still had yet to do so made her crazy. She curled her fingers at the thought of touching those oddly colored markings and tried to push past the image of her lips running over them.

A man shouldn't be this sexy or so damned irritating.

"You don't understand a damn thing," he informed her. "If you weren't constantly running scared, maybe I wouldn't have felt like an animal chasing a rabbit. You ran from me every chance you had."

"I simply stood aside to keep from being trampled by the hordes of lusting women," she bit back acerbically.

But she had been frightened, and she knew it. Frightened of the strength of her desire as well as the past that she feared he would never forget or forgive her for.

"You were scared, just as you're scared now." There was a hint of censure in his tone. "When have I ever made you believe I would hurt you, Cassa?"

She was silent at that question. He had never done anything to make her believe he would lay a hand on her. Unless she were the enemy, and then there would be no saving her from him.

God, wasn't that a cheerful thought, considering the fact that she had been the reason for the worst betrayal of his life and still he hadn't given any indication of the amount of blame he assigned to her.

"You've done nothing to make me believe you would hurt me, Cabal," she answered wearily. "If you sensed fear, maybe it's for other reasons."

"Your husband?" He cast her a brooding look. "That wasn't in the investigation Jonas had done on you." She guessed she should congratulate herself for having hidden the abuse she'd suffered so well that no one had guessed. If anyone had suspected, then the Breeds would have had that information. They knew every damned thing. Sons of bitches couldn't keep their noses out of other people's lives.

"Then what makes you think it was my husband?" she asked archly.

He grunted at that. A completely feline sound of irritation.

"I read the report on you as well as that of your husband, Douglas Watts," he informed her. "He wasn't exactly a prize,

Cassa. You could have done much better. Just because there was nothing in there about abuse doesn't mean it didn't exist."

That was no joke.

"But there was nothing in that report about it," she reminded him.

His hair brushed against his shoulders as he gave his head a quick shake before maneuvering the vehicle onto the main road.

"And you're being too evasive, that's answer enough for me." There was a latent growl in his throat, one that sent shivers of both pleasure as well as dread racing down Cassa's spine.

"Believe what you want to," she told him coolly. "There are much more interesting matters in my life right now than a husband long dead. How long do you think it will take Jonas to figure out where that drug came from?"

Thick dark gold lashes narrowed on her as he cast her a quick look before turning his attention back to the road.

"Soon" was the only answer he gave. "Our main concern at this point is to catch our killer. Find him and we'll find the origin of that drug."

"Jonas thinks he can control a rogue, doesn't he?" She could well believe Jonas was that arrogant.

"Jonas thinks he could control the wind if he put his mind to it," Cabal snorted. "He's that damned hardheaded. But in this case, he most likely can."

Cassa shook her head at that thought. "I saw those pictures, Cabal, just as you saw the bodies. That amount of rage can't be contained. Jonas could end up on the wrong end of a rogue's fury."

"He's been there before." And from the sound of Cabal's voice, it hadn't been any more pleasant then.

◆   ◆   ◆

Cabal breathed in the scent in the Raider and restrained the need to snarl in anger. He still couldn't catch her scent or his mark upon her. It enraged him that something so elemental had been restrained within her body. Her scent, so uniquely hers, had been completely wiped away. There was nothing to reassure the animal inside him that she was his, that his scent covered her body. There wasn't even the scent of arousal to salve that primal need.

Added to that insult was the knowledge that his accusations against Watts were correct and she was still trying to hide it. Watts had admitted to beating her, abusing her. During his interrogation after Cabal's escape from the hellhole of the pit, Watts had admitted to it. Just as he had admitted that Cassa had known nothing about his betrayal. That he had played her. He had laughed at how eager she had been for that illusion of love, of belonging.

Cabal had wanted to kill him. So many times. So many ways. But forcing the bastard to live was a salve to Cabal's pride as well. As much as Cabal wanted him dead, this way Watts was actually paying for his crimes rather than resting in peace as it were.

Cassa's fears were instinctive, and though Cabal understood that, still he couldn't get past his anger that she would fear him.

He was her mate. He would rather harm himself than harm her. That was more than instinct, that was a part of him. No male could call himself a man if he gained his sense of power from harming those weaker than himself. Especially his woman.

Glancing over at her, he grimaced at the continued lack of scent. It should have lasted only approximately two hours, she had told them that morning. It had been quite a bit longer than that.

He couldn't smell her, and a part of him needed that connection to her. Removing one hand from the wheel, he reached out to her and enclosed the soft delicacy of her hand as it lay against her thigh.

Her response was a stiffening of her body as the slightest tinge of surprise wafted through the air. She looked from where he clasped her hand back to his face.

"What are you doing?" she asked suspiciously.

"Isn't this what lovers do?" he asked her as he continued to hold her hand, drawing it from her lap to his hard thigh. "Hold hands."

She blinked back at him silently. He'd managed to shock her. Damn, he thought he might feel a little pride in that. Cassa rarely allowed herself to be surprised or shocked.

She stared at their hands again, as though uncertain what to say, or how to act. To throw her further off balance, and simply because he enjoyed the feel of her soft flesh, he allowed his thumb to run over her fragile knuckles, to caress and warm her flesh.

A little tremble went through her fingers and raced up her arm. He swore she acted like a woman unused to touch.

"Beginning nearly forty years ago, escaped Breeds were making their way to areas they felt would shelter and protect them. They came here, to Glen Ferris," he told her softly. "A few, one here, one there, until over two dozen amassed together. Then, about twenty years ago, out of those few, there would be disappearances. Rumor would make it back that the bodies of those missing Breeds had been returned, lifeless, to the Council. There was a hunting party that called themselves the Deadly Dozen, and they were preying on escaped Breeds."

"Some of those Breeds were sold to Brandenmore Research before being returned to the Council," Cassa remarked, a tone of relief in her voice. "Since Phillip Brandenmore and Horace Engalls were arrested for crimes against the Breed society, information has begun trickling through linking them to illegal research."

"Exactly." Cabal nodded. "Our rogue Breed made his first kill about three months ago, just before Brandenmore and Engalls were caught in Sanctuary attempting to steal Breed medical information. Since then, five others have died, each rumored to be connected to the research and pharmaceutical family."

Cabal continued to hold her hand, his grip firming each time she tried to draw it free. He found he enjoyed holding her hand, feeling her skin against his, her warmth encased in his.

"It's obviously a Breed with a grudge," Cassa pointed out. "A friend or family member lost to the Deadly Dozen. Perhaps a mate."

Cabal shook his head at that. "A Breed would never wait twenty years to exact revenge against a lost mate. There are few instances of matings before the Breeds revealed themselves. Each time, the Breed left behind went feral and was killed."

Cassa breathed out roughly. Glancing at her as he drove into Glen Ferris, Cabal took in the light frown between her brows and the concern in her dark gray eyes.

"Myron knows something." She shook her head as she glanced back at him. "There was something about his reaction to my questions that didn't sit right. It wasn't in character. It made me wonder if he didn't know what was going on here and why."

She worried about her friendship with Myron, but she worried as well about the Breed community and the killings now taking place. Myron knew something, and that something could mean the difference between catching a killer and the safety of the Breeds.

"He lost his mate here, just before the revelation of the Breeds," Cabal stated. "A Lion Breed female. She was barely eighteen. She was killed while helping to escort an escaped Breed through the mountains. Nearly a dozen Breeds died that day in the same valley where we found Alonzo."

"Do you think there's a connection?" She could feel the connection.

Cabal wanted to believe there was, simply because he needed easy answers.

"A Breed is making these kills," he told her. "Not a human. Myron might suspect someone, but he's not the killer."

"Meaning you've already checked on the possibility," she stated.

Cabal smiled at that. "See how well you know me, Cassa? Mating with you might well be more fun than either of us anticipated. It could get very interesting."

She rolled her eyes at him.

Cabal had no doubt it was going to get interesting, just as soon as he got her back in the bed. That damned pill was slowly wearing off, and the sweet scent of her arousal was beginning to drift to him. Her arousal as well as the hormonal mark he had left on her body. Finally, the animal inside him could breathe easier.

That pill was dangerous. As Jonas had stated, there wasn't a Breed alive that was safe from the Council now. There would never be an assurance of safety because they could no longer depend on being able to scent their enemies.

"Where are we going first?" she asked as he turned off the main road onto one of the side roads.

"Sheriff Lacey," he told her. "Today's her day off. I called earlier to let her know we were coming by. Her father was one of the leaders of the groups that protected the Breeds around here. She was friends with most all of them. I'm hoping she'll know something about the group that was killed in the valley. It's not a coincidence that we found Alonzo's body there."

"But no other bodies were found there," she pointed out.

"They've been scattered, and Banks's body still hasn't been found. Someone had to have seen something," she mused. "There could be more than just a rogue Breed, but also one or more persons protecting him."

He'd already checked that angle, just as he'd investigated every Breed in the county. He hadn't questioned the sheriff enough yet. She might have more information he wasn't getting from others.

"Lacey seems cooperative," Cassa ventured carefully.

Cabal almost grinned at the hint of jealousy he could smell now.

"Her family has always protected the Breeds that made it here," he told her. "She's an important contact to have."

But he hadn't slept with the sheriff. Danna Lacey was cooperative and friendly, but there was a reserved air about her that practically screamed at a man to hold his distance.

Cassa didn't say anything more. Cabal drove the Raider to the turnoff to Danna's small house, just inside the forested tree line that surrounded the small town.

The sheriff was waiting at the door, a cup of steaming coffee in her hand as she leaned against the frame and watched them leave the vehicle and move to the house.

She was dressed in jeans and a large flannel shirt, with her hair pulled back into a braid, while her green eyes gleamed with amused interest.

Her gaze flicked to where Cabal recaptured Cassa's hand after getting out of the Raider. His prickly little mate still wasn't certain about the affectionate side of the mating she was now involved in.

He'd given up on remaining distant from her. He needed to touch her, needed to hold her.

"Good afternoon." She greeted them as they stepped up on the porch. "Come on in. I just made a pot of coffee. Decaf if you don't mind it. My doctor thinks I need to cut my intake of caffeine." She snorted at the thought.

"Decaf is fine," Cabal assured her as they moved to the long kitchen table. "Thanks for seeing us on your day off."

"That's not a problem," she assured him. "But I am curious. What do you need to know that it couldn't wait until I returned to the office?"

Cabal lifted the brown envelope he'd carried from the Raider and laid it on the table before extracting the aerial shot of the valley where H. R. Alonzo had died.

"This valley." He pointed to the area. "Twenty years ago a pride of Lion Breeds were killed there. What can you tell me about those who were mated?"

♦ ♦ ♦

Cassa watched as the sheriff moved slowly to the table and picked up the aerial shot. Her expression transformed for the briefest second into lines of pain before she took a deep breath and shook her head sadly.

"There were ten Breeds," she said as she looked up. "They were headed by Patrick Wallace, an escaped Breed from the UK. He'd banded most of the Breeds together into his pride. He took ten of them that night. The youngest was a little Lion Breed female. She was only eighteen years old but she was one of the fiercest fighters they had."

Danna moved from the table, poured coffee, then returned with cups for both Cabal and Cassa before she took her seat.

"What was significant about the female?" Cabal asked.

Cassa knew before the sheriff answered, but she listened, and ached at the regret she heard in the sheriff's tone.

"I was twenty-three myself then," Danna sighed. "The girl's name was Illandra. She had just married one of our group's young men, Myron James." The curve of her lips was tight with sadness. "They were escorting a Coyote Breed through the forest. He was wounded, too weak to get over the mountain on his own, and they couldn't risk taking him by vehicle or allowing him to stay in the area. They went on foot instead, thinking they could avoid the Council Coyotes and soldiers that had been sent for them."

"What made this Coyote so special?" Cabal asked her. "At that time there were few Coyotes that opposed the Council."

"Maybe that was what made him special," she stated as she shrugged heavily. "I didn't know who he was, or why he was there. We rarely did. Patrick was pretty secretive."

"They were caught in that valley though?" Cabal pressed her.

Danna nodded. "They were caught in the valley by a group of men sent to hunt them. Most of the male Breeds were killed. Illandra and the other female in the group were captured and taken away."

The sheriff reached out and pulled the picture toward her once again. She sat staring at it as Cassa watched her face. She had obviously known the Breeds who had died there well.

"Illandra was Myron's mate, you said?" Cassa sked.

Danna looked up, her lips pressing together painfully. "She was so vibrant. She had only just started laughing. Myron would make faces at her, bring her flowers and candy. He was always spoiling her, always trying to make up for the horrors she'd experienced in those labs. He was devoted to her."

"What about the other female?" Cabal asked. "Was she mated?"

Danna frowned at that. "She was mated to one of the Breeds in the group. He was killed as well."

"No one survived?" Cabal questioned her again.

Danna smiled sadly. "If anyone survived that night, I would have known about it. My father searched those mountains for months looking for some sign of where they'd been taken. Finally, Illandra's body was returned to the lab she was created in. We did get word of that. Most of the males were returned as well. From what we later learned, those that never showed up again, there was nothing left of them to return. The group that captured them had sold them to an independent scientist who used most of the body parts for various experiments."

"Were there any rumors as to who that scientist was?" Cabal asked her.

Danna laughed at that. The sound was hollow and bitter. "Not until recently. There are rumors it was Brandenmore." She shook her head at that. "He and Engalls kept an elaborate cabin in the mountains, but we had no idea it was being used for anything like that until he was arrested last year by your people. I heard there was a research facility beneath the cabin?"

There had been. Cassa had seen the pictures of the underground lab, and it had horrified her. Not that there had been any proof that Breeds had been tortured there; they had been smarter than that. But the extent of the equipment found there, and its uses, horrified the imagination.

"Danna, have you heard any rumors of vengeance strikes by a Breed against the group of men who attacked the pride that night?" Cabal asked the sheriff then.

Cassa watched the sheriff's gaze flicker between the photo

and Cabal before she frowned back at him. "You think Banks was part of that group? And that he was a killer?" she asked curiously.

She was sharp, Cassa gave her credit for that.

"I know there were rumors that he was a part of the Dozen, but I didn't take them seriously." There was an edge of a laugh in her voice. "You didn't know David Banks then. He was a bully, yes, but he puked at the sight of blood. I don't think it's possible."

Cassa disagreed with her. David Banks would have no more fainted at the sight of blood than Cabal would have. The man had been hard-core evil, despite the compassionate facade he often used.

"We've definitely tied him into the Dozen," Cabal assured her.

Danna's frown deepened. "You've found his body?"

"Not yet, but we will." Cabal shifted his shoulders as he blew out a hard breath. He pulled the photo back toward him as he lifted the envelope.

"What else do you have there?" Danna leaned forward as the edge of several other photos peeked free at the top of the envelope.

Cabal looked up as though in surprise. Cassa knew better. Breeds were rarely surprised by anything or anyone, especially Cabal.

It was interesting to watch these two together. Beneath her calm facade, Danna was obviously irritated that information was being held back. It was also clear that she was well aware that something was going on in her county. It would be impossible to miss with Banks's disappearance and the sudden influx of Breeds running around.

Cabal pulled several more photos free of the envelope as Cassa watched Danna's face. The other woman paled at the sight of the first bloody picture. The features were indistinguishable, but there was no doubt that the victim had been horribly mauled.

It was a photo Cassa had seen herself. It had been in the file that had included the crime scene photos of Dr. Ryan Damron. Where he had been murdered Cassa didn't know, but she had a feeling it was in the same mountains where H. R. Alonzo had died as well.

"My God," Danna whispered as she raised shocked eyes to meet Cabal's. "Who is it?"

"Dr. Ryan Damron," Cabal said quietly. "Did you know him?"

He pulled free another of the pictures, in which the sheriff could see the body and the ground around the doctor. There was an eyeball by his left shoulder. His tongue had been sliced off and laid on his mauled chest.

"Ryan Damron." Danna inhaled deeply. "I knew of him. He visited with Brandenmore and Engalls during the summers fairly often. Especially during hunting season."

Cabal slid the pictures back into the envelope.

"You think he's tied to David Banks," she guessed. "Were they both killed by the same person?"

Cabal shook his head at the question as though he were uncertain. "The only tie we have is the fact that the good doctor was missing for several months before we found his body. The kill was fresh. The Bureau received information where the body could be found, and nothing more."

"And Banks's body hasn't shown up either." Placing her hand on her hip, the sheriff turned away before pacing to the other side of the room.

"I knew Banks," she sighed. "I didn't like him much, but I knew him. Damron I was only acquainted with." She turned back to them, her dark green eyes flickering back to the envelope that held the pictures. "They were both tied to Brandenmore and Engalls though, I do know that."

"Damron, Banks, Brandenmore and Engalls were all hunting buddies," Cabal stated. "Do you remember anyone else that hunted with them, or visited with them here often?"

Danna lifted her hand and tapped at her lips with her index finger as she frowned thoughtfully for long moments.

"There were several others," she finally said. "A police officer, Aaron Washington. A quiet guy, kind of plain. An attorney out of D.C., Elam March, he came in maybe once a year and made a nuisance of himself. There was a sheriff from out west somewhere I think, Jason Douglas. And that damned H. R. Alonzo. He was a pest even then." She shook her head. "There were others, but I'd have to ask Myron about them. He was more social than I was, even then. He'd know more about Brandenmore's buddies than I."

Myron. Cassa felt her stomach sink at Danna's words. After his reaction yesterday morning to her questions, she was beginning to get a bad feeling that he was more involved in this than she wanted to believe.

"Thanks for your time, Danna." Cabal rose to his feet as Cassa followed more slowly. "If you think of anything else, let me know."

"Cabal, what the hell is going on here?" Concern lined the sheriff's face now. "What was Banks involved in? A Breed wouldn't wait this long to kill over a murder that took place over twenty years ago."

"I'm not sure, Danna." Cabal's gaze was somber as he watched the sheriff, and Cassa thought perhaps she detected a shadow of regret in his voice. Did he suspect, as she did, that Myron could be involved in the killings?

She didn't want to believe it, but she'd learned to be suspicious, and she'd learned that even those closest to you could betray you in the worst ways. She and Myron were friends, but that didn't mean he wouldn't be seeking revenge for a mate that had been murdered and possibly tortured to death.

Danna's jaw clenched as she gave an abrupt nod, obviously sensing that Cabal wasn't going to tell her anything more.

"Let me know if I can help you any further then," she told him. "I'll keep looking for information on Banks as well. His disappearance is still an open case. There were a lot of people around here that liked him though, so be careful how you ask your questions."

"Thanks for the advice, Sheriff." Cabal nodded once again before turning and heading for the door.

"Thanks for the coffee, Sheriff," Cassa said quietly.

"You're welcome, Ms. Hawkins." The sheriff's voice was stiff now, concern lining her expression as Cassa turned away from her and followed Cabal out of the house.

As she stepped into the chilly air and felt his warmth next to her, she had to restrain a shiver of sudden need.

She wanted to keep her mind on this investigation; she wanted to find the killer whose acts might destroy the Breeds and learn why he'd committed such destruction on the bodies of his enemies. What was driving him, and who was he? A Breed or someone intent on destroying the Breeds?

The need to understand drove her to try to answer the questions roiling through her mind. But another need was beginning to burn through her as well.

The need for her mate.

CHAPTER 16

There was nothing as confusing as a damned Breed, especially Cabal. He'd gone from refusing to hold her at all to refusing to release her.

He held her hand out of the sheriff's home. When they were back in the Raider, his large hand cupped her knee as he drove. He acted as though he couldn't stand to take his hands off her.

Was he trying to distract her? Throw her off balance? What the hell was up with him?

She gave him another suspicious look as they drove through town. The Raider itself drew an incredible amount of attention as it eased through the light traffic of Glen Ferris. Not that the town was large enough to actually slip through without being noticed. The Breed insignia on the door of the vehicle didn't help matters much.

Breeds drew attention wherever they went though. The world still wasn't used to, or certain of, this strange new species that man had created.

"The Breed Freedom Society that hid the Breeds in the area. Do you know the identities of all its members?" she asked as she tried to think past the feel of his fingertips rubbing against the inside of her knee.

"No one knows the identities of the Freedom Society," he answered her, and he didn't seem concerned by it.

She stared back at him in disbelief. "Right," she answered mockingly. "No one knows their identities. You haven't checked into it. And I'll just bet Jonas doesn't have a clue either."

His lips quirked at her snappy words. "What Jonas knows pretty much stays with Jonas," he stated. "Who knows what he knows?"

She almost snorted at that, but found herself staring at him in disbelief instead. He was joking with her? The stoic, sober, dangerous Cabal was cracking jokes? Since when?

"You're making fun of me," she accused him suspiciously.

The look he turned on her was one of confusion. "Making fun of you? Why would I do that?"

"Because you can," she sighed, attempting to move her leg from his touch and failing. Not for the first time.

"I've never attempted to identify all the members of the Freedom Society for a reason," he explained. "They've struggled to remain anonymous, even to the Bureau. I've tried to respect that."

"And if they're hiding a killer now?" She turned to him as she asked the question. "What if they're aware of the rogue, aware of the murders?"

He stared through the windshield as she watched him with a hint of anger.

"Danna is a member of the Freedom Society, we know that." She held up a single finger. "Walt. I'd bet he was part of it, and high ranking at that."

"Why Walt?" His hand slipped higher on her leg, his fingers rubbing, caressing, interfering with her thought process.

She could barely manage to control her breathing. If his fingers went much higher, she was going to lose her breath entirely.

"Why Walt?" She looked down at his hand, watching as his darkly tanned fingers continued to smooth, to rub over the denim that covered her legs.

There were chills chasing up her legs, frissons of sensation beginning to sing through her nerve endings, to strike higher, to wrap around the sensitive bud of her clit.

She was growing wetter, more sensitive. She could feel the tender flesh of her pussy heating, preparing for him.

All she wanted to do was to slide across the console, straddle his lap . . .

And what the hell was stopping her? This was her mate, right? He was her man. He could touch. He could kiss. He could do whatever the hell he wanted to do.

Her jaw tightened at the thought. Well, maybe she should try doing what she wanted to do for a change. They were close enough to the hotel. Hell, for that matter there were any number of places that he could pull off the road, darken the windows and just have his way with her. If he were of a mind to do that.

She wondered if she could put him in the mind to do it.

"What the hell are you up to?" She slid around in her seat, watching him closely now, wondering if she had the courage, if she dared to be so bold.

"Me?" He stared back at her in surprise. "What do you think I'm up to?"

His fingers were moving higher, only inches from the wet, desperate flesh that vibrated with need for him.

"You're trying to distract me." She could be naughty. She could be bad. She would be, because she was sick and damned tired of this particular Breed thinking he could, and that he would, control her.

She let her fingers touch the back of his hand, the pads barely caressing his flesh as he paused on her thigh.

"You think you can control me, don't you, Cabal?" she asked him softly, the accusation weighing heavily between them. "You don't want me asking questions. You don't want me investigating this story. So what are you doing?"

He glanced over at her in disbelief. "What am I doing?"

"You're using the mating heat and the sex to distract me," she answered him. She should have been furious. She assured herself that she would be later. For now, she was going to be what she wanted to be. For once, she was going to do what she wanted to do. For once, she was going to distract rather than be distracted.

She decided that was a mate's job. At least when a woman had a mate such as Cabal.

"I wouldn't do that." He cleared his throat as she moved her hand from his and laid it on his thigh. Her fingertips danced over the denim that covered the hard muscle there, moving close, then drawing away from the bulge of his hardened cock.

She watched as he took a deep breath, his chest expanding as she released her seat belt and moved in her seat.

"Hell," he breathed out roughly as she slid one leg over his thighs and moved until she was straddling him, her body braced between him and the steering wheel.

"I'm sure this is illegal." His voice was suddenly guttural, harsh.

"Have you ever cared about the legalities of what you do?" she asked, her head lowering to his shoulder, her lips touching his neck.

"Only if I could get caught." His hand gripped her hip, his body tightening as she raked her teeth along his neck. "We could get caught."

"What are we doing?"

"Driving and riding in an illegal manner?" he questioned her. "I'm sure there's a law somewhere."

"I'm sure," she murmured, suddenly distracted by the taste of his flesh as her lips caressed his neck, her tongue stroking over it.

She felt a surge of power racing through her as Cabal's hips lifted, shifted, his cock pressing into the vee of her thighs as she moved over him. He wasn't pushing her from him. He wasn't denying her or ridiculing her.

"Damn, Cassa." He was groaning instead, as she pulled his shirt from his jeans, her hand smoothing over his hard abdomen, feeling the muscles flex beneath her palm.

He was warm. So warm and hard. He made her feel soft, female, in ways she had never realized before.

"If I wreck, we're going to be in trouble," he warned her, but he wasn't ordering her away. He wasn't calling her names; he wasn't cursing her for her temerity.

He was aroused. And he was holding her to him.

How many times had she fantasized about this? About being brave and bold with him. She had dreamed about being the woman she had never been able to be before. The woman she hadn't known how to be.

"Don't wreck, Cabal," she whispered as she nipped at the hard flesh of his neck.

"Easy for you to say," he groaned, his hand moving against her hip, shifting her against him as he rocked in the cradle of her thighs.

"Very easy for me to say." She sighed in bliss at the feel of the hard ridge of his cock stroking against her sensitive folds.

"What the hell has come over you?" His moan was a strangled breath of lust as his head turned, his lips stealing a quick kiss before he turned his gaze back to the road. "I thought you were going to fight this with every breath."

"You were the one fighting."

She leaned into the curve as he took the turn that led back to the cabin he had rented. Her knees tightened on his thighs, her hand stroked his chest.

"Cassa, baby, you're destroying my control."

And what had happened to her control? Where had her common sense gone or her sense of self-preservation?

It had disintegrated in his hold. It had disappeared with his first kiss.

"I own you." She sat up on his lap as the Raider gained speed up the steep incline to the cabin.

She watched the amber in his eyes flare, watched the flush that stained his cheekbones and the lust that flared in his expression.

Her hands moved between their bodies, her fingers tearing at the closure of his jeans. She needed him. Ached for him.

"Damn you," he growled. "What you do to me should be illegal."

"Take it up with the ruling cabinet," she gasped, speaking of the group that oversaw the Breed community and its laws.

"I'll take it up with you, mate."

His breathing was as harsh, as heavy, as hers when the Raider slammed to a stop outside the cabin. Before she could draw more than one harsh breath, his lips were on hers, his tongue swirling over hers, spreading the spicy taste of the mating hormone and setting fire to an arousal already growing quickly out of control.

She tightened her arms around him; her knees gripped his hips and she held on to his shoulders and his kiss as he stepped from the vehicle.

She wanted to laugh in sheer pleasure as she felt his hands grip her rear, holding her to him. But she was consumed by his kiss instead. She moaned into the kiss, her hands tearing at his shirt, pulling at it, desperate to feel his bare flesh as she felt the door at her back, felt Cabal struggling to release the security lock.

"You've pushed too far, mate." He was growling with lust now, his voice thick, deep, as the door pushed open.

Cassa took her own kiss this time. Melding her lips over his, she dug her fingers into the long strands of his hair, holding him to her as she teased, stroked, as she loved.

Here, within the lust that consumed them both, she could hide the love that welled so deep inside her and spilled over into each touch she gave him.

Here she could hide each emotion, disguise it in her own lust and hold on as tightly as she needed to hold.

"You make me mad to touch you. To taste you."

She had no idea how they made it from the door to the living room. She only knew that as he lowered her to the couch, her shirt was being jerked from her, tossed aside. The lacy bra was shredded and his lips were covering a torturously hard nipple.

His hands were tearing at her clothes, dragging his jeans and boots from his body, even as he lashed at the nipple with his rough tongue, sucked it into his mouth and had her crying out in blistering need.

It was exquisite. She could well find herself living for this, aching for this even when the mating heat wasn't torturing her body.

She dug her fingers into his hair, twining the thick, heavy strands around her fingers as her back arched and she fought to get closer to the wicked, knowing tongue that licked and stroked at first one nipple, then the other.

Cassa could feel the vortex of sensation, of pleasure, as it began to swirl, to twist inside her. She was naked before him, arching into his embrace and needing so much more than his teasing strokes were allowing her.

"Cabal, please," she whispered the plea with a soft sob as his hand smoothed down her stomach.

"I'm going to please you," he rasped. "I'm going to please both of us, baby."

His fingers slid into the thick, slick moisture between her thighs as he began to kiss and nip his way down her stomach.

A startled cry tore from her lips as he suddenly lifted, reclining her back on the couch and spreading her thighs before him as he sat on his knees before her.

She had no time to grasp the significance of the move before his head lowered and his tongue was burrowing into the clenching, desperate grip of her pussy. Licking, thrusting. He ate her with wicked decadence as he lifted her legs, propped her feet on the cushions and opened her farther to his touch.

Cassa tried to fight back the scream of pleasure as his tongue licked through the narrow slit, then sucked her clit into his mouth, but there was no holding it back. She was flying through a turbulent wash of sensation so violent it shuddered through her, causing her to writhe on the cushions in suspended ecstasy.

It was too much. She was dying. Right there in the living room with the sun pouring through the large tinted windows, she was dying. Burning alive in his arms and rushing headlong into the flames.

The orgasm that rushed through her left her crying out his name as he pushed from between her thighs.

Cassa opened her eyes as he untangled her fingers from his hair and placed them on his shoulders. They both watched as he gripped his cock with one hand and tucked the wide, flushed head against the wet entrance of her sex.

"Damn, baby, that's sexy." His rumbled voice sent shivers of pleasure racing through her.

Cassa watched, eyes wide, as he pressed forward, eased back, pressed in again. The head of his erection entered her slowly, stretching her flesh as a low, moaning cry fell from her lips. Her lashes drifted closed as she arched into the penetration, relishing the slow, exquisite burn of entrance, the stroke of his cock through tender tissue.

Her head rolled against the cushions, her nails tightened into the skin of his shoulders as her legs wrapped around his hips to draw him closer.

Each slow thrust, each powerfully controlled stroke of his flesh inside hers sent her senses spinning. Electric impulses of pleasure pulsated through her pussy, causing her to tighten around the shuttling flesh, to fight to hold him inside her as he continued to thrust slow and easy.

"So sweet," he rumbled, his voice rough. "Damn, Cassa, so fucking good."

Too good. She was reaching, her muscles gripping him, her nails digging into his flesh as he leaned into her, thrust deep and hard. His hands gripped her hips, his lips went to her shoulder and she knew what was coming. She could feel her climax building, tightening in her womb.

It was a conflagration. Heat and flames swirled around her, through her, until they exploded into a mass of such exquisite sensation that nothing else mattered.

When she thought she could bear no more, it got better. The feline barb became erect, locked inside her and spilled Cabal's release in spurt after spurt of liquid heat.

She was locked in a world of sensation, of pleasure. Her legs gripped his hips, her neck arched, and when the bite came, she exploded in a series of orgasms that stole her breath and shook her mind.

She was left holding on to him with a desperation she had never known in her life. Holding on to him to retain some semblance of order, some measure of security.

His arms around her, his flesh locked to hers, his body sheltering hers—he was her security. Her port in a storm that threatened to destroy her with the violence of the pleasure. She had sworn she would never depend on anyone, that no man would be the center of her universe, her port or her security.

Even Douglas hadn't meant that much to her. He had never been imperative to her life, or to her pleasure. In this moment, awash with ecstasy, Cassa admitted, to herself at least, that Cabal was exactly that. Even without the mating heat, this man was imperative to her heart.

"Easy." She heard his voice whispering at her ear, and only in that second did Cassa realize that she was crying.

Her head was buried against his shoulder, her arms locked around him, and she was losing her mind, because she was insane enough to let him realize what he meant to her.

He was a Breed. He wasn't a normal male. He could sense, scent emotions. He would know what she refused to say. He could smell what she refused to feel. And right now, she was feeling plenty that she shouldn't, that she had sworn she wouldn't.

"I have you." His lips pressed against her neck, his hands slid up her back, the calloused palms stroking over her flesh, soothing the tremors racing through her.

She didn't want the comfort. She didn't want to depend on this, didn't want to look forward to it only to have it taken away from her later. Because it always went away. It never lasted for long.

She fought to steady her breathing as he slowly withdrew from her before lifting her in his arms and rising to his feet. Legs around his hips, her arms holding tight, Cassa rested her head on his shoulder as he carried her up the stairs to the huge bedroom above and the bed that still held their scent.

"You make me lazy," he said softly as he laid her in the bed, then followed quickly, pulling the sheet and comforter over them as he drew her back into his arms.

"Yeah. Lazy." The mockery in her voice fell far short of what it should have been. She hadn't met a Breed yet that was anywhere close to lazy.

"You make me want to stay right here, Cassa, for as long as I can stay."

His head settled into the pillow beside her as she turned to stare into the somber gaze directed at her.

"Why couldn't you?" she asked. "Unless you have something to do that you don't want me to be a part of."

He continued to stare back at her silently, the gold flecks in his gaze brightening knowingly as he watched her.

"We're mates," she pointed out. "There should be nothing you do that I can't be a part of."

She had been saving that trump, hoping to use it at a time when it would actually work. She didn't know all the specifics of Breed Law, but one thing she was damned sure of: If she didn't want him endangering his life, then he was required to cease and desist at once, for a period of one year.

She would hate to pull that one on him; truth be told, she probably couldn't bring herself to do it, unless he made the mistake of trying to take her out of her job.

"You know, I've always been aware of the fact that you knew how to play dirty," he stated musingly, without anger.

He was actually pretty calm, surprisingly. Terrifyingly so perhaps.

Cassa arched a brow. "Play dirty? I merely stated that I should be a part of whatever you're doing, however you're doing it. How is that playing dirty?"

He snorted at the comment as he shifted to his side and propped himself up on an elbow. "We both know Breed Law."

Her eyes widened. "Do you think I'm threatening you, Cabal?" She blinked for added effect. "I wouldn't ever."

"I was hoping you wouldn't," he drawled. "You seem like a

very intelligent woman, Cassa. That's why you're going to stay out of this now that we've mated. I won't risk you."

She laughed. Right there in his face, amusement welled inside her until it erupted past her lips and left her shaking her head at his arrogance.

"Yeah. That's exactly what I'm going to do," she promised with all the sarcasm she could muster as she rose from the bed and jerked the wrinkled sheet from the bed to wrap around her naked body.

She didn't care much for the frank male appreciation in his gaze at that moment. Nor did she care for the mockery that lingered in his expression.

"Cassa." He didn't bother to cover his nakedness, or his arousal, as he crawled over the bed. "This isn't a joking matter. Whatever the hell is going on here is about to get fucking dangerous."

"You cover my back and I'll cover yours." She glared back at him fiercely. "But I won't be leaving, and I won't drop what I'm doing here."

"Just what the fuck are you doing here?" His voice rose, not a lot, but a lot for Cabal, who normally kept his tone calm, even. "Besides endangering your own life."

"Getting the story," she informed him coldly.

"Why?"

"What do you mean 'why'?" she exclaimed. "The killer sent me information, Cabal. Should I just ignore it?"

"What are you going to do with the information or the answers once you get them?" he asked her, his expression fierce. "You know we're going to cover this up, bury it as deep as possible. Why write a story that will never see print, Cassa? Why do that to yourself?"

Why? She stared back at him in confusion. She knew the answer, but it wasn't one she could give him.

"What if you're wrong about covering it?" she whispered. "What if someone else finds out? Or the killer sends the proof to another reporter? You'll need the answers. You'll need someone to write a story that will show your side of it, and cast a better light on the Breeds."

"That can be accomplished without putting you in danger," he stated. "Why are you here?"

"I want the answers," she bit out angrily. "I need to know why."

He shook his head. "You need to absolve yourself. That's the reason you've done this all these years. It's the reason why you've always fought to see the Breeds as heroes and victims rather than the killers we were created to be. It's why you put yourself in danger time and again for the Breeds. You can't make up for what Watts did."

Cassa flinched. The pain of his statement traveled through her until she was amazed that she was standing on her feet. It was like a punch of agony centered in her soul that spread out through her entire being.

She couldn't make up for what she had allowed Douglas to do. For what she hadn't realized he was doing. She'd known that all along. Known that there was no absolution, no forgiveness for the crimes he had committed. The crimes she had unknowingly committed in trusting the man she had been married to.

There was no way anyone else could forgive her either. There had been two dozen Bengal Breeds. To her knowledge they had all died but one. Cabal. The most fierce, the most dangerous of them all.

"That has nothing to do with this," she argued, aware that her voice as well as her argument was weak.

It was no more than she had thought herself. She fought to make the world see what she saw once she had gotten to know the Breeds. Men and women fighting for survival. It didn't matter what they had been created to be. What mattered was what they were, honorable, strong.

"It has everything to do with this, Cassa," he growled as he jerked a pair of jeans from a dresser and pulled them on. "You think putting yourself in the line of fire will make anyone see you differently?"

Cassa whirled around so he wouldn't see the pain in her face. It was exactly what she had hoped. That the Breeds, should they ever learn the extent of what Douglas had done, would believe that she hadn't been a part of it. She had hoped that it would ease the hatred she feared Cabal felt for her.

"Whether they see me differently or not doesn't matter," she said quietly as she turned back to him and fought to bury the pain deep enough that even his Breed senses wouldn't detect it. "What matters is how I see myself. And I wouldn't like what I saw in the mirror every morning if I just walked away from this."

She walked away from him instead. She didn't bother to stalk out of the room; she didn't think she had the energy for that. She just walked away, returned to the living room and the clothes scattered across the floor.

Her clothes as well as his.

Shaking her head at her own feeling of failure, she hurriedly dressed before picking up the pack she carried as a purse and leaving the cabin.

The walk was going to suck, but it wouldn't suck near as bad as staying here and staring into his eyes, knowing that nothing she did, no matter how much she loved him, would ever make up for what her ex-husband had done. Or for how much he blamed her for the chance that Douglas had had to deceive the Breeds.

The air was chilled, the late winter weather moving in hard on the mountains as the temperature began to drop. It would be a long, cold walk back to town. But it couldn't be any longer, or any colder, than the past that stretched out behind her.

· C H A P T E R   1 7 ·

He followed her. Cassa had expected it. He was her mate. He was her hormonal, biological match. She would have snorted at that thought if she weren't so pissed off at him.

The walk back to town was a chilly one, but it gave her a chance to think, a chance to put things in perspective a bit more than she had already. Not that she had anything worked out, because she didn't.

When he pulled up next to her and the passenger door of the Raider slid open, she turned, looked at him for a long moment, then slammed the door closed.

She was here for a story; she wasn't here to be psychoanalyzed by a Bengal that had no idea the torment she had lived through because of his suffering. And she wasn't here to fight for the heart of a man who obviously didn't want to open his heart to her.

When she hit town, her legs were burning, her anger was building. She was nearing the entrance to the Kanawha Falls when a wicked, powerful black Harley pulled in from the parking lot and drew to a stop.

Dog.

His smirk was mocking, amused, as he glanced from her to the Raider.

"Want a ride?" he asked.

"I won't ride with him, why would I ride with you?" she snapped.

"Maybe because I'll give you answers, and he'd die and go to hell first?" he asked as she drew to a stop a second before Cabal did.

"Better hurry, here he comes," Dog laughed as the Raider drew to a quick stop.

Cassa pushed aside her misgivings about Dog, jumped on the back of the Harley and crossed her fingers with a prayer that she'd survive the ride.

Dog wouldn't hurt her so blatantly, she told herself, as she heard Cabal's vicious curse behind her and Dog roared off.

"Answers," she bit out furiously. "As you said, we don't have much time."

"You've been fucking up, Ms. Hawkins," he called back to her as she gripped the leather jacket he wore rather than wrapping her arms around him. She couldn't bear the thought of embracing him.

"No kidding," she said tersely. "Now tell me something I don't know."

Dog took the curves through the little town faster than she would have liked. The motorcycle vibrated and hummed like a powerful beast between her thighs and reminded her of the fact that she shouldn't be here, not like this, not with this Breed.

"Something you don't know?" he called back. "Something you don't know, Ms. Hawkins, is the same thing that your Bengal is figuring out."

"Just keep me in suspense, why don't you?" she called back as they neared the inn. "And if you don't mind, don't pass up my lodging."

His big body vibrated with a chuckle as he turned into the inn's parking lot, pulled around and parked close to the entrance, as Cabal pulled in behind them.

"Ask him why the killer contacted you, Ms. Hawkins," Dog suggested as she slid off the motorcycle. "Because he knows why you're here."

His statement had her stopping and staring back at him, her eyes narrowing, aware that Cabal was jumping from the Raider and moving toward them.

"Why?" she snapped.

"Because Watts was part of the Dozen, Cassa. He was part of it, and he's the one the killer wants."

With that surprising statement, Dog gunned the motor on the Harley and shot out of his parking space a second ahead of Cabal reaching them.

Cassa stared up at her mate, shock resounding through her as she saw the suspicion in his eyes, the knowledge. It was there, in the brilliant pinpoints of amber that gazed back at her. He had a piece of the puzzle that she should have had. He'd known something that important, and he hadn't told her.

"What would make your rogue killer think I can bring Douglas back from the dead? Or does he just think I should continue paying for his crimes?" Her voice was hoarse with tears she refused to shed, with an anger she refused to let free.

"Fuck!" The muttered curse was a testament to the rare honesty Dog had become afflicted with.

A part of her had hoped it was a lie, that the Coyote Breed didn't know what he was talking about. Dog wasn't known for his loyalty to the Breed community, quite the contrary. He was known for working with their enemies. In his own way of course. Rumor in the past year was that even Dog's handler wasn't always certain which side he was playing on.

"Yes, fuck," she stated with cold emphasis on the curse. "Fuck all of it, Cabal."

Turning, she stalked away from the Bengal, ignoring the need just for his touch. It wasn't sexual this time, and it should have been. Mating heat was reputed to always be sexual.

No, the need twisting inside her now was a need for his touch, for his hold. A need to curl against him and, for once in too many years, just heal a little.

She'd been alone since her parents' deaths, twelve years before. On the heels of that had been her marriage. Douglas had moved in, taken over and slowly destroyed the self-confidence Cassa had had within herself.

How easy she had been, she thought as she pushed into her room and tossed her pack on the nearby table. She had thought she loved him when she married him, but as the months went by, she realized it had been her grief that had had her leaning on him.

By then, it had been too late. Douglas had integrated himself into her life and had already begun sowing the seeds of her destruction.

She cursed her own ignorance with him. She'd been cursing it for eleven years now. She had made the mistake in trusting him, and she was still paying the price for it.

Sometimes she wondered if she would continue paying until the last breath she took. And beyond.

◆   ◆   ◆

Death watched the light flicker on in the room at the inn. How warm and inviting it looked from the opposite bank of the river. How many memories it brought back.

Too many memories. They were stacked from one end of the mind to the other, flickering across the imagination as pain ripped through a soul that had felt shattered for too many years.

Valentine's night. It had all happened then. Another anniversary was moving in quickly. Another year without a mate that had brightened every corner of a life that had been dark before that mating.

Death rubbed at arms that were still sensitive, that still ached for touch. There wasn't a cell that didn't miss the presence of the mate. It was like a disease, a steadily building fever that eventually destroyed the mind.

It never ended.

Once there had been warmth, laughter. There had been a place to belong. None of that existed now. There was no longer that place to belong or those arms to be held by. There was no longer the kiss that was needed to still the hunger that never stopped growing, never stopped tormenting or torturing the body or the mind.

It had created Death. This horrifying, gnawing emptiness that never went away. That never eased. The agony never eased, it never went away. It pulsed and echoed through the spirit until insanity would be a relief.

Many would think it was insanity now. It wasn't. Insanity was the inability to accept that what one did was wrong. Death was very well aware there was nothing right here. It was simply justice. And justice was all that mattered for the lives that had been taken. For the lives that could never be returned.

"You were once a handsome man." Death turned and stared at the bound, gagged victim who lay at the edge of the water.

His eyes were narrowed and filled with loathing. Filled with fury.

A smile crossed Death's lips. It was a brutal smile. One that flashed with razor-sharp teeth and intent.

Yes, Cash Winslow, a former CIA agent. He had once been a very handsome man. Tall and fit, his hair dark and silky, his eyes deceptively friendly. Once he had been someone Death had trusted. Trusted and been betrayed by.

"I remember that fishing trip we went on," Death said quietly, looking at the man Cash Winslow had aged into. "Do you remember?"

There were muffled sounds of rage behind the duct tape that covered his mouth.

"I caught the bigger fish. That big ole catfish. You ate with us, planned with us. We ate that big ole fish, tough as he was." And they had laughed, planned for Breed freedom and lives that were far different from the danger they had faced then.

Death turned back to Cash then, stared into those eyes. Those deceptive, lying eyes.

"You betrayed us all."

The chill from the river wrapped around a body that had been far colder than this on many nights. Nights when blankets didn't ease the chill, when even the memories couldn't warm the ice growing inside.

Death tapped gloved fingers against Winslow's forehead. His hair was gray now. He was a little over sixy. Aging. He wasn't as quick as he used to be, nor was he as intuitive. It had paid to allow time to pass before exacting revenge. The victims weren't nearly as agile as they used to be.

"I remember how close you were with so many of them," Death sighed painfully. "All of us."

Muttered sounds came from beneath the tape as Cash struggled desperately. It was pathetic really. He had once been fit and hard, muscular and rather handsome. He was now just a paunchy, overweight, balding old man. With a fishing line around his neck.

He had been bait once before. He had drawn them to the Coyote Breed that had supposedly escaped and needed help over the mountain.

"You came to us. You swore he was a victim, you argued for

his freedom and his safety. And you were our friend, we believed in you."

Standing straight and tall, Death stared down at Winslow with a heavy, broken soul.

"We believed in you."

There was no more time to waste. Gripping him beneath the shoulders, it was no hardship to lift him and scoot him the small distance to the edge of the river, to the boulders several feet away.

He struggled, but that was okay. The struggle was preferable. That meant there was still some life left in him. When he went under the water, he would suffer. He would know pain, for a few moments at least.

"The water is very cold. Cold enough that hypothermia will come fairly quickly. Which is really too bad. I was hoping to make you suffer just a while longer. I was hoping to taste your blood, but this is the wrong time for that, isn't it?"

Blood would have been nice. Ripping his throat out would have been so much better than simply watching him drown. But his death needed to leave a message. Bait. There were many who would know what this meant. Many who would see the significance, but none who would know the answer.

"Loyalty," Death whispered. "It's repaid. Just as death is avenged. You killed us all."

He was struggling, fighting. It wouldn't do any good. There was only one place on the bank that he could reach safety, and she had that covered. He was going to die, and she was going to watch him die.

"You and Watts." The hiss was filled with hatred, with the brutal need for blood. "You and Watts planned it. You executed it."

A strong, hard kick to his back sent him tumbling into the water. The splash wasn't nearly as satisfying as the sounds of screams when their throats came out, but it was better than watching him breathe. It was better than knowing he lived so much as a moment longer.

Gripping the line looped around Winslow's neck, it was an easy matter to keep him in the deep pool of water chosen for his deathbed.

Wickedly sharp canines flashed in the night as a smile pulled at chilled, chapped lips. He was struggling, fighting the line, searching for a toehold, a way to draw in air, and there was no way to do so.

Tugging at the line, Death hummed a little melody and stared into the cloud-laden skies. It would snow by morning. The Breeds would find an icy corpse, and no trace of the murderer. That was the best way to kill. Without a trace. No DNA. No evidence, just the body to show the passing of life.

As Winslow's struggles ceased and his body became a dead-weight against the line, Death knelt on a boulder and stared into the murky water at the body below.

"Roses are red. Violets are blue. I remember, mate, and how I miss you."

There were tears in the voice that whispered the words. Tears and grief. Had it truly been more than two decades since life had turned so dark and bleak? It hurt as though it had happened yesterday. An hour ago. It hurt until the agony was like an open, festering wound that refused to heal.

"I miss both of you."

Death wiped at a face without tears. They had stopped falling so long ago.

Moving slowly, the fishing line was attached to a sturdy limb of a nearby tree, and on its end a photo was attached.

Let them make of this what they would.

Turning to stare into the well-lit window of the room Cassa Hawkins had taken, bleak eyes narrowed and rage built again.

She had mated that Bengal. Damn her. She had mated a Breed. That made it harder. It shouldn't have. Death hadn't thought it would. But it did. There was regret, but so little remorse.

A mate would have to be sacrificed. But so many had already been sacrificed, did another really matter? The end result was what mattered. The end result, and the death of those who had destroyed so much.

"Good-bye, Cash Winslow," Death whispered with a feeling of relief. "Seven down. Four to go. And one to die again."

CHAPTER 18

*Because Watts was part of the Dozen, Cassa. He was part of it,
and he's the one the killer wants.*

Dog's statement ran through Cassa's mind through most of
the night. Pacing the floor at the inn, she fought to understand
why a rogue Breed would think she should pay for what Douglas had done so long ago.

He had been part of the Deadly Dozen. She pulled up the
old, faded picture on her laptop and concentrated on the faces of
the twelve men in poor focus. One face in particular had always
caused her to pause, though she had never been certain why.

Now she knew why.

Douglas.

She squinted her eyes and stared closely at the face. It could
easily be Douglas when he was younger. The same blunt, squarish features. The same narrow, almost cruel lips. He was much
younger. At least ten to fifteen years younger than he had been
when Cassa was married to him. He'd been several years older
than her.

The murders during the Valentine's night massacre had taken
place eleven years before the revelation of the Breeds. About
twenty-two years, Cassa surmised. Valentine's night, no more than

a few weeks from now, would be the twenty-second anniversary of that massacre.

"God, Douglas, what did you do?" she whispered as she closed out the picture before logging into the Bureau of Breed Affairs History section.

There were no stories on that night, nothing to shed any light on what had happened. The truth of that event would have to come from a local source. And she needed something more than the sheriff had given them.

Danna Lacey had been a part of the Breed freedom movement in Glen Ferris. She had been part of the group that had fought beside the Breeds and attempted to provide some measure of security to those who escaped there.

She hadn't been a part of the leadership though. She would have been too young. No, whoever had led those Breeds with Patrick Wallace would have to be much older now. Such as Walt.

In this little town there were so many secrets where the Breeds were concerned. The citizens that had been a part of the movement had kept close vigilance on the Breeds, and the Breeds themselves had made certain they stayed hid in those days.

Even now, they stayed in the background.

Tapping her finger against the laptop for a second, Cassa pondered the best way to get the information she needed.

She would love to track Dog down for more questioning, but she had a feeling that wasn't going to happen. Cabal was keeping a close eye on her, and meeting with another Breed would be just about impossible to accomplish.

Maybe.

She pulled her sat phone from the pocket of her jeans, flipped it open and keyed in a number.

"Mordecai." The Coyote Breed presently affiliated with the Feline Breed compound, Sanctuary, answered on the first ring.

"I'm calling in a favor," she stated.

Silence filled the line. She could almost feel the intractable Breed mulling over possibilities and wondering which favor she would call.

"You have a surplus," he finally sighed. "Will it get me killed?"

She almost grinned at that. She couldn't imagine Mordecai contemplating death, let alone worrying if it would affect him.

"I guess anything is possible," she mused. "You backing out?"

He grunted at that. "Life's too long sometimes anyway. Who do you want me to kill?"

"No one this week," she promised.

Actually, she had never wanted him to kill anyone, he just always seemed so enthusiastic to do so.

"Too bad," he muttered. "Go ahead."

"I'm in Glen Ferris investigating the Valentine's night massacre that occurred around twenty-two years ago. A dozen or so Breeds were murdered, along with mates. Do you know anything about that?"

Sometimes Breeds knew things. Information was carried between them, held close to their chests, but there if the right question was asked at the right time.

"Bits and pieces," he answered. "Nothing that could help you, I'd imagine. A dozen or so as you said, some were mated, there was a rumor that there were unborn children murdered."

"Dog is here. He knows something."

Mordecai cursed. "Stay the fuck away from Dog, Cassa. He's bad news."

"Which side is he on?"

"His own side," Mordecai grunted. "That's where Dog has always been and where he will always be. If he's in Glen Ferris fuckin' in Cabal's and Jonas's business, then clear out."

"I need to talk to him, Mordecai."

And Mordecai owed her. She was the one who had tracked down the location of several Breeds that were taken from the labs where he was held, just before the rescues. She had found his natural brother and told no one but Mordecai of his location.

There were other favors the Coyote owed her for. Information she had given him when needed. Papers she had provided him that were illegal. A few small exchanges among friends.

"Bad news," Mordecai muttered. "You are in the mood to get me killed this week."

"You can arrange it," she told him. "Contact him. He knows I'm here; he tried to talk to me once, but Cabal interrupted us."

"And he'll keep interrupting."

"Not if Dog has my sat phone number. Not if someone gives it to him. I'll take care of the rest."

She had two of the pills left that she hadn't given to Jonas. Just in case she needed them. She would use them if she had to. If Cabal forced her into it.

"Hell," Mordecai cursed. "Contacting him directly isn't exactly easy, sweetheart."

"I have confidence in you." Cassa moved back to the window and gazed across the river.

She almost smiled at the sight of the small fire on the opposite bank. A fisherman, no doubt, though it was damned cold to be fishing.

She frowned as the blaze flickered in shades of red and gold. It was close to the falls, where the water ran swifter, faster. An odd place, and an odd night, to be fishing the treacherous waters.

"I'll see what I can do," Mordecai finally sighed. "If he's going to call, you'll hear from him soon though. Dog's not predictable. And you be damned careful."

"As always, my friend," she assured him. "When dealing with Breeds, one learns to be real damned careful."

She almost laughed at his little grunt of acknowledgment. Flipping the phone closed, she slid it back into her jeans pocket and continued to watch the blaze in the distance for long seconds, as she tried to pinpoint why it bothered her.

She was drawn out of her reverie by the muted alarm on her laptop. The email alarm was set for one email address specifically.

That of a killer.

◆　◆　◆

Cabal stood at Jonas's side, a communications link at his ear, tuned to the quiet chatter of the enforcers securing the perimeter as the body was pulled out of the water.

There were no lights this close to the scene of the death. The fire had been doused the moment he and Jonas arrived on the scene, and as Cabal glanced toward the darkened sky, he only prayed they could clean everything up before daylight painted its first rays over the water to reveal the murder none of them wanted seen.

He turned his gaze from the sky to the inn across the expanse of the river, his eyes narrowing on the window of Cassa's room.

What was she doing now? No doubt going over the pictures a killer had sent her, tracking the location, making plans to arrive here as quickly as possible. The moment he received notice of the killing himself, Jonas had attempted to intercept the email he had known she would receive. It hadn't worked. The email had been delivered, and the program attached to it didn't allow for remote corruption or deletion.

The rogue wanted her to know about this. He wanted her involved in this. She was a pawn in a very dangerous game, and he was growing sick of it.

"She's been informed," Jonas said quietly as Cabal glanced over at the director. "Confirmation just arrived. The email has been read, pictures downloaded. The remote tracker we have on her laptop is working at least."

"Traced?" Cabal asked, though he knew better.

Jonas shook his head. There was no mockery, no sarcasm this time. This was the second email they'd tried to trace through Cassa's connection, to no avail.

The director's expression was somber, brooding and filled with icy fury. Jonas was at his most dangerous in this mood.

"No trace," he bit out in clipped tones. "The program we installed isn't going through. The email itself is embedded with a program that doesn't allow for it. Dane hasn't been able to crack it yet."

Dane Vanderale, Jonas's nemesis and half brother, as well as the heir to the powerful African Vanderale empire, was a natural born Breed and a thorn in all their sides. But he was the best they had at cracking codes and tracing information.

"He'll crack it." Cabal shrugged.

Cabal turned his gaze back to the bank then and the body Rule and Lawe had pulled from the water. The fishing line around the victim's neck had cut into the skin, leaving a slender wound. Tape covered his mouth. Pale eyes bulged in horror; pale features were creased into lines of pain, suffering.

Someone, something, had made this man suffer.

"Cash Winslow," Rule stated as he crouched next to the body before staring up at Jonas. "We've been watching him. Ex-CIA. He worked for Brandenmore as a security specialist."

Jonas moved closer to the river-soaked body and hitched up the legs of his slacks so he could get down on his haunches and look at the features revealed by the slender illumination of Lawe's flashlight.

"He was working on a special assignment from what we were able to find out," Jonas mused quietly. "We were trying to track him, trying to figure out what the hell Brandenmore was up to, when he flipped off our radar last week."

Cabal's brows lifted. It was rare that anyone flipped off Jonas's radar.

"No rumors as to the assignment?" Cabal asked.

Jonas stared back at him. "He was searching for someone, that's all we knew. Someone Brandenmore was certain could help him with this case we have against him and Engalls."

The attempted murder and illegal research against Breeds. Phillip Brandenmore and his brother-in-law Horace Engalls were coming closer to the day of reckoning and possible Breed Law sanctions for their actions over the past year. How the hell they thought anyone could help them was beyond Cabal.

"Any idea who?" he asked.

Jonas shook his head. "All we knew was that he supposedly had information against the Breeds that Brandenmore wanted to use as a bargaining tool. We were trying to find him when our killer sent the message that he'd beaten us to him."

Cabal breathed out deeply before wiping his hand wearily over his lower jaw. Hell, this was becoming more of a mystery by the day.

"He was meeting Brandenmore or Engalls here?" Lawe questioned the director quietly as he motioned to several enforcers to collect the body.

"Not here he wasn't." Jonas straightened before staring around the wooded area with a frown. "There wasn't a chance of them escaping the men the Bureau has watching them and they know it. They wouldn't have risked it."

"Then who was he meeting?" Cabal asked.

"Our killer." Jonas's voice was cold, hard steel, a clear indication that the rogue they were searching for was beginning to try the director's patience. "Unfortunately for him, or for us, our rogue chose the wrong mark this time. I had plans for Winslow. I'd have preferred to mete out my own justice rather than clean up after another's."

Cash Winslow had information. Information Jonas was hoping to use against Brandenmore. Information Jonas would have paid for by granting Winslow his own freedom from prosecution once they had him brought in for questioning.

According to their investigation, over the past several years Cash had been involved in the kidnapping of several Breeds that the pharmaceutical owners had used for their research. According to their sources, it was also possible that Winslow knew the location of an infant that had been taken from a mate's body just before her death.

That child was one of the few naturally conceived children that were the hope for the Breeds' future. A child that would be used for research, nothing more, if it wasn't found. Finding that child drove Jonas, Cabal knew that, just as it had driven the rest of them for the past year. The thought of a babe, created naturally by the hand of God rather than the hand of man, suffering the horrors they had suffered, gave them all nightmares.

"They'll take care of the babe for the first few years," Lawe mused soberly. "They're too delicate after birth. They won't risk its death."

"Yet," Rule growled. "Winslow knew where the fuckers stashed that child. As far as we know, he's the only one besides Brandenmore and Engalls who knew."

And they sure as hell weren't talking.

Cabal turned away from the director as well as the two enforcers that were now a part of his own team to listen to the reports coming over the link.

"There's nothing on-site." He turned back to Jonas. "No sign of anyone. No tracks, no scents, no vehicle tracks."

"Fucking ghost," Jonas cursed.

"Or so he'd have us think." Cabal shrugged as his gaze moved back to Winslow's lifeless body. "Seven down. Four to go and one to die again," he stated, repeating the message that had come through Jonas's personal sat phone several hours earlier.

Jonas stared back at him silently, and understanding the look wasn't a problem for Cabal.

"We know the last one," Jonas stated. "Help me with the other four, Cabal. Tell me you have names by now. Something."

"Ivan Vilanov, former Russian intelligence officer, a double agent for the CIA. He was one of Winslow's assets at one time. I identified him from the picture last night with some help from a few new buddies I found at a bar near Gauley Bridge. He was a regular here more than twenty years ago, during his assignment to the Russian Embassy in D.C. Hunting weekends with Brandenmore and Engalls both here in the States as well as in Europe."

Jonas rubbed at the bridge of his nose in disgust. "He's missing. Son of a bitch. A report came through Homeland Security less than twenty-four hours ago. He slipped away within hours of being picked up for questioning in the case we have against Brandenmore and Engalls."

Cabal grimaced at the information. "I have some other names, but I'm running them. Banks's body hasn't turned up yet. Walt Jameson thinks he's still alive. I think its possible. Whoever this Breed is, he would have left the body to be found within twenty-four hours of his death, just as he has the others."

"Does Walt have any idea who this could be?" Jonas bit out furiously.

Cabal shook his head. "It's obviously connected to the massacre that took place in the valley we found Alonzo's body in. The Breeds that were part of that group that night were all killed though, according to all the information we've been able to come up with. Walt gave me the names, I ran them. There's no one unaccounted for."

Each Breed on that list had either arrived back at the labs dead, head intact, or just the head had been returned and payment collected.

"Any way someone fucked up?" Jonas asked.

Cabal rejected the suggestion. "If they fucked up, then I haven't found proof of it. There was DNA proof of each kill. That's damned hard to fake."

"Someone fucked up somewhere," Jonas assured him. "Forward that list of names to my sat. I'll go through them myself. I want to know every man and woman in that group, Breed or human, and their connection to everyone in this fucking town. And I want it yesterday."

"It was forwarded just before I left the inn to meet with you here," Cabal informed him. "Good luck with it."

Jonas was silent once again, his expression brooding, uncomfortably cold as Cabal watched him.

"We know who the last one is," he finally said. "The one that gets to die again." He narrowed his eyes on Cabal. "Tell her."

"No." Cabal realized the instant refusal was more instinct than intellect.

"If you don't, the killer's going to," Jonas told him. "What then?"

"He can't prove a damned thing," Cabal growled. "There's no way to get proof and no way to get to him. Forget it, Jonas. It's not happening."

Jonas shook his head. "The best laid plans," he sighed. "This isn't going to end up well, Cabal. You're fucking up."

"Then it's my fuckup."

Douglas Watts was dead to the world, and as far as Cabal was concerned, he was going to stay dead.

"How did our rogue Breed know Watts was still alive?" Lawe asked, the question barely a breath of sound. "That information was contained to just a few Breeds."

Jonas shook his head. "I suspect it was information Winslow was sent to find proof of. We know his last assignment took him overseas. We lost him for a while there. Weeks later the first killings began. It's tied in." He turned back to Cabal. "You know it's tied in. And you know where it's leading."

He'd known all along where it was leading, but that didn't mean he had to like it, and it damned sure didn't mean he had to handle it however Jonas dictated.

Cassa was his mate, plain and simple. Period. Nothing was going to change that, and there was no reason that he could think of to muddy the waters of the mating with the knowledge that the man she had believed she was married to was still alive.

Watts had lied to her, cheated on her. He had betrayed her trust in the most elemental fashion from the beginning. The wedding had been no more than a farce, because Watts didn't believe in contracts or promises. The preacher that had married them had been no more than an actor hired to act the part. The papers signed, the marriage license—the whole deal was no more than a collection of props.

Watts liked drama. He liked ceremony. He had enjoyed fooling everyone so effectively. It had been his own private little joke, and now the joke was on Watts. The woman he had thought he would hold through lies now belonged to one of the creatures he had so despised. One he had thought he could destroy.

"Drop it, Jonas," Cabal warned him as he watched the eerie silver of the other man's gaze shift thoughtfully.

Jonas was studying the situation, considering it, coming up with the most effective way to ensure that Cabal moved to the correct spot on the mental chessboard he was certain Jonas often used.

Jonas shook his head. "Hell of a way to start a life together," he stated. "You can't hide something like this forever. It always ends up biting you on the ass, my friend."

"It's my ass at risk." Cabal shrugged.

Jonas's lips had parted to say more when a warning hiss echoed across the communications link.

Cabal felt the premonition in his gut, knew exactly who the enforcers were stalking before the name ever came across the line. He was only surprised that it had taken her this long to get here. She must have been damned careful attempting to slip past the perimeter patrol.

"Reporter." Mordecai spoke quietly through the link. "Bengal's mate."

Damn. He didn't want her here; she had no business here. It would only entrench her deeper in the danger he could already feel swirling around her.

Cabal clenched his teeth furiously before sprinting away from Jonas and heading for the tree line. He could smell her now. There was no breeze rippling through the trees, which had given her the advantage in slipping through the forest toward the murder scene.

She was clearing the edge of the forest at a fast clip as he moved toward her. Dressed in black, her long hair pushed beneath a cap, her expression furious, she found him instantly with her stormy gaze, even as the enforcers securing the area converged on either side of her.

"This isn't going to work," she snapped immediately as she pushed past enforcers reluctant to force her back as long as her mate was in the vicinity.

And there was no missing the fact that she was his. The mating scent, as well as his scent, wrapped around her, infused her. It was more effective than a brand, that scent. It held the other males back, had them watching her as well as Cabal warily.

"What the hell are you doing here?" he growled, his fingers wrapping around her upper arm as he drew her to him, then turned her to head back down the bank in the direction they had parked the Raiders.

She jerked at the hold he had on her as the scent of her anger slapped his senses. She was pissed, and he could feel his senses reacting to that aggression and the mating heat that surged between them.

She was endangering herself, placing herself in the line of fire, and for the first time in his life Cabal felt true fear that he could lose his mate.

"What the hell do you think I'm doing here?" she retorted as she began digging her heels into the sand and resisting his hold. "Let's see, exactly why am I here? What brought me here? Could it have been those nasty little pictures a killer is sending me? Could it be that you have a rogue killer on the loose who's threatening to send those pictures to a list of reporters who couldn't give a damn if the Breeds survive this particular story?"

Cabal came to a hard stop. "What did you say?"

A mocking smile curled her lips. "Let me guess, you didn't get that little message? Let me ask you this one, did you get the audio file of his death?"

Somehow, she knew he hadn't. Cabal knew he hadn't, just as he knew that Jonas hadn't received it.

"You brought it with you?"

There could be clues in an audio file. Clues they could use to find the killer. Not that he expected that this particular killer had left much in the way of clues. He had been too smart so far.

"Did I say I brought it with me?" Her eyes narrowed on him. "Don't play games with me. I want to know what you've found here, and I want to know who the hell the killer is talking about when he says that the last one to die is one who was dead and will die again. What the hell kind of game is being played here, Cabal?"

CHAPTER 19

Anger was a horrible emotion. It stayed, lingered, brewed and built inside until Cassa felt as though she were going to explode.

Two days after the discovery of Cash Winslow's death, she watched the news report of the supposedly fiery car crash he had been involved in while driving from D.C.

His vehicle had hit ice—plausible, there was a light snow in the mountains—and plunged through the guardrail to explode at the bottom of a treacherous mountain cliff.

Dozens were mourning the loss of the security advisor, the reporter related. The ex–government agent was suspected to have been drinking and driving.

"Could you have used anything more clichéd?" she muttered as Cabal paced the room behind her, his narrowed gaze drifting to the reporter before turning back to her.

"It's clichéd because it works," he growled.

She shrugged nonchalantly as she continued to watch the news report, her gaze keeping track of the time at the corner of the television screen.

Two days. She'd slept in her own bed during those two days, alone. He'd taken her, but if any dared to call it making love, then she would have become violent. Not that that made it much different from the first time, or the times after it. She was merely noticing that there was definitely more and more Cabal was holding back.

Was it tenderness? He was always gentle with her, always careful . . . Perhaps that was it. He was too careful. Too conscious of each touch, while keeping her helpless in a sensual maelstrom that didn't allow much of a chance for her to assert her own sexuality.

Mating heat and a mission that Cabal was refusing to allow her to be a part of weren't going hand in hand here. And she was tired of bitching over it. She hated to whine, and begging wasn't her style.

"I have a meeting to go to." The deep rasp of his voice sent a thrill of response down her spine.

Of course he had a meeting to go to. Jonas was waiting for him two floors above, along with whatever evidence they had taken from her computer and the latest crime scene.

"Figures." She gave another shrug and kept her attention on the television, carefully controlling her response to him as well as her own plans.

"I'll be a while." There was an edge of impatience to his voice now.

"Take your time." She waved him away, allowing just enough of her own anger to show to allay any suspicions that she might be hiding something or have a meeting of her own planned.

Text messaging was a wonderful, wonderful invention. And Dog was so sneakily efficient that he even avoided messaging while Cabal was in the room with her. That was damned scary. It made her wonder if he had an eye in her room, or an ear, that Cabal might have overlooked.

She glanced over at her mate to catch him watching her silently. On second thought, she doubted he'd missed anything, especially not an electronic bug in either of their rooms.

"Look, Cassa, I know you don't understand my need to protect you . . ."

"Don't start." She held her hand up in a halting motion. "I'm not fighting you any further."

His lips thinned in irritation. For the past two days she had refused to discuss his stubborn insistence that she wasn't a part of this investigation. She wasn't arguing anymore.

"We're going to have to discuss it." The words came from between gritted teeth. Poor little Bengal, at the rate he was going he wasn't going to have any molars left by the time he left Glen Ferris.

By the time she left him.

"You mean I'm going to have to agree with you and turn my independence over to you sooner or later," she retorted sweetly. "Nope, sorry, my pretty striped tiger, it's not gonna happen."

A frown jumped between his brows at her mocking pet name for him. He hated any references to those sexy-as-hell stripes. Too bad, because she rather liked them herself.

"That wasn't what I meant." There went another layer of those molars.

"Don't you have a meeting to go to?" She turned the television up louder as she settled more comfortably in her chair and directed her attention to the weather for Glen Ferris for the next week. Looked like it was going to be colder than normal. Big surprise there.

Behind her, Cabal blew out a hard breath. "I'll be back in a few hours. Maybe we could go downstairs for dinner when I get back."

She shrugged. She had no desire to eat with him, not when she was getting ready to share burgers with a Coyote who had information.

Damn Cabal. Did he think the thought of a meal with him was going to make up for what he was trying to take away from her?

"Cassa." He was in front of her before she could move away, bending until he could stare into her eyes, his knees bracketing her legs as the backs of his fingers brushed against her cheek.

The curiously gentle caress had unbidden tears threatening to moisten her eyes. And that, after she had promised herself she wasn't going to cry.

She stared back at him coolly. He might be able to smell the turmoil brewing inside her, but that didn't mean she was going to allow him to see it. And it sure as hell didn't mean she was going to beg.

"What?" Her voice was husky, a measure of the emotion slipping free to roughen the tone as the very nearness of him affected her senses.

"I'm not trying to steal your independence."

Oh yeah, she believed that one. She could see the proof of his statement. Yeah, boy. Sitting right here as big as life and as ignorant as a rock was Cassa Hawkins. Slammed right out of an investigation that involved her more than it likely did any Breed that Jonas Wyatt had brought in to investigate it.

None of those Breeds had been married to the man the killer wanted. A man who was dead.

She stared back at him silently. Refusing once again to argue her own points or the dishonesty of his statement.

His hand cupped her cheek. She expected him to kiss her, to pull her to him, to infuse her senses with the taste of the mating hormone that she knew would fill the kiss. Instead, he leaned forward, his head lowered, and his lips pressed against the sensitive flesh at the bend of her neck and shoulder.

The kiss was poignantly tender and filled with all the warmth, the need, that she had wanted to feel when his body covered hers at night. It held everything he had refused to give her at any other time.

"I just want you safe," he whispered, his forehead pressing against her shoulder then. "Just that, Cassa."

She shook her head as she stared across the room miserably. "You can't lock me up. And that's what you're doing, Cabal. You're doing the one thing you would kill to keep anyone from ever doing to you again."

He tensed, then slowly pulled back from her. The amber in his eyes glittered with anger. She'd pricked his arrogance, his male assurance that he knew what was best for her. She didn't need him making such decisions for her, and she didn't need his so-called protection.

"You don't know nearly as much as you think you do," he assured her, his voice harsh as he rose to his feet, towering over her. "This isn't a case of wanting your goddamned independence, Cassa."

"Then it's a case of you wanting everything your own damned way, Cabal," she burst out with, pushing to her feet and pacing across the room. "Look, just go to your damned meeting. I have work here to do, and I sure as hell don't need your help."

She stalked to her laptop, stared at the screen and tried to fight back the fear she couldn't keep from building inside her. The fear that somehow the past was darker, harsher than she had ever believed.

The information she had found in the past two days on Douglas, information she hadn't had before, hadn't bothered to find, was beginning to give her panic attacks. Reports on the Deadly Dozen, from Breeds who had survived being captured by them, were violent, vicious. Among those reports were those of a single male and the horrifying acts he had practiced on the female Breeds that were captured.

Not just the acts, but also his pleasure, the joy he'd found in practicing them.

"You don't need anything from anyone, do you?" he growled, coming behind her, his large body bracketing hers, shocking her with the sudden heat that poured through her.

Mating heat and anger didn't mix. She could feel the blood pounding through her system just that fast. She could feel the heat of his flesh beneath his clothes, the warmth of his palm as it settled on her stomach.

"This won't fix anything." She tried to keep her voice strong, sure, but there was too much awareness, too much need for him.

She sucked in her breath as his fingers found the button and zipper for her jeans. They released, too damned slowly.

Cassa closed her eyes, drew in a hard, deep breath and fought the wave of dizzying need that assailed her.

It was always like this. Her nails dug into the top of the small desk as his hand slid into her jeans and found the wet heat between her thighs.

"You want me," he accused her roughly. "How can it not fix at least this?"

Yes, she wanted him.

Her head fell back against his chest as his fingers parted the plump folds of her pussy, delved inside and filled her with the exciting rasp of his fingers caressing her.

Behind her, she could feel him releasing his jeans, felt the hard, jutting length of his cock pressing against her lower back, and she knew what was coming. She knew, and she couldn't stop it.

"Bend over, baby." His voice was rough, sensual, as one hand pressed against her back. "So sweet, Cassa. You make me drunk on the taste of you, the touch of you."

If only she could make him fall in love. If only she could make him respect her. If only . . .

She bent for him instead, her upper body lowering as she braced her shoulders on the top of the table and felt her jeans and panties sliding over her hips.

God, this was so primal. Sexy. She had never been taken like this, hadn't imagined she would want to be until she heard his broken breathing behind her and the heated little growls that escaped his throat.

"Fucking you is like flying." The head of his cock pressed closer, slid through her juices and found the entrance it sought. "Like dying, Cassa. The sweetest escape in the world."

Her back bowed as she felt the thick flesh pressing inside. Tingles of electric, ecstatic energy sizzled through her, inside her. They surrounded her clit, struck at her nipples. She trembled beneath the force of the energy and fought to keep from crying out as he stretched her slowly, easily.

His hands gripped her hips, holding her in place. She wanted to see his face, but she was feeling something she hadn't felt the other times when she had lain beneath him. She felt more now. As though he were letting go of something he'd held inside.

His hips moved with a smooth, pumping rhythm. Each stroke of his erection inside her pushed the pleasure higher, pushed her closer to the center of sensation and bliss.

Cassa could feel herself tightening, close to coming apart with the pleasure. She was riding a sensation so desperate, so filled with ecstasy that she wondered if she could survive it.

She wanted to scream but couldn't find the breath. She wanted to cry out his name, to beg, to plead for more, and couldn't find the strength. She could do nothing but hold on to the wood of the tabletop, lift to her tiptoes and silently plead for more.

As though he could read her mind, he gave it to her. Harder, faster strokes. The thrusts of his cock inside her stroked hidden nerve endings, revealed others. It stretched and burned, and as the pace increased to a driving, desperate rhythm, her orgasm began to tear through her.

It exploded in her clit, ricocheted to her womb, then detonated in the center of her pussy and left her trying to scream, to cry out with such a surfeit of sensation that shudders began to race through her.

She was lost in him. So lost that little else mattered, nothing else made sense for long, agonizing moments. Until she felt his release pour into her, felt the barb extend from beneath the head of his cock, locking him into her and creating another climax that completely stole her breath.

He was there with her. Through the violent tremors, he held her to his chest, arched over her, sheltered her from a storm that wrapped around her as well as inside her.

His fingers tugged her hair, turned her head to the side, and as she fought to hold on to the last shred of reality, his lips covered hers. His tongue licked over her lips, stroked them, then slid inside and spread the fiery heat of the mating hormone into their kiss.

It infused the last pulsing tremors of her orgasm, intensified it, tightened her muscles and left her shaking rather than trembling, left her arching to him, desperate for more.

His lips slid from hers despite her whimpering cry. He kissed and licked his way down her neck, then before she could prepare herself, his teeth bit down on the mating mark at her shoulder and his tongue rasped over it.

Shivers began to course through her, quaking through her body as a muted scream tore from her throat. Finally, there was the emotion. Now, when she couldn't see it on his face, couldn't define it. When it couldn't soothe the pain racing through her heart.

She wanted to cry at the unfairness of it. Because she knew once it was over nothing would change. She would still be relegated to being the protected rather than the protector she had been for so many years. She would be behind him rather than beside him. And beside him was where she longed to be.

"I'd die without you," he whispered at her ear, his voice rough, dark, rasping with an emotion she wished she could define, could see on his face. "Do you understand that, Cassa? If anything happens to you, then I'm nothing."

Because she was his mate. Because once mated, there was never another for them.

Of course he would fear losing her. He would want her behind walls, locked away from danger, safely in his bed.

She had to fight back tears long moments later as the barb receded and he eased from her. She could still feel the pulse and throb of his cock inside her in the echoes of her release. The heat of him was a memory that even her flesh couldn't let go of.

"I'd do anything to protect you, Cassa," he swore as he helped her straighten her clothes.

She kept her back to him. She couldn't look at him, not yet. She couldn't let him see her tears, or her regrets. Loving him wasn't going to be enough and she knew it, because she knew she could never be what he needed.

"I don't need your protection." She fought to keep the pain out of her tone even as she kept her back to him. "I never asked you for that."

"It's here anyway," he promised her. "I can't do anything else."

There was an edge in his voice, not really of anger, irritation perhaps.

Cassa shook her head. "It doesn't matter, Cabal, we're never going to agree on this. And until we agree, nothing is going to change."

She couldn't allow him to win this battle—if he won this one, then she would never know a moment's independence again.

She moved slowly from the table back to her chair, before taking her seat with a sense of weariness. Suddenly, she felt tired, uncertain. She had no idea where to go from here or how to convince him that he would end up destroying her.

She turned her head, watching as he straightened his clothing, his gaze glittering with amber frustration.

"I'll be back later. We'll discuss this then," he stated as he stalked across the room to the door.

"Of course we will." Her smile was tight, sad. "I'll just sit right here and wait on you like the good little mate you think I should be."

"Is that what I ask from you?" Anger was invading his tone now.

"Have you asked anything else from me?" she asked quietly.

The door slammed behind him in response, a clear indication that his temper was riding the same thin line as the arousal that bound them.

The sarcasm in her voice should have warned him. If it hadn't, then he would learn in time, she assured herself.

Pushing back the fear was the hard part. The fear that defying him would earn her more than his arrogance or harsh words. That it would earn a slap, or something worse.

She wasn't a coward, but she had been taught her limits of physical endurance years before, during one of the most hellish periods of her life.

God, what had made her think that Douglas wouldn't betray his own career then? He had betrayed her, over and over again. His career wouldn't have mattered any more to him than she had. Selling the Breeds and their rescuers out to the Council wouldn't have caused him to lose a moment's sleep. What had ever made her believe otherwise?

And what had made her think she would ever be free of him? There wasn't a chance of being free, not ever again.

She watched the news for a while longer, keeping careful track of the time as she did so. She was to leave her room at precisely three minutes after four. No sooner, no later.

She rose from her chair at two minutes after, pulled on her jacket and moved to the door. As the time changed to three minutes after, she opened her door and stepped out as she slung her pack over her shoulder.

Striding to the elevator, she checked the time. Dog had given her exactly two minutes to make it to the back entrance of the inn.

As she stepped into the elevator, she had to fight the feeling that she was going too far. Contacting Dog wasn't a good idea— if Cabal ever learned of it . . . Meeting with him was an even worse idea.

How else was she supposed to get the answers she needed? How else was she supposed to find out why a killer thought he could kill Douglas again? Unless he meant to kill him through her.

She shook her head at the thought. The killer wasn't insane. There wasn't even a hint of insanity in what had transpired so far. Vengeance, yes. Anger, perhaps. But there was nothing crazy.

Did the killer think Douglas was still alive?

The thought almost froze her in her place as the elevator doors opened on the lobby floor, depositing her in the deserted hall.

Douglas wasn't alive. She had seen him die; she knew she had. There on the floor of that horrible lab, a steel spike driven into his back.

She stepped into the hall, her steps slowing as she moved to the back entrance of the inn.

She hadn't actually seen him die. She hadn't seen his body at the burial. It was a closed casket funeral, supposedly at the request of family.

She'd wondered at the time, What family? Douglas had never mentioned family to her.

Lifting her head, Cassa paused at the back entrance, her hand clenched around the strap of her pack as she fought with the questions raging through her mind.

This killer was smart, methodical. He had managed to get seven men to return to Glen Ferris after word would have spread that the Dozen was being picked off, one by one. He knew what he was doing, and he knew how to do it.

He wanted Douglas. He wouldn't be satisfied with Douglas's wife.

She felt her heart racing in her chest now, and this time, it wasn't from arousal. It was from horror. Terror.

She could feel herself shaking her head, feel the knowledge burning into her soul as surely as the mating heat burned through her body.

"Turning back, Ms. Hawkins?"

She turned with a gasp at the sound of Dog's rough voice.

Eyes widening, she watched as he stepped from the doorway of one of the offices. Dressed in black leather, his silver and black hair framing his savage features, he looked like a demon come to collect souls.

Was her soul the one he had chosen? Or merely her life?

"You were supposed to meet me outside," she said, feeling the fear as it rose inside her with a vengeance.

"So I was." His brow arched with curious amusement. "And you were supposed to actually step outside that door thirty-five seconds ago. You're late."

"So I am." She stepped back as he moved a step forward.

What had she done? She had known even as she stepped from that elevator that she was making a mistake. That she should have never agreed to this meeting. Now she could feel that certainty to the very marrow of her bones.

She should have never allowed herself to be drawn away from Cabal so effectively. She should have fought this out with him rather than trying to solve things the same way she had done all her life. Her way. Silently. Stubbornly.

Douglas had once told her that her stubbornness was going to cause him to kill her. Maybe, in a way, he had always been right.

"So much fear." Dog scoffed mockingly as he watched her,

his head tilted to the side as one thumb rested just inside the pocket of his snug leather pants. "You should have thought of the wisdom of this meeting before arranging it perhaps."

No shit.

"I'm considering it now," she retorted. "Let me pass, Dog."

"Going to run back to your little Bengal then?" He grinned as he asked the question. "Tell me, Cassa, have you figured it out yet?"

Had she figured it out? She had a lot of suspicions and a lot of questions. But she had a feeling that Dog didn't have as many answers as he thought he had.

"What's there to figure out?" she questioned him instead. "Cabal will kill both of us if I leave here with you."

"Well, he'd kill one of us anyway." His lips quirked in a rueful smile. "Somehow, I doubt you'd be so lucky as to escape that easily though."

Somehow, she guessed he was right.

"We're not leaving the inn," he finally told her as he glanced up the hall before turning back to her. "I have no desire to end my existence quite yet, despite repeated attempts by others to hurry it along."

Cassa swallowed tightly as she stared back at him and wished to hell she had stayed in her room.

"What was I supposed to have figured out by now?" She returned to his previous question.

He shook his head slowly. "Mordecai seemed pretty confident that you were smarter than you're letting on," he sighed. "Tell me, Cassa, haven't you figured out yet why the killer drew you here? Why your Bengal refuses to allow you to be a part of what he's involved in?"

"Dog."

Cassa started, swinging around as Cabal stepped into the back hallway.

Talk about being caught between a rock and a hard place.

Her gaze swung between the two men as the eerie sense of danger began to wrap around her.

"What was I supposed to figure out?" she asked the Coyote as she ignored her mate. Ignored the man she loved and tried to ignore the suspicion that was beginning to make her sick inside.

"Drop this, Dog," Cabal warned quietly. "It's gone far enough."

"Perhaps it has," Dog sighed. "If the truth hasn't slapped her upside the head by now, then it isn't going to." He inclined his head toward her. "Next time you want to talk, Ms. Hawkins, try going through regular channels. It's normally safer for my ass that way."

"He's alive."

Dog froze. Time froze. Behind her, Cassa heard Cabal growl.

"Isn't he?" she whispered and turned back to stare at Cabal. "My husband is still alive."

CHAPTER 20

"He's not your fucking husband!" The words tore out of Cabal's mouth before he could stop them. For the first time in longer than he could remember, he spoke without thought, without considering the words that fell from his lips.

He hadn't meant to say it, not just like that. But he couldn't handle it. Hearing her call Watts her husband was too much for him to stand.

The pain in her eyes, in her scent, nearly overwhelmed him. The need to comfort her, to wrap her in his arms and shelter her from this knowledge, was like a stake through his soul.

"Get out of here, Dog," he snarled.

That bastard Coyote. The son of a bitch had to be related to Jonas, because he was nothing but a manipulative troublemaker, rather like the Bureau director himself was.

Dog watched them silently, his expression brooding, heavy.

"Let her face it," he said softly, his gaze going to Cassa as she stared at Cabal with betrayal in her eyes.

The betrayal hurt the worst, Cabal acknowledged. As Jonas had warned him, this secret had come back to bite him on the ass.

"You knew." Her voice was husky with a pain he had no idea how to ease for her. "You knew he was still alive."

"And I know it doesn't matter." He'd had enough.

Cabal stepped forward, gripped her arm and pulled her toward the elevators. "We'll talk about this upstairs."

"The hell we will." Jerking her arm out of his grasp, she stared up at him, waves of fury beginning to pour from her now. "What else have you been keeping from me, Cabal? How many other lies have you told?"

"More than you want to keep track of," he bit out in self-disgust. "Do you want a fucking list?"

He pushed her gently into the elevator, blocked the exit and stared down at her implacably as the doors slid shut behind them.

"Locking me up again, Cabal?" she sneered at him.

He couldn't blame her for her fury. She had every right to it. As Jonas had said, this was a secret he shouldn't have kept from her, but neither had she needed to know. Until this assignment. Until the mission that Cabal had no doubt would require that he kill Watts again. This time for good.

"You would only slip out," he growled. "You can't stay in place, can you, Cassa?"

"Go to hell!" she yelled furiously, her face flushing a becoming pink. "I'm not some weak-kneed little bitch you can order around. Not anymore."

"So instead of fighting me for anything, you go to Dog?" he snapped out, the anger beginning to burn in him as well. "To a Coyote, Cassa?"

"At least he was willing to tell me the truth."

"Perhaps I would have been willing if you had dared to fight for it," he accused her roughly.

"Fight for it? I should fight for it?" She looked like she was ready to shoot him. "Why should I fight for a respect that you should have given me willingly? For God's sake, Cabal. You should have let me stand at your side without having to fight you for it, simply because I was your mate. You should have wanted me there."

He stared back at her in silent shock, seeing in her gaze the betrayal she felt, and for the first time understanding why Cassa had never fought him for respect and acknowledgment when she had never hesitated to go head-to-head with other Breeds.

It had bothered him, he admitted that now. It was something

he hadn't wanted to admit before. Just as he hadn't wanted to see what it was doing to her. He wanted to protect her. He had wanted her to demand her rights from him as he had seen her do with others she went up against. He had wanted her to challenge him. He hadn't realized until this moment how she *had* been challenging him. Daring him to be a true mate. Daring him to be *her* equal.

As Cabal struggled to make sense of the mistakes he had made, the elevator came to a stop with a muted little ping and the doors slid open on Cassa's floor.

The hall wasn't empty. Waiting for them were Jonas, Lawe, Rule and Mordecai. And they didn't look happy.

"We have a situation," Jonas stated, his tone cold, implacable. "We need you for this."

Cabal clenched his teeth together furiously as he turned to Cassa.

"Like hell." She pushed in front of him. "I know Breed Law and don't think I won't use it." She stared back at Jonas. "Where he goes, I go." She shot Cabal a hard, angry look. "It looks like the only way to get the truth out of him at this point."

Jonas's brows lifted in surprise as the other members of the team stared back at Cabal in shock.

Cabal kept his expression carefully blank, though he didn't doubt the arousal pouring through him was clearly detected. Mating heat was surging through his system, pumping in his veins. She was taking her place. She wasn't asking for it. A part of him was exultant, another part was terrified. He couldn't protect her if she was in the line of fire. But she was also proving that protection wasn't what she wanted.

Was this what he had been pushing for all along? he wondered. A mate who would fight to stand beside him rather than behind him?

It didn't matter, and he wasn't questioning it at the moment. Later, they would discuss this. Just as they would discuss her penchant for getting information from Dog rather than her mate. If she needed information, then she could damned well challenge him for it.

"Very well." Jonas shot Cabal a warning look. "We'll take the elevator to the top floor. The meeting room is set up there."

The same meeting room Cabal had been headed to when

Mordecai had waylaid him in the upper hallway to inform him that Cassa was meeting with Dog.

A meeting Mordecai had set up to repay a debt he owed to Cassa. Cabal understood the repayment, just as he appreciated the loyalty the Coyote had shown in informing her mate of that meeting.

He had accepted certain facts the second Mordecai had informed him that Cassa was meeting with Dog. First and foremost was his own mistake in not working with her. He had thought he could quell that independent nature enough to allow him to protect her. He'd been wrong about that, he admitted it.

Breed society was much different from that of human society. Respect wasn't given, it was taken. She had earned the respect of every Breed she had worked with but had held back with him. She had expected that respect to be given. She had demanded it in her own way; he had just been too dense to understand. And now it was hers.

Above all else though, he had wanted to save her from the truth of what was going on here, the truth of her own past and the parts that were not as dead as she had believed they were.

"In here." Jonas led the way into the suite he had taken.

The meeting room was still set up from earlier. Pictures were displayed on a holographic board while several holographic vids still played of previous hunts the Deadly Dozen had been on. The videos had been saved from Council archives that had been discovered in some of the labs that were rescued over the years.

There weren't many of them, but there were enough to show the horrifying measures the Dozen had taken in catching their prey.

Cassa stopped inside the room, her gaze on the images displayed across the electronic board.

The Deadly Dozen had been rumored to have taped some of their hunts. It was how they sold their services to the Council and the individual labs seeking to reacquire their escaped Breeds.

Actually seeing proof of it was horrifying though. Seeing the Breeds as they fought to run, to hide, to escape a dozen hunters that had lain in wait for them.

She heard the door close behind the four men, and she was aware of them moving around her, watching her as she stared at the images on the screen.

"They were too good," she whispered as she watched the video for long moments. "There was a Breed with them."

"Two. They weren't part of the Dozen," Jonas stated quietly. "That was always part of the deal. The labs would loan them two Coyotes to help track during the hunt."

She shook her head slowly. "They led them where they wanted them to go. They watched. Waited."

"Some of the hunts lasted for weeks, a few months at a time," she was told. "They stalked their prey."

Like a safari hunt, she thought. They knew what they wanted, where it was. They knew their prey's habits and how they tracked, hid. As she watched, she could see that. They knew their prey intimately.

"This particular hunt was one of the first," Jonas told her, and she felt Cabal moving behind her, his hands settling on her hips, pulling her against him.

The clasp was intimate rather than sexual. Comforting rather than arousing.

"We found this one in a lab in New Mexico," Jonas continued. "The hunt took place approximately twenty-seven years ago. The Breeds they were hunting were a male and two females from that particular lab. They caught the first female a week before this hunt."

She sensed what Jonas wasn't saying. That she didn't want to know the particulars of that capture. She probably didn't want to know this one either.

As she watched the footage, she caught a few glimpses of the hunters themselves. Black-masked and black-clothed. It was impossible to tell who was who.

The dark landscape was illuminated by the thermal and night-illuminating capabilities of the video. She could see the male Breed, a Lion Breed if the brown eyes and tawny-colored hair were an indication, as he attempted to keep the female in front of him.

Both Breeds were cunning and swift, but the hunters had them surrounded. They played with them. They built the rage in the male and the fear in the female until the first shot was fired.

Cassa flinched at the sound and the sight of the bullet as it impacted the male's back. There was a moment of stunned agony, of resignation on his face, before he went to the ground.

The female raced to him. Tears tracked down her face as a roar of rage tore from her lips. Her canines flashed in the darkness as the hunters advanced on her, their laughter echoing through the night.

"She's a pretty sight," one of them called out.

"Let's not damage her too bad quite yet," another suggested and Cassa nearly cried out in agony at the familiar tone. "I have a few plans for her."

Another jeered. "I still say it's like fucking an animal."

"It's like fucking a wildcat," Douglas laughed back as he moved toward her. "Let's get her down. He can watch while I fuck his pretty little pussy."

Cassa tore herself out of Cabal's grip, turned her back on the video and had to fight to hold in the sickness rising in her gut.

She was trembling, shaking her head as she cupped her hand over her mouth and swore to herself she wouldn't throw up.

Behind her, the sound cut out. There was silence in the room, but all Cassa could hear were the screams as the hunters tried to pull the female Breed from her mate.

If the female Breed had mated, then any other males' touch would have been agony. Such agony that it was like daggers tearing through the flesh. Cassa knew. Something as simple as the brush of another man against her in a crowd was so discomforting since the mating heat had begun that she avoided it at all costs.

The day she had ridden from the park back to the inn on the back of Dog's Harley, she had been careful not to touch him, and he had made certain he hadn't touched her.

The agony that female mate would have endured, because of Douglas, sliced through Cassa's soul like a dull knife. Her husband. And he was still alive.

She shook her head as Cabal tried to pull her to him again. She couldn't allow him to touch her now, not yet. She needed to think, and she couldn't think if he held her. She needed his comfort, needed his touch too much. She wanted to burrow into him and forget that reality existed.

He had tried to shelter her from it, she realized that. He had wanted to protect her, and she had refused to allow him to do it.

Was it better to know? she wondered as she swallowed back the tears that filled her chest. Or would innocence have been better?

"Why is he still alive?" Her voice was hoarse as she realized that she wanted Douglas dead. Not for what he had done to her, but for what he had done to the female Breeds. The mates that had dreamed of nothing but freedom, safety.

She turned to Cabal, glaring at him, demanding an answer.

"Why?" she repeated. "Why is he still alive?"

She remembered as though it were yesterday. Watching that stake hurl through the air, burying into his spine and sending him to the metal floor as he screamed out in agony.

The screams had cut off. Blood had pooled on the floor. How could he still be alive? Why was he still alive?

"You let him live," she whispered painfully. "You let him live, didn't you?"

"He deserved to suffer." The statement was more a growl, a primal snarl of complete rage as he glared back at her, the amber glints in his eyes like fire in a background of forest green.

"You let him live." She had to fight the tears, and still two fell. "All these years, he's lived while you ignored me. Is that why?"

His jaw clenched. "That has nothing to do with why I didn't claim you, Cassa. It didn't matter if he was alive or dead."

"He was my husband," she cried out. "He *is* my husband."

Fury contorted his face and narrowed his eyes.

"Like fucking hell!" he yelled back at her. "That bastard was never your husband, Cassa. He made certain there were no true ties. The marriage wasn't legal because the minister that married you wasn't a minister. He wasn't licensed to marry anyone, and Watts knew it."

Cassa felt what little blood was left in her face recede. They hadn't been married? It was relief more than anything else. She didn't doubt Cabal's word; he wouldn't bother to lie to her about this. But it was the shock of it. Yet another betrayal that Douglas had dealt to that stupid, innocent little girl who had thought she loved him.

They hadn't been married. That information shot through her head like a bullet, nearly bringing her to her knees.

And Douglas was still alive.

"Where is he?" she whispered. "What did you do, Cabal?"

An enraged growl sounded from his chest.

"Does it matter where he's at?" he bit out furiously.

"It does actually." Jonas answered the question for him.

Cassa swung around to where Jonas was watching them, his gaze narrowed, his expression calm, watchful.

"Watts escaped four hours ago."

Tension snapped into the room. It filled the atmosphere, making the air thick as it tightened Cassa's chest and sent trepidation skating down her spine.

"Watts has been confined in a small prison in the Middle East that Breeds now control," Jonas told her. "We've had him in confinement since the night of Cabal's release."

Cassa swallowed tightly as she stared back at the director of the Bureau of Breed Affairs.

"And you allowed him to escape." Her voice was raw, thick with tears she couldn't shed.

Jonas's lips quirked. "We may have made it a bit easier for the Coyote team that rescued him to get to him." He shrugged. "He's been a little irate since he learned you and Cabal had mated. It seems he still believes he has a hold on you, Ms. Hawkins."

Cassa wrapped her arms across her breasts and shook her head. Douglas no longer had a hold on her. He had nothing more on her than old, bitter memories.

"What purpose did it serve to allow him to escape?" she asked acerbically.

The master puppeteer. That was Jonas. Always conniving, always manipulating. Always with a plan.

"The rogue Breed we're after contacted you, drew you here, hoping to draw Watts out," Jonas told her. "We believe he's a mate that's gone feral and now he's killing the men who killed his mate."

"And Douglas raped her." She had to force the words past her throat.

Jonas nodded. "About a year and a half ago word leaked, somehow, to the Council that Watts was still alive and was being held by us. How the rogue got the information, we're not certain yet." He moved back to the table set up in the middle of the room and took his seat with an outward calm she doubted he truly felt.

"We believe," he continued, "that he bribed one of the human guards we had working there. Several months later, the first victim, Dr. Ryan Damron, was killed after he called Phillip Brandenmore requesting a meeting. They were to meet here at the hunting cabin Brandenmore keeps in the Hawk's Nest forest."

Once again, Cabal moved behind her. His warmth surrounded her, like a blanket to hold out the cold, a solace against the pain she could feel raging inside her and the hatred that boiled black and ugly.

"Dr. Damron disappeared before he could reach the cabin. He was found several weeks later, several states from here, mauled and bled out. Since then, six other suspected members of the Deadly Dozen have turned up dead."

"The information Damron carried was the suspected location where Watts was being held." Cabal spoke quietly behind her. "Damron was still working for the Council, and we believe Watts had demanded that the Council facilitate his release."

"You should have killed him," she whispered.

She wondered if she would burn in hell for that one. If he were dead, then perhaps the Breed now killing wouldn't have turned feral. And she wouldn't be facing her past or the weak person she had once been.

"He had information," Jonas explained with a shrug. "And death would have been an easy punishment. I don't like making it easy on my enemies. Neither does Cabal."

She well believed that. Jonas didn't even like making things easy for those he considered his friends.

"So you arranged to allow for his release." It was an accusation. "To what purpose?"

She didn't want to believe he was still alive. Hell, she hated the thought that suddenly he was again breathing the same air she was breathing. That he was on the same planet. And a part of her was terrified as well. Douglas was a vicious, cruel man, and any and every weakness he could find he knew how to put to good use.

"To allow us to capture the rogue we're after now," Jonas told her. "We believe Douglas knows the identity of our rogue. When he learned of the killings, he became more determined than ever to escape, when he should have been eager to stay. After all, he's the one the killer ultimately wants."

"And how do you know this?" She pushed away from Cabal, her head turning to catch the expression of regret on his face before he wiped it away. "How do you know the killer is after Douglas?"

"We suspected when we learned he had contacted you," Cabal answered. "We learned Watts was part of the Deadly Dozen years ago, but we'd never learned the identity of the others. That was information we were trying to get out of him when the killings began."

"And after eleven years you still didn't have that information?" She scoffed furiously. "Bullshit, Cabal. What were you doing, playing with him? Don't tell me you couldn't have learned what you wanted to know in this amount of time."

"The truth serums we've developed couldn't be used on him because of his weakened physical condition," Jonas stated. "We didn't want him dead, not quite yet. And he'd never fully recovered from that steel stake Cabal drove into his back." A mocking quirk of his lips accompanied the statement.

"Do you have any suspects?" She had to stay focused. Cassa felt as though she were going to shake apart from the inside out. Anger and fear ate at her insides, tearing at them until she felt the raw, bleeding wounds in her soul. If she didn't focus on something besides that pain, then she might not survive, she might not get out of this room before humiliating herself and breaking down entirely.

"As of now, we have no fucking clue." Disgust flickered in his gaze and on his face.

Cassa believed him. Not that she wasn't certain he would lie about it if he did have a suspect, but that flash of self-disgust and anger in his eyes convinced her that he truly didn't know who the killer was.

"That's why we allowed Watts to escape," Cabal stated. "To draw the rogue out. If we watch Watts close enough, then we'll be there when the killer goes for him."

"And you're certain he's headed here?" she asked as she turned to her mate, to the man she had hoped would eventually love her. Now she wondered if she had a chance. If she had ever had a chance. She kept forgetting the fact that she had been involved with the most horrifying event of his life. The deaths of his family. And now she wouldn't be the only one facing that past, he would be as well. And there was no way he couldn't remember exactly the role she had played.

She had allowed Douglas in. She had been the reason he had the information, she had given him the chance to sell the information on the rescue of that facility. Because of her, Cabal had lost so much.

"Positive." Cabal nodded as he broke into her thoughts. "But he's not coming for a killer, Cassa. Watts is coming for you."

CHAPTER 21

Death watched; Death stalked. But as Death sat in the woods across from the inn and watched the shuttered windows, there was an edge of weariness that crept through the mind and through the soul.

Blood stained not just the hands, but the soul as well.

"He escaped." Myron James sat to the side, and in his voice Death heard the same weariness, the same old bitterness. "He's on his way here."

Of course Watts was on his way here. It was here that it had all begun, here that the Reaper had had his greatest triumph.

Three women. Three beautiful women that had been destroyed by his evil.

"Cabal's going to try to stand in our way," Death informed the other man. "He'll keep guard over the reporter, that's going to throw a wrench in it."

"Not if we draw her away from him." Sheriff Danna Lacey's voice was fraught with agony.

God, so much pain. It beat at him, tore into the center of his being and lashed at the animal he had always kept careful control of.

Drawing Cassa Hawkins away from her mate wouldn't be that easy. The animal known as Death knew this. The man, the man understood it, regretted it.

Suddenly, there was so much regret. So much blood scenting his entire body that sometimes he wondered if there was a way to survive the fallout.

Watts would be dead soon, he would make certain of it. There was nothing left to live for except the executions to come. There was no reason to worry about a future or roads not taken. There was only this, only Death.

"She's not to be hurt." He hardened his voice, injected the steel needed to ensure that his orders were carried out.

"Since when do we care about her?" Danna was the only one foolish enough to question him. "She came here. She made the decision to place herself in danger."

"Because we drew her here." He straightened from his crouch, his eyes still on the inn.

He could sense the four men inside, plotting, maneuvering to learn who he was. He was a dead man. He was Death. He would remain the shadow they could never identify, his life depended on it.

"Are you certain the Coyotes that rescued him will keep us apprised of his location?" Myron straightened as well, his voice rough with his own memories, his own pain.

"They know the cost if they don't." Death shrugged. "Either way, Watts will die, even if I have to go hunting myself."

He stared back at Myron, seeing the pain on his face and in his eyes. That pain had only grown over the years since Illandra's death. Since his mate had died on that ill-fated mission. A mission Death had selected her for.

The guilt that weighed him down was heavy. It stacked on his shoulders until there were days he felt as though he would collapse under the strain.

God help him, it had been too long, too many years that he had lived as a shadow, waiting, watching.

"We should take her before he arrives." Danna's voice was thick with unshed tears, her scent was thick with a pain she never allowed free.

Death shook his head. He felt the breeze as it moved around him, feathered through his hair, and suddenly the memories were so clear, so crisp. The feel of soft hands rubbing at his scalp, the whisper of her kiss, her laughter. The knowledge that she had betrayed him.

So much betrayal. His life had begun in betrayal, and it would end with it. He had known that for far too many years. Had accepted it.

Serena had died by the hand of those she had betrayed him to, and their child was paying the cost, even now he feared. The child they had cut from her body.

Pain fueled rage. It bit inside his soul with sharpened fangs and tore at his guts with rapier claws. Damn her to hell. She had thought she would be safe, that the bastards that searched for them would keep their word to her. She had never paid attention to the blood they had spilled or the proof of those that had already been betrayed.

Where was the child? Only Watts knew the answer to that. He had taken the baby with him. The Council had never known of the child that disappeared that night. But Watts did. Death demanded its due. The child was all he had left to live for—the child, and the deaths to come.

"Rick, we have to get her away from them before Watts arrives," Danna argued. "She's what he's coming for."

He shook his head. "That's what he wants us to think. That he's coming for her. That he's coming to take back what belongs to him. Watts has no feelings for this woman, and he doesn't care one way or the other who she fucks or mates. No, he's coming back here to save his own ass, Danna, and we both know it. He's coming here to kill me. Because he knows he'll never be safe as long as I live."

And now that he was free, Watts would want to ensure that freedom. The only way to ensure it would be to kill the one man he knew he would never escape.

Patrick Wallace. Death.

"Cassa walked into this with her eyes open," Danna snapped. "She knew she would be facing a killer."

"She doesn't deserve to die," Myron argued heatedly. "For God's sake, Danna, we've both lost mates. Do we really want to force another to live as we have?"

"Did they care when we lost our mates?" Patrick kept his voice low, commanding. "We're still at war, Myron, don't let propaganda tell you any differently. We use the weapons at our dis-

posal, and that is all Ms. Hawkins is here, a weapon against
Watts. How or if she survives isn't my concern. Finding my child
and killing that bastard is my concern."

"Will it bring them back?" Myron was the one Patrick had
always known would falter at this point. He would falter, but he
wouldn't betray them. For that reason he was still alive.

"Nothing can bring them back," Danna whispered, and they
both looked to him, as though he had the power to turn back
time and return the laughter to them.

"Nothing can bring them back," he told them. "All we can do
now is make them pay. With each one we kill we learn more.
There's four left to go besides Watts. I want them all dead. Every one of them."

He would never live to see that final closure. The Breeds
would stop him; Jonas Wyatt would eventually figure out who
he was. The pills Danna had managed to steal from Brandenmore's labs wouldn't last forever.

Patrick had taken a risk in sending the pills to Cassa Hawkins. It had been a calculated risk, but it had drawn her here. She
was now distracting the Bengal he was having problems with,
distracting Jonas, and soon she would distract Watts. That was
all he needed. Just one moment of time to strike.

"If we kidnap her before he arrives, before Jonas has a chance
to throw a net around her, then we can draw Watts straight to
you," Danna argued. "If we wait, we could lose out on the goal
we've been fighting for."

He stared back at her, his heart heavy. How much she had lost.
Not just her mate and her child, but her very soul. Sometimes he
felt the vacancy within her, and knew the pain this would have
caused his treasured baby brother.

How Raine had loved this woman. His first smile had been
because of her laughter. His first night without nightmares had
been because of her presence in his bed. His first tears of joy
had been the day they had learned she carried his child.

The night Raine died, a part of Danna had died as well. The
night those bastards had held her down and the Reaper had stolen her soul, and the life of her child, Danna had ceased to exist
as a woman. She had emerged from that hell broken, irrevocably
damaged and without the mate who could have eased her spirit.

They had buried Raine without his head, but Patrick had
known they had buried Danna's soul with him.

"Taking her before Watts arrives would be a mistake," he finally ordered them both. "We wait until he's here."

"The risk is too great," Danna bit out fiercely. "Rick, they'll be ready for us then."

"They're ready for us now." He shrugged. "They'll be more distracted once Watts arrives and so will she. We wait."

He moved away from them, heading up the hill, using the trees to hide his presence, knowing he would blend into the forest in a way that even another Breed couldn't track.

He was good at hiding. He was damned good at what he did. He was even better at it than he'd been twenty-two years before. And he had been good then.

He should have followed his first instincts that night and taken that Coyote youth through those mountains alone. He shouldn't have listened to his own mate. He should have left her safe at their farm, he should have known it was a trap.

The youth was wounded, in pain, desperate to reach the location where he knew he would be safe, where a litter mate had promised him haven.

He was also one of the Council's prized creations. One of their most advanced engineered Breeds.

He hadn't listened to his instincts though, and because of that, so many had died. And still suffered.

"Rick, don't walk away from us."

The hold that materialized on his arm drove him into action. A snarl tore from his lips, vicious and primal, before his fingers wrapped around Danna's throat and he was pushing her into the heavy trunk of the bare oak tree behind her.

The smell of fear and submission filled the air, though it was tinged with anger and pain. She gazed back at him furiously, her eyes watering with tears, and suddenly he saw her sister. Sweet, soft Serena. The betrayed and the betrayer.

"Back off." He pushed away from her, enforcing his calm, enforcing Death rather than the man that wanted nothing more than to lie down and give up the fight that he knew was never ending.

Rick. Patrick. Patrick Wallace. Death. He was a man without a soul, pretty much as Danna was a woman without her own.

He had hoped at one time that they could console each other, but it had never happened. There was no touch but Raine's that she could tolerate. And for him, there was only the memory of the woman he had thought Serena was.

"You can't just walk away," she argued, grabbing his arm even as he tried to do just that. "We have to decide now what we're going to do."

"We aren't going to do anything," he snarled back at her. "I will kill Watts, just as I killed the others. That simple."

"Not this time," she cried out. "I have the right to be there. Myron and I both have the right."

They had the right, but he had the authority.

"You forget one thing, little cat," he bit out coldly. "I give the orders here. Not you, not Myron. I'll take care of Watts."

Neither Danna nor Myron had any business being any further part of this. Their hands weren't stained with blood yet; he wouldn't have them stained with Watts's blood. That was his responsibility, just as it had been twenty-two years before. He had failed then, he wouldn't fail now.

"I have the right." She glared back at him, her eyes stone hard. Eyes like Serena's, the same color, nearly the same face. But she wasn't Serena. She wasn't a betrayer. She was the one that had loved, that had lost and that had suffered through the years after that loss.

"Little cat." He sighed the endearment. Her mate was pure Lion. Raine had been as wild as the wind and just as impulsive. "Let me take care of this."

"Like you took care of that damned Coyote," she suddenly sneered. "You just had to save him, didn't you, Rick? Just had to help him. You knew the whole fucking pride would follow you, and you just had to do it."

He shook his head. "As I would have any Breed, Danna. You know that."

He wouldn't excuse it. That was his responsibility as well.

"A Coyote," she cried. "A dirty fucking mongrel that didn't have the right to live."

"We all have the right to live." He removed her fingers from his arm and stared back at where Myron watched, his gaze filled with such pain, with such regret.

Even the love of his wife Patricia hadn't been able to dim the pain that festered inside him. That love had eroded over the years because of something Myron had been unable to help. Because of an affection he couldn't give the woman who had given him her heart.

So much waste. And he accepted the fault for it. It lay on his soul and he had learned to live with it.

"I'll take care of this," he told them both then. "Then I'll take care of the others. The Breeds might have been unwilling to kill Watts by using the truth serums on him, but I have no such fear. I promise you that."

He would get what he needed, and he would watch the man die. Slowly. Patrick wanted to savor his death. He wanted to watch each labored breath until Douglas Watts took his last and then no more.

He lived for it. Ached for it.

Turning from them, he left them where they stood, though he wasn't confident they would obey the order he had given to stand down. He needed Watts alive for just a little while, just long enough to get the names of the final members of the Dozen. Names that those who had died previously were unaware of. It seems they hadn't even trusted one another. Not all of them. None of the men knew exactly who all of their hunting party was. They weren't disguised just on hunts, but at other times they'd met as well.

They had been paranoid about their protection, but not paranoid enough. Elam March had trusted Ryan Damron. Ryan Damron had trusted Aaron Washington, and so on. Now he had only four other names to acquire. Once he acquired those names, his job would be done. His life would be done.

What was there left? He doubted his son still lived, but he had to be certain. They had killed Serena and cut their child from her while he had been with his pride escorting the Coyote through the forest.

Beautiful, lying Serena. Sweet, sweet Serena.

He still didn't understand. He doubted he ever would. He simply lived with the consequences of her actions. And he would die with them.

CHAPTER 22

Cassa sat through the rest of the meeting Jonas had with Cabal, Lawe and Rule. They laid out their plan for keeping up with Watts and identifying their rogue. They also named those they believed were possibly involved in helping the rogue.

Walt Jameson, Myron James and Danna Lacey.

That explained the tension that had poured from Danna when Cassa and Cabal had met with her. Danna had been part of the Breed Freedom Society all those years ago. And according to Jonas and his Breed senses, Danna had, at one time, been mated.

"The scent is barely there," he revealed. "Nearly undetectable except in periods of stress. She's obviously been without her mate for some time, just as James has been."

"Myron is married. He has children," Cassa interjected. "I thought that would be impossible if he had mated."

Jonas shook his head. "We don't know that for sure, Cassa. We're less than twelve years into researching mating heat. Our doctors and scientists still don't know what the hell they're dealing with here."

And neither did those who were mated or would be mated in the near future.

She sat back, watched and listened as they went over their plans. To watch Douglas, make certain he had no chance to get to Cassa, simply because they thought that would piss him off, make him mess up.

It was too clichéd. Douglas didn't give a damn about her one way or the other. He was after something else here. There was something else, someone else, he was after rather than Cassa. She just had to figure out who it was and why.

She knew Douglas. He hadn't loved her. She hadn't even truly been a possession to him. She had been the means to an end, nothing more.

He wasn't here for her. She just had to figure out what he was here for. Unless he knew who the killer was.

He had to know who the killer was; he wouldn't be headed here otherwise. If he didn't know who and what he was facing, then he would have stayed where he was safe. Douglas would be more concerned with eliminating the threat to his own life, and the lives of those who could help him now. Namely, the Deadly Dozen. She would be nothing but an afterthought, and then for amusement only.

He was alive though. All these years she had believed herself free of him, of the part he had played in her past. Only to learn he was still alive, and he was still determined to kill the Breeds.

As the meeting wound down, the information was stored and Jonas rose from his chair to stretch lazily. Cassa's gaze drifted back to Cabal. He had watched her through the meeting, his gaze lingering on her for long moments before his attention would return to the information scrolling on the holoscreen.

She could see the heat building in him. She could feel it. Just as she felt it building in herself.

Anger. Fear. Emotion of any sort affected the hormones that ruled the mating heat. But Cassa realized that something more was driving both of them.

The earlier confrontation. Her insistence on meeting with Dog had broken through a barrier she hadn't known existed between them. She didn't even know what that barrier was; she still wasn't certain.

But it was as though something had been freed within her, a part of her that she hadn't known existed and that had nothing to do with the hormones he had infected her with.

This was pure defiance.

How dare he keep this information from her. How dare he, for all these years, ignore what he knew was between them while keeping these secrets. And then, to push her so effectively from an investigation that she was so much a part of?

Hell no. This wasn't happening. It would never happen again.

Her head lifted as her gaze met his, eye to eye, defiance meeting pure male arrogance. He might be a Breed, but she was his mate, and those who had drafted Breed Law regarding mating hadn't done so without an eye to the pure stubbornness that epitomized Breed males.

She had her own rights. Rights she hadn't enforced or threatened him with. This changed things. Never again would she be made to cash in on a valued favor because he wanted to play the protective, silent male.

If he wanted to continue playing with Jonas, then by God he would do so under a new set of rules.

"Gentlemen, be prepared," Jonas finally sighed. "We'll receive word several hours before Watts hits Glen Ferris. I want everyone in place and prepared." He looked to Cassa. "We know where he'll focus, so let's keep our attention there."

Watts wasn't focused on her—not that they were willing to see that. Because Breeds focused so highly on their women and their mates, they sometimes forgot that humans weren't nearly that loyal. Not even close.

She had faith in them though. Give Jonas a little time—if he hadn't figured it out by now, then he would. Cabal no doubt already had his suspicions. She had watched his face through the meeting. He knew. Just as she knew. Or at least, she hoped he knew. If he didn't, then he wasn't as intuitive as she thought he was.

She rose silently from her seat, collected her pack from the floor and headed to the door, eager to return to her room. She had some research to do herself, some answers to find. Now that she had a bit more of the information that she needed, perhaps she could get her own line into this. There was even a slight chance that she could figure out at least one or two of the missing members of the Deadly Dozen.

She might even have an idea where Douglas would head. One thing was for sure: If she was on his list, then she was last on his list.

As she left the suite, she was aware of Cabal following her

and the tension emanating from him. As though there were a wire connecting them, tuning them in to each other. The closer they came to the elevator, the tighter it became.

She moved into the cubicle, standing close to the rear as Cabal stepped in and punched the button for the lower floor. The doors slid shut. Cassa blinked.

The next thing she knew she was in his arms, plastered between his body and the wall of the elevator, as his lips closed on hers, pushing into the suddenly hungry depths of her mouth.

The taste of him. It was nectar. It was spicy and sweet, cinnamon and sugar. It was a fire in the middle of winter and seared her to her soul.

Her arms wrapped around his shoulders, the once muted desire flaring to an open flame, spreading through her body, blistering her senses.

The mating hormone she had been taking for so many years had kept it repressed, did keep it repressed, until he kissed her. Then it was like a hunger that had waited too long. A starvation that flared to life and overwhelmed.

"Damn you." He nipped at her lips, licked over them. "You make me insane, Cassa. Like a madman that can't get enough of the madness."

He would have kissed her again. She knew it was coming, she was reaching for it, when the electronic beep of the elevator indicated their floor.

He drew back from her, took a hard breath, then gripped her hand and pulled her into the hall.

"Impatient?" she gasped.

If he wasn't, then she damned sure was. As though all the pent-up anger and resentment didn't matter any longer. As though the fierce fury that had thundered through her blood had suddenly morphed into something else. Arousal burned through her now. It hardened her breasts, pulsed in her clit and sent her juices spilling between her thighs.

She was wet and hot. Spoiling for a fight and spoiling for his touch.

"With you? I stay impatient," he muttered as he shoved the key card into its slot and pushed the door open.

Any other woman might not have noticed how he quickly inhaled, the small pause before he entered, the way he used his senses to ensure the room was safe before pulling her inside.

"Great, now you have a key to my room. Tell me, Cabal, do you have keys to my car as well?" She knew he had keys to her apartment; he had surprised her more than once as she stepped inside to find him awaiting her.

"Probably. Somewhere," he growled before he pushed her against the wall and took her lips again.

Nectar. Paradise. His kiss was almost an orgasm in and of itself. He took quick, hard little kisses, then settled his lips over hers and sipped delicately, then greedily. It was a smorgasbord of sensations and caresses.

One hand fisted in her hair, the other gripped her hip. Cassa was beyond shame or reticence. Her legs wrapped around his hips, tightened on him. Her hands were in his hair, and her lips and tongue caressed and stroked in turn.

The hard ridge of his cock notched against her sex—a heated, heavy weight that rubbed against her, ground into her and stroked her clit to a pinnacle of sensation.

She was burning for him now. The need had been an ache before he touched her, but now, now it was a flame searing her from the inside out.

"Burn, baby," he growled against her lips. "Burn for me, Cassa."

She was a flame in his arms.

Cabal had never known anything as hot, as sweet as Cassa. Her kiss. Her touch. The way her fingers threaded through his hair, tugged at it, pulled him closer. Her lips moved beneath his with heated demand, and what he didn't give her, she tried to take.

Her tongue rubbed against his, and as he followed those wicked strokes, she drew his tongue into her mouth and sucked at it with delicate greed.

Cabal felt his entire body tighten, felt his cock jerk and harden further as he ground himself against the heated mound of her pussy.

"Cabal." She breathed his name against his lips, then her sweet little tongue stroked across them, eluding his kiss as it moved farther away to stroke down his neck.

The rasp of her teeth had a growl rumbling in his chest. His hands tightened on her rear, clenching in the bunched muscles there as he lifted her closer, pressed her harder to the wall and ground his cock powerfully against her pussy.

He was on fire for her. Son of a bitch, he was burning for her.

"You're going to push me too close to the edge." He was almost panting, the need for her growing so sharp, so desperate, that holding on to his control was becoming no more than a wish.

"You already pushed me past mine." She bit at his neck, and damn if the pleasure didn't intensify tenfold. Those sharp little teeth of hers nipped, her silken little tongue stroked and pleasure struck his balls like a bolt of lightning.

"Let me down." She wiggled in his grasp. "Let me go, Cabal."

He released her rear, allowed her legs to slide down and tried to catch her lips with his once again.

"Not yet." She slapped at his hands as he glared at her, outraged.

"What the hell do you mean, 'not yet'?" He could barely push the words past his lips as her soft hands slipped beneath his shirt.

Sweet God save him. His stomach clenched as her nails raked over his hard abdomen.

"Exactly what I said." There was an edge of feminine command to her tone that had his hackles rising even as his cock took notice with a hard jerk of interest.

She pulled at the metal tab of his jeans.

"Damn." He breathed out the curse as the zipper rasped down.

"I want to lick those stripes."

Cabal stiffened at the moan in her voice, and the desire she voiced.

He had never allowed any woman to caress those stripes. Until this moment, they had been his personal shame. Now, hell, if that's what it took to get her tongue on him, then he was fucking all for it. Let her lick. Let her lap. Sweet heaven. She could bite if she wanted to.

He sucked in a breath as his jeans pushed past his hips. Watching her, he narrowed his eyes, seeing the complete absorption in her face as the hard length of his cock sprang into view.

She wasn't distracted. Fuck. He was praying she would become distracted.

"Hell." His head nearly slammed into the wall behind him as she licked one of those fucking stripes. Her tongue was a lash of fire, and he promised himself she was going to pay for the torture.

Soft, delicate, her tongue ran over the stripes, exciting the sensitive flesh. As though the nerve endings were closer to the skin in that area, each wash of her tongue was like a flame of excitement burning across the area.

"You'll pay for this, Cassa," he promised her.

"Promises promises." She nipped at his thigh, then moved to the other.

As she tortured, tormented the area where the flesh was striped darker, Cabal toed off his boots, worked his jeans over his legs and tore off his shirt.

He watched, his jaw clenching in greedy hunger, as her tongue licked and stroked, coming close enough to his oversensitive cock that he could feel her breath.

He was going to feel more than her breath. He promised himself that. Tonight, he was going to feel that hot little mouth wrapped around his cock.

His fingers tightened in her hair, tugged at the silken strands, and he nearly growled at the soft little moan that left her throat.

"Stop teasing me, Cass," he ordered her roughly.

"You tease me." She was panting for breath, kneeling in front of him and driving him crazy with the proximity of her mouth to his cock.

He gripped the base of his cock with one hand, her hair with the other. Pulling back, he watched as he rubbed the thick crest against her moist lips and swore he was going to come from that sheer excitement alone, when her tongue peeked out to rake against him.

Sensation shot through the shaft straight to his balls. Never had anything been so good, or so tormenting. He wanted her mouth on him. Wanted the moist warmth wrapped around the sensitive crest, wanted to feel her suck him, lick him. Just one more time. He was going to burn alive if he didn't have her.

"Cass. Now." His voice was a rough, primal groan.

Her lips parted as her lashes lifted to watch him. The crest slipped inside as her tongue lashed at the underside, stroking sweet fire across the sensitized flesh as she sucked him into her mouth.

He was dying. The suction of her mouth was taking the life right out of him. Soft, heated bliss. Fiery hunger. Her tongue stroked and licked, while she sucked him deep. Soft fingers wrapped around the shaft as far as they would go, pumped it, caressed it, as her other hand moved between his thighs to stroke the taut sac that held his tortured balls.

Never had he needed to come so badly and yet fought the release with such desperation. He wouldn't come in her mouth. He wouldn't allow himself to. He wanted to be buried deep inside her, feeling her pussy clench and tighten around him as he pumped into her.

"Fuck, your mouth. Hot. Sweet." He was muttering, growling. It was an ecstasy he could barely stand to endure.

"Yeah, baby. Suck it." His thighs tightened as his hips began to move, to pump shallowly inside her hot little mouth as he fought to relish the sensation of her sweet suckling.

If he could just hold on a few more seconds. One more minute. Just a little while longer.

He watched her face as she sucked him. The way her cheeks hollowed, the flush over her face, her reddened lips. She wasn't just sucking his cock, she was loving it with every stroke of her lips and tongue. Relishing it. Tasting him with all her senses.

"Enough." He couldn't take any more. One more stroke of her tongue against his cock and he was going to come.

He pulled her head back. Forced her head back as he ignored the mewling little protest that slipped past her lips.

He had to have her. Nothing mattered at this point but taking her. Slipping inside her, feeling the heat and soft acceptance she always gave him.

That was it. The acceptance. Without lies, without asking for anything but pleasure in return, she accepted him.

And he needed it now. Needed her. Beyond the mating heat, because it had begun long before he had ever felt that torturous heat moving through him. He needed her. Her touch, her laughter, her softness. Her acceptance of who and what he was.

Lifting her into his arms, he carried her to the bed. Laying her on the soft blankets, his lips covered hers as he made short work of the clothes that kept the sweet perfection of her body from him.

God, he loved touching her. Just touching her. Stroking her skin, tasting her kiss, loving her.

He loved her.

That knowledge slipped past his soul from that shadowed corner where he had kept it hidden. Even from himself.

"Sweet love." He pressed his lips against the mating mark on her shoulder as he moved over her.

She tasted so good there. Each touch he gave her she responded to as though she had been made for him alone. She was his mate. Nature had created her just for him, for no other man in this universe. Her skin ached for his touch; his kiss fueled her desire, just as hers fueled his. She was the other half of his soul, not just his body. Not just his heart.

"Cabal, don't tease me." Her breathy tone sent shards of impatience tearing through him.

The soft brush of her thigh against his cock had pre-cum spilling from the tip. He was on an edge he had never known before. The need to savor her body versus the need to spill inside it. God only knew which hunger would be sated first.

Moving lower, he couldn't help but swipe his tongue over one hard nipple, then the next. A single taste would never be enough though. He drew the tight tip into his mouth, sucked at it, laved it with his tongue and tasted her until she was arching to him and crying out his name.

Then he couldn't have one without having the other. He sucked the mate into his mouth with greedy hunger. Sucked it. Worshiped it. God help him, but he couldn't get enough of her.

"Cabal, you're killing me," she cried out, but the pleasure in her voice was enough to spur him on.

He moved lower. Stringing kisses down her torso, along her stomach, he spread her legs and inhaled the sweet, delicate scent of arousal. Of pure heated female.

And he had to taste there as well. The scent of her was pure fucking bliss.

"You taste like summer," he groaned as he lowered himself between her thighs. "Hot and sweet."

His tongue swiped through the narrow slit, drawing her juices to it, tasting the incredible need that flowed from her. Never had a woman tasted so sweet or so damned innocent.

She wasn't tainted by another man's touch. No other male's

scent lingered on her flesh. She was pure. Fresh. And he needed more of her. So much more of her.

He licked the soft folds, drew them into his mouth. Each taste of her pushed him higher, and he swore he could feel his cock thickening, growing harder. It felt like pure hardened steel between his thighs, burning to find the haven that only she could provide.

His hands gripped her thighs as she twisted against him, pushed her pussy closer to his lips and gave him more of her. Her clit was swollen, drawing his tongue. It tasted as sweet and hot as the rest of her. He was burning in the grip of the hunger that filled him now. Every cell in his body was focused on one thing only—Cassa. Her touch, her taste, the feel of her need, the husky murmurs of her desire.

As her fingers buried themselves in his hair, he allowed her to draw his lips back to the swollen little bud of her clit. He licked it. Teased it.

"Suck it." The needy command had his blood pressure rising. Hell, his blood was going to pound right out of his flesh at this rate.

"Please, Cabal. Oh God. Please."

His lips enclosed the hardened knot of nerve endings as he sucked it in and allowed his tongue to flicker with the utmost gentleness over the responsive bud.

She writhed beneath him. Her hips pumped, her thighs tightened and he could feel her release building inside her. He could smell it. She was close. So fucking close that he knew it would take so little to push her right over the edge.

And that was where he wanted her. Flying in his arms.

Tightening his grip on her thighs, he sucked her clit deeper into his mouth, harder. His tongue stiffened, flickered harder, faster over the flexing flesh, and within seconds her ecstatic cries were filling his head as she exploded beneath him.

He couldn't wait. Her orgasm was burning over his tongue when he jerked upright, lifted her legs and pressed the burning crest of his cock into the saturated folds.

They enclosed him. He swore her sweet pussy sucked him in as he worked the thick flesh inside her. Flexing, silken muscles tightened around him, stroking that violently sensitive crown, then the hardened shaft, until he was seated fully inside her, surrounded by fiery heat.

Primal hunger filled him now. There was no stopping. There was no way to halt the inferno overtaking both of them. He could smell it in the air, infused with emotions he couldn't decipher, and needs as instinctive as nature itself.

Gripping her hips, he pulled back, trying to move slow, fighting to relish every stroke, every caress. Her nails bit into his wrists as she held on to him. Her head was arched back, her hips lifting to him.

Fuck it. God, he couldn't hold back. He needed too much, needed her too desperately.

Moving over her, his lips took hers as he began to stroke inside her. His hips pumped, churned as he fought to work every inch of the burning shaft inside her with each stroke. She was tight. A heated, snug grip that made him mindless with the need for release.

Holding on was torture. Control was barely a thought, focused solely on holding back his own release for hers. She had to come. He had to feel her orgasm tightening around him, flowing around him. It was imperative. Nothing else mattered.

Her whimpers beneath their kiss assured him it was building again. Each stroke inside her and he swore she was growing tighter, wetter, slicker.

He couldn't kiss her and breathe. He couldn't stop kissing her. His tongue pumped inside her mouth as his cock pumped inside her pussy, until he couldn't bear much more. He couldn't hold back. He was losing control, losing thought and his sanity inside her.

Jerking his lips back from hers, he buried his head at her shoulder, his teeth clamped on the mating mark, and then he felt it. She tightened, drew taut in his hold, as a shattered cry fell from her lips and her orgasm exploded through her.

Cabal couldn't hold back the growling snarl that tore from his chest. He plunged inside her again, again. Felt her orgasm rushing around him and lost himself to his own.

The barb beneath the head of his cock pressed out, became erect, violently hard and locked him inside her at the moment of his release. With each spurt of semen he felt the shudders of furious pleasure tearing through, ripping through his soul, opening it for her.

He held her close, one hand buried in her hair, to hold her to his heart, as he fought to breathe through the ecstasy.

She was his. His woman. His mate. His life.

Nothing in this world would ever matter as much as Cassa.

Not his life or others. He would die without her. And by God, he would have no compunction in killing to protect her.

She was more than just his heart. Cassa was his soul.

CHAPTER 23

"I'm not going to sit here in this room and wait on someone who's not coming."

Cassa made her announcement the moment she stepped out of the bathroom, freshly showered and dressed. She wasn't a patient person when it came to pacing the floors. She would just as soon be pacing the sidewalk adding to her story or hunting down sources.

Hunting down sources was her primary concern today. She had several in mind, for information she needed. Chief among the questions she had was in regards to any surviving members of the Feline pride that had been massacred on Valentine's night twenty-two years ago. Who was left? Who would be taking vengeance now?

She knew Walt Jameson had information, and there were the two Breeds that had been in the café the morning she had met Myron there. On closer thought, those Breeds had been a little too curious. They were watching her that day, listening to her conversation. Which meant they were most likely involved.

She was going to find them and simply have a nice little conversation with them. Maybe mention Valentine's Day. Maybe mention Douglas.

She felt armed for battle. Dressed in jeans, her favorite dark gray long-sleeved T-shirt and boots. Her long hair was pulled back in a ponytail, and a light dusting of makeup had been applied where she felt it was needed.

Last night had held too many revelations, and too many surprises. She wasn't a sitting duck for anyone, especially Douglas Watts. She had put that behind her the day she thought Douglas had died, and she wasn't returning to it.

She watched Cabal as he turned from the window to stare back at her. She took in the hard expression, but paid attention to the glitter of amber in his forest green eyes.

Those eyes almost had the power to mesmerize her. She could stare into them for hours, lose place and time and never regret a moment of it. If she let herself.

"What do you think you can do before Watts arrives?" He crossed his arms over the dark gray cotton shirt he wore, as his gaze flickered over her.

"There's any number of things I can do." She shrugged. "High on the list is finding Walt Jameson. I'd like to talk to him a bit more."

"Why?" Suspicion hardened his eyes.

"Because I suspect he's more involved in this than even you know," she informed him. "And he offered me information. I intend to take him up on that."

"He's close to Myron and Danna," he informed her. "Anything you talk to him about he's going to talk to them about."

"Then I'll just have to talk to him discreetly." She shrugged. "I am aware of how that's done, Cabal."

And she needed to get out of this bedroom, away from him. The night before had thrown her off balance. Not just in terms of the revelations she had learned, but also in terms of things she had learned about herself as he held her in his arms.

She had felt more last night than she had ever felt in her life. Each touch he had given her, each kiss had sunk clear to the core of her spirit. It had been like flying. Like being reborn. And now she felt off balance, uncertain. She needed time to think, time away from his touch to make sense of it.

"I have no doubt that you can question him very discreetly, Cassa." He blew out a rough breath as he pushed the fingers of one hand through his hair, feathering it back from his face only to have the silken strands fall back into place. "I just know Walt.

If Danna and Myron are involved in this, he's going to protect them. And if they're involved, then no doubt he is as well."

"I'll talk carefully," she stated. "But I will talk to him."

She moved to the desk and quickly stored her electronic notepad in its case before pushing it into her pack. Sitting here waiting wasn't something she could do. She had to get out of this room, she had to put some distance between herself and her need to stroke Cabal from head to toe.

Her hands were tingling with the need to just pet him. Just touch him. And she knew damned good and well where that would lead.

Her body was already heating in response to that thought. It seemed that the more she touched him, the more she was touched by him, the more she wanted.

"You think you're leaving here without me, don't you?" he asked with an edge of amusement in his tone and his expression as he watched her.

Cabal personified male arrogance. She could see it, feel it pouring off him. She might think she was going to go without him, she might even want to go without him, but as far as he was concerned, it wasn't going to happen.

It was a damned good thing she had decided she was better off with him than without him at this point. She was stubborn, and she liked her job, but she had to admit that with the information she now had, things might be just a little too dangerous for her alone.

"Actually, I more or less assumed you would just follow along," she replied blithely. "So come on, Bengal. Let's get to work."

She didn't miss the narrowed eyes or the look of male outrage in his gaze. Well hell, if she was going to have to put up with his male attitude, then he better learn to take her female adjustments. It was that simple.

"You know, Cassa, we're going to have to discuss this penchant you have for pricking my ego," he stated as they left the room.

"Really?" She couldn't help the laughter in her voice as she glanced back at him. "You know, Cabal, I was just thinking the same thing about my ego. Sounds like a lengthy discussion to me. Are you certain you have the patience for it?"

The sound he made behind her was between a purr and a growl. Almost one of anticipation.

Funny, she thought, she had heard that Feline Breed males would purr for their mates, normally after sex. She hadn't heard a single purr yet. And here she had been looking forward to it.

Another discussion they might be having soon. She made a mental note of that one.

Start as you mean to go on. That was the advice her mother had always given her where men were concerned. Weigh each confrontation and ensure you can handle years of it before you decide to bow down and let a man have his way. Because give him an inch and he was going to take a mile. Or in Cabal's case, an interstate.

As they left the inn, she felt his hand settle in the small of her back as he led her to the black Raider normally designated as a law enforcement or Breed vehicle. The high-profile, four-wheel-drive vehicle was rated for normal road use, but designated for off-road efficiency.

She'd often heard that it could almost climb a tree if it had to. The Bureau of Breed Affairs loved the vehicles.

Having opened the door with the keyless entry remote, Cabal helped her step up into the seat. She didn't miss the way his hand caressed the outside of her thigh, or the heated look he gave her. It was enough to make her wonder if perhaps she should have postponed this little outing for a bit more inside playtime.

She almost laughed at the thought, as well as the almost giddy euphoria she could feel moving through her. She felt . . . happy. And why she felt that way didn't even make sense.

It had something to do with the night before. The way he had held her after taking her, the feel of his lips as he kissed her head while cuddling her to him.

Last night he hadn't budged from her side. He hadn't let go of her. He hadn't given her a chance to feel the familiar chill of loneliness that usually afflicted her while she was on assignment. His arms had been strong, his big body warm. And Cassa had felt almost cherished.

It was a good feeling. A fool's dream perhaps, because only a fool could believe in happily ever after considering the past she and Cabal shared. But it had been nice. It had been satisfying.

As he got into the driver's seat and closed the door behind him, she caught the look he shot her and had to restrain her smile. It would have been a very self-satisfied smile. Because his look lacked that complete male confidence he'd always had until now. As though he was questioning his opinion of her or their relationship.

Her lips had parted to make a laughing comment when a strange beeping began to sound through the vehicle.

She saw Cabal's expression first. Complete disbelief.

"Fuck! Get out!" Between one breath and the next he was throwing her door open and pushing her out.

Stumbling, adrenaline coursing through her body, Cassa went to her knees before scrambling to her feet and running.

"Cabal!" She screamed out his name as the Raider exploded behind her.

A wave of heat, shocking, searing, threw her to the ground as smoke began to roll and thicken the air. She could hear the squeal of tires, voices raised in alarm, seconds before rough hands latched onto her arms and she was tossed again.

Screaming, kicking, trying to bite, she fought the hold as she literally bounced against a metal floor and a door slammed shut.

Smoke still filled her lungs as she fought to cough, to drag in needed oxygen, as she pushed herself to her knees and swept her hair back from her face.

Terror surged through her as she felt movement. In one second a thousand impressions assailed her. She was in a van—the cold metal floor beneath her knees, the chill of the air, the dank scent of the interior. It was shadowed, closed off. There were no windows, but she wasn't alone.

Her eyes swept around the interior until they landed on the man who inhabited the van with her. Long, dark brown hair, dark brown eyes and a dark complexion. For all his unassuming coloring, his features were memorable, and unmistakable. He was pure Lion Breed. She'd seen him in the picture left on the bank where Cash Winslow had died. She had seen him in other pictures as well. In the vids Jonas had displayed the night before. Pictures of the pride of Felines that was murdered Valentine's night, twenty-two years before.

"Cabal will kill you," she whispered hoarsely.

His lips quirked into a faintly amused grin.

"You don't care?" She did.

"I'd have to be alive to care, Ms. Hawkins," he said, his voice torn, raspy. More animal than man. "And we both know, I'm not really alive. Don't we?"

She was staring into the face of a dead man.

◆　　◆　　◆

Roars of rage echoed in the parking lot of the inn as smoke billowed from the destruction of the Raider. Flames leapt from the burning vehicle, searching for dry tinder, finding none. They sputtered on the pavement, in the street and the damp bank of the river that flowed on the other side.

Guests rushed from the inn. Sirens screamed through the small town, and Breeds rushed from several points shouting reports to Jonas as he raced from the building, followed by Rule and Lawe.

Cabal fought through the haze of smoke to find his mate, knowing she wasn't there. He'd heard the vehicle, heard her screams. She'd been taken. He could feel it in the very marrow of his bones, and the knowledge enraged the tiger that lived just beneath the flesh of the man.

"St. Laurents, you're wounded." One of the Breeds rushed to him, dared to lay hands on him.

Cabal turned to him with a silent snarl of pure primal fury. Satisfaction raged through him as the Breed paled and backed away. He knew what the other man saw. At any other time he would have hated it, would have fought back the animal to hide it. Now he let it free, knowing that the dark stripe that ran from his forehead, slashed across his eye, nose and opposite cheek was an anomaly—the animal raging too close to the flesh, the spirit of the beast overtaking the man. He didn't care. Let the animal free. The man had been weak. He had let his enemies live as he searched for answers. He had allowed his mate to be endangered as he searched for vengeance. No longer. Blood would spill. The enemies would die. There would be payment for this day.

"Cabal. Stand the fuck down." Jonas's order was a distant command, one he ignored as he surveyed the area, taking in the scents, drawing them in, separating them.

He knew the scent of the vehicle. There was a hint of something he had smelled once before, in only one particular place. The sheriff's home. Danna Lacey was partial to cinnamon scents. The scent of cinnamon had been heavy in the small house she owned. It was more subtle in the van, but proof enough that she was acquainted with it.

He raised his head as the sounds of the sirens drew closer. The sheriff's cruiser was the first to pull in. Cabal narrowed his gaze, watching as it slammed to a stop and Danna Lacey jumped from the vehicle.

There was no surprise at first. There was knowledge. Her eyes showed her knowledge of what had happened here before she replaced it with shock and began shouting orders. An ambulance rolled in, fire trucks. He paid little attention as he stalked toward her, aware that Jonas, Rule and Lawe were coming on his rear fast.

"Cabal. Are you okay?" There was true shock now. There was always shock when the unwary saw the proof of the tiger streaked across his face.

He didn't answer. He could feel the blood at his shoulder, the slice across his flesh. It was there. It wasn't fatal. An inconvenience, nothing more.

He bared his teeth in lethal fury. It wouldn't stop him from killing this woman.

As the Breeds converged around them, his hand went out, his fingers locking around her throat as he slammed her against the side of the car.

Not enough to hurt her. The male was weak; he was merciful where the animal wanted nothing more than to rip her lying throat out.

"Return my mate." He kept the order simple. Words weren't as easy as they had once been, not with the growls that were tearing from his chest.

"Get him off me, Jonas." Her voice was rough, filled with fear as she stared up at him.

She stank of terror and guilt. And he wanted her blood. He wanted to taste it, feel it pouring over his fingers and know that any fear his mate was feeling at this moment was felt tenfold by this woman who had instigated it.

"I. Want. My. Mate." His roar was an ugly, furious sound.

He saw Jonas's reaction, smelled the wariness that emanated from the Breeds around him.

God help him, he was terrified himself. All he could think about was Cassa. She would be frightened. She would be waiting for him to save her. He would save her. Or he would kill anyone he suspected to be involved in her disappearance.

"I don't have your mate," she wheezed, her nails clawing at his wrists. "Let me go, Cabal. I don't know where she is."

"Cabal, let her go," Jonas hissed at his ear. "Stand down. Now."

He turned on the director, snarling in rage.

"Now, Cabal!" he barked.

"You back off." He drew back, the rage solidifying into ice, into primal, feral determination. "Fuck you. No more games, Jonas. Not again. I'll find her myself."

He turned and loped across the parking lot, slammed his way back into the inn as he ignored the curious bystanders. He needed to get to his room. Weapons and needed supplies had been destroyed in the Raider, but he had more. He never went into an assignment without additional weapons.

Jonas, Lawe and Rule followed him. It was no more than he could expect. Jonas had his games to play, and it was Rule and Lawe's job to keep him alive while he played them. He might not live much longer though, if he continued to play them with Cabal's mate.

"Cabal, the van she was taken in is being tracked," Jonas informed him as they followed him into his room. "We have a team on it now, keeping close behind. We'll have her location soon."

"Now." Cabal threw open the closet door and pulled out the duffel bag he had carried in with him earlier.

"Cabal, we don't have it now," Jonas snapped. "For God's sake, if you mated bastards don't stop going apeshit like this, then I'm going to start shooting you."

"Remind me not to tell Jonas if I get infected," Lawe murmured to Rule.

"Better yet, don't get infected," Rule grunted. "I'd hate to have to shoot you myself when you start acting stupid."

Cabal stared back at them in icy distain before pulling out the weapons he would need. There was a knapsack packed with ammunition and clips. He strapped a dagger to one thigh, a handgun to the other. From the back of the closet he pulled free a rifle stored in its weatherproof bag and pulled the strap over his head and shoulder to allow it to lie comfortably along his back.

"Dammit to hell, Cabal, we have this covered," Jonas cursed furiously. "Let's handle this the right way."

"Your way you mean?" he asked coldly.

"That's usually the right way," Jonas informed him.

Cabal shook his head slowly. "Not this time, Jonas. Not this mate. You can ignore yours as long as you want. I've claimed mine." He paused, pain streaking through his soul. "She claimed me."

He brushed past the three men as he stalked from the room.

Watts hadn't had time to reach Glen Ferris; Cabal couldn't imagine he'd had anything to do with this kidnapping. The Coyote spy they had on the team that had broken him out of the prison would have reported it first thing.

Who had taken her?

He slipped silently out of the inn, a shadow, a lethally trained ghost that had once known nothing but the hunt and the kill.

Sliding around the edges of the commotion still ongoing outside the inn, he pinpointed Jonas's people, and those who weren't.

There were three Breeds, well trained to blend in, but not blocking their scent as well as they thought they were. How the hell had they gotten the drug that blocked the Breed scent and left only the human scent? The drug Cassa had given them had been tested at Sanctuary. The hormones in it were developed to block scent in Breeds, not humans. Though in humans they blocked all scent, as shown in Cassa.

Breeds were another story though. The drug left only the human scent, and human scent within Breeds was often known to change under duress.

As he watched from the hill above the inn, he saw the sheriff's subtle looks toward the three Breeds. They took orders from her. She was directing them.

He watched, eyes narrowed, his senses on alert. Danna Lacey was a mated female, though obviously her mate had died, because his scent barely registered on her now. According to the information Jonas had managed to find, her mate had been killed the same night Myron James's mate died.

And speaking of the reporter, the supposed friend to Cassa, James pulled up, parking his car in the far corner of the inn's parking lot before getting out slowly.

Sheriff Lacey glanced over at him. There was fear on her face, and indecision. She was still looking around, as were the Breeds that had arrived.

Cabal watched Jonas's enforcers as they talked to firemen, filled out reports. There were others watching, just as he was. But the explosion had revealed the Breeds. Whoever else might be watching would know how many there were now, and had most likely identified them as well.

Ice filled his veins at the thought of Breeds working against Breeds. These weren't Coyote, they were Lion and Jaguar, and if he wasn't mistaken, there was a Cougar Breed down there as well. These were men who weren't registered with the Bureau or with Sanctuary.

That made them a target.

Someone had taken his mate, and someone was going to pay for it. God help them all if she was harmed.

Memories of the murdered members of the Dozen flashed through his mind. The horror in their expressions, the pain they had suffered before they died. Cash Winslow had died fighting to breathe. There had been no mercy in his death. There had been pure vindictive hatred in it.

Was Cassa suffering?

Agony streaked through him at the thought.

He hadn't told her . . . He shook his head. He hadn't told her that she made him warm inside. That the ice that had filled him for so many years had begun unthawing at her touch.

He had wanted to tell her. As he held her last night. As her soft breaths had caressed his chest and the pads of her fingers had rubbed against his waist, he had wanted to tell her what she was to him.

As he had fought the purr that wanted to rumble in his chest, he had fought the words, held them back, because he didn't know how to tell her. Didn't know what to say to her.

And now she was gone, frightened, taken away from him. And he couldn't tell her.

What had he done? He had wasted so many years because of his own pride, his own stubbornness. He had always known she'd had nothing to do with Watts's actions, but the very fact that he saw her as his weakness had held him back.

Because of this. Because the thought of losing her was destroying him inside. It was eating away at him in ways he couldn't fight, couldn't push back in that icy corner of his soul. Because there was no ice left. Cassa had warmed it, melted it, softened parts of him that he hadn't even realized were stone hard.

She had made him proud of his stripes as she kissed and licked them. She had made him proud to be a man, to be a Breed, with each soft touch of her hands, each whispered cry of longing as he touched her.

She didn't know how she had touched him, and that was his fault. She didn't know how important she was to his life. Hell, he hadn't known himself until he had heard the countdown to that explosive and realized he could lose her.

She was his mate. She was his heart.

"Cabal, tell me you're using the comm link." Jonas's voice came over the secure link he had placed at his ear.

"I'm watching," he replied almost silently. "There are three unregistered Breeds taking silent direction from Lacey. James is in sight, for the moment watching only."

"We have eyes on them as well," Jonas reported. "Were you detected leaving?"

"Negative."

"I have two enforcers that didn't show themselves during the explosion. Mordecai and Tarek Jordan. What's your location?"

"Close" was all he revealed.

Jonas cursed bitterly. "I need more than this, Cabal."

"Fuck what you need," Cabal stated bitterly. "I know what I'm doing. I don't need direction or orders from you, Director."

He'd had enough. For ten years he'd followed Jonas, worked with him, and though he highly respected the man, he didn't trust his mate's life in anyone's hands but his own.

"We don't know who has her, Cabal," Jonas reminded him softly.

"No, we don't," he agreed. "But I sure as fucking hell know how to find out."

And he knew where to go. Who to wait on.

Disconnecting the link, he moved from his position and began his trek up the mountain. The sheriff's house was about twenty miles away. An easy run for a Bengal Breed. An easy run for a man racing to save his own soul.

His mate.

CHAPTER 24

"I don't want to have to touch you. I know you've mated the Bengal and I know that would be painful. So I'm going to ask you to cooperate and walk into the cabin yourself."

Cassa stared at Patrick Wallace for long moments after he made his request. There was nothing dead about him. He was living, breathing, a man tortured and playing a very dangerous game.

"I hate to see you die for this," she said softly. "Let me go now. I'll call Cabal and he'll come for me. He'll tear through this mountain like an avenging angel."

His lips quirked mockingly. "Nothing's going to stay St. Laurents's hand at this point." There was the faintest shrug of his shoulders. "I may as well continue with my plan."

"And that plan is?" She was curious about this part. She hadn't figured that out quite yet.

He reached past her and threw the van door open, exposing her to the cold mountain air and the front of a rough log cabin.

"Don't make me force you inside the cabin," he requested again. "Neither of us would enjoy your pain."

Breathing in roughly, she stared at the opened door.

"Are you going to kill me?" She stared into his eyes, eyes that flickered first with ice, then with regret.

"I won't harm you, Ms. Hawkins," he told her quietly. "That was never my intention."

"Then why kidnap me?" she asked.

She hated to admit that she was actually afraid to leave the confines of the van and enter the unfamiliar territory of the cabin waiting just outside its doors.

He sighed deeply as he stared back at her knowingly. "I'll make a deal with you. Get out of the van and come into the cabin. We'll discuss it over decaf coffee and chocolate cake."

She almost smiled. Breeds did love their chocolate. Somehow it almost made it seem less threatening. Not quite, but almost.

He was lethally dangerous. She could see it in his face, in his eyes, in the resignation in his voice. He was a man who didn't care if he died, and that made him more dangerous than any other.

Hiding the shaking of her hands in the pockets of her jacket, she moved slowly from the van. Gravel crunched beneath the heels of her boots as she moved slowly along the walk to the opened cabin door. Damn, she felt like she was going to the gallows rather than the warm confines of a cabin.

Drawing in courage with a deep breath, she stepped across the threshold and entered a rather homey, spotless kitchen. There was a pot steaming on the stove. Chili if she wasn't mistaken. A long table sat in the middle of the room, a checkered cloth covering it. The windows were covered with dark blinds, but the modern appliances and well-waxed wood floors assured her it was a well-cared-for room. Most likely a home.

"Come on in, Ms. Hawkins."

She jumped, startled, as Walt Jameson stepped in from another room, his somber expression heavy as he moved into the kitchen.

"Let me guess, Myron and Sheriff Lacey aren't far behind?" she asked as she did as he'd suggested and moved into the room.

Behind her, Patrick stepped in as well as the young Breed that had driven the van. The door closed and locked behind them, sealing them into the warmth of a home that suddenly seemed more sinister.

"Not that I'm aware of," Walt answered as he moved to the stove and stirred the contents of the pot, before turning back to her.

Dressed in a checkered shirt, jeans and boots, he looked just as friendly, just as unassuming as he had that morning in Glen Ferris. In his case, looks were definitely deceiving.

"I see you've met Patrick." There was a wealth of affection in his voice as he nodded at her kidnapper. "Behind him is Keith. I trust they took good care of you."

"Don't place too much trust in them," she suggested. "They're severely inconveniencing me."

Walt glanced behind her in surprise before a light chuckle escaped his lips. "Yeah, they have that small habit."

"It's going to be a fatal habit in this case," she informed him. "You know Cabal, Walt. He'll kill them both."

Walt shook his head, though his face was lined with resignation. "He'll be killing us all then." He sighed heavily as he waved his hand to the table. "Sit. I'll get you some food, maybe some coffee, and we'll talk."

She moved to the table and sat down, though she ignored the food and coffee set before her. She instead watched warily as Patrick and Keith each took a seat, then Walt. They had no problem digging into the chili or drinking the coffee as she watched them silently.

"Watts is in Virginia." Patrick's head lifted from the steady concentration he had been giving his food. "He's been held in a prison in the Middle East since he was captured at that facility in Germany. One of Jonas Wyatt's pet prisoners."

Her brows lifted. Did everyone but her know about this prison?

"So I just learned." Her hands clenched in her lap. She was almost shaking with nerves, with fear. The murders that had been committed in this small town had begun here. Perhaps all three men had been involved in them. They had been cold-blooded and bloodthirsty. Without mercy.

Patrick shook his head. "We're not going to harm you, Ms. Hawkins, unless we have no choice." His eyes were hard now. He would, if he had to, that was the message he was giving her. If she didn't cooperate.

"Cabal's going to start with Myron or Danna," she said softly. "He's going to hurt them, Mr. Wallace. Myron was a friend of mine; I'd hate to see that happen to him. But unless you let me go, nothing is going to stop it."

"Myron knew the risks involved in this plan," he told her quietly. "I just hope your Bengal knows that harming either of them will come with a price."

She would be harmed. She was getting real damned good at reading between Breed lines here.

"So why don't you just tell me what this genius plan of yours is?" She crossed her arms over her breasts and glared at the three of them. "Don't tell me you actually think Douglas is going to come for me?"

Patrick's smile turned thin and cruel. "Do you think he will?"

She rolled her eyes at that thought before staring back at him steadily.

"You're just a distraction," he finally admitted. "And a bit of insurance. Jonas has a leash on Watts in the form of a Coyote Breed on the team that helped him escape. I just want to make certain he loosens that leash and gives Watts his head a bit."

She shook her head. "It's not going to work. Cabal won't be distracted."

"He's not looking for Watts; he's looking for you." Patrick shrugged. "Jonas is trying to cover Cabal's ass as well as keep up with Watts and look for the Dozen's killer." His grin was self-depreciating. "That would be me of course."

"Of course," she murmured as she sat back in her chair and watched him. "And you just want to be the one to kill Watts."

"No, Ms. Hawkins, he wants to be the one to rip the identities of the last of the Deadly Dozen right out of Watts's lying throat."

She whirled around, eyes widening, lips parting in shock at the sight of the former mayor of Glen Ferris as he limped into the room.

David Banks had a bandage extending from his thigh to his ankle. There were healing wounds on his face, bandages were obvious beneath the loose T-shirt he wore, and as he limped forward on crutches, it was easy to see that whatever had happened to him had nearly been fatal.

She jerked around in her seat to face Patrick. "He was part of the Dozen."

Patrick nodded slowly. "He was."

"And he's here? Why don't you stop making me guess what

the hell is going on here and just tell me? Because I'm getting damned sick of coming up with the questions and getting none of the answers."

"That's possibly my fault." David eased himself into the chair at the other end of the table, wincing as he stretched his leg out in front of him.

Walt rose from his seat and collected another bowl of chili and cup of coffee before setting it in front of David.

"That's Walt," he sighed before looking back to Cassa. "The Deadly Dozen were real bastards. I was a part of a small group of FBI agents tracking down information on the Council and the Breeds. I managed to infiltrate the Dozen when it first formed. Brandenmore and Engalls funded the group at first, because they wanted Breeds for research. The Council allowed the Dozen a certain number of live specimens on the condition that they returned either the live Breeds or their heads as proof that they were no longer free."

Cassa covered her mouth with a hand, staring back at him in horror.

"I couldn't tell anyone here what I was doing, because I never knew who I could trust. At that time, there was someone in the Breed Freedom Society sending information to the Council. I didn't know if it was a human or Breed, so I kept my mouth shut and did my job. However, my interests always lay with protecting the Breeds."

His expression twisted in pain, in grief.

"What happened Valentine's night?" she asked.

David shook his head. "There was a Coyote Breed. A young one. He'd managed to escape his lab in Yugoslavia and he made it here. But he had Council soldiers on his ass the whole way. He was wounded, feverish. The kid was next to dead when he finally made it to Glen Ferris and managed to contact Walt." He nodded to Walt. "He was a new genetic design. That was all the information we were given. The Council was desperate to get him back. The Dozen was called in when they received word from their spy that he was here."

He looked up at Walt and Patrick. "I tried to send them a warning, but it was intercepted."

Patrick rose from his seat and moved to the window. Bracing his hands on the window, he stared outside as David continued.

"They were ambushed. I didn't even know the hunt was on

that night. They'd gotten word at the last minute and I wasn't in town. If I had been . . ." He swallowed tightly. "So much would have changed."

"Your husband raped and killed Myron's mate." Patrick's voice was toneless. "Before the hunt they found my cabin. They killed my mate and cut our child from her body as we were trying to escort the Coyote through the mountains. She was in labor. She and the midwife both were killed." His shoulders were tense, his voice thick with emotion. When he turned back to her, his eyes were like brandy flames in the depths of his sun-darkened flesh. "Your husband knows where my child was taken. He wasn't taken to a lab. He wasn't even reported as being alive. Brandenmore and Engalls didn't have him. Watts and three others of the Dozen hid him. I want to know where my son is. If he's alive or dead. Ms. Hawkins, I will know, or Douglas Watts will know pain as he's never imagined it."

Fury throbbed in his voice. An icy sharp rage that sent shivers racing down her back.

"Why didn't you contact Jonas Wyatt?" she asked, her voice thick. "Why didn't you tell him? He would have helped you."

Walt shook his head. "This ain't Wyatt's fight. It's ours. The Dozen killed our people. Patrick's mate and his younger brother. His brother was Danna's mate. Friends and loved ones, Ms. Hawkins. This ain't Sanctuary. And by God, we take vengeance for our own."

Anger lined Walt's face now, anger and grief. He shook his head and sniffed back his emotion. There were no tears; the burning rage inside him would have dried any moisture, Cassa thought. There was nothing left now but the need for blood.

"What happened to you?" she asked David.

A bitter little laugh escaped his throat. "I made the mistake of asking the wrong person about the child that was taken that night. About six months ago, the Dozen came after me. Ryan Damron had managed to get the names of a few of the members. He was bringing the information and the proof of it to me. But he didn't come alone. Elam March was with him as well as a Coyote soldier. They were going to kill me, Ms. Hawkins. Damron had betrayed me."

"David was smarter than he used to be though," Walt grunted. "He came to me. I called Patrick, and he and Keith shadowed that meeting."

"That's when I decided I liked the feel of their blood on my hands." Patrick's smile was hard, cruel. "I'd been searching for their identities for years. I'll have them when I find Watts. I'll find my kid, and I'll finish killing the rest of them once I do. This isn't Wyatt's or St. Laurents's fight, nor is it yours, Ms. Hawkins."

"But you drew me into it," she reminded him angrily. "You sent the emails, the pills, and you drew me here. Don't deny it."

"I did exactly that." Suddenly, he was before her, his hands flat on the table, the fury flickering in his eyes. "To distract your mate. That was your only job. To keep him out of my damned way. But you had to go and decide you were going to get your answers anyway. You couldn't let well enough alone."

"Bullshit." She came to her feet, glaring back at him. "You knew I wouldn't leave it alone. You knew I'd do everything in my power to get this story."

His brow lifted. A sardonic curl of his lips attested to the truth of her accusation as he eased back from her. Manipulating bastard.

"I could fail." He straightened, drawing to his full height as he stared back at her, the chill in his gaze once again. "If I fail and word leaks to the world of the killings that have taken place here, then I want someone with influence to know the truth." He shook his head wearily. "It's not my desire to destroy the Breeds in the public eye, Ms. Hawkins."

"Why did you draw Wyatt in if you didn't want his help?" She wasn't finished, and she didn't care much for his explanation. "Why did you leave it to him to clean up your mess?"

"Because I knew he would." He shrugged easily, as though it really didn't matter to him one way or the other how Jonas was forced to clean up after him. "And if anyone knew where Watts was being held, then Wyatt would. I knew he was alive. There have been too many rumors, too much information against the Council that's come out, that only he would have known. I knew Wyatt had Watts, and I wanted him. There was no way to keep Wyatt out of it."

"Breeds and their schemes," she sighed. "You've made a mistake, Patrick. Your own arrogance and need for blood is going to destroy you."

"They already have," he said simply, solemnly. "Years ago, Ms. Hawkins. They did that years ago."

♦   ♦   ♦

Cabal entered the woods surrounding Sheriff Lacey's home just as she was pulling into her driveway. Myron James pulled in behind her, his expression creased with anger as he got out of his car and slammed the door furiously.

"He said he wasn't going to do this." He was in the sheriff's face within seconds, the freckles standing out on his pale face as he confronted her. "What the fuck is going on?"

"He didn't do this." She pushed back against his shoulders, jerking away from him and glaring back at him. "He would have told me before he did anything this fucking insane in my county."

"I told you he was out of control," Myron continued to argue. "Who else would have done it, Danna? There's no one else that would have kidnapped Cassa like that. No one else is that fucking crazy."

"Crazy" was a good description of any man that dared to touch Cabal's mate, let alone take her from him.

"He wouldn't have done it." Danna shook her head furiously as she turned and stalked to the house.

Cabal eased in closer, moving in along the house, listening carefully as they entered.

"Who else could have done it, Danna?" Myron yelled, the anger thick in his voice. "You know he did it."

"He's not answering his sat phone. Again." Frustration filled her voice. "Rand and Jason were on-site, they haven't heard from him either. No one can contact him."

There was a note of fear in Danna's voice now.

"God! I checked the cabin. He's not there either." Myron paused. "The cabin was cleaned out, Danna. Everything. It's empty as hell."

Silence filled the house as the scent of fear and sadness seeped from the building. As though they were mourning him.

"He's okay." Danna was fighting to believe that. Cabal could hear it in her voice. "He has to be okay, Myron."

Myron didn't say anything for long moments.

"Have you called Walt?" Danna finally asked. "I couldn't reach him earlier."

"He wasn't answering," Myron stated. "And he has David. If Walt and David are missing, then the rest of the Dozen could have figured out that he's still alive. If they have, then he's screwed."

Cabal snarled silently, gripped the doorknob and in one smooth motion opened the door and stepped into the sheriff's kitchen.

He had his weapon on them even as Danna reached for hers.

"Now, we don't want to do that, Sheriff," he drawled as he watched both of them pale.

He knew what they saw. The stripe across his face, and the other stripes now running down his body. The markings of his genetics that only surfaced when the animal inside him rose to the fore. When a killing fury was on him. And there was a need for blood now. A need to kill.

Danna eased her hand back from her weapon as Cabal stepped forward and jerked it from its holster.

"So Banks is alive?" He stepped back. "And good ole Walt is taking care of him." He eyed them both with a hard smile. "Where has he been hiding him?"

Danna and Myron glanced at each other, fear thick in their scents and their expressions.

"Come on now, let's keep the bloodshed to a minimum. I'd hate to have to hurt one of you."

Danna shook her head. "He doesn't have your mate, Cabal. We would have known if he did. Rick was insistent that he wouldn't strike at her. She was just here to distract you."

"Consider me distracted." He smiled thinly. "Now, where is Walt's cabin? Don't make me go looking for it. You wouldn't like the consequences and neither would they."

"Cabal, we weren't involved in this." Danna's voice broke with fear and nerves. "This wasn't planned."

He lifted his lip in a curl of anger, revealing the canines at one side of his mouth. The stripes on his face darkened with his rage, only barely contained.

"Do you want to die today, Sheriff?" he asked her before he turned to Myron. "Do you want to see your daughters grow up and have children of their own? I could make certain you don't live to see that if you prefer."

He would make certain of it. He'd stood back and denied his mate for too many years. Out of arrogance, out of stubbornness, for whatever reason. Now that he had claimed her, he wasn't willing to lose her. Not for any reason. Especially not a rogue Breed's hunger for vengeance.

He turned his head, staring around the house, inhaling slowly. He could barely detect that hint of cinnamon in the sherrif's house now. The same scent that had caught his senses before when he had been here. The same scent he had detected in the air during Cassa's kidnapping.

"Who is Rick?" He turned back to the sheriff, the name filtering through his mind for possible Breeds that he could identify.

Danna inhaled swiftly at the name, perhaps only now realizing she had used it. She shook her head slowly, her eyes sheening with tears.

"Rick," he mused, a picture flashing before his mind. A picture found on the bank of the river where Cash Winslow had died. A picture of a Breed who should have been dead.

"Patrick Wallace?" His eyes narrowed on the sudden dilation of her pupils. She wasn't trained to lie. She was good. Damned good. But still an amateur. Easily read and easily deceived. "Where is he, since it's obvious he's no longer dead?"

Danna stared back at him levelly. "Patrick Wallace died twenty-two years ago."

Cabal tilted his head and stared at her before straightening and roaring back in her face in rage. "Where is he?"

He could sense the lie. He knew a liar when he sensed one.

"Oh God." Terror raced through her; the stench of it was nearly overwhelming.

"Get back, Danna." Myron pushed in front of her, using his own body to shield her as Cabal advanced on them. "Look, Cabal, we don't know shit!" he yelled back. "Whatever the hell happened to your mate, we don't know shit about it. We don't know where Walt has Banks, and we don't know where Rick's at."

"Who is Rick?" he snarled in Myron's face.

"Patrick Wallace," he answered truthfully. "But in the labs he was known as Azrael."

Cabal almost blinked back at him in surprise and in shock. Azrael had killed himself, six other Breeds and an entire lab of soldiers and scientists more than thirty years ago. He had been created in a hellhole in Libya. His Lion genetics were crossed with the genetics of a young woman rumored to be a descendant of an ancient, bloody pharaoh.

Each DNA sequencing that had gone into the creation of Azrael had been precise. Nothing had been left to chance. He was their prize. He had become their death. And it was believed he had become his own death due to feral fever.

"Azrael," Cabal murmured. He had been a legend among the Breeds when he lived. There had been no Breed bloodier, or more merciless, than he.

Eyeing them both for long moments, he reached out first to jerk Myron's sat phone from its belt clip, before pushing past him and taking Danna's.

Opening the call log, he shook his head and muttered. "Amateurs."

The numbers were clearly displayed, giving him all he needed.

Tucking the phones into the narrow pocket on his mission pants, he smiled coldly. "It's been a nice visit, but it's time for me to go now."

He had no compunction about knocking them both out. It was that or kill them, and the need to kill was already rising hard and fast within him.

After making sure they were unconscious, he pulled two pressure syringes from his pack and a vial of sedative. They needed to stay out for a while. He didn't have the time or the patience to deal with the interference they would cause.

Using the sheriff's restraints, he secured them by the wrists and ankles and left them lying on the kitchen floor. If either of them had an ounce of intelligence, then it wouldn't take them long to get free. But it would give him enough time to do what he had to do. They were going to nap for a while anyway.

Cabal reengaged the comm link as he left the house, and pulled the sat phones free again as he hit the secure line to Jonas's link.

"I'm going to kill you when I find you," Jonas promised with lethal deliberation.

"You have a bigger problem. Azrael is alive."

There was a long silence, dark and dangerous, across the link.

"That's not possible," Jonas finally answered, his voice cold. "His DNA was identified at the scene."

"You said yourself when we found Alonzo that these kills reminded you of Azrael," Cabal reminded him. "That's because they are his kills. I suspect the six Breeds he led are here with him as well. You need to get an accounting of your Breeds, Director. All kinds of problems are beginning to crop up here," he finished sarcastically.

"It's not Azrael." Jonas denied it again. "He's dead, Cabal. Whoever this is is just doing a damned good job of impersonating him. Do you have anything else?"

Cabal shook his head. Jonas didn't want to admit Azrael was out there, simply because there would be no controlling that particular Breed.

"I guess giving you the sat phone number I have for our god of death would be a bad idea then," he drawled. "I was hoping you could trace it, but I think I can handle that little chore now."

"Don't make me kill you painfully, Cabal," Jonas warned him, and it wasn't an idle threat.

There would be payment for literally going rogue on the director of the Bureau of Breed Affairs. That wasn't usually a wise move. However, in this case, it had been Cabal's only possible move.

"Sorry, Director. Some things are more important than the bottom line." He disconnected the link as he mulled over Jonas's insistence that Azrael was indeed dead. The director should have learned by now that nothing was definite where Breeds were concerned.

There had been too many Breeds that were believed dead but had turned up alive in the past few years. It wouldn't surprise Cabal in the least to learn that Azrael was indeed still alive.

Moving away from the sheriff's house, he pulled one of the small remote sat detectors from his pack and plugged the sat phone into it. Pulling up the numbers once again, he chose the one he figured was most likely the rogue he was searching for. The number dialed the most often.

Tucking the unit back into the leather holder, he loped through the forest to the area where he'd stored his rifle and larger pack before entering the cabin. He should have the location he was searching for soon. Once he had that, he would have his mate's kidnapper.

His muscles were tense, and rage still thundered through his blood as he fought to hold on to his much needed control. Now wasn't the time to let the animal free, to allow the killer to hunt.

The man had to keep a measure of control for the time being. Until his mate was safe. Then the animal could have his vengeance.

God help all of them if Cassa had been harmed. There would be no force on earth that could save any of them. Danna Lacey, Myron, Azrael or whoever the hell he was—it wouldn't matter. If Cassa was harmed, then Cabal had no reason to live.

He almost paused at that thought. Living had always been the one hunger that had gotten him through the hellish existence of the labs. Nothing had mattered but survival. When most of his pride had died, when he had realized there was no way to save them, even then, survival had been paramount.

It was humbling to realize that if Cassa didn't live, didn't breathe in his world, then he didn't want to be a part of it.

He paused, breathed in hard and deep and fought back the emotion clawing at his chest, at his throat. God help him, just to smell her scent, to hear her voice, to know she lived . . .

He couldn't bear the not knowing. Wondering if she was suffering. If Azrael lived, then he was the one Breed that wouldn't care if she suffered. If he had deemed her a threat, or a pawn in this game, then he wouldn't care if she hurt, if she cried. If she was innocent. Nothing would matter but the plan he had in store for her.

If that were the case, then nothing would matter to Cabal but his blood. Azrael might be the god of death, but Cabal would ensure he died.

As he reached the store of supplies he had stashed for the visit to the sheriff's home, he felt the muted vibration of the tracking unit in its pack against his thigh. He smiled, a cold, hard curl of his lips, and drew the device out.

And there it was. The location of the sat phone he was searching for. And, he prayed, the location of his mate.

"Rick, I can't reach Danna or Myron on their sats." Walt moved back into the kitchen a few hours later, a frown creasing his brow. "They were calling every few minutes, then it just stopped. I can't reach them now."

Patrick turned from the open window above the sink, his gaze going immediately to Cassa, his eyes turning hard and cold.

"Keith." He turned to the Breed that waited silently at the other side of the room. "Contact Rand and Jason. Have them check on it."

Keith nodded before pulling free the sat phone and making the call. His voice was low as he spoke, filled with pauses, but little expression on his face.

"I'll let him know," he finally said before turning to Patrick. "They're under surveillance," he reported. "Do you still want them to continue?"

Patrick looked at her again, as though it were her fault or she could do something about it. Finally, he nodded slowly. "Continue and report back to me."

Keith relayed the order before disconnecting and storing the small phone in his jeans pocket.

"If he's hurt them, you'll hurt," he stated coldly. "He knew that before he laid hands on them."

"If your mate was taken, what would you do?" she asked him. "Who would you hurt? They knew the risk when they helped you in this."

"And he knows the risks in striking against them." He lifted his shoulders heavily. "So be it."

So be it.

Cassa shook her head at the statement. This was the part of the Breed world that she didn't always understand. Though she knew she should by now. In some ways it wasn't that dissimilar to the human psychology, and yet in others, they were poles apart.

She was a pawn between Patrick Wallace and Cabal whether she wanted to be or not. She was insurance that Cabal wouldn't strike out against his friends, as well as insurance that he would stay suitably occupied while Patrick killed again.

"Once Douglas is dead and you've found your son, what then?" she asked him. "What's left, Patrick?"

He didn't answer her immediately, but she saw the stiffening of his shoulders, knew he'd heard her and that the question had impacted.

"There are four more," he finally answered. "If Jonas doesn't kill me, then I'll finish the job."

"Jonas?" She stared back at him in surprise. "Jonas is the one you have to worry about killing you?"

"Jonas is the only one capable of killing me," he informed her with mild amusement. "Your Bengal is good, Ms. Hawkins; he's damned good. But he's not a primal Bengal. He's a recessed Bengal."

"Really?" The question was mockingly phrased. "So there are two different kind of Bengals?" That was news to her.

He turned back to her then. "There are in every Breed species." He lifted his hand, flexed his fingers, and Cassa felt her stomach almost heave as she watched claws extend and push out beneath the nails.

"I'm a primal Lion Breed." He smiled. "The skin on each side of the human nails is no more than cartilage. Beneath the nail is a claw. It's really rather interesting, though damned confusing to the scientists as well as the few primals that exist. There's no pain, but sometimes, if the claws aren't exercised, there is some blood during retraction. All in all, it's really quite amazing. Primal Lions have been noted to have that ability. It's rumored that primal Bengals display their stripes, especially across their face during a hunt. The small hairs at the nape of their neck become thicker, their sense of smell sharper, their rage is like icy fury. I saw one killed in the lab before my escape. It fought with true fury. Took out several Coyote soldiers as well as trained pit bulls. It was an incredible sight."

It sounded terrifying to her. Cruel and horrible. And this man had called it an incredible sight.

"But they don't have the retractable claws?" she asked. She had seen Cabal's stripes, she had sensed the animal he tried to hide.

"They do." He nodded. "All primal Feline Breeds have the retractable claws."

She turned away from him. Cabal didn't have retractable claws, she knew that. At least, she didn't think he did. She had to admit she hadn't actually asked him about them.

"Jonas is primal," Patrick revealed. "Few realize this, and he definitely wouldn't want the public to know. But he was created to breed. To be a stud for a new army." He chuckled at that. "He was primal from birth."

"You know Jonas?" She turned back to him, searching his expression.

Patrick shrugged. "I know of Jonas. I knew the rumors that circulated of his genetics, and I knew what the scientists were working on before I escaped myself. It wasn't hard to figure out who and what he was once I began checking into it."

"You investigated Jonas before starting this. As well as Cabal," she guessed.

"I did." He nodded. "As well as Rule Breaker and Lawe Justice." He grinned at the names. "Even they aren't quite what you would expect. Mordecai, that Coyote Jonas keeps on a leash, is more dangerous than he knows. Coyotes aren't always forthcoming, you know, even to those they give their loyalty to."

She shook her head. "And you're going to defeat them all?"

"I don't have to defeat them all," he sighed. "I just have to get Watts. He's probably in town by now. I wonder if he'll ask about you. Do you think he's forgotten about his lovely wife in the years Jonas has kept him imprisoned?"

"No doubt," she said, mocking him. "Especially considering the fact we weren't really married."

"There was that." He nodded. "At least you know where you stand with Cabal. No divorce. And the words 'till death do us part' take on a whole new meaning, wouldn't you say? When your mate dies, a part of you dies with them." There was an edge of bitterness there, one that didn't belong with a man's feelings toward his wife. Or his mate. There was almost a hatred, a cold, hard core of pure resentment.

"Does innocent blood appeal to you, Patrick?" she asked him. "Is that why you don't mind using an innocent in your games?"

"There are no innocents," he grunted as he turned back to the window, obviously assessing the breeze and the scents that flowed from the mountain. "And there's no innocence. We just pretend there is."

Cassa parted her lips to argue that statement, but as she began to speak the sat phone at Patrick's belt beeped imperatively.

Pulling the phone free, he checked it, quirked his lips mockingly, then flipped it open. "Good evening, Douglas. How nice to hear from you." He turned to Cassa, his brows lifting in surprise. "Actually, I do have her." He paused. Listened. His expression darkened. "A trade? Very well. The information I want for your wife. Where would you like to meet?"

For one horrifying moment she felt fear cascade inside her and felt any hope she had of surviving this diminish. He was going to trade her for information on his son. He was going to trade her to a man that they both knew would kill her. There was no way Douglas would allow her to survive.

God, where was Cabal?

◆   ◆   ◆

Douglas Watts stared at the sat phone in his hand, then at the commander of the Coyote team that had broken him from the prison Jonas Wyatt and Cabal St. Laurents had kept him in for more than eleven years.

He hated Breeds. It didn't matter what kind they were or whether or not they were loyal to the Genetics Council. He just flat-out hated them.

H. R. Alonzo had phrased it perfectly. They were an abomination against mankind. Whatever had possessed scientists to think they could control these creatures, he didn't know.

Now they were mixing in the general population, *mating* human, God-created women and infecting them with the DNA that had created the Breeds and making inhuman little monsters.

"Were you able to track the call?" he asked the commander, as the Breed stared at the display on the tracking device he used.

The Breed shook his head slowly. "The signal's bouncing. It wasn't a direct line." He folded the device and slipped it into a pocket of his olive green mission pants.

Douglas inhaled slowly. Deeply. Patience, he warned himself. The Council contact that had arranged the breakout had warned him that these Coyotes didn't understand subservience the way Coyotes used to understand it.

Kill them all, he thought. That was what they should have done.

Clenching his teeth, he looked down at his legs and moved them again. At least there was some satisfaction there. The metal supports on his legs gave them strength, and the neural disc that had been implanted just after his escape gave him movement, sensation.

Damn, he was a man again. He was even fucking horny. He hadn't had a hard-on since that son of a bitch St. Laurents staked him in the spine the night Douglas had tried to ensure his death.

If it just hadn't been for that stupid bitch, Cassa. God, he was glad he hadn't actually married her. The woman was dumb as a fucking brick. She wasn't even a nice fuck. Not that she couldn't have been if she had just put a little effort into it. The little prude.

He snorted at the thought. He bet she would move that little ass the next time he got his dick inside her. Being mated to that Bengal. He almost chuckled at the thought. He'd heard about mating and what it did to a woman, how they couldn't tolerate another man's touch. Hell, he'd even seen it for himself. Twenty-two years ago, in the mountains of this little town. He'd had the pleasure of raping one. She'd screamed. Screamed in agony. Begged and fought him like a lioness. And finally, she'd died. He'd fucked her until she lost the little animal she was carrying and died right there in his arms.

He was going to fuck Cassa like that too. Fuck her until she screamed and cried, fought and begged. And if she was carrying St. Laurents's kittens, then he'd make sure she wasn't carrying them when he finished with her.

Moving slowly, he rose to his feet, almost moaning with the

welcome pain he felt in his legs. It would take a while to regain
the muscle he'd lost in the past eleven years, the surgeon had
warned him. But it would happen. He had his legs back, he
had his manhood back.

And he had to piss.

Even that feeling was almost ecstasy. Soon, he'd be back to
his old self, and once he was, he'd tell the world, show them the
brutality of the Breeds.

They had reported Douglas Watts dead. Wouldn't the world
be surprised when he showed up, not just alive, but with proof of
what they did to their enemies and the horrors they subjected
those against them to.

"We're meeting them in the valley then?" the commander
asked, his voice chillingly polite.

"Isn't that what you heard me arrange?" Douglas grunted,
wishing he could slap the bastard down as he should have been
able to do.

"There have been Bureau patrols around them," the Coyote
reminded him. "Just because the meet was stated for there
doesn't mean we can't change it."

No, the valley was perfect. He almost rubbed his hands together in glee. There was a reason he and his friends had chosen
that valley to ambush the Breeds in. There were plenty of places
to hide and not as many to break through. The bastard that had
dared to try to kill off the Deadly Dozen, and Douglas himself,
would learn that he wasn't dealing with some country bumpkin.

Good Lord, why hadn't Phillip Brandenmore taken care of
this mess in Glen Ferris? He practically owned this town, but
still, Breeds lived and were probably breeding here. Like rats.
Or cockroaches.

"I gotta take a piss," he told the Breed commander. Damn if
he could remember his name. "Get your men together. Have
they moved to the valley yet?"

"My men are in place." The answer wasn't rude, but it was
just shy of it.

Douglas glared back at him. "Remember who's paying you,"
he bit out angrily. "If you don't succeed, you won't get a penny."

The Coyote's grin was rueful. "And I'm all about the money,
man. It's the only reason your white-trash ass is still alive."

Fury nearly strangled Douglas. He was not white trash. He
could trace his family tree back beyond the *Mayflower*. He was

a descendant of kings, and this bastard dared to talk to him this way.

"You remind me of a braying jackass," Douglas sneered. "You bastards used to remember your place."

The Coyote laughed at that. "At your back, with a blade? Man, you'd be bleeding from your throat, not your back, if you weren't worth more to me alive than dead. Now take your piss so we can get started."

The Coyote shook his head as he continued to chuckle. Let him enjoy his little laugh. He would be next, Douglas promised himself. There were plenty of pure blood societies willing to be trained to kill these animals. And Douglas knew just how to train them. Just how to work them. And this Coyote commander would be first on his list.

Brimstone might think his shit didn't stink, but Douglas would be the man to show him better. Soon. Very soon.

♦   ♦   ♦

Cabal took the pill he had saved back from those he had given Jonas. It wouldn't eliminate the human side of his scent, but it would at least hide the Breed. If he stayed downwind of the location he had tracked the sat phone to, then it wouldn't matter anyway.

He just had to find Cassa. He would deal with Patrick Wallace, or Azrael as Cabal suspected him to be, after Cassa's safety was assured.

God help the bastard if she wasn't okay.

Shifting the pack on his back, he scaled one of the low-lying cliffs that led along the path to the location he was searching for. There wasn't time to go around it. Cassa said the pills lasted two hours; that should be time enough for what he had to do.

As he slid along the top of the cliff, he stayed low, listening to the steady hum of the near silent heli-jet cruising overhead.

The specially designed mission pants he wore would hide him from the thermal imaging the craft had. He'd disconnected the locator the pants carried, ensuring that Jonas couldn't pick him up on the specialized radar the heli-jet was equipped with.

As it passed overhead, Cabal rose to his feet and moved quickly along one of the narrow paths that animals or hikers had made on the mountain. He checked the sat phone locator beacon often, noticing that it hadn't moved. At least not yet.

Though Jonas had sent a message that Douglas Watts was definitely on the move, and that worried Cabal. Because Watts was heading this way.

He ignored the slight chill that pressed through the mission suit and ignored the snow beginning to swirl around him.

As he topped the rise, he crawled to the edge of a ravine and looked over, his eyes narrowing at the slightest glow of light through the darkness.

He checked the tracker on the sat phone, and was certain that this was the cabin he was searching for. He watched, inhaling the scents blowing toward him, searching for some sign of Cassa and finding nothing on the cold breeze.

He was going to have to get in closer, but with the way the cabin sat and the position of the ravine, it was going to be damned near impossible to slip up on another Breed. His Breed scent might be masked, but if the pill did indeed allow the human scent through, then he could be fucked. Because Azrael would be able to detect him coming.

He would have to stay low. The lower he was, the less chance there would be of the breeze betraying him. The winds were swirling, but for the moment they were coming down, curling and moving along the edge of the valley. If they stayed as they were, a big *if* there, then there would be a narrow window of movement that he could use to advance on the cabin.

Plotting his course, he gave the breeze time to die down before he took off. Using one hand to hold the rifle secure at his back, he ran, body low, using the speed that had been built into his genetics to race the wind.

As he drew closer to the cabin, he knew something was wrong. He could smell Breed scent; Walt Jameson's scent was there as well as a scent he knew belonged to David Banks. But the scents weren't fresh. They weren't there.

Enraged, a howl tore from Cabal's lips as he went through the front door. Glass and wood crashed into an immaculate kitchen. There was chili on the stove, coffee in the pot. All fresh. Cassa's scent was there at the table, an untouched bowl of food where she had sat.

But there was no Cassa.

"You fucker!" he screamed. Fury burned like fire in his blood and tore through his senses, darkening the stripes now bisecting his face and running down his body.

"Jonas," he barked into the comm link. "They're not at the cabin I tracked the sat phone signal from. What the fuck is going on?"

"Watts is moving," Jonas growled into the link. "If you'd keep the goddamned link turned on, you might know that. There's movement at the valley where Alonzo's body was found. We can't slip in with the heli-jet. We're moving in on foot."

Cabal didn't wait to question. The clearing was a good half hour's hard run from where he was currently at. The distance could be shortened if he shot over the cliff behind him. If he could scale it quickly enough.

It was a second's thought, quick calculation before he ran for the cliff. The leather gloves on his hands protected his palms, but nothing could protect the gloves as his nails retracted, the strong claws beneath shooting out to grip the stone.

He scrambled up the narrow cliff face, using every ounce of strength in his arms and legs to move himself quickly along the jutting stone and the weathered erosions that pitted it.

Within minutes he was jumping over the top and was running. Son of a bitch, he hated running with this damned suit on. He couldn't feel the breeze, couldn't smell it either, couldn't sense friend or foe as he could without the protective outerwear.

Without it though he would be easily detectable to Breed or human devices. The fabric blocked some scent; hopefully the anti-scent drug he had taken would completely block the Breed scent. If he was lucky, damned lucky, then he just might be able to slip in.

"Cassa's been sighted, Cabal. She's alive. Patrick Wallace has made a deal with Watts according to the information our spy within the group had gotten to us. He's trading Cassa to Watts for information on a missing son."

"What missing kid?" he snarled into the link.

"The Valentine's night massacre," Jonas relayed. "Wallace's mate was in labor when the Dozen found her. She was alone with the midwife. Both his mate and the midwife were killed. Her child was cut from her body and taken. Watts took the boy. Wallace is hunting for his child."

Then he should have come to Jonas. Hell, he could have come to Cabal at any time and received every resource they could use to find Wallace's missing child.

No, what this man had done was insanity. He had killed,

risked the Breed community and then dared to attempt to trade Cassa for information.

He was a dead man, Cabal promised himself. There was no way in hell Cabal was going to allow such mercilessness to survive.

"Cabal, we have a team moving in," Jonas informed him. "Brimstone is commander of the Coyotes that broke Watts out of the prison. That team is not to be touched. Those Coyotes are friendly. I repeat, they're friendly. Do not engage. Son of a bitch, you stubborn-assed Bengal. I know what the fuck I'm doing here!" Jonas finally yelled in frustration when Cabal didn't respond.

Engage, his ass. Then they better not get in his damned way. He liked Brimstone just fine. Second-in-command of the Coyotes that had joined the Wolf community of Haven, he was a fine man. He was a damned good Breed. But if he stood in Cabal's way, then he was going to be a damned good dead Breed. It was that simple.

CHAPTER 26

Patrick Wallace didn't touch her, Cassa had to give him that. He made certain she was given breathing room, she wasn't crowded in the van that he, Walt, Keith and David rode in.

David didn't continue the full distance. They met another vehicle not far down the mountain.

"Protection," Patrick murmured as Cassa watched the several Breeds from the other vehicle help David Banks into the four-wheel-drive. "David has proof and information against the members of the Dozen that have been identified so far. It's been a process of elimination for the past few years."

Cassa turned and stared at his profile. His expression was quiet, reflective. His face was cast in shadow in the low light of the dash, giving him a somber, dark-angel appearance.

"You won't find the identities of the final four," she told him quietly. "Cabal will kill you for this, Patrick."

She was shaking inside. She could feel the fear moving through her, building in her mind. If Cabal didn't find her soon, and she knew he was looking for her, then she was screwed. God only knew what Douglas would do to her once he got his hands on her. From the videos she had seen of those hunts, it was something she didn't want to contemplate.

Patrick shook his head slowly.

"My mate betrayed me and mine to those hunters," he said quietly. "My best fighters were massacred. The females of my pride were either killed or returned to their labs. I learned then: You do what you have to do. My loyalty is to my fallen pride and those who still survive. You're a pawn, Ms. Hawkins. Cabal was a pawn. And Watts will become a fatality. However I have to effect that end, that is what he will be. Whether you live or die all depends on how intelligent you are, and whether or not you've learned how to fight in the past eleven years." She stared back at him, knowing there was going to be no mercy here. He might not want to hurt her himself, but if she was harmed, he wouldn't cry over it.

"I hope this is worth the hell Cabal will ensure you endure," she whispered.

"There is no hell greater than the one I've already endured." He sighed as he slid the vehicle into gear and drove the van out of the wide spot he'd used to pull off on.

Cassa was certain a worse hell awaited her though if she didn't find a way to escape it. What had he said? Her ability to survive this depended on her own intelligence. And what exactly did he mean by that?

"Rick, everyone's in place," Walt informed him quietly as he disconnected the sat phone he had held to his ear for long moments. "Watts is moving into the meeting area."

Patrick nodded. "Keith?" He glanced at the Breed in the back.

"In place." Keith was quiet, his voice rough. "The players are all heading to the field."

The tension mounted in the van now.

"Don't do this," she whispered again.

"I was born to do this," he said heavily. "Live or die. It ends with Watts tonight."

Cassa stared into the darkness that gathered around the van as they drove deeper into the mountains. The bare trees danced in the wind as snow began to swirl in the air. The chill outside seemed to seep inside the vehicle, to sink into her flesh.

She needed Cabal. She ached to burrow against him, to feel the warmth of him just once more. She should have told him, she thought. She should have told him that this mating meant so much more to her than she had ever imagined it would. That through the years she had run from him, just as hard as he had run from her, because she had been frightened. Because she had been afraid he could never forgive her for the deaths of his family.

Not just his pride. Those Breeds were more: They were brothers and sisters, born of the same mother, bred from the same genetics.

She loved him. She had always loved him. That night as she stared into his eyes, feeling his fingers wrapped around her throat and seeing the amber rage in his gaze, she had also seen the mercy. The struggle within himself. The certainty that he would never hurt her, no matter the fury that tore through him.

He hadn't left the first mark on her. Not a single fingerprint or bruise. He hadn't hurt her. He would never hurt her. In that single moment a part of her heart had opened and Cabal had filled it.

And now she could lose that forever.

Where was he? She stared out into the night, knowing he was there somewhere. He was looking for her. He was fighting to save her. She might have to save herself for a while first though.

She could do that. Whatever it took to ensure that she had the future she had always dreamed of with Cabal. Whatever it took to ensure that she didn't have to live so much as another hour without knowing that he understood the faith and the trust she placed in him.

Had she ever told him that? She hadn't. God, this had all happened so fast. The mating, learning to adjust to a heat that really wasn't as bad as she had heard it was. Actually, she thought and frowned, it was rather tame when compared to the trials she knew other mates had faced.

Though the physical symptoms were lighter than with other mates because of the hormones, she could still feel the bonding. She could feel the need to be close to him, the need for his warmth, not just his lovemaking. She needed Cabal, just because he was Cabal. Her wild Bengal Breed.

"Get ready," Patrick warned them as they pulled into the wide clearing she had used herself when searching for the valley where Alonzo had died.

Get ready to die.

Cassa could feel the tension rising inside her. As Patrick stepped out of the van and slid open the door by her seat, she met his gaze calmly.

"You can't trust Douglas," she told him. "He always has a backup plan."

"As do I." He shrugged. "Let's go. We'll get this taken care of as quickly as possible. Perhaps you'll get lucky and you'll see your mate before the night is over."

Cassa inhaled slowly and stepped into the cold. She could feel it wrapping around her, prickling over her flesh despite the coat Walt had given her to wear.

"Move out." Patrick urged her forward, but she noticed that he, Walt and Keith surrounded her.

There was no sense of safety here though. There was a heavy sense of danger instead. As though she could feel evil surrounding her, coming closer to her. Or rather, she was moving closer to the evil.

Her chest hurt with the knowledge that blood was going to spill, one way or the other, tonight. There was no way to stop it. Whether Douglas lived or died, the Breed that had dared to kidnap her, to attempt to trade her, no matter the reason, would become the hunted rather than the hunter. Cabal would see to that.

"Keep your head up." The Breed that had spoken little through the day and evening, Keith, spoke to her softly as he walked beside her. "Watts fears strength. Don't be surprised by him, don't be fooled by him. He's not going to be as strong as he wants you to believe."

"Enough, Keith," Patrick cautioned him, both their voices low and calm as they led her through the forest to the meeting Patrick had set up. "She'll survive by her own wits. To be a Bengal's mate, she'll have to learn now."

"And a Bengal's mate is different how?" she asked him.

She wished she could forget where they were going, what awaited her.

She stared through the night again, her heart whispering for Cabal, aching for him. She had never been so frightened in her life, or so uncertain. She wasn't the least bit ashamed to admit that she was way over her head here. "And if Cabal gets here before this is over, stand behind me," she told the younger Breed. "I might be able to keep him from killing you."

Patrick chuckled, more at the fact that she hadn't offered to stand in front of him, Cassa figured. He could stand on his own, he'd proven that. She had a feeling he was a little overconfident when it came to Cabal though. Primal Breed or not wouldn't matter in Cabal's case.

Stilling the shudders that wanted to wrack her body, Cassa

kept her eyes opened, watching, waiting for a chance to run. No doubt they would find it rather easy to chase her down, but she would never be able to ignore the opportunity if it presented itself.

Cassa could feel her palms sweating as they moved closer to the valley that she had been directed away from before. Sliding through the thick growth of pine and bare trees, a single narrow path led through the dense growth of thicket, boulders and wild roses.

Tiny thorns caught at her borrowed jacket, and she stumbled more than once over the large, hidden stones beneath her feet.

She felt as though she were walking through another reality, a different dimension. She could feel the clash of fear and disbelief rocking through her, shortening her breath as panic rose inside her.

The past was catching up to her with a vengeance, and she wanted nothing more than to escape it. Just as she had prayed to escape Douglas when she believed he was her husband.

Escaping him wouldn't have been easy. He was manipulating, controlling, and Cassa had been too young, too uncertain of herself at that time to defeat him. She would have, she assured herself, in time. Douglas wouldn't have had the power to hold her indefinitely. But he hadn't wanted to hold on to her, she reminded herself. She had been a tool he had needed at the time, nothing more, and she was suddenly thankful for that.

They came to a hard stop as Patrick moved ahead of the group and lifted his hand imperiously. She could feel the indrawn breaths around her, sense them testing the wind.

"Four Coyotes and one human," Keith murmured.

Patrick shook his head slowly, his head lifting as though searching for answers in the very air itself.

As he turned to Cassa, his teeth flashed in the darkness. "You shared the little gift we sent you, didn't you?"

The gift? The pills. He was talking about the scent-neutralizing pills that had been sent to her before she left for West Virginia.

Refusing to answer him, she stared back at him coolly instead, wondering if he could smell something in a way that Jonas had not anticipated. Was there a way for a Breed to detect others who were taking the neutralizer? She'd assumed it blocked all scent.

Patrick shook his head slowly as he chuckled in amusement.

"I would have enjoyed having time to get to know you better, Ms. Hawkins," he finally said. "I have a feeling you would have increased my understanding of humans in a few small ways."

"Humans?" she asked him. "You're human as well, Patrick."

He shook his head at that.

"He looks like a human. He walks like a human. He speaks with the voice of a man." His eyes seemed to glow red in the dark for the briefest moment. "The animal is loose, Ms. Hawkins. There is now nothing but blood for drink and death for peace." He turned to Walt then. "You know what to do if all does not go as planned."

Walt sniffed and nodded slowly. "I'll take care of your boy, Rick."

Patrick nodded before inhaling slowly and turning to Keith. "Return with him."

"That wasn't the plan," Keith reminded him, his voice colder now than before. "I'll fight by your side, Rick."

Patrick shook his head slowly. "This is my fight. She was my wife. My mate. Too many have paid the price already for her deceptions."

"Then I'll fight by her side." He nodded to Cassa. "You have enough blood on your soul, brother."

Patrick turned away from them long seconds before finally nodding. When he turned back to them, she warily tried to step away from him. The spare light of the moon caught his eyes, and the animal was indeed loose. His eyes flashed red, and she swore his facial features had tightened, turning more animalistic than they had been moments before. Cruel purpose slashed across his face and drew his body taut as he bent closer to her.

"Your friends are in place, your mate isn't. Good luck, Ms. Hawkins. If you survive, remember one thing. We are all a product not of our environment or our training. We are a product of the deceit of man."

With that he turned from her. Walt stood aside as they moved forward, and she swore she saw a tear in the old man's eyes.

Swallowing past the panic welling inside her, Cassa moved between Patrick and Keith through the thick underbrush and heavy boulders. Minutes later they stepped to the edge of a large clearing.

"We're here, Watts." Patrick's voice echoed through the valley.

They were still sheltered by several thick, ages-old oak trees. Patrick Wallace was no man's, or Breed's, fool.

"Did you bring the Bengal's whore?" A light illuminated deeper into the clearing.

As Cassa watched, a figure stepped into the beam of light. As he moved closer she recognized the arrogant swagger of the walk, and then the form of the man she had once called husband.

"I've brought our lovely reporter," Patrick corrected him. "Do you have what I require?"

Douglas came closer, and only then did Cassa see the two Coyotes that walked with him. Her eyes widened in recognition of the one at his left.

Brimstone. The second-in-command of the Coyotes that had only recently sought asylum in Haven, the Wolf Breed compound.

What the hell was he doing here? At Douglas's other side was another Coyote she recognized. Mutt, part of Dog's team. She looked between the two Breeds, her throat tightening in dread.

"Hello, wife," Douglas drawled as he moved closer.

His steps were a bit stiff, his expression furious.

Cassa lifted her head and smiled. "Wife?" she asked. "I much preferred widow."

He sneered back at her as she noticed the large envelope he was tapping against his thigh.

"Send her over here," Douglas snapped.

"Not yet," Patrick drawled. "I believe you have something for me first. Let me see the proof, then we'll see about the trade."

"Do you think I'm a fool?" Douglas snarled.

"I do," Cassa forced the insult past her lips. Nothing was guaranteed to incite his rage faster than her smart mouth. She remembered that well from their so-called marriage.

"You little bitch." He slapped the envelope into Brim's hand. "Take it to him. Then bring that little whore to me."

"Once a whore always a whore I guess," she quipped. "Really, Douglas, that insult doesn't have the power it used to have. You should have learned something new in the past eleven years."

"Locked up like an animal in that cage your lover stuck me in?" His voice throbbed with anger now. "You're spreading your fucking thighs for a damned animal. You can pay the price for that now."

"Whatever your price, Cabal was well worth it," she snapped.

"A man for a change was a pleasant upgrade from the monster I thought I was married to."

Brim stepped closer and handed Patrick the envelope. No one was paying attention to her except Douglas. No one cared if she ran, if she fought to escape. Patrick wouldn't come after her. She didn't think Keith would. Brim might, but she was starting to wonder about that one. He was an enforcer under Jonas's command. Could he be undercover now?

There was nothing left but to find out.

"I'll make you pay for this, Cassa," Douglas promised her.

"You'll have to catch me first."

She took off before the words had left her lips. She was running, crashing through the undergrowth and clamoring over the boulders that ringed the valley.

She could hear Douglas screaming behind her, then, seconds later, the labored chase he was giving.

God, he was crazy. A true hunter he wasn't. Didn't he take the time to know his adversary? To pay attention to the fact that the men helping him were no more friends of his than Cabal was?

At least, that was what she prayed.

She ran through the forest, panting, her heart racing, remembering the last flight she had taken through here.

Where was Cabal? Patrick had warned her that Jonas was near when he posed the question about the pills. He had to have smelled something in that valley that assured him the director was there.

Where was Jonas at least?

She could hear the pursuit behind her, and knew that despite his halting steps in the valley, Douglas was determined. Determined enough that he was actually gaining on her.

"Cabal!" She screamed out his name now. He had to be close. He wouldn't leave her here like this. He'd been here when Dog and his men had chased her. He had saved her then, he would save her now.

A sharp retort sounded behind her. Cassa screamed when a bullet shaved the tree next to her as she flew past it. Ducking, tears finally falling from her eyes, she cried out for Cabal again.

Snow was falling faster now, covering the ground beneath the trees and making it treacherous. She slipped, fell and rolled before scrambling to her feet once more. When she glanced behind her, wild terror seared into her brain at the sight of Douglas pausing and aiming the handgun he carried toward her.

She raced behind trees, barely escaping another bullet as she glimpsed the dark forms moving with Douglas. He wasn't alone. Was that Brim or Mutt? Either of the two she felt she had a chance with.

Panting, sliding down the slick, mountainous slope, Cassa prayed for a miracle now. She couldn't let herself be killed. God forbid she was actually unlucky enough to be caught.

Slipping again, she found herself facedown on the ground, fighting to find traction, to find her feet again. She was kicking off to sprint again when cruel hands gripped her arm.

Wild-eyed, she stared back at the Breed that gripped the heavy arm of her jacket. His eyes were black, his hair blond. Determination marked his features and filled her with terror.

The Coyotes weren't good. None of them. Those at Haven were betraying the very vows they had made to protect the society as a whole. Proof was in this man, their leader, the mate she had watched take his vows just weeks before. Del-Rey Delgado.

"No!" She screamed out the rejection, fighting him, tearing free as the coat slipped from her shoulders and she raced down the mountain.

Another bullet clipped a branch overhead. Behind her, she could hear Douglas cursing, ordering. The mountain was alive with terror, running feet and shouted orders.

She wasn't going to make it. Oh God. She wasn't going to escape this. There was no way to get far enough ahead of them. No way to save herself.

"Enough!" A hard bicep wrapped around her waist as agony streaked through her from behind.

This was pain. This was the most horrendous pain she had ever known. Every place that the hard male body touched burned in agony as she kicked, shrieking in fear and fury as she was tossed to the ground.

Rolling to her knees, she fought to find her feet. Sliding against the snow and mud, she rose shakily, only to face Douglas.

A second later a hard strike against her face sent her back to the ground again as she heard a furious growl echo around her.

"Touch her again, Watts, and I'll kill you myself," Delgado warned him. "We didn't sanction harming another Breed's mate."

"My wife!" Douglas screamed. The next second Cassa

barely deflected a kick aimed to her ribs as she rolled out of reach. "She's my wife. She's not that dirty fucking Breed's anything."

"Don't touch her again." Brim moved between them.

Another shot was fired. Cassa glimpsed Brim flinching as she made it to her feet again and started running.

Down the mountain. She just had to make it down the mountain. Then to the road. Maybe they'd all kill each other behind her.

"You fucking bitch."

Douglas tackled her from behind. They crashed to the forest floor as Cassa fought. She kicked, screamed. Her nails tore at his face, and for one incredible second she thought she'd actually be free.

"Fucking Breed whore." A hard fist to the side of her head froze her.

Stars erupted behind her closed eyes, and for a second Cassa swore she was going to lose consciousness. Then rage kicked in. Pure, unfettered rage. It boiled through her stomach, raced through her brain and sent adrenaline surging through her system.

Years of brief, almost amusing episodes of "training" with Breeds rose to the forefront of her mind. They had made a game out of teaching her this little trick and that little trick to get herself out of trouble. Several of her "instructors" had claimed with rueful smiles that someone had to teach her, considering the fact that Cabal was gone so often.

Cabal had arranged that training. She sensed it. She knew it.

Bracing herself against the ground with one foot, she kicked out with the other. She didn't try any sissy moves. She didn't go for the cool little ninja maneuvers. She kicked out hard and swift, her boot slamming into Douglas's crotch and stealing his breath as she prayed she'd crushed his nuts.

She was only dimly aware of the enraged roars that filled the night. Along with feet crashing through the forest, the sound of a heli-jet and someone screaming out orders.

Coyote howls, there might have even been a Wolf in there. Human screams. She heard several of those. The night became centered, the cold disappeared. Cassa came to her feet in a smooth jump, facing Douglas as he slowly straightened.

His face was white, his eyes were filled with inhuman rage.

"You're a whore!" he screamed. "A dirty stinking animal-fucker."

"And I'm loving every minute of it." Her croon was harsh, filled with her own fury.

He had once made her go to her knees and beg for mercy. This man who had taken vows with her, who had sworn to love the young woman she had once been. He had made her beg and then he had slapped her so hard she had blacked out.

There had been no mercy.

"I'm going to kill you." His arm lifted.

Too much happened at once. Too many impressions, too many sounds. An animal scream of pure demonic rage echoed through the night. Cassa went flying, thrown to the ground by a shadow with amber eyes, as a gun fired.

Rage was a scent. It was a feeling, like rain washing through the night. It was the smell of blood and a scream like nothing she had ever known.

Rolling to her knees, she pushed her hair from her face and stared in shock at the sight that met her eyes.

There were lights now, streaming down from the heli-jet that hovered overhead. Dressed in shadowed colors, his face streaked with black, his eyes glowing amber in the night, Cabal stood over Douglas's writhing form.

Screams poured from Douglas's throat, raw, brutal, agonizing screams. His upper body writhed on the ground, his hands clawed into snow stained heavy with blood.

"You fucker!" he screamed, pain burning in every word as tears spilled from his eyes now. "Do it, you son of a bitch. Motherfucker. Do it. Kill me."

Cabal roared in his face as Douglas covered it with his hands and sobbed in pain and fear.

"Don't take me back." His screams were rough now, demented. "No. You can't take me back. Please."

Cassa stared at Cabal in shock. The marks on his face weren't face paint. They were tiger marks bisecting his savage features. His hands were tipped with claws, bloodied now, and his eyes glowed gold in the night as he turned, his gaze raking in a slow circle before falling on Patrick.

"Azrael." His voice was a harsh growl. An animalistic sound that had Cassa flinching.

Patrick inclined his head as he stepped back. "Another day, Bengal."

The night swallowed him as Cabal roared his fury and started after him.

She couldn't let him leave. She stumbled for him, her leg going out from under her as a startled cry left her throat. Pain streaked through her now, a burning hot lance of fire tearing through her body as she went down, collapsing on her side.

◆　　◆　　◆

His mate. Cabal jerked around, his gaze locking on her pain-filled eyes, his senses registering more than pure fury now.

Blood. His mate's blood. He rushed for her even as the others moved to where she had fallen.

Del-Rey, the Coyote Breed alpha. Wolfe was there, alpha of the Wolf packs, even Callan and Tanner were racing for her as they tore through the forest.

"Cassa." He slid to the ground beside her, fear suddenly tearing through him.

He had raced here for her. He had used more than what he had once thought was every ounce of strength he possessed to find his mate. Had he failed her in the end?

"Baby." He knew the sound of his voice was demented, he saw the shock that filled the Breeds around him.

He had never told even his brother Tanner of the gifts he shared with such a very few other Breeds. The claws, the markings, the heightened senses. The ability to run and track as no other could. He was a primal Breed. He had hidden it, knowing that even other Breeds feared the primals.

His claws retracted, the strong human nails sliding back into place as he touched her, his hands racing over her chilled flesh until he found the wound at her side.

"Cabal." Tanner was there.

He stared up at his brother for a brief second before his shaking hands touched the blood at her side.

"Get her ready to fly!" Jonas was there. Breeds were pouring through the woods. Some were securing Douglas despite his screams as he fought to find sensation in his legs.

The impulse regulator in his spine had been dissolved. The temporary fix to his legs had been deactivated by Jonas. It had melted through flesh and bone, leaving him now with no hope of finding sensation there again.

"Cabal." Her sweet voice was weak, her fingers latched onto his arm. "I'm sorry."

He shook his head. "Sorry?"

Pain was like a burning brand in his chest now as he stared into her white face.

"Your family," she whispered tearfully. "He used me to kill them. I trusted him. Oh God." She lowered her head as sobs tore from her. "I'm sorry."

"No." Gripping her chin, he lifted her face, his eyes locking on hers. "So many lived because you fought for them," he swore to her, revealing something he had revealed to no one else. "You saved four, Cassa. They thrive. They fight to survive. You saved us."

She stared back at him, confusion filling her face before it cleared. The tears still fell as she lifted a shaking hand to his face. "I love you. I loved you for so long."

"Cassa, stop." Fear raked hard and deep inside his soul. "Tell me later. I'll hold you close. I'll keep you warm, baby, and give you the words I've feared for so long."

She shook her head. "I just love you, Cabal." Her voice was weaker, more distant.

"Cassa. Stay awake." Terror gripped him now, a terror unlike anything he had known, even in the labs. "Stay with me, Cassa."

Her fingers, stained with her own blood, touched his face.

"Hold me now," she whispered, her lashes drifting closed. "Just hold me now."

CHAPTER 27

Cabal had never known such a hellish experience in his life. Even watching his family die hadn't impacted him, hadn't destroyed him, the way watching Cassa drift away from him had.

The heli-jet ride across the mountains to Sanctuary, the nearest facility with the equipment and doctors to save her, had been a waking nightmare.

Now, standing outside the operating rooms, his gaze locked on the doors that Dr. Morrey would use to enter the room following the surgery, he felt the rage and pain burning inside his soul.

He had waited too long. He had held himself back from her for too many years. He had fought what he felt for her, what he needed, and now he was paying the price.

"Cabal." Jonas stepped back into the waiting area, his face heavily lined and somber as his secretary moved in behind him.

Rachel wasn't timid, but she was quiet. Her gaze was filled with compassion, her composed expression saddened.

She was Jonas's mate. Cabal had known it the moment he met her, and he was sure Jonas knew it as well.

"Ely's certain she's going to be okay," Cabal stated, though he didn't really believe it. He'd always feared that fate would steal her from him. Now he was terrified he had been right.

"Ely knows what she's doing," Jonas said quietly. "Watts has been transferred back to the Middle East. We'll be questioning him next week in regards to the remaining members of the Deadly Dozen, as well as Azrael's child. If we can find the child, then we'll find the father."

Cabal growled at the thought of the Lion Breed that he blamed for Cassa's injuries. If Azrael hadn't kidnapped her, hadn't decided that she could be traded for the information he wanted, then she wouldn't be in surgery now.

"I'll kill him for this, Jonas. He had no right to involve her this way."

Rachel spoke up then. "She's not a doll. You won't put her on a shelf and dictate how she can or cannot live. If you do, Cabal, you'll lose her."

He glared at her, noticing absently how Jonas moved to block sight of her with his own body.

Hell, he knew better than to growl at her. She might not realize it, but Jonas was like a damn dog with a bone when it came to his little secretary.

"I don't need any advice at this point," he warned her instead, when he knew that what he might need was a miracle.

He hadn't protected his mate.

He hung his head, refusing to look at either of them further. He couldn't look at them. He had failed his mate, and that was even worse than failing his pride and his family.

"We know Azrael is alive now," Jonas finally stated. "We need him alive."

Sucked to be Jonas.

"You need everyone alive," Cabal said. "You just like killing them yourself."

"There is that," Jonas agreed. "But we won't have to worry about a funeral for anyone anytime soon. If Ely says Cassa will be fine, then she will be just that."

Cabal clasped his hands between his knees, his grip tight. He prayed. As he had never prayed in his life, he prayed that Cassa survived.

He rubbed his hands over his face, still feeling the sensitivity of the marks across it. He hadn't lost the stripes. Rage was still burning inside him; fear was still a metallic taste in his mouth.

As he lifted his head to glance back at Jonas, the door swung open and Ely stepped through. Her face was somber, but it always was now. Her eyes were dark and almost emotionless. That too was normal for her lately.

"She's doing well." She was wiping her hands. Cassa's blood still stained the front of her surgical gown. "We had a few tense moments during surgery, but it appears the bullet didn't do any lasting damage. Entered and exited through her right side. A few weeks' recuperation and she'll be . . ."

Cabal didn't hear the rest of it. He pushed past her and followed the scent of his mate to the recovery room, set deep beneath the estate house that served as the main base of Feline Breed affairs.

He stepped quietly into the curtained-off room and stood by the bed that held his mate.

She was pale. Her hair was streaked with blood. A light sheet was pulled up over her bare breasts and the mating mark he had given her was clearly displayed on her shoulder.

Cabal reached out, his finger barely glancing it.

"You have stripes." Her weak voice drew his attention as her hand tried to lift, only to falter and fall back to the bed.

He knew what she wanted. She had been fascinated with the stripes on his hips and thighs. These on his face would be no different.

He lifted her hand to them as he slowly sat down on the small stool next to the bed.

"These will be gone soon," he said quietly. "It won't be long now."

She smiled as her lashes drifted closed, then opened once again.

"Ely pulled me through, huh?" There was an edge of wariness in her voice. "Everything is okay?"

"Everything is okay." He turned her palm into his kiss. "You're okay."

She stared back at him, her gray eyes somber, drowsy.

"I didn't protect you," he said quietly. "This won't happen again, Cassa."

"Don't cage me, Cabal."

He shook his head at that. "I can't cage you. You'd die, just as I would. But from now on, we work together. No more assignments apart." It was the best way to ensure that she was never threatened again.

She grinned at that. "Tame little assignments, huh?"

"By my standards perhaps. I doubt others would see it that way."

She stared back at him silently for long moments, and he knew what she was waiting on, what she needed.

He lowered his head as he dragged in a hard, desperate breath.

"I never blamed you." He finally lifted his head and caught her gaze once again. "Never. Not even that night when he accused you of knowing, I knew you couldn't have."

She frowned at that statement.

"Your scent," he explained. "It was one of innocence, of desperation and sorrow. There was no guilt in you, Cassa. There never has been. From the moment I smelled that innocence, I wanted nothing more than to taste it. To touch it. To hold it as my own. All these years, I've longed for that alone, and I've been too damned scared to reach out for it. Too scared that fate would tear you away from me and take you forever."

Terrified she would die. A part of him had always feared that this incredible gift that God had given him would be taken from him just as quickly.

"No more running." Her fingers caressed a stripe.

"No more running, Cassa," he swore. There was no place he wanted to be other than right here by her side. "I've loved you since the moment that sweet tongue licked across my blood. Since the night I watched you fighting so desperately to save me. I've loved you, Cass, and I've been terrified of losing you."

Her fingers paused in the slow rubbing caress of the tips against one narrow stripe.

"Terrified?"

"Shaking in my boots." He leaned closer, his lips against hers. "So terrified I ran as far and as fast as I could."

She stared up at him, her eyes wide, so filled with hope. His Cassa. His brave, adventurous Cassa.

"No more running?"

He licked across her lips, tasted her, loved her. His hands framed her beloved face, his thumbs stroking across her jaw. He was nearly shaking with the need to assure himself she was fine. That she lived. That she was his.

"No more running, baby."

He eased onto the bed with her, thankful that it was so damned big. They had to make room for large men in pain when they made the beds for the Breed intensive care facility. It was just large enough for him to lie on his side beside her, to hold her, to feel her warmth, to soak in the fact that she still lived. That she was still his.

"I love you, Cassa." He gave her the words he knew she needed, and felt that last barrier toward her collapse.

If she died, he would follow her. He would avenge every moment of pain she felt, and then he would give up his life to be with her in death.

"Always?" she whispered.

She had always loved him. She would always love him. He knew it, felt it to the ends of his soul.

"Always, baby." He brushed the hair back from the side of her face, lowered his lips and touched hers once again. "I'll always love you."

She would always be his mate. She would always be the Bengal's heart. Man and beast, they existed for her alone.

"I love you, Cabal." She sighed against his lips, drowsiness finally taking her as she went to sleep to his kiss.

"I love you, Cass." He lowered his head beside hers and let his own lashes drift closed.

She was safe. She was his. She was the Bengal's heart, the man's soul. And forever the mate he would cherish.

· E P Í L O G U E ·

Jonas entered the interview room of the maximum security prison that held the prisoners they didn't want the world to ever know about.

There was a scientist in a cell. One of the most brutal and yet one of the most brilliant to ever live. She had bypassed genius level in her teens and was now considered one of the most dangerous creatures alive, even by Genetics Council standards.

There were several trainers here who had once worked for the Council and even a billionaire who had disappeared years ago behind the walls of this fortress, never to be seen again.

It wasn't truly a harsh place to be. It just wasn't a nice place to be. It was cold at night, a little warmer in the day. There weren't a lot of conveniences, but there were doctors to oversee the health of the prisoners and there was nutritious food. Might not necessarily be food the prisoners were used to, but they were alive and they weren't abused.

It was better than could be said of the treatment received by the Breeds that most of the prisoners had once overseen.

But none of those was the one he had come there to talk with now.

Jonas sat silently in the interview room and stared at the defeated pose Douglas Watts now used when facing him. His face was down. Once, he'd kept his person immaculate, his hair washed, his body in shape. In less than two weeks the hair had become dank and oily and the skin sallow. He was a man who had lost the will to fight.

"Are you in pain?" Jonas asked, though he knew Douglas wasn't.

Douglas shook his head. "I feel nothing."

Literally. From the hips down he was once again paralyzed, this time with no hope of recovery.

"The surgeon warned you that it could happen?" Jonas asked. He'd commanded that Douglas be given the warning.

Douglas nodded. "I was warned."

The chip implanted needed months to interact with the nerve endings. By pushing himself as he had physically, Douglas had been the cause of his own demise.

"Then we'll proceed," Jonas stated. "I want the names of the final four of the Deadly Dozen."

He was surprised when Douglas gave him the names. Three of them anyway.

"The fourth died," Douglas sighed. "I heard about his death after I escaped. Ivan never was very smart. He pissed off the wrong man in his own government and paid for it."

Ivan Vilanov, the former Russian elite officer that had once been an attaché to the United States.

"And the child of Patrick Wallace?" Jonas asked. That was the information he needed, what he wanted more than anything else.

Douglas lifted his head. "A boy. He was sold to this couple." He gave their names easily. "They died. The report I have is that he has an older sister that disappeared with him a few years ago. I wasn't able to find out more." And Jonas believed him.

Jonas nodded as he checked the voice recorder he carried to make certain it was still recording everything.

"Did you know who Patrick Wallace was?" he asked Douglas.

Once again the other man nodded. "Azrael. The angel of death. We knew. He disappeared after that hunt. I knew he was wounded. I hoped he was dead. I was wrong."

And now he was gone.

"And Brandenmore and Engalls?" Jonas questioned him. "Tell me what you know about their part in the hunts and the Genetics Council."

There was two hours' worth of information. Douglas didn't pause, he didn't argue or hide anything. Any question Jonas had, he answered. He was broken. There was no fight left in him because there was no longer a chance of escape, no longer a chance of enjoying the brutal games he had once enjoyed.

When Douglas had finished, Jonas turned off the recorder and rose to his feet. Douglas lifted his head then, his gaze piercing.

"You promised." His voice was rough. Raw. "You promised I'd die if I told you everything. You promised mercy, Wyatt."

He had. And he'd lied.

Jonas stared back at him coldly. "You don't deserve mercy, Douglas."

"And you do?" There was no anger, no rage, just dejection. "Kill me. You swore you would."

"I lied."

Douglas stared back at him as his eyes filled with tears. Jonas watched as the liquid overflowed, and wondered at the small spike of regret he felt.

"They know who you are," Douglas whispered. "They know what you are. They'll destroy you and all of your kind, Jonas. And you'll deserve it."

At that, Jonas could only quirk his lips ruefully. "They might destroy me, Douglas, but never the Breeds as a whole. Haven't you figured it out yet? We're here to stay."

"You'll die," Douglas predicted.

"And of that, I have no doubt."

With those parting words, Jonas left the room, closed the door behind him and walked the long expanse of hall back to the control room.

Douglas's screams followed him. Enraged now, finally. Filled with pain, filled with broken, hollow anger. And Jonas had no mercy.

He was created to know no mercy. He was created to know no love. He was created to destroy his entire species, and he was damned if he would allow that to happen.

Turn the page for an exclusive look at the
next title in the Nauti series
by Lora Leigh

ΠΑVΤİ DECEPΤİΟΠS

Coming soon from Berkley Sensation!

Now, how had she known the day was just going to suck. Caitlyn Rogue Walker watched as Principal Thompson entered the class-room after her freshmen students had left for the day. Following him were no more than the self-righteous Nadine Grace and her bully of a brother, Dayle Mackay.

She knew what was coming. Somehow they'd found a way to punish her for coming to a student's defense the month before. She had been waiting for the shoe to drop, and she had a feeling when it fell, it was going to be an earthquake in her little life.

At least she didn't have to worry about it coming any longer.

Maybe she should have heeded her father's advice about coming here to his hometown to teach. He had wanted her to stay in Boston, he'd wanted her to be a lawyer rather than a teacher. Or better yet, the wife of a lawyer would have suited him fine.

Being the wife of a lawyer didn't suit Caitlyn Rogue though. She wanted to teach, and she wanted to teach in the picturesque little town her father had told her so many tales of.

Perhaps she should have heeded the tales he had told her of Dayle Mackay and Nadine Grace though, as well as his warnings to make certain she stayed off their radar. But staying off their radar hadn't been as easy as she had thought it would be.

And as her father had warned her, they would target her simply because she was a Walker. Nadine Grace and Dayle Mackay had tried to destroy her father when he was younger, and it seemed they were more than determined to destroy her.

She had lived in Somerset for one short year. Long enough to know she loved it here. Long enough to grow a few quick roots, to dream, and to meet the county's beyond sexy sheriff.

The schoolteacher and the sheriff. What a fantasy. Because within months, she learned that her father hadn't been exaggerating about Dayle and Nadine. At the end of the school term the year before, she'd been forced to enter their radar to defend one of her students against Nadine's accusations that he had cheated on an exam that she had overseen as a member of the Board of Education. Caitlyn knew the boy hadn't cheated, just as she knew that no defense would help her now.

As her gaze met the two, she could feel her stomach tightening in warning as her heart began a heavy, sluggish beat.

Brother and sister resembled each other in too many ways. The same black hair, the same squarish features. Nadine was built smaller, and her eyes were hazel rather than green. Dayle Mackay was taller, with thicker black hair and forest green eyes. He would have been handsome if the evil that was a part of his soul didn't reflect in his eyes.

Neither Dayle nor Nadine spoke as they entered the room with the principal. Rogue remained in her seat, watching them cautiously as Nadine moved forward and slapped a small stack of pictures down in front of her.

The first one was enough to know exactly how Dayle and Nadine intended to destroy her.

Caitlyn stared down at them, feeling shame, mortification, defeat. She had never known defeat until she stared down at the pictures that she knew she could never refute. Not because she hadn't done it, but because she had been unable to stop it.

Fanning the pictures out slowly, she had to bite back a cry that tightened her chest and had her hands shaking. She had somehow known that one night that she couldn't fully remember had been a setup. She had sensed it then, but she knew it now, and the rage and pain festered in her chest like a wound she wasn't sure would ever heal.

Rogue swallowed back the bile that rose in her stomach and ordered herself not to react, not show pain, fear, or anger. She had her pride and she would be damned if she would let these two know how much they were hurting her with these pictures. How much they were stealing from her.

"As you can see, Ms. Walker, there's no way we can allow you to remain within the educational system," Principal Thompson informed her with chilling morality. "Such actions cannot be condoned."

No, they couldn't be, Caitlyn would be the first to agree with him. If she had done it voluntarily.

The pictures showed her half undressed, her skirt raised well above her thighs, her legs spread for the male going between them. Higher, her blouse was undone and a female, her long hair obscuring her face, obviously caressed Caitlyn's bare breasts with her lips.

Caitlyn blinked down at the photos. There was no fighting them, though she knew, whatever had happened that night, she hadn't had sex. When she had awakened in the unfamiliar hotel room, the first thing she had done was schedule an emergency appointment with her doctor. But the school board wouldn't care about that. No more than they would care about the blood tests that had shown that whatever happened, she hadn't gone into it willingly. Rogue had been drugged, and betrayed.

She was still a virgin, but she would be branded as a whore.

She could fight it. She could call her parents. Nadine Grace and Dayle Mackay had no idea how powerful her parents were now, how eloquently they could seduce a jury, how enraged they would be if she ever let them know what had happened here. Brianna and Calvin Walker would descend upon this county like wraiths from hell with all the powerful Bostonian wealth they had amassed behind them.

Her grandparents, the Evanworths, were like icons. Her mother's parents would destroy Grace and Mackay without a thought.

But her father had warned her and she had promised him. She was a big girl, just like her brother and sister. She would carve out her own future, and she would succeed. She had promised him that there was nothing this county could do to destroy her.

She was going to teach, marry and raise babies in the mountains. That was her dream. And her dream was crumbling beneath her feet. She felt her world shifting on its axis, felt the shame and the rage building inside her until she wondered if her head would explode with it.

Nadine sniffed. "You have a week to leave and we'll not resort to putting the pictures on the Internet."

She stared back at the pinched-face bitch that so hated Shane Mayes simply because he was the sheriff's son, and the sheriff refused to kowtow to her or her brother. It was rumored Sheriff Zeke Mayes kowtowed to no man, or woman.

"I really don't give a fuck where you put them." She turned back to Nadine. It wouldn't do her any good, Nadine would do as she wished anyway. "I'm not leaving Somerset."

"My dear Ms. Walker, your employment here—" the principal began.

"Is obviously at an end." Caitlyn smiled tightly as she picked up the photos and shoved them in her case. "I'll clear my desk this evening, Mr. Thompson."

"You'll leave town," Dayle Mackay stated, his voice like ice.

The man was a viper. His son, the town's bad boy, had a heart of gold. But this man, he was black, evil. It was in his eyes, in his face. It was almost enough to send a shiver down her spine. But she didn't shiver, her spine straightened and pure Walker arrogance and stubborn pride kicked in. Her father had once warned her that her pride would be the death of her.

"Go to hell, Mackay." She could barely speak. Fury was ripping through her, tearing at her.

"Your reputation will be less than nothing by time we finish with you, Caitlyn." Nadine's tight-lipped, superior smile looked like a viper's curl of the lip. Anticipatory. Ready to strike. "You don't want to stay here."

"No, you don't want me to stay because you're terrified that if one person stands up to your viciousness then others will," she stated calmly. "I'm doing more than standing up to it, Nadine. I'm warning you now, you can't hurt me."

Nadine's smile was cold. "Your position within the school system has been terminated, Ms. Walker, and your standing in this county will be history." Her tone assured Rogue she felt she had done the damage she wanted to do.

Caitlyn forced herself to laugh. Her father had taught her how to be strong, her mother had taught her how to be a lady. But her grandmother, ah, her grandmother had taught her how to be a bitch and made Caitlyn enjoy every lesson.

Bess Evansworth was a force of nature and a law unto herself. And Caitlyn had been her favorite. She had always allowed Caitlyn to tag along with her and her cronies to their luncheons and teas. And Caitlyn had learned.

"Put them on the Internet." Caitlyn's smile was all teeth. "I dare you. Better yet, mail a set to my grandparents. Their address is easy to find. Evansworth. Taite and Bessamine Evansworth, Boston. I'm sure my grandmother will get a tickle out of it. Though, Daddy might return to Somerset." She shrugged as though she didn't care. "You could take your chances."

She shoved the few possessions from her desk into her bag. She didn't have much. They hadn't really given her time to settle in. She could fight the school board, but who really wanted to. She'd come here with dreams, and over the past months she had learned how ineffectual those dreams were in these mountains.

Somerset was beautiful, inspiring and filled with dark, poisonous little creatures just waiting to strike. She had sensed that during the first few months settling in. She knew it the moment she had met these two, and now she felt its swift, sharp retribution.

The pictures were in her purse, but she knew that meant so very little. Simply that she had her own copy. Damn them.

"Staying here will serve no purpose," Dayle Mackay snorted. "You're not wanted, you little bitch, any more than your ignorant father was wanted or any of the Walker clan. The lot of you are nothing but white trash whores and drug guzzling bastards."

Oh, one day, he'd pay for that one. They would both pay for that one.

"Oh well, far be it from me to prove you wrong," she replied mockingly. "Do whatever the hell you want with the pictures. But"—she paused as she picked up the oversized bag at her side— "be watching for me. When you least expect it." She looked between the two. "When you very least expect it, I'll be there. And it won't be trumped-up photos that are used to break either one of you. It will be the truth."

She left the school, and she left her dreams behind her. She refused to call her parents. This was her life, and the thought of dragging them into the mess she had allowed to develop made her cringe.

It was her fault. She should have done as her father warned her and let his friends who managed the bar he still owned in town know who she was when she went there, rather than hiding

from them. It wouldn't have happened then, because they would
have watched out for her.

The problem was, she hadn't wanted anyone to watch out
for her. She had been too confident that she could watch out for
herself. She was an adult. She was able to defend herself. In the
arrogance of youth she had convinced herself that nothing and
no one could touch her.

She had entered that bar as confident and arrogant as any
young woman that had just turned twenty-one, watched the excitement and fun with a sense of anticipation and she had let
herself be betrayed and nearly used. She had made that mistake.
It was no one's fault but her own. She would live with it.

She wasn't about to leave Pulaski County though. As she
drove home, she stared out at the mountains, watched the sun
blaze full and bright as it began its descent in the evening sky,
and she knew she couldn't leave.

She had been raised in the city, but these mountains, they
were a part of her. From the moment she had entered them, she
had known she had come home, and she'd known she never
wanted to be anywhere else.

But now, she knew an adjustment would have to be made.

Her eyes narrowed, her jaw clenched. Damn Nadine Grace
and Dayle Mackay. She wasn't going to be run out of town. She
wouldn't be defeated like that. They had won this round, and
those pictures would probably be on the Internet within hours.
But that didn't mean they had beaten her.

Her hands clenched on the steering wheel as she drew in a
hard, deep breath. Her father had always called her his little
Rogue. He would smile fondly when she dressed in her 'good girl'
clothes as he called them, and his eyes would always twinkle as
though he knew something she didn't.

"You're as wild as the wind," he would tell her, and she had
always denied it.

But now, she could feel that part of herself burning beneath
the surface of the 'good girl'. The dreams of teaching had always held her back. A teacher had to be circumspect. She had to
be careful. But Caitlyn Rogue Walker was no longer a teacher.
She no longer had to worry about being circumspect. She didn't
have to worry about protecting a job she didn't have.

She flipped on the car's turn signal and took the road that
headed to the little bar outside of town. It had begun there, and

if her father knew what had happened, he would burn it to the ground. Unfortunately, she had loved being in that damned bar.

She had sat in the corner, watched, devoured the atmosphere and longed to be something more than a "good girl" while she had been there.

There was an apartment overhead. The manager, Jonesy, was a good friend of her father's, as were the bouncers that worked there. She only had to walk in, announce who she was and take over ownership.

Had her father somehow sensed her dreams would go awry here more than he had told her? Because he had offered her the bar. Told her that when she got tired of playing the political games that filled the educational system that she could always run the bar. And his eyes had been filled with knowledge, as though he had known the wildness inside his daughter would eventually be drawn free.

Her reputation had been destroyed because of whatever had happened there the one night she hadn't been cautious enough. Now, it was time to remake that reputation.

Rogue was young, but she was pragmatic. She was bitter now, and she knew that bitterness would fester until Nadine Grace and Dayle Mackay had paid for what they had done. But she wasn't going to let it destroy her. She wouldn't give them the satisfaction of destroying her.

She smiled in anticipation, in anger. Nadine Grace and Dayle Mackay had no idea what they had done. They had destroyed Caitlyn Walker, but nothing and no one could destroy the Rogue she intended to become.

ΘNE WEEK LATER

Sheriff Ezekiel Mayes eased from his current lover's bed and moved through the bedroom to the shower. The widow he was currently seeing slept on, oblivious to his defection as he showered and dressed.

It would be the last night he spent with her, he knew. Zeke insisted on privacy in his relationships. He didn't publicly date. He didn't claim any woman. There was no room in his life, his heart or his secrets for such a woman. And she was steadily pushing for more. He knew if he didn't break it off now then it would only become a mess he didn't want to face.

He didn't want ties. He didn't want the mess that came from claiming any woman as his own. He didn't want the danger he knew a woman of his could face. He was walking a thin line and he knew it. He wouldn't make his balance more precarious by taking a lover that could become a weakness. Calvin Walker's daughter was definitely a weakness, simply because of her affiliation with the Walkers and others' hatred for them. The job he had set for himself demanded a fragile balance at the moment. Maintaining that balance would be impossible if he gave in to the needs clawing at his gut right now for one innocent little school teacher.

As he moved from the bathroom Mina rolled over and blinked back at him sleepily. Slumberous dark eyes flickered over him as a pout pursed her full, sensual lips.

"It's not even dawn yet," she muttered, obviously less than pleased to find him leaving.

She should have expected it. He always left before dawn.

"I need to get into the office early," he told her. And he did, but it could have waited.

Mina Harlow was a generous, warm lover, but she wanted a relationship, and Zeke wasn't ready to complicate his life to that extent. He hid enough of himself the way it was, he wasn't interested in hiding it on a regular basis.

"Whatever." She stretched beneath the blankets before eyeing him with a glimmer of amusement. "Oh, I forgot to tell you. That little school teacher that looks at you with stars in her eyes, Miss Walker. The school board fired her last week."

He didn't want to hear this particular piece of gossip again. He sure as hell didn't want to hear the satisfaction in Mina's tone at the fact that the little schoolteacher had been hurt. Mina was gloating over it, simply because Caitlyn hadn't hid her interest in him.

This was bullshit. Catty, snide and hurtful. He'd thought better of Mina at one time.

"I don't like gossip, Mina," he reminded her.

She gave a soft little laugh. "Come on, Zeke, it's all over town and now it's hit the Internet. Pictures of her in the cutest little threesome with another couple. Who would have guessed she had it in her."

Zeke wouldn't have, and he still didn't believe it. He'd heard about the pictures more than he wanted to. He refused to look at them.

"Miss Goody Two Shoes got caught having her fun," Mina said smoothly. "I can't believe she thought she could get away with playing like that here. She should have known better."

Zeke's lips thinned as he sat at the bottom of the bed and pulled his boots on. Dammit, he didn't need to hear this again. He could feel that edge of burning anger in his gut, the one that warned him he was letting a woman get too close.

Caitlyn Rogue Walker was nothing to him, he told himself. He couldn't let her become something to him either. She was too damned innocent, no matter what those photos might show. Not to mention too damned young.

"Too bad the camera person didn't take a few more." Mina yawned then. "Miss Walker wasn't even fully undressed, but she was definitely getting ready to have a good time."

His jaw bunched. The innocent Miss Walker had pissed off the wrong people, and Zeke felt responsible for that. Hell, this was just what he needed. He had steered clear of her for the express purpose of making certain she was never targeted for any reason, because of him, and she had ended up as a target because of his son instead.

She had caught the attention of two of the town's worse inhabitants. A brother and sister who delighted in destroying anyone they could. She had caught their attention by defending his son at school.

He felt responsible. It was his son, and despite his knowledge that she had been set up, he still hadn't managed to find a way to punish those who had hurt her or to tamp down his growing interest in a woman he had no business touching.

He could feel the curling knot of anger, a hint of territorial possessiveness where the teacher was concerned, and squelched it immediately. Miss Walker was too young, too innocent. She wasn't a woman that would accept a sex only relationship, nor was she a woman Zeke would be able to hide the darker core of his sexuality with, as he did other women. Women such as Mina. Women who touched only his body, never his heart. Miss Walker had the potential to touch the inner man, and he refused to give her the chance.

He'd failed to protect one woman in his life already, he wouldn't make that mistake again.

"She's Calvin Walker's daughter, you know," Mina continued. "Hell, I thought he was dead. What's he doing with a daughter?

Damned Walkers have never been worth crap, so it shouldn't be surprising."

Zeke rose to his feet and turned back to her. "I'm heading out Mina. Take care."

This relationship was over. He could barely manage civility now. Mina had always seemed like a kindhearted woman. She had a ready smile, compassionate hazel eyes, a gentle face. And a mean streak a mile wide. He'd learned that over the past few months. When it came to other women, younger women, anyone she considered a threat to what she might want at the time, then she turned viperous.

"And you're not coming back." Her expression lost its amusement now. "Did you think I didn't know your attention was waning, Zeke?"

"We had an understanding, Mina." He'd made certain of it before the relationship began.

She sat up in the bed, unashamedly naked, her short brown hair mussed attractively around her face.

"Your attention hasn't been worth shit since you met that girl," she accused him snidely. "You go through the motions but I don't doubt you're thinking of her when you're fucking me."

His brow lifted. "Jealousy doesn't become you, Mina, and it's not a part of what we had. In this case, you're wrong. There's nothing between me and Miss Walker."

And there never could be. She was too young, too tender. Zeke didn't mess with women whose innocence lit their eyes like stars in the sky. Caitlyn Walker was the forever kind, and Zeke simply didn't have that to give her. Forever required the truth. It required parts of himself being revealed, and he'd learned at a young age that the truth wasn't always acceptable.

"There's nothing between the two of you because you're a closed-mouthed bastard intent on making certain you never give so much as an ounce of yourself," she snapped. "What's wrong, Zeke, can't anyone match the memory of that paragon you were married to? Or did you simply spend too much time in Los Angeles partying with all the gay boys?"

Zeke stared back at her silently. Prejudice in the mountains was still alive and thriving, he'd known that before he'd come home.

"Goodbye, Mina."

He turned and left the room. He'd be damned if he'd let himself be drawn into an argument with her, especially one she could use against him at any time in the future.

Zeke had a lot friends that still lived in L.A., and yeah, a few of them were gay. He and his past wife, Elaina, hadn't felt that sense of prejudice that thrived here. He didn't give a damn what a man or woman's sexual preference was. He hadn't cared then, and he didn't care now.

As he left Mina's little house outside town, he reminded himself that he was here to do a job, not to make friends or to find another wife. He'd been born and bred in these mountains. He knew every cliff and hollow, every breath of breeze and sigh of the wind. And he'd missed it like hell when he'd been forced to leave. Not that he'd had a choice at the time. It was leave with his mother or face the further destruction of his soul.

At fourteen, his life had changed forever. One moment in time had cursed him, and had caused his parents' divorce. Moving to L.A. with his mother and meeting Elaina, the woman he'd married, had changed it further. At seventeen he'd become a father himself, and through the years he had learned the hard way that he couldn't run from his past. It had found him, and his wife had died because of it.

He was back in Kentucky because of it. Because he was tired of running, tired of fighting to forget what couldn't be forgotten.

Damn, he loved these mountains though, he thought as he started his truck and pulled out of Mina's back drive. The sun was rising over the peaks of pine, oak and elm that filled the rolling hills. There was a mist in the air that drifted off the nearby lake, and the scent of summer filled his senses.

The vision of Rogue—he just couldn't see her as Caitlyn—filled his head, no matter how hard he tried to push it back. He was thirty-two years old, a grown man next to her tender twenty-one. She was so damned tiny she made a man second guess his own strength, and so damned innocent that all a man could think about was being the one to teach her how to sin.

Someone else would have to teach her, he thought, if someone hadn't already. He was staying just as far away from that land mine as possible. She would be the one woman that would tempt him, he thought. If he dared to touch her, if he even considered taking her, he'd never be able to give her only a part of himself. And because of that, he could never have her. There wasn't enough of him left to give. Sometimes he felt as though he had never completely found himself, and never would until the demons of his past were destroyed.

Securing that end wouldn't be easy, he had known that from the beginning. Navigating the waters of deceit could come with a very high price. It was hard enough protecting his young son from it, he couldn't deal with protecting a woman as well.

Vanquishing those enemies meant doing the job alone. And until one little school teacher with violet eyes, he hadn't minded paying the price.

DON'T MISS

Lora Leigh's

NEW YORK TIMES BESTSELLER

COYOTE'S MATE

For six years Anya Kobrin worked with Del-Rey
Delgado—the genetically altered rebel known
as the Coyote Ghost—to free a group of coyote women kept in her father's lab. As Anya
matured into a woman, she and Del-Rey grew
close…but then he broke his promise and shot
her father. Now she must deal with her uncon-
trollable desire for the man who betrayed her.

Don't miss

Tanner's Scheme

Part of the Feline Breed series
by *New York Times* and *USA Today*
bestselling author

Lora Leigh

After the Feline Breeds' main base is attacked,
Tanner desires revenge. So he kidnaps Scheme
Tallant—the daughter of a one-time high-
ranking member of the Genetics Council. But
when Tanner discovers that Scheme herself is
a target of her father's ruthless mission, his
vengeance takes a backseat to saving the life
of the woman he hopes to claim as his mate.

penguin.com

Fourth in the *New York Times*
bestselling Nauti Series from

LORA LEIGH

Nauti Intentions

Since he first saw Janey Mackay taking a dip in
her bikini, Major Alex Jansen has had to quell the
fire she ignites in him. Even touching her would
mean death at the hands of the Mackay men.
Until now, the girl of his dreams—and fantasies—has lived in a vacuum of affection, shying
away from the danger she thinks men represent.
Alex sets out to prove her wrong, with his torturously slow caresses.

But when someone starts leaving spine-chilling
notes, Alex won't rest until she's completely safe.
And completely his—body and soul.

New York Times and *USA Today* bestselling author
Lora Leigh invites you into an intriguing world
where genetically altered Breeds and the
humans who created them commingle—and
sometimes cross the boundaries of desire...

Megan's Mark
By Lora Leigh

Cursed with the extraordinary power to feel
other people's emotions, Megan Fields has
tucked herself away in a remote corner of
New Mexico, working as a small-town sheriff's
deputy. She finds solace in the silence and heat
of the desert. But when Breeds begin dying
on her watch, Megan realizes that the secrets
from her past can't stay buried forever.
Someone is out for blood—her blood.

**"WHEN I'M IN THE MOOD FOR A STEAMY
ROMANCE, I READ LORA LEIGH."**
—Angela Knight

M203T1107